Awaken the
Highland
Warrior

Anita Clenney

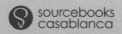
sourcebooks
casablanca

Published by Sourcebooks Casablanca, an imprint of Sourcebooks, Inc.
P.O. Box 4410, Naperville, Illinois 60567-4410
(630) 961-3900
FAX: (630) 961-2168
www.sourcebooks.com

Printed and bound in the United States of America
QW 10 9 8 7 6 5 4 3 2 1

This book is dedicated to my brilliant editing partner, Dana Rodgers, who spent endless hours and months editing and brainstorming with me. Without her I would be lost.

Prologue

August 1860

"Bury it." The whisper rasped against darkness as lightning split the sky.

"But Master, the storm—"

"Now," Druan roared.

A grimy hand, fingers unnaturally long, lowered the vault lid and turned the key, locking the prisoner inside.

"Mark this place, and guard the key."

The night flashed, illuminating a dozen men digging furiously in the earth, rain running in rivulets down mud-streaked faces, as the vault disappeared into the ground. The soft thud of dirt on metal was lost to the crash of thunder, and another bolt ripped through the heavens, as if God himself raged against the desecration taking place below.

Skin stretched, bones cracked and popped. A scream of triumph pierced the night as the last shovel of dirt fell.

It was finished.

Nothing could stop him now.

Chapter 1

Present Day...

BREE'S FINGERS TIGHTENED AROUND THE METAL DISK as she ran through the graveyard, zigzagging past leaning headstones. Her lantern swayed, throwing shadows on the crypt looming before her, its stone walls the color of bones. Thick vines crept over it, sealing in cracks left by time, while gnarled branches from the twisted oak hovered like outstretched arms. Protecting... or threatening?

An owl screeched overhead as Bree scurried up the crumbling steps, wishing night hadn't fallen, when shadows twisted into monsters and spirits came out to play. The burial vault lay open near the back of the crypt, waiting. Blood roared past her ears, like the sound of all the angels' wings beating in unison. She moved closer and peered at the chest inside. It was ornate, made of metal and wood, with green gemstones embedded in each corner. It looked ancient, like it belonged in a museum or a pyramid, or perhaps Solomon's Temple. The beauty of it struck her again, as it had when she'd first discovered it.

She set the lantern on the edge of the burial vault and studied the markings on the chest. Swirls and shapes like writing shifted in the amber glow. Stretching out a finger, she touched the surface. Warm? She yanked her hand back and hit the lantern. It crashed to the floor, throwing the top of the crypt into darkness. Dropping to her knees, she scrambled for the light. A sound cut through the silence, scraping, like fingernails against stone. She grabbed the lantern, not daring to blink, then remembered the wind outside and the claw-like branches of the old tree.

She placed the lantern securely on the vault cover she'd pushed onto the alcove and unfolded her hand. The metal disk she held was three inches in diameter and appeared to be made from the same metal as the chest, not silver, not gold. One side had deep grooves; the other was etched with symbols. With trembling fingers, she lined up the disk with the matching grooves on top of the chest and pushed. There was a series of clicks as the notched edges retracted.

A voice brushed her ear. *What lies within cannot be, until time has passed with the key.*

Bree whirled, but she was alone. Only stone walls stood watch, their secrets hidden for centuries. It was sleep deprivation, not ghosts.

She pulled in a slow, steadying breath and tried to turn the disk. Nothing. Again, this time counterclockwise, and it began to move under her hand. She jerked her fingers back. A loud pop sounded and colors flashed… blue, orange, and green, swirling for seconds, and then they were gone. Great, hallucinations to go with the voices in her head.

Her body trembled as she gripped the lid. This was it. All her dreams held on a single pinpoint of time. If this ended up another wild goose chase, she was done. No more treasure hunts, no more mysteries, no more playing Indiana Jones. She'd settle down to a nice, ordinary, boring life. She counted.

One.

Two.

Three.

She heaved open the chest.

Terror clawed its way to her throat, killing her scream.

The man inhaled one harsh breath and his eyes flew open, locking on Bree. A battle cry worthy of *Braveheart* echoed off the walls. Bree jumped back as metal flashed and a rush of air kissed her face. Petrified, she watched him crawl out of the burial vault, a wicked-looking dagger in his hand. Her scream tore loose as she turned and fled.

Fingers grazed her shoulder, and she glanced back. The last thing she saw before her feet tangled with the shovel was the dead man reaching for her. She fell, smashing her face against the stone floor, and then lurched to her feet. He towered over her, blocking her escape, so close she could see his pulse throbbing with life, even though he'd just climbed out of a tomb.

"Where's Druan?" His voice was a growl, body taut, like a lion ready to pounce.

Bree stumbled backwards, but he followed, his eyes as hard and cold as the dagger at her throat. He scanned the shadows as if he expected a horde of demons to appear, before his fierce gaze settled on her again.

A thousand disjointed thoughts tumbled in her head as the blade pressed harder. "Who are you? How did you get here? Are you a ghost?" She wasn't sure she believed in ghosts, but she also didn't believe in dead men rising from their graves, and this one was wearing a kilt.

"A ghost?" Dark brows drew into a flat line. He

lowered the dagger, opened his other hand, and stared at it. "No." He didn't sound sure.

She wasn't, either. He looked too muscular for a spirit, but there was no doubt she was talking to a man who should be dead. And he was standing between her and the door.

The blade flashed, and Bree screamed. A trickle of red appeared on his palm. She pushed past him, but he caught her arm, spinning her around. A jolt shocked her, and they both flinched. His blood was warm and sticky against her skin. She decided she'd die fighting.

Pulling free, she grabbed the shovel from the floor and swung it at his head. He stopped it with one hand, tossed the shovel deep into the crypt, and shoved her against the wall. She flailed with her fists and then lifted her knee. He pinned it between his thighs. She was trapped. She sagged against him, waiting for the blade to plunge, but the only thing she felt was a hard body in damp clothes holding her still.

"Impossible," he muttered, releasing her. He stepped back, the dagger still red with his blood. "Who are you?"

"I'm Bree. Who are you? Why did you do that?" she asked, staring at his hand.

"To be sure." He wiped the blade on his kilt and slid it into a sheath at his side. "Where's Druan?" he demanded.

"I don't know anyone named Druan," she said, wincing as she touched her stinging face. At least he'd put the dagger away.

He frowned and leaned closer, studying her cheek. She stood, not breathing, as warm, calloused fingers brushed her face and dark eyes reflected the lantern's golden glow.

"It can't be." He stared at his hand as if it had betrayed him. "You fell hard," he said, his voice softer, with an accent she couldn't place. "Are you okay?"

No, she wasn't okay. There was a dead man talking to her. And he looked familiar. "You tried to kill me."

"I'm sorry."

Sorry he'd tried, or sorry he'd failed?

"Where am I?" he asked, muddy fingers grazing the crypt wall.

"Where? New York, near Albany…" She gulped. "Earth."

"How did I get here?"

"New York, the crypt, or earth?"

"How did I get in a crypt?" he asked quietly, and she knew the question wasn't intended for her. A better one would be how he'd gotten out—alive. She looked at the disk, still in the lock. Locks weren't made just to keep things out. They also kept things in. Her stomach took a hard dive. A ghost would be one thing, but ghosts didn't bleed.

He spun back toward the burial vault. "What year is this?"

She told him, watching as the color drained from his face.

"No." He rubbed his hands across his forehead, leaving a streak of blood. "A hundred and fifty years." The words were barely a whisper. Clasping his chest, he moved toward the open door of the crypt. He didn't move like a normal man; he flowed, like water over rocks in a stream. As if each muscle moved in perfect harmony with the others.

"It's still here," he said, staring into the night.

"What's still here?" Before the question left her mouth, an image of charred earth, smoking and desolate, reared up like a serpent from a forgotten dream. One of her premonitions? She was still reeling when he walked back to where she stood.

"How did you find me?" he asked, his voice gruff again.

For someone who'd just been freed, he wasn't very gracious. "I followed the map. Who are you? How did you get inside that chest?"

"Chest?" He looked at the burial vault. "I can't remember," he said, licking his lower lip.

He was lying. Bree knew it as surely as she knew she wasn't dreaming and he wasn't dead. This man wasn't a ghost. He was a thief. He'd probably stolen her treasure when she wasn't watching. He couldn't have locked himself inside, which meant someone had left him for dead. An accomplice? Or was it a joke? He *was* wearing a kilt.

"Where's my treasure?" she demanded. She'd searched too long to let anyone steal it.

He swayed and grabbed the wall.

"What's wrong?"

"The time vault... I need to lie down."

Time vault? Did he mean the burial vault? "Are you hurt? Do you need a doctor?" Thief or not, she couldn't refuse him help if he was injured.

"No." He grabbed her arm, and she felt the strength held in check, although he looked ready to drop. "You can't tell anyone about me."

Was he hiding from the person who had locked him in the chest? She'd seen a man in the woods several days ago and a shadow in the graveyard earlier tonight. Then there was the shriek last night that made her skin feel like it had turned inside out.

He leaned his head against the stone. "Need rest."

Rest? Where? If she called the police she'd have to tell them about her treasure, and she couldn't take him inside. He didn't look capable of walking, much less hurting anyone, but that dagger proved he was dangerous.

The man's eyes closed and his face paled. She'd made countless bad judgment calls in her life, and this might be the worst, but she couldn't let him pass out here, and she wasn't about to lose her treasure. The thief must know where it was hidden or who'd taken it.

"Let's get you inside the house." It wouldn't be the first time she'd taken a risk. Besides, her friend Jared should be back from his trip soon. He could give her a hand. Bree retrieved the lantern and carried it back to where the man waited. He raised his head, giving her the first grateful look since she'd freed him. "Do you need help?"

He nodded stiffly, his expression grim.

She moved closer, and he dropped an arm over her shoulders, leaning his body into hers. He smelled like dirt and leather and rain. A feeling settled in her chest, like recognition, and she wondered if she was dreaming. She put her arm around his waist. Solid. Real. Wet? How had he gotten wet? It hadn't rained in weeks.

"Wait," he whispered. "The time vault. I have to cover it… can't leave the key."

Why? Questions bombarded her, but she left him leaning against the wall and approached the burial vault. Bree reached for the lid, and her breath caught when she saw the inside of the chest. It was green, like the stones on the outside, but there was no time to explore. She'd have to come back later. She closed the lid and pulled the disk from the lock. Nausea rose in her throat as the metal grew hot in her hand. She wanted to hide the disk, bury it where it would never be found.

After the queasiness subsided, she struggled with the stone cover, then he was there, pulling with her. The lid scraped as it dropped into place. If this was his weakened state, she couldn't imagine him full strength. She was crazy to consider taking him inside, but if he was going to kill her, he would've already done it when he had the dagger against her jugular vein. He not only hadn't hurt her, he'd even seemed concerned about her fall. Or was she making excuses because the mystery of a lifetime stretched before her, beckoning like the yellow brick road?

He leaned against the vault, and a trickle of water dripped from his hair onto his face. There was a knot on the back of his head. "How did you get hurt?" she asked.

"I don't remember."

The knot looked big enough to cause amnesia. Maybe he wasn't lying.

He held out his hand. "Give me the key."

"The key?" She looked at the antique disk that had hung on her great-great-grandmother's mantel for generations. "It's mine."

"Please."

She didn't know why he wanted it, but judging from the pallor of his face, if they didn't get inside soon, she'd have to drag him or call for help. She could get her disk back after he fell asleep. He put it in the worn, leather pouch hanging over his groin, a sporran. She'd never seen a real man wear one, but then again, she'd never seen a real man in a kilt.

He slipped his arm around her shoulders again, and they staggered into the still September night. No frogs croaked or crickets chirped. No owl's eerie call. A stab of unease prickled her spine at the lack of sound. They were both panting by the time they made it to her back porch. Having him pressed to her side, body to body, was doing strange things to her senses, and his scent made her long for something she didn't understand. She opened the back door, and they moved into the kitchen. "Do you want something to eat? Water?"

"No. Lie down." He slumped lower, his chin bumping the top of her head.

Bree grabbed the arm he'd slung around her shoulders to keep him from sliding to the floor and debated where to put him. The house had eight bedrooms, but only one assembled bed and a single set of sheets. She hadn't replaced the ones she'd tossed out when she moved in. Living in a dead person's house hadn't bothered her, nor had sleeping in a dead person's bed. Sleeping on a dead person's sheets—even Grandma Emily's—that, Bree couldn't handle.

And here she was with a man she'd pulled out of a crypt draped around her like a shawl. Her mother was right, Bree had missed normal by light years.

She guided him to her bedroom, thankful it was on the first floor and that her mother lived half a dozen states away. She nudged on the light switch with her nose, dragged him across her hand-loomed rug, and dropped him onto the bed. "What's your name?"

"Faelan," he said and fell backwards like a downed tree.

Faelan? Unusual name. Bree shook his arm. "What happened to the treasure in the chest?"

His eyelids fluttered. "Not… treasure… chest."

"Not a treasure chest? What do you mean?"

If the box wasn't a treasure chest and it wasn't a casket, what was it?

Chapter 2

FAR ACROSS THE OCEAN, A WOMAN WOKE, BREATHLESS and sweating. It wasn't one of those annoying, erotic, Duncan dreams. She pushed aside the long strands of red hair plastered to her forehead and lay still in the darkness, seeking the source of her dread. Her hand touched the metal growing warm at her neck, and she allowed her mind to drift, searching for somewhere to anchor. Blurred pictures flashed in her head, a dark-haired woman and a handsome man, then four more.

A round object came into focus, and she bolted upright, her nails digging into the bed.

The key.

For more than a century they'd searched for it, bled for it. Died for it.

The lost key.

"What do you mean it's not a treasure chest?" Bree had a treasure map and her great-great-grandmother Isabel's journal to prove it. She shook Faelan's shoulder and lightly slapped his face. He didn't move. Was he dead? She checked his heartbeat. It was a little fast, and his skin felt too warm. Should she take him to the hospital? Awkwardly she searched the sporran, but he had no wallet, no ID, only her disk, a strip of leather, and a smooth white stone. Who was he?

She replaced the items and studied him. He lay cross-ways on her bed, arms at his sides. A red and black kilt was belted at his waist, where the dagger still hung. His shirt was white, or had been at one time. It was smeared with mud, as were the beige socks—kilt hose—folded below his knees. She had to admit the costume looked authentic, except for the boots. They looked like something from the Civil War. Her specialty.

But it wasn't his clothing that drew her. It was his face, strong jaw, straight nose, dark hair hanging to his shoulders, and most puzzling, his eyes. They had been uncannily familiar, but uncanny was her norm. Even as a child, when other girls were talking about schoolboys and planning sleepovers, she'd been dreaming of... whatever it was. She couldn't put a name to it, although she often felt it had a face. A face! The painting.

Bree ran to the library, crossing the freshly sanded floor to the Davenport desk she'd pushed against the wall. Opening a drawer, she took out a small portrait she'd put there for safekeeping until she finished the room. The Highland warrior in the picture could have been Faelan's twin, from the kilt and white shirt to the broadsword at his thigh.

She'd found the painting in an antique store while visiting her grandmother a couple of years ago. There was no signature, only a smudge at the bottom like a four leaf clover. Bree couldn't have left the painting any more than she could've left a child, and it embarrassed her to think how much time she'd spent staring at it, like a young girl daydreaming over her first crush.

That was before Russell blew back into her life like Prince Charming incarnate. He hated the painting the minute he saw it. She should have taken it as an omen, but what man wouldn't feel inadequate compared to a warrior like the one in her portrait?

Bree carried the painting back to her bedroom, where Faelan still slept. Her Highland warrior. *He isn't yours*, she scoffed. But he belonged to someone. Maybe someone's husband or lover. Someone's son. Side by side, his resemblance to the painting was shocking. Could it be one of his ancestors? There were Scots in the area, and Faelan's voice did have that sexy lilt, almost a brogue, although his name sounded Irish. The painting was obviously old. Bree knew old. She'd spent her life pursuing it, analyzing it. Old documents, old relics, old books.

No, it was too far-fetched, even for her, to think he could be related to the warrior in her painting. Stick any dark-haired man in Highland clothing, and he would probably look the same. Bree slid the portrait inside a drawer by the bed and ran a fingertip over Faelan's arm. Whoever he was, he was stunning. She pulled her hand back with a sigh. No matter how rotten her love life was or how much he looked like her Highlander, she wouldn't sink to caressing an unconscious man, especially a thief. For a moment she debated whether to get him out of his clothes, since the covers were getting damp, but he had a feral look about him that made her suspect he wouldn't appreciate waking to find he'd been stripped. She could at least remove his muddy boots. Muddy? She looked at the footprints tracked across her wide-planked floor and handmade rug. Where did the mud come from?

She needed answers. He'd need food. If the way to a man's heart was through his stomach, maybe the path to his trust was there too, but for now, she didn't want any more mud on her quilt or her favorite rug. She knelt at his feet and tugged on one boot, then removed the other, taking great care not to use her vantage point to see what he did or didn't wear under his kilt.

After she gathered a first-aid kit, thermometer, damp washcloth, and towel from the bathroom, she left it by the bed and went to the kitchen for soup, bottled water, and an ice pack for his head. She started from the kitchen, when a crash sounded from her bedroom. Gripping the tray, she ran down the hall, coming to a halt in the doorway.

He was naked, sprawled face down on the bed, as bare as the day he was born. The lamp was overturned, his clothes piled on the floor next to his dagger and boots. He'd tried to turn the covers back, but now they were trapped underneath him. Bree set the tray on the table beside the bed.

He wasn't the first naked man she'd seen, but he might as well have been. Taut skin covered muscle so defined it made her want to weep at the raw beauty. Several faint lines ran across his back and shoulders and a couple along the side of his hip. Scars.

Bree gave one lingering look from thick, dark hair to sexy feet, then averted her gaze and poked his shoulder with her fingertip. "Faelan, wake up."

He didn't move. She took one more look, leaned down, and shook him again.

He grunted and flipped over, pulling her flat against him. He rolled again, and the air whooshed from her lungs as he slammed her into the mattress, his forearm braced against her windpipe. "Druan," he said, looking through her, "stop the war."

She lay still, trying not to panic. "Faelan. Let me go," she wheezed. When he didn't, she tried to put her knee into his groin, but with her legs pinned under his it proved as ineffective as it had in the crypt. He groaned and moved his arm from her throat. She was so busy sucking in air she didn't notice his fingers threading through her hair until she calmed enough to realize he was still on top of her, stomach to stomach, where her shirt had ridden up. Her legs, bared by shorts, were tangled with his. His skin felt hotter. He had a fever. And that wasn't his dagger rubbing against her thigh.

His head lowered, damp hair brushing her cheek as he whispered strange words that made every cell in her body sizzle. Gaelic? His look was more alarming than before, as if she were water to his thirst. This was a look she could die in, a look that made her want to trash logic for a slim chance at bliss. His lips touched hers.

She was too stunned to stop the kiss and too captivated by the feel of his mouth on hers to pull away. The soft nibble, a mere testing of flesh against flesh, deepened to lips parting and a flick of his tongue. Just when she thought she'd lift off into space, he raised his head and blinked at her, then rolled off so fast she grabbed fistfuls of the quilt to keep from falling off the bed. She sat up, too dazed to move, and tried not to gape.

She'd thought the back view was good…

He lay next to her, his chest rising and falling, covered with the most beautiful tattoos, mystical, like some sort of ancient text. The symbols started below his collarbone, coming to a point above sculpted abs. A necklace lay in the center, held by a brown leather strap. Something inside her shifted, a memory edged in, then slid away. She dragged her gaze from his tattoos and forced herself to concentrate on his face. It held no threat, only remorse.

"I'm sorry," he said.

"You were dreaming. You have a fever."

"Need rest," he mumbled, eyes drifting shut.

"Wait. Do you need a doctor? Food?" She started to stand so she could cover him, but he grabbed her hand. The tingling started again.

"No doctor… rest… disease…"

"Are you sick?"

"Find it… destroy…"

Bree leaned closer. "Destroy what?"

"The world… stop… war."

She felt a shiver creep in, but he was asleep. She pulled the sheet over his lap and checked his temperature. High, but not dangerous. She put the ice pack on his head, cleaned the blood from his face, then moved the cloth down the thick column of his neck and over the symbols on his chest. She wasn't brave enough to clean the smudge low on his stomach, next to the faint line of hair that disappeared below the sheet.

Another scar crossed his left bicep, larger than the others. She ran her finger along the raised ridge, wondering what had put it there. Chill bumps appeared on his skin and rose on hers as a faint sound echoed in her ear, like the distant clang of a sword. She turned her attention to his necklace. It was unusual, round, about the size of a silver dollar. She couldn't identify the metal, but it looked old. She touched it. Warm, like the vault had felt just before she opened it. Symbols were engraved on the front, similar to the ones on the treasure chest and the disk. Warning bells rang in her head.

How could the symbols on his necklace look like the ones on the treasure chest and the disk? Her disk?

Faelan's head jerked against the pillow. "Sorry."

Was he apologizing again for choking her? For kissing her? Stealing her treasure?

His hands gripped the covers. "Father… shouldn't have sent them away…"

Sent who away? His father? Was this Druan person his father? "It's okay," she said, stroking his arm, but all this talk of disease and war was making her uneasy.

His hand unclenched and reached for hers. He pulled in a quick, shallow breath and calmed. Dried blood covered the cut on his palm. Picking up the washcloth, she wiped away the crust exposing a thin, pale line. A scar.

Her throat went dry. She dropped his hand. Less than an hour ago, she'd watched him cut it with the dagger. No one could heal that fast, except a superhero. Or Dracula.

Vampire!

Bree sprang off the bed, clasping her throat. He'd crawled out of a crypt at night. He was strong, mysterious, and healed inhumanly fast. But vampires didn't exist, did they? She'd always wondered… the eternal undead, shapeshifters. She had to do something. What? A stake through the heart? A silver bullet? No. Silver bullets were for werewolves. Why hadn't she waited for Jared? He'd know what to do. Archeologists loved dead things.

Light. The overhead light was on, and he hadn't burned. Was that why he passed out? She needed something stronger. Bree yanked the shade off the lamp and held the bare bulb close to his face. His lashes flickered, but he didn't scream, didn't start cooking. Didn't even moan.

The legends varied, but they were consistent on one thing: vampires needed blood. If he was so weak, why hadn't he drained her in the crypt? Where were his fangs? With that dagger, who'd need them? Maybe he was good and drank only from animals. Or maybe she'd read too many paranormal stories. Vampires were just a legend, no matter how intriguing the idea. She'd felt Faelan's heart beating and the warmth of his skin. And who ever heard of a vampire with a fever? Who was he, then?

She picked the dagger up off the floor, examining it for the first time. It looked even older than his clothes. A dirk, at least early eighteenth century, similar to one she'd authenticated last year for a prince. The narrow blade was about ten inches long, the rounded hilt made of bronze. She checked his clothing piled on the floor, disappointed there was no *sgian dubh* tucked inside his kilt hose or hidden in his sleeve.

Where did he get this outfit? Not the local costume store. *Okay, Bree. You love mysteries and puzzles. Think.*

His clothes looked old, his dagger even older. He had an accent like nothing she'd heard and an uncommon name. His necklace had symbols similar to the disk that had been in her family for generations, a disk that turned out to be an elaborate lock. The chest—time vault, he called it—had felt warm before she opened it. He'd muttered something about 150 years, and he healed inhumanly fast. On top of it all, he was wet and muddy, but it hadn't rained in weeks.

A wide yawn nearly dislocated her jaw. She needed a good night's sleep to sort this out. There was probably a good explanation for everything, like he was a Scottish thief who'd heard about the treasure. There were lots of caves and lakes nearby where he could have hidden it and gotten wet. He probably had an accomplice who double-crossed him and left him inside the chest to die. But how would he have known about the disk? Cousin Reggie? He'd always been as fascinated with the disk as Bree had. He could've found the map and entry in Isabel's journal years earlier, the sneaky little twerp. He could have even made a copy of the disk. It sounded crazy, but it was saner than her vampire theory.

Bree pulled the covers up to Faelan's chin and started cleaning the tracks that had dried on her floor. Next she tackled his clothes—noting the lack of underwear—cringing as she applied Spray 'n Wash to his linen shirt and his kilt. She hand-washed away the dirt and blood. Even if the garments proved to be relics, he needed something clean to wear. She headed for the bathroom, trying to forget about sizzling kisses and fangs and mud that shouldn't exist.

Thunder rumbled in the distance as she reached for the blinds. A storm was coming. A flash of lightning streaked the sky, and something moved at the edge of the woods. A deer. Or a camper. A few campers always showed up here lost. Since Grandma Emily thought she was a cross between Martha Stewart and Mother Teresa, it wasn't unusual for the visitors to stay for hours.

What if it was the person who locked Faelan inside the burial vault? Had he seen her dragging Faelan across the backyard? Could Faelan's weakness have been a ploy to get inside? Thief or ghost, his fever was real. So was the lump on his head. Bree locked the window and closed the blind. Still, it might be wise to hide her valuables. Her Civil War collection was on loan to one of the universities. She doubted anyone would want her books or artifacts. The only real thing of value to a thief would be the two-carat diamond earrings Grandma had given Bree before she died. The earrings had been in her family as long as the disk.

Out of habit, Bree touched her ears and found the left one bare. She hurried to the mirror, confirming her fear, and got another shock at her appearance. Her cheek looked like a microdermabrasion treatment gone bad, and her diamond wasn't the only thing missing. A few inches below her ear, a chunk of hair had been sheared. She stared at the thin, pink line where the dagger had grazed her throat. Her missing earring was the least of her worries. Was she insane to take this risk?

Something bothered her about this whole thing, more than the peculiarity of finding a live man buried in a crypt.

She wasn't comfortable leaving him unguarded, so after showering, she dressed again, removed his ice pack, and pulled the rocking chair close to the bed. The wind howled outside as she listened to the steady rhythm of the chair and tried to collect her thoughts. The walls faded and the room disappeared.

Grandma's rocking chair creaked softly, making nine-year-old Bree sleepy at last. Her eyes were still swollen from crying, and her nose felt like a balloon. Her dad was in heaven now, Grandma had told her after they rescued Bree from the crypt, but she'd already known. She held her ragged panda closer, staring at the candle flame as she listened to Grandma's fairy tale about big strong warriors who could destroy terrible demons—maybe even rotten cousins who locked girls inside crypts. It was way better than Snow White and a bunch of goofy little men.

"Time vaults," Grandma whispered, "that hold demons until Judgment."

Bree's lashes drooped...

"Now, Bree." Grandma's voice was shaky but loud.

Bree opened her eyes as the window pane rattled and a flash of lightning lit the room. Grandma stood near the bed, but her dark hair was gone. She was gray, her skin wrinkled.

"Find the book, Bree! Help him." Grandma vanished.

Bree launched out of the chair, the scent of lavender strong in the air. She stared at the naked man tangled in her sheets. Twice he'd called the chest a time vault.

Forget vampires... there was a demon in her bed!

Chapter 3

GRANDMA'S STORY WAS NO FAIRY TALE. THE LEGEND of warriors and demons battling for the fate of mankind was true. Bree had opened the demon's prison, tucked him into her bed, and let him kiss her.

She grabbed her tote bag, car keys, and the dagger. Halfway down the front steps, she stopped. It wasn't because she was barefoot and it was the middle of a stormy night. This was her home, where she'd spent nearly every summer growing up. Her haven. She wasn't running away. She'd done too much of that the past few months. No one would make her leave again, not even a demon. There must be some way to send him back. Her heart gave a funny little wrench when she thought about his kiss and how much he looked like her Highland warrior. But a legend was one thing; playing hostess to a demon was another.

Bree put down her bag, keys, and the dagger and punched in the number to Jared's cell phone. She should've told him about the map before. He was her best friend. After leaving a jumbled message asking him to call, she started to dial 911, but there was no way anyone would believe Faelan was a demon who'd been locked in a time vault awaiting Judgment. She wouldn't, if she hadn't opened the darned thing.

Holding the dagger in front of her, she tiptoed down the hall to her bedroom. His dark head rested against her pillow, hand curled low on his stomach, where the sheet had slipped. She was struck by an insane desire to crawl in next to him, cuddle up and... cripes! Was he manipulating her mind in his sleep? She yanked the door closed, smashed her finger, and bit back a yelp.

Her grandmother had said to find the book. What book? She had as many as Bree. Bree headed to the attic, where the books were being stored while she finished the library. Help Faelan? How? She crossed the dusty floor, passing decades of history she hadn't fully explored. Every minute she wasn't working on the house she'd spent tending the graveyard, reading Isabel's journal, or watching the archeologists dig. She hadn't written in her own journal in months.

After searching several boxes, Bree was about to give up when she heard a thump a few feet away. A book lay on the floor. *Secrets of the Afterlife*. Grandma's favorite. Why had it fallen? Bree dug through the box. Near the bottom, she found a thick leather-bound book with straps. Grandma's journal? Bree had seen it only once. She'd surprised her grandmother, who quickly hid the book underneath a pillow. Bree had been searching for it when she found Isabel's journal and the map.

Bree unclasped the straps, opened the book, and stared at the name written in faded ink on the yellowed page. *The Book of Battles of Clan Connor*. This was not Grandma's journal. In smaller print underneath was written *By the order of...* The rest of the sentence was smudged. Bree sat on the attic floor, eyes growing wider with each page. She learned about secret clans and talismans of great power and ancient time vaults that held demons until Judgment. According to the book, the time vaults could be opened only after 150 years, the number Faelan had whispered in the crypt.

Her blood hummed. Was it possible? All those summers she'd visited as a child, had he been in there waiting for someone to wake him? She read on and found names and dates. *In the year 1749, the Demon Mour was suspended by Warrior Malcolm…* The last name was impossible to read. This was a record of battles between demons and warriors of the Connor clan. Bree quivered with excitement. Demons and warriors… it was real. How had Grandma gotten it? Why had she never mentioned it?

The book said warriors had talismans. Was that what Faelan wore around his neck? Was he a demon who'd stolen a talisman, or a warrior who'd hijacked a time vault? Bree ran her finger down the entries, searching for his name, but there were so many, and the writing so hard to read it could take days, weeks. Several pages later, she found something that made her mouth drop. *In the year 2053, the demon Lor was defeated by Warrior Darius Ander.*

In the year 2053?

Regardless where Grandma had gotten the book, this was more incredible than Stonehenge or the Lost Colony of Roanoke. The last few pages were missing; only jagged edges remained, and the one that had survived was written in a language she didn't recognize. Bree's head swam, and an image started to take shape, but a noise sounded below, and the vision fled.

She put the book back in the box and closed the top.

Gripping the dagger, she crept down the stairs, faintly registering the scent of lavender clinging to the air. She eased her bedroom door open, expecting to see something out of *The Exorcist*. He didn't look like a demon. He looked like a man caught in the throes of a nightmare. His head tossed back and forth, damp hair clinging to his neck, sheets tangled with his legs. He mumbled a word here and there. "Druan." The name from before, and another, "Alana."

Alana? A wife? Had Bree kissed a married man? Let him rub his naked body against her? Was he a man? Did demons marry? If he had been married, his wife would be nothing but dust. Of course he'd have nightmares. Bree moved closer. A sheen of sweat covered his body. The fever had broken. He uttered one small sound that blew common sense away. He whimpered. If he was a demon, she was doomed.

She put the dagger on the table and took the cloth to the bathroom to dampen it. When she returned, his forehead felt cooler, and he seemed more at ease. She untangled the sheet from his legs and wiped the sweat from his face. And because she simply had to, she smoothed the tiny line between his brows. Moving the rocking chair to the corner of the room, she sat close enough to see him or hear if he called out in his sleep and near the door, in case she needed to run. Staying here was dangerous, but any treasure hunter worth her salt knew great discoveries required great risks. If this stranger had somehow traveled through time, she had to know why and how.

—∼∼—

Faelan crouched behind the crumbling chimney of the burnt-out farmhouse. He could hear the worried breathing of the man beside him and hoped the coins jingling nervously in the man's pocket were enough to buy his loyalty. The full moon was covered by clouds, and there was a thickness in the air that didn't sit well, but he attributed it to the coming storm. Even the horses, hidden in the nearby grove of trees, neighed and stomped uneasily.

It was madness to take on a demon as powerful as Druan without other warriors to protect his back, but Faelan couldn't wait for his brothers to arrive, not after what he'd discovered last night. In truth, he didn't want his brothers here. While it was brave of them and the other warriors he'd sent away to offer their help, it was too dangerous for them to face an ancient demon without being assigned. One mistake could mean death. He wouldn't risk their lives. He'd already warned his accomplice to flee as soon as Druan showed. Faelan felt the warmth of his talisman and hoped he wouldn't have to use it. The time vault waited behind the trees, ready to suspend the demon, but if he had to be destroyed, so be it. One way or another, this would be finished tonight.

The wind kicked up, slapping his kilt against his legs. The first fat raindrop hit his nose, followed by the second and third. A jagged flash of lightning split the sky. Faelan flinched. "You sure Jeremiah's coming?" That was the name Druan went by these days.

"Should've been here," the man said, fretting. "Probably ran into the storm."

It came fast, the sky blackening as wind howled through the trees. There was a loud crack, and sparks *flew from a nearby pine. Faelan heard horses approaching, hooves pounding the ground like an army from hell. He gripped his sword. "You said he'd be alone."*

"He was supposed to be."

At least a dozen riders entered the clearing, mounts snorting as the night flashed. There were too many. He could take Druan or the others, but he couldn't take them all. If he tried and wasn't strong enough, wielding the talisman's power would kill him. He should have kept the other warriors with him, instead of trying to capture Druan alone. He would have to retreat.

Then Faelan saw them, sitting in the midst of the others, four figures taller than the rest. Like the four horsemen of the apocalypse. Druan rode in front, flanked by the other three, faces any warrior knew from the time he could lift a sword. The demons of old, the ancient ones. Tristol, Malek, and Voltar.

What were they doing here?

He heard a gasp. His accomplice hadn't run. The man stood frozen, staring at the ancient demons. The sky lit violet, and Druan's yellow eyes found Faelan. The demon rode closer. Tristol, Malek, and Voltar followed, in demon form as well. They seemed puzzled to see Faelan. The remaining horsemen, halflings, and demons, closed in around them.

Faelan shoved the man behind him. He'd have to destroy Druan by hand and save the talisman's power for the rest. It wouldn't be strong enough to kill them all, but it might give the man with him a chance to escape. There was no way out for Faelan. He would die. His only hope was to take Druan and as many with him as he could. "As soon as they're distracted, run," he *whispered over his shoulder. "I'll try to hold them off until you're safe."*

"Did you think you could stop me, warrior? Stop my war?" Druan hissed as Faelan raised his sword.

"I will stop you, you bastard," Faelan yelled over the storm. "We both know this isn't about war. The war's just a distraction for this disease you've created. You're planning to destroy every human on earth." And by the time his clan and the other warriors got the message, it would be too late. Everyone would die.

Druan's eyes widened. His thick, gray skin quivered.

"What disease?" Tristol roared, turning on Druan. Where the others were hideous, Tristol was striking. Long black hair flowed from a face that looked almost human, except for a slight bulge in his forehead. He was rumored to be the closest to the Dark One, hell's favorite son. What was he doing with Druan?

"Lies. He tells lies." Druan looked over Faelan's shoulder. "What are you waiting for, Grog?"

"Grog?" Faelan tensed and started to turn as a jarring blow struck his skull. He'd been betrayed. It was over. The world was doomed.

<hr />

He woke hard, chest heaving. He was here, not in the clearing. Not in the time vault. He was in a bed. He remembered the woman opening the vault and helping him inside the house. One minute he'd felt his skull explode, the next, he'd looked into terror-filled green eyes. Human eyes. It seemed an eternity had passed in between. It had, if the woman told the truth, and she must have, or he couldn't be here.

Grief hit him again, as it had in the crypt. His mind clawed at the darkness, searching for faces forever lost. A woman's smile and a lassie with dimples, two lads wrestling in the dirt.

What had he done?

A tear formed, but didn't fall. He had no time for grieving, there was work to do, and he couldn't ask forgiveness from the dead.

He touched the talisman. If he wore it, how could the world still stand? Or did it? He'd seen only one human, if she was that. Were there others? What he'd seen outside looked normal, not the wasteland he'd expected. And who'd sent the woman to wake him? Druan? Or one of the other ancients: Tristol? Malek? Voltar? No one else would have known where to look, and Druan had the only key. Someone with knowledge was behind this.

Faelan flexed his muscles, testing. His strength was returning, though his head felt like a split watermelon. That bastard he'd hired had betrayed him. Probably a bloody minion. He thought of the woman again. She'd saved him, for sure. If not, he could have been in that vault until Judgment. By freeing him, she'd saved mankind. Who was she? She couldn't be a full demon and enter the graveyard. Was she a halfling? She didn't smell like one. Or a minion? Then why wake him from suspension, offer him food and a bed? He'd keep quiet and see what part she played in this game. He wouldn't think about what he'd seen in her eyes. It must be the time vault messing with his senses.

He sat up and the sheet fell away. He was naked. Her doing, or his? Pushing the covers aside, he stood, his body hard, aching. He needed a woman. Her. He'd dreamed of kissing her, his tongue dancing with hers, but it hadn't felt like a dream. Was she entering his thoughts like Michael did? No minion could do that.

Faelan looked around for his clothes and saw a box with glowing numbers beside the bed. He cautiously touched it, but it wasn't warm. Some kind of timepiece, judging by the number shown and the lack of daylight at the window. His clothes lay folded next to the box. Another kindness. But halflings and minions would use any means to carry out their master's evil.

A quick search revealed he had one less thing. His dirk was missing. He should've hidden it with the key. The woman's scent caught his nose. He tuned his vision and saw her in the corner, asleep in a rocking chair. He could just make out her face, but it didn't matter. Every inch of her was etched into his brain. His body grew harder. He walked over to where she slept, her dainty hand holding his dirk. Did she understand the danger that came with waking him? Or did she hold it in protection against him? Who was she?

She was perfect, that much he knew. Long dark hair like strands of silk. Bonny eyes as green as the hills of the Highlands, and a soft, feminine mouth that made his water. Her breasts were full. He wanted to fill his hands while he tasted her. He'd start with her lips and move on until he'd had every part of her. He longed to feel her skin, her legs entwined with his, lifting around his waist, her body opening to him. What if she had a husband?

Did it matter, he wondered, reaching for her.

Chapter 4

HIS FINGERS WERE SIFTING THROUGH HER HAIR WHEN she woke. She gasped but didn't move, just watched him with wide, wary eyes as her hand tightened around his dirk. He wished it were tight around something else. He let her hair fall but stayed where he was, inches away, neither of them uttering a sound.

She glanced at his groin, level with her face, and he sensed her pulse quicken, her skin growing warm. He wanted to be inside her, so deep they were one. He reached for her again, and a flicker of panic crossed her face. Some vestige of control hovered within reach. He made a desperate grab for it, knowing if he didn't, he'd do something unforgivable.

Turning, he rushed from the room and found himself in a parlor with chairs and tables and some other things he didn't recognize. It was lit by a strange lamp near the door. He sat on a chair, heedless of his nakedness, and gulped in air.

What was happening to him? In his twenty-seven years, he'd never hurt a female. He'd always defended them. Would he have taken one against her will? How could he even think about a woman after what he'd lost? He shouldn't be thinking of women at all. It was against the rules.

A throat cleared from the doorway. She stood there, eyes averted, his clothes in her hand. He started to stand, but figured manners wouldn't count if he was naked.

"It's almost six. You'll need to eat. I washed your clothes last night. You can clean up there." She pointed to a door down the hall. "I'll be in the kitchen." She put his things on the floor and left.

He stared at her retreating back. What kind of woman gave hospitality to a man who'd done what he had? He was surprised she hadn't stabbed him with his own dirk, or worse, he thought, looking at his naked body, still aroused. The women of his day would've fainted dead away or had him jailed. If she had a husband, he'd probably kill Faelan before he regained his strength and save Druan the trouble. Perhaps she was a prostitute. Or did she play a deadlier game? He needed some distance from her so he could think. And he needed to piss.

He could hear—and smell—her near the back of the house. He dressed and put on the boots he'd bought from a young soldier after he wore a hole in his own. Passing boxes shoved against the wall, he made his way to the front door. Was she moving out or in? Outside, he focused his vision to the darkness and moved around back. He could see a graveyard and the outline of a crumbling church. It looked like the old chapel near the Wood place. It had been a bit rough, but not in ruins.

Why would Druan put the time vault in a graveyard? Faelan needed to find his clan, but he had no means of traveling to Scotland. Other than his talisman and his dirk, he had nothing. No coin. No horse. No sword. He listened to the birds greeting the morning and considered his options. Getting to Scotland wasn't possible now. He could take to the woods or find a nearby town and try to blend in while he asked around. But more than a century had passed. Everyone who'd lived then would be dead.

Feeling the pressure of a full bladder, he looked for a privy. All he found was an old tool shed. Moving around to the side, he lifted his kilt. He'd just finished when the birds hushed their singing. A prickle ran up his back. He shook off, dropped the front of his kilt, and scanned the wood line. He couldn't see it, but he could sense it. Something was out here. Maybe an animal. Maybe not.

What if she'd stumbled on him by accident? If so, she'd unleashed the gates of hell in her own backyard. Her blood would be on his head. If he stayed, he could find out who she was. If she was helping Druan, she would have to be killed, but first she would lead him to the demon.

In the meantime, something had to be done about this burning he felt for her. He'd spent years honing his self-discipline, but this went beyond lust. His stomach rumbled. She'd offered food, and he was near famished. Perhaps he could distract himself from one appetite by feeding the other.

He watched the woods a minute longer and then slipped around to the front door. The smell of food cooking made his stomach growl again as he made his way to the room where she'd told him to clean up. He opened the door and found another shock, this one pleasant. He spent ten minutes pushing buttons and turning knobs until he figured out how to make the water flow out of the wall. He picked up a square cake and sniffed. Flowers. Was this soap? He didn't relish smelling like a flower, but it was better than mud and sweat. The warm water rolling over his body like a gentle rainfall was an unexpected pleasure, as was the soft cloth he dried himself on.

He dreaded facing her after acting like an animal, but it was that or sleep in the woods, and whatever she was cooking smelled bloody good. After dressing once again in his clean clothes, he followed his nose to the kitchen. At least he thought it was a kitchen. The room was large, with old wooden floors covered by colorful rugs. A big oak table sat in the center. But there were things here he'd never seen in a kitchen, such as a woman in trousers.

She took a container of something that looked like milk out of a tall, white box and reached for a glass, leaving a strip of skin bare at her waist. He could already see every curve of her body. There was a name written on a wee square, right at the top of her arse. Levi Strauss. Was this some sort of family crest? Unusual place to display it.

Her arms were bare, along with most of her shoulders, and if he looked hard enough, he could see the swell of her breasts. Her skin was smooth and creamy, all over, as far as he could tell. And there was a lot of it to see. Did all women dress this way now?

His body started to harden. Damnation. He'd just gotten it down. He shifted his sporran and cleared his throat.

She pulled in a quick breath and turned, thick hair swinging around her shoulders. Their gazes locked and held. It was powerful, this feeling. Did she sense it? A flash of fear showed in her eyes, and he remembered who she might be. If so, she'd do well to fear him. Then he saw the scrape on her cheek and the thin line marring her throat… from his dirk. If her unlikely story was true, he'd come close to killing an innocent woman. If it wasn't, the next time, he wouldn't fail.

"Breakfast is ready," she said, swallowing nervously, forcing a smile.

Whatever else she was, she was brave. Faelan smiled in return, but it felt like a sneer.

"I'm Bree," she said. "You must be starving."

He stifled a growl. She had no idea.

"I hope you're not lactose intolerant," Bree said as Faelan drained his glass of milk without stopping to breathe. He frowned at it, discreetly sniffed, and then wiped a drop from his chin. Milk in his day wouldn't have been pasteurized or two percent, just straight from the cow.

He stuck his fork in the scrambled eggs and shoveled a bite into his mouth.

"It's hot—"

His eyes widened. He took a gulp of milk and did it all over again. Burning hot food, cold milk. It sounded like he moaned, but there wasn't enough room in his mouth for the sound. She studied him as he ate, not surprised he looked even better in daylight. Just her luck. She was avoiding men like poison ivy, and she'd condemned herself to solitary confinement with the sexiest man alive. Or dead?

"So you've decided I'm not a ghost?" he asked, smothering a quiet burp behind his napkin.

"I don't think a ghost could eat this much." She wasn't sure about demons.

"My manners aren't usually so poor, but I don't recall ever being so hungry." Faelan glanced at her breasts and knocked a biscuit onto the floor. He picked it up, blew on it, and stuffed half in his mouth. "I haven't thanked you properly," he said after he'd swallowed. "For freeing me, the bed, food. I didn't expect hospitality." A half smile touched his lips, making her insides twitch like she'd been hit by a stun gun.

He was gorgeous. And his voice. She took a breath and tried to gather her wits. He was a puzzle to solve, not a potential boyfriend. "I couldn't let you starve." Or she'd never find out who he was. She'd tried searching for the Connor clan, but her computer wasn't cooperating.

If she truly believed he had amnesia, she'd mention the name and see if it jogged his memory, but she suspected he knew exactly who he was, and he was trying hard to hide it from her. And if he was the demon, and thought she knew too much, he might kill her and be done with it, which probably made her the stupidest woman alive for bringing him inside, but what kind of historian would toss out a living, breathing, walking history book?

"I'm indebted to you," he said, spearing a chunk of fresh pineapple with a small knife, popping it in his mouth. "I have nothing. Not even a horse."

A horse? She bit back a smile. The only payment she wanted was answers. "So you still have no idea who you are or how you got inside the chest?"

He shook his head, his mouth too full to answer.

"You must remember some snippet of something. Children? A wife?" If Alana was his wife, did that kiss count as cheating?

"I wasn't… I don't think I was married." He licked his lips, drawing Bree's attention to his mouth.

"Brothers? Sisters?"

He shook his head, the movement so small it could have been a tic. If she hadn't been watching his mouth, she would've missed the flicker of anguish that tightened his face.

"We should tell someone. We could put up pictures of you, see if someone recognizes—"

"No." He banged his glass on the table and leaned forward, his face rigid. "You can't tell anyone about me. No one."

"You've remembered something?"

"No. It's just a precaution."

"You know your first name but not why you need all this secrecy?"

His brows flattened. "I only remember that one thing."

"And someone named Druan."

Faelan went still, staring at her as if she'd asked him when he last had sex. "It's all muddled," he said and attacked his food again.

"And that you needed to keep the disk safe."

He stopped chewing and scowled at her.

"And you called the chest a time vault. That's a lot of memories for someone who doesn't have any."

He gave her a glare that curdled the sip of milk she'd drunk. "Who are you?" he asked, his voice almost a snarl.

"I told you who I am."

"How do I know you tell the truth?"

"I can show you my driver's license."

"What's a driver's license?"

His memory loss might be real, but he wouldn't forget what a driver's license was. "It means *I'm* not lying. I can prove who I am." She raised her head and looked him dead in the eye. She didn't want to accuse him, but she needed answers. There was a slim chance he was just a thief, but she'd bet her Mustang he'd been in the crypt longer than she'd been alive.

He stared back, neither of them blinking, then he let out a breath and picked up his fork. "You ask a lot of questions."

If she had a penny for all the times she'd heard that, she'd never have to work again.

"I appreciate all you've done," Faelan said, his voice sexy again. "But until things are clear I'll ask you to keep this quiet."

He wasn't *asking* anything, but she let it slide. It was going to take patience to earn his trust. Lots of patience. Bree had lots of things. Too much of some. Patience wasn't one of them.

"Does your husband work with horses?" he asked as if the distressing conversation had never taken place.

"Horses?"

"I saw them on your family crest. Is Levi Strauss your husband?"

"Levi? Oh, no, I'm not married."

"You let a man who's not your husband put his name on your ar… backside?"

"It's a brand."

"Brand?" He looked confused.

"A label. The name of the person who made the jeans."

"Jeans?" he asked, then his face went blank, as if he knew he'd revealed too much.

"Denim. Dungarees." Bree felt another shiver of excitement at his ignorance. More evidence that he was old.

"So you live here alone? There's no male here to take care of the place? To protect you?"

"Do I need protection?" She'd hidden his dagger in one of her boots, and Grandpa's old gun was here somewhere. Not that it would help; warrior or demon, Faelan probably knew a hundred ways to kill her with his bare hands.

He speared another chunk of pineapple. "Don't all women?"

Bree put a hand to her throat and stared at the knife, remembering the crazed look in his eyes as he leapt from the vault.

"But my brother… uh, Biff, Big Biff, I call him, because he's so big. And strong. He stops by sometimes. A lot. Probably tomorrow."

Faelan's shoulders stiffened. "Tomorrow?" He glanced at the door, his body tense as an arrow ready to fly. He'd be gone before lunch if she didn't intervene.

"I forgot. He's not coming until next week."

He relaxed, but still watched her closely. "You never explained how you found me, where you got the key."

"The disk? My great-great-grandmother Isabel found it when they were building the house. She hung it on the mantel for luck. Of course, no one knew it was a key." She and her cousins had made up stories about it. She'd secretly believed it opened a time portal. If the book in the attic was right, her theory wasn't far off.

"You did." His tone was accusing.

Not until last night, when her fingers touched the grooves on the chest and she'd clearly seen the disk in her mind. How could she explain that or the words that had brushed her ear as the disk turned in the lock? "The opening on the vault had the same shape, the same grooves, and it's made of the same metal."

He grunted his disbelief. "What about this map you mentioned?"

"I found it in a trunk in the attic. There was a riddle on it."

"What kind of riddle?"

"'It lies hidden close to God, in a place where evil can't trod.' That's what it said. Then I read in Isabel's journal that a man came by in the 1800s searching for lost treasure, and I've always figured anything worth hiding is worth finding—"

"He came here?"

"His name was McGowan. He was murdered before he found what he was looking for."

"Murdered?" Faelan asked.

"He and another man with him."

"What year?"

"Early 1860s. After I read the journal, I remembered seeing McGowan's name on the box holding the map. The map resembled the graveyard. The riddle said 'close to God,' and the graveyard is close to the chapel. I thought someone had buried coins or jewels. Then I noticed the crypt was missing on the map, the biggest and oldest thing there. I figured it had to be a clue. And there was no place to hide anything except inside the burial vault."

"Can I see the journal?"

Bree started to refuse, thinking it would be invading Isabel's privacy, kind of like opening her underwear drawer and waving her bloomers around, but Faelan seemed very curious about Isabel's visitors, and Bree wanted to know why. "Sure," she said. She found it on the floor beside her bed, where it usually fell after a long night of reading, and carried it back to the table. "I'll read it to you."

> "The most dreadful thing has happened. McGowan and another man were robbed and murdered last evening as they walked through the woods to town. The bodies were found early this morning. Frederick tried to keep it from me, but I overheard the men talking about the vicious attack. There was speculation that someone else was also searching for McGowan's treasure, or it may have stemmed from an argument over this impending war. Someone in the area has been helping slaves escape to Canada. The men did seem rather intense. The older one in particular was disturbing. I think Frederick regretted inviting them to stay."

"War?" Faelan asked, his voice hollow.

"The American Civil War." If he wasn't from this country, or had been locked in the time vault prior to 1861, he wouldn't know about it. "With your memory loss, you probably don't recall what a terrible time it was for this country. Brothers killing brothers. More than six hundred thousand soldiers died."

He sat back in his chair, looking ill. "How long did it last?"

"From 1861 to 1865." She knew everything there was to know about the Civil War. Her childhood obsession had become her passion. It was the reason she'd become a historian. "Shall I read more?"

He nodded, and she continued.

"Today was one of the saddest I have known, watching McGowan's son remove the bodies from the crypt. I could feel his grief. I would not admit it except in these pages, but I think even before McGowan arrived I sensed death. Perhaps it is the reason I wanted the disk for a good luck charm, something to ward off evil. I should have known those things don't work. Frederick watches me as if I will have a nervous breakdown. I suspect he knows I'm reminded of my grandfather's tragic, untimely death. He was also robbed and brutally killed. Father was a baby then, and according to his mother, barely escaped with his life.

"Perhaps Frederick is right, and the pregnancy is making me emotional and restless. I am not the only one unable to sleep. Even as I write, I can see a lantern moving in the graveyard. Ghosts? Or McGowan's son searching for his father's treasure? I feel certain I have seen the son somewhere. I remember now—"

"The next page is missing," Bree said. "I'd kill to know what Isabel remembered—"

A scream sounded outside.

Bree jumped to her feet, and the falling journal struck her plate, dumping the contents on her jeans before it hit the floor.

Chapter 5

FAELAN GRABBED THE KNIFE AND LUNGED AT BREE. She yelped, but he was there before she could jump clear, shielding her from the door. She tried to peer around broad shoulders, but all she could see was a muscular forearm and long, lean fingers gripping the blade. He'd put himself in front to protect her. She felt a quiver that had nothing to do with the horrible scream.

"Where's my dirk?"

"In the bedroom."

"Stay here," he ordered. In three strides he was at the door. Whoever he was, he was used to being obeyed.

"What was that sound?" she asked, but he was already gone. She ran to the window and watched him move through the pale pre-dawn, one hand gripping the knife, the other clasped to his chest. He stopped and lowered his head, then trotted along the path like a bloodhound scenting a trail, as he disappeared into the woods.

What if he didn't come back, just kept going? Bree jerked open the door and took off after him. She found him in the clearing near the dig, standing tall and motionless, like a valiant protector of an ancient Scottish realm.

"Did you see anything?" she asked, panting.

He whirled on her, his expression fierce, the kitchen knife still in his hand. "I told you to stay inside."

She jumped back, alarmed, but she didn't care what

time he came from, she wasn't his dog. "Excuse me?" Her glare was wasted.

His eyes scoured the forest like a predator, concentrating on one spot beyond the tree line, before moving back to the empty holes nearby. "What's this?"

"It's a dig. My friend is an archeologist. He thinks this was once an Iroquois settlement."

Faelan frowned. "How long has he been digging?"

"A few months. He's working from notes an old trapper left. Grandma opened the site to him before she died. She loved Native American history. He hasn't found much, only some arrowheads and a beaded necklace." Jared was going to kill her when he found out she'd gone treasure hunting without him.

Bree caught a glimpse of Faelan's talisman as he moved closer to the holes. She'd feed him as much as he could eat, if he'd let her examine it. "Be careful," she warned, when his foot neared the edge. "Those holes are dangerous."

"These wee holes?"

"I sprained my ankle in that one." She muttered to herself, "The same ankle I broke in the cave."

He gave her a look that bordered on insulting. "What were you doing in a cave?"

He not only healed fast, he had ears like Superman. "Exploring." She shuddered at the memory, running her hands through her hair. "Did you figure out what that sound was?"

"No," he said, glancing at his dusty boot.

Bree saw a footprint in the dirt smeared with something... red?

Faelan nudged a rock, covering the print, and turned his attention back to the trees.

"Does this place seem familiar?" she asked.

He shook his head. "Do you get many trespassers?"

"Just campers," she said. "There's a campground a few miles through the woods. Every year a few of them get lost." Several since she'd moved in. "I think I saw one last night." She nodded toward his boot. "Is that blood?"

Faelan gripped her arm. "You saw someone last night? What did he look like?" His accent was stronger now, the brogue more distinct.

What did it matter, since he couldn't remember anything? "I'm not sure it was even a man. It was dark outside."

"Do you have a horse and carriage?"

"I have a Mustang—"

"It'll do," he said, pulling her across the grass, his longer legs forcing her to jog to keep up. His eyes never stopped scanning.

She wanted to ask what he was looking for, but she was almost certain she wouldn't like his answer. "Where are we going?"

"We need to leave."

"Why? Did you see something back there?"

He didn't answer, just kept pulling her forward.

"I guess we could ride around the area, see if you remember anything." While they were out, they could get extra sheets and get him some new clothes. Nothing would be open this early except Walmart, but if secrecy was so important, he was going to have to lose the kilt. Probably best. Knowing he was naked under it wasn't doing her any good. "Let me change clothes and get my bag."

"Do you have to change?" he asked, eyeing the glob of food on her jeans.

"I'm wearing jelly," she said panting. "Can you slow down?"

He did, but not much. "Has this place been in your family long?"

"For generations," she said, looking at the house coming into view, faded, yet grand, like an old woman who'd once been a beauty, and now only character remained. Like Grandma Emily. "My great-great-grandmother's family owned the land. Her father gave it to her and Frederick, her husband, as a wedding gift. Frederick built the house for Isabel when she was only eighteen. The chapel was already here. A lot of my ancestors are buried in the graveyard. There was a village through the woods. This path was the road back then. My great-great-great-grandfather had a farmhouse not far from here. It burned down a long time ago."

For a man whose movements were so smooth, the hesitation in his stride struck her as extraordinarily clumsy.

"What was his name?"

"Samuel Wood. Does that ring a bell?"

He didn't answer, just watched the trees as if he expected them to attack. They hurried past the orchard her grandmother had planted near the house. "Look out!" Faelan said, as Bree's shoe caught the edge of a log Jared's men had carried over from a tree they'd cut near the dig.

She felt herself falling, and then she was in Faelan's arms, her breasts plastered to his chest. His heart hitched. Or was it hers?

"Are you okay?" he asked, untangling their legs. He didn't let go. He searched her face, blinked a few times, and jumped back as something poked her stomach. She didn't have the courage to look down and see if it was his sporran or something else.

"I think so. Thanks. You're fast."

His lips twitched. "Now I understand how you fell in that wee hole."

Let him fall in one and see how little it was, she thought, checking to see if she'd torn one of her favorite shoes. "I meant to split the wood a few days ago but never got around to it." She'd gotten sidetracked by McGowan's map. "I love a fire in the winter. I may have to hire someone."

Faelan scooped up an apple, cleaned it off on his kilt, and took a bite.

"Take all you want," she said, looking at the fruit wasting on the ground. "Grandma used to make apple-sauce, but I never got the hang of it. All I can manage is a pie."

"Apple pie?" he asked, wiping a drop of juice from his chin.

"I'm not the most graceful person alive, but I make a pretty good pie. I suppose I could bake one for dessert tonight." Maybe a full belly would loosen his tongue.

"Hurry and get what you need," he said as they reached the back porch. He hurled the apple core into the trees so far it would've put a major-league baseball pitcher to shame, and posted himself at the door like a guard.

What did he think was out there? She changed into a print skirt and grabbed her tote bag before meeting him outside. His eyes roved over her legs, looking as shocked as if she'd slapped him.

"What's wrong?"

"Nothing."

She led him toward the azaleas and pines hiding her red 1968 Fastback from view, dropping back a few steps when he kept glancing at her legs. "There's my Mustang—"

He stopped so fast, she plowed into him. "I thought you meant a horse," he said, finally looking at something besides her knees. He approached the car like she would Noah's Ark, running his hands over the hood, smudging her wax job, pressing his nose to the window like a kid who'd crash-landed in the North Pole.

More proof he wasn't a demon. All human males were as fascinated with cars as they were with breasts. Faelan appeared to be no exception.

"It's yours?"

"It was my dad's. He died when I was a kid." One day the car would be hers, he'd promised. One day he'd teach her to drive. He hadn't.

"You loved him," Faelan said.

Bree heard sympathy in his voice. Did he miss his father as much as Bree missed hers? She and her dad had done everything together, Civil War re-enactments, metal detecting, exploring caves. The only time he'd let her out of his sight was to visit her grandmother. Bree had never understood why she wasn't allowed to attend summer camps and have sleepovers like the other girls. She asked him about it once. He'd smiled a little sadly and said fair damsels had to be protected. That was before she found out about her dead twin.

There was a rustling in the trees, followed by a shriek, and something white flew overhead. Faelan grabbed Bree's arm. "Let's go."

She opened the car door, and he shoved her inside. What was he so afraid of? "Was that an owl?" she asked after he moved around to the other side. "I've seen a huge one hanging around. That could be what we heard earlier."

"Maybe."

She showed him how to work the seat belt, then started the car. The engine roared to life, and Faelan's eyebrows rose. At the end of her long driveway, she pulled onto the road and hit the gas. Faelan's shoulders were thrown back as he gripped the seat. Bree played tour guide as they drove, but he wasn't listening. His gaze was everywhere—on the car, the scenery, the traffic—but his hand never strayed from the bump where the necklace lay under his shirt. They passed a massive rock sticking out of the ground, and he twisted around. Bree saw the look on his face. Recognition.

"Is that a talisman you're wearing?"

He clamped his hand over the necklace, as if she might leap across the seat and rip the thing from his neck. "How do you know about talismans?"

"I have all sorts of useless knowledge floating up here," she said, tapping her temple. "Who gave it to you?"

"Mi… my family."

"The one you can't remember?" Touché. She saw a muscle in his jaw twitch. "If you knew your last name, we could search for them on the computer."

"Computer?"

She could tell by the way he formed the word that it was the first time he'd uttered it. "You can find anything you want on a computer, and some things you don't, but I need a name first."

"Hopefully I'll remember it soon. I have nothing. No home, no horse, no food."

She was pretty certain he'd remember when he wanted to. "I wanted to talk to you about that. Since you can't remember anything, you're welcome to stay here until we figure out who you are."

He looked at her as if she'd offered him cyanide. "You'd do all this for a stranger after…" He shook his head. "Why?"

"You have an odd way of showing appreciation."

"You're too trusting. I could be dangerous."

She knew he was dangerous, but he was also the key to a mystery. "I woke you. It seems the right thing to do, in here." Bree patted her heart, and Faelan stared at her breasts. With Russell calling every day, it wouldn't hurt to have a strong man around, even one she'd found in a crypt. Russell would think twice before coming after her with Faelan here.

"I'm becoming more and more indebted to you," he said, not sounding pleased about it. "I can take care of the farming and chores until your brother gets here, then I'll leave."

Leave? She'd just found him. "I don't have chickens or cows, but there's work to be done, that's for sure." Isabel's journal had distracted Bree from remodeling.

"I'm surprised you don't have someone to help you with the place." His tone gave away what he didn't say. That she was too old not to have a husband. Unmarried at twenty-six would have been a spinster in his time.

"I don't have much luck with men." She didn't realize she'd spoken aloud until he lifted one sexy eyebrow in disbelief.

"You can't be serious?"

"I can't find a *good* one." With those ears of his, she'd have to be more careful what she said. She had a tendency to talk to herself, something Jared teased her about. Jared. "You know, the archeologists will be back in a few days. You'll have to stay hidden."

"Aye. We can't have your reputation sullied."

Her reputation sullied? "I was thinking of someone asking questions." She glanced at his kilt. "You said no one could know about you. I could say you're Cousin Reggie. He owes me." She pictured the crypt rising from the weathered gravestones, the old tree hanging over the top like a shroud, and remembered the crippling fear. Screams. And blood. The memory stopped there, as it always did.

"What in tarnation is that?" Faelan asked, looking out the window at a silver glint in the sky.

"An airplane."

"Airplane?" The word sounded as strange on his tongue as *computer* had. He watched the white line cut through the clouds, and she could see a thousand questions in his eyes. His astonishment erased any lingering doubts. She took pity on him, knowing he must be dying of curiosity, too.

"It's remarkable how much travel has changed in the last century. We've gone from carriages and hot air balloons to airplanes that can carry hundreds of people anywhere in the world in less than a day."

"You jest?" he murmured, obviously forgetting his amnesia as he watched the plane disappear, his expression a mixture of fascination and alarm.

If he wasn't the demon, why didn't he admit who he was?

When the last of the policemen had gone, the tall man slipped from the woods, carrying the shovel he'd taken from the dig. He hurried through the graveyard, stopping at the back of the crypt. Counting off five paces from the corner, he approached the third grave. Just as the paper had said, a headstone with no name. He heard a cry and something white swooped overhead. A huge owl settled in the gnarled tree, tucked in its wings, and watched with steady, round eyes. Was this a bad omen? Swallowing, he raised the shovel and drove it deep into the earth.

Chapter 6

DRUAN STOOD IN FRONT OF THE ANTIQUE MIRROR inspecting his human form. He leaned closer, peering at a tiny line in his forehead. The furrow surprised him. Was that a wrinkle? He'd been here too long. The humans were rubbing off on him. It wouldn't be much longer. Soon all the pieces would be in place. He wouldn't fail this time. He couldn't, not with the Underworld watching to see if he would outdo his father's plague and Tristol still gloating over his precious HIV.

This new virus would make Tristol's AIDS look like child's play. Druan's shell started to shift just thinking about Tristol. The demon was even more despicable than the humans. Demon? Druan sneered. He knew Tristol's secret. Druan had caught him in the act. If only he were free to reveal it. But he had secrets of his own to protect. A knock sounded. "Enter."

"You called, Master?" This minion was new, not one he'd seen before.

Come to think of it, there had been several new faces in the last few days. He'd killed so many, he supposed Grog had found it necessary to replace them. "Did they find it?"

"No, Master, but we found a coffin."

"A coffin?" Druan let out a frustrated roar and then forced himself to inhale and exhale, slow and steady. In human form, he'd found deliberate intakes of oxygen to be calming. He'd found it necessary too much of late. Here he was, ready to wake the warrior, and both the vault and the key were missing. He should have killed the warrior when he had the chance, but he'd needed to test the time vault. If it did what he suspected, he would have more power than he'd dreamed. "This wasn't a coffin."

"Are you sure this is the place?"

"I saw it buried myself." He'd watched the lid close and the key turn in the lock.

"Maybe it's been moved," the minion suggested.

No one knew where it was except those who'd buried it, and most of them were dead. Tristol, Malek, and Voltar weren't there. Druan had waited until they were gone before burying the time vault. Had one of them spied on him? Tristol? Had Tristol stolen the time vault? He'd probably dug it up and replaced it with a coffin for spite. He was near. Druan was sure of that. This morning he'd found another minion slaughtered on the front lawn. If this kept up, someone would notice the vultures.

Druan turned to the minion. "If the time vault has been moved, it couldn't have gone far. It was heavy as a ship." He'd tortured a young warrior decades ago, attempting to discover how they transported the vaults, but the warrior had stayed loyal until death.

Another knock sounded, and Malek walked into the room without waiting for permission. The minion dropped his head in deference as Malek passed.

"The human is here," Malek said, brushing the streak of silver adorning his thick, auburn hair.

"Let him wait," Druan said, wishing he could throw Malek out, or at least figure out why he was here. But he couldn't refuse hospitality to one of the League. He turned to the minion. "Time's running out. Find the vault or you'll be *replaced*."

He would've checked on it sooner, but he'd been so busy with the war and trying to salvage his lost virus, while convincing the rest of the League that the warrior had lied. He'd never dreamed someone might move the damned thing.

The minion kept his head lowered. "Yes, Master." He followed Malek from the room, and Druan thought he saw a smirk.

That one needed watching. With minions, you never knew when they'd turn on you. If this wasn't over soon, he'd get rid of the lot of them and start fresh. He knew a demon in Haiti who could supply as many as needed.

He moved back to the mirror, concentrating, but all he could see was himself. That oaf of a sorcerer. He frowned, growing angry when he realized how often he was slipping into human expressions, even when there was no one around to see his disguise, although he was glad it had remained intact after all this time. He admired the front and then turned away from the mirror, spinning his head around backwards.

Yes. That side was holding up, as well.

⌇

It was worse than trying to keep up with a child. Bree tucked the receipt in her wallet and searched the street for Faelan's dark head. A warrior should be easy to spot. She hoped he was a warrior. A demon couldn't look that good.

Then again, Satan couldn't have been too ugly, or Eve would've run screaming from the Garden of Eden instead of listening to his lies. And Lucifer, the morning star, the signet of perfection, full of wisdom and perfect in beauty—yikes—until his pride corrupted him and he tried to become greater than God. The dark angels, demons disguised as angels of light, all beautiful. Like Faelan, who was hiding everything but his name. He probably would've hidden that too, if he hadn't been half unconscious when she asked.

Bree spied a bakery, and a few stores down, a lingerie shop. Food and sex. She hurried toward Margaret's Bakery, since it was closest. An assortment of delicious aromas teased her nose as she opened the door. A round, pink-cheeked woman smiled from behind the counter.

"I'm looking for a man—" Bree started.

"Aren't we all, dear? All I got's bread and doughnuts, but they're the next best thing."

"I don't know about that… well, maybe doughnuts. I've lost my… friend. He's tall—six four—longish dark hair, wearing a kilt."

"Oh, him." She smacked a hand over her heart. "I'd take him over doughnuts any day. He just left. Ate all the banana nut bread samples and headed for the lingerie—"

Bree's feet were already in motion as she shouted thanks over her shoulder. The door slammed on the woman's reply. Bree speed-walked down the street, dodging the morning shoppers, her tote bag with Faelan's new clothes bumping her thigh.

Faelan in a lingerie shop? He'd have a heart attack. In his time prostitutes would've worn more clothing than the average woman today. Bree burst through the door, and there he was, in all his kilted glory, standing near the edible panty display, holding a tiny piece of material in his hands.

"Go ask if he needs help," one of the slack-jawed girls whispered to the other, both staring at him as if he were Attila the Hun.

"You do it."

They were probably afraid he'd ravish them. Bree wasn't sure he wouldn't, but she wasn't about to stand idly by and let him ravish someone else. She set her bag down and cautiously approached him like an animal in the wild. "Faelan?"

He looked up, eyes so dark with passion that her heart moaned. Before she could blink, he pulled her into the dressing room behind him. The door slammed and his lips came down on hers, his body pinning her against the wall. Bree put her hands against his shoulders to push him away, but the feel of hard muscle and warm skin was too much. His mouth moved to her neck, biting and licking until her knees gave out, and all that held her up was his leg wedged between her thighs. He tasted every bit as delicious as she'd remembered, desperate with a touch of divine.

"Do you need any… help?" a timid voice asked from outside the closed door.

They both froze. Faelan dragged his mouth from hers. He looked at her body astride his leg. "I'm sorry," he whispered, his voice rough.

"Everything's fine," Bree croaked, her back still pressed to the wall. Faelan steadied her and backed away, his expression grim. He rearranged his kilt and sporran as Bree pulled her skirt down and ran her hands over her hair, hoping it didn't look like they'd been doing what they had.

"Let's get out of here." She'd done some stupid things in her life, but since she'd found Faelan, she was off the chart.

He took her hand, and they exited the dressing room. An elderly woman waited outside the door, holding two thick robes. Next to her, the salesgirl was trying to cover her shock.

"Well, I never," the woman said, glaring at Faelan from head to kilt over the top of her bifocals. "What kind of place is this?"

"Ma'am." Faelan tipped his head, the edible panties still in his hand.

Bree snatched the panties and put them on the counter. "They didn't fit." She scooped up her bag and yanked Faelan outside. He took the tote bag from her, and they trudged in silence for a block until they came to a bench on a quiet street.

Bree sat, and Faelan joined her, putting a large space between them. "I'll leave as soon as we get back. I need my dirk."

"Where will you go? You'll starve."

"I can hunt."

"You have to have a license to hunt. You probably need food. Let's try that taco place. You can change clothes in the restroom. You're drawing too much attention in that kilt. Then, we're getting you a cell phone or a leash. I'm not losing you again."

"Do you need a doctor?"

Faelan's hand was pressed to his chest, his face pale.

Bree took his arm. "I'm taking you to the hospital." She could tell them she'd found him on the street.

"No." He pulled away, walking toward the brightly colored fruits and vegetables, floor-to-ceiling shelves of food, cereal boxes, pastries, and breads.

"I thought you were having a heart attack," she said, hurrying after him. He didn't hear her. He was already halfway to the bananas. Shopping with him would be fun.

Half an hour later, she'd changed her mind. "Stop eating the grapes, before they throw us out of the store," she hissed. The produce manager watched them from the corner of his eye while pretending to stack oranges.

"I'm hungry."

He couldn't be hungry. He'd just eaten ten tacos and half a pound of grapes. "Here, eat a granola bar. We can pay for it. I'm going to get another cart," Bree said. They'd already filled one. "Don't eat anything else."

Faelan stuffed his mouth with granola like a starving toddler and moved down the aisle with the loaded cart. Bree grabbed an empty one and squeaked back. She rounded the corner and stopped. Faelan wasn't chewing. That was a good sign. The package he was reading wasn't. He glanced up, mouth parted, eyes dark, and the hand holding the box of extra large condoms darted behind his back.

"Ice cream. We need ice cream. Meet me in the freezer section." Her cart thumped along, squeak, bump, squeak, bump, as she fanned her heated face. She yanked out a carton of Caramel Delight, and a reflection appeared in the glass, right there beside the Chunky Monkey. Her heart froze. Russell! She whirled, searching the aisle for his dark blond head. It couldn't be Russell. He was in Florida.

"Hello, Bree."

She yelped and spun again, and the carton of ice cream shot out of her arms like a torpedo. "Peter!" Peter Rourke was a homicide detective. One of her grandmother's dearest friends.

Peter chuckled, retrieved the ice cream from the floor, and placed it in her cart. "I swear, you remind me of Emily. Haven't seen much of you since the funeral. You doing okay?"

"Good as can be expected." Bree glanced toward the aisle where she'd left Faelan and saw him park the cart near the restrooms. "I still miss her. I think I always will."

"Me too." He sighed. "I'm glad I ran into you. I stopped by…"

She tuned him out, her thoughts racing. She had to get rid of Peter before Faelan got back. She took a couple of steps backward so she could see Faelan coming before Peter spotted him. Thank God they'd put the tote bag with his old clothes and boots in the car. How would she explain that? How would she explain Faelan? She wasn't even sure who he was, what he was.

"…strangers in the area."

"What did you say? Strangers?"

"You sure you're okay?"

She nodded. "What about strangers?"

"A couple of campers saw something suspicious near your place."

"Suspicious?" Breathe in, breathe out. Had someone seen her dragging Faelan out of the crypt? If the world found out about him, she'd lose him. Someone else would solve her mystery.

"This morning, before sunrise. They were pretty shaken, rambling a bunch of nonsense about... well, it won't do any good to go into that. Must have been watching too many scary movies, but we had to check it out." He paused and leaned closer. "We found a body in the woods behind your house." His voice dropped to a whisper. "It was bad, Bree. I've never seen anything like it."

Bree's legs felt like a paper doll's. A dead body? In her woods? Was that the scream they'd heard? "Who was it?"

"Don't know yet. We're talking to the campers. The man was... torn up," Peter said. "Or else an animal got him. He'd been dragged through the woods."

She remembered the shadow outside the bathroom window. Had she seen the killer?

"Whatever or whoever did it was big. And strong."

Strong. Like Faelan, who'd looked ferocious enough to uproot a tree with his bare hands when she'd followed him? And she was almost certain he'd tried to hide a bloody footprint. But he was with her when they heard the scream, and he hadn't been out of her sight long enough to kill someone and drag him through the woods. "I haven't seen anything."

Maybe he had. That might explain his desire to leave.

"Call me if you do. Better yet, why don't you stay with me for a few days? I'd feel more comfortable if you were away from there."

"Thanks, but I'm expecting some books I have to sign for. I'll be careful."

"Just like Emily," he said with a wistful smile. "You could fill a room with all those books. Well, promise me you'll be careful. We're trying to keep this quiet, but your grandmother would come back and haunt me if I didn't warn you. Maybe get that young man of yours, the archeologist, to stay for a few days. We're patrolling the area, but it wouldn't hurt to have a strong man around."

She had a strong man around, but was he the one they were looking for?

"Did you know they have toilets on the wall—" Faelan stopped short when he saw Bree wasn't alone. His gaze darted between Peter and Bree. He was still several feet away, but it was too late to pretend she didn't know him.

"And this is?" Peter asked quietly, his shrewd cop eyes assessing Faelan and the loaded shopping cart.

"Faelan. He's here for a visit."

"Unusual name. Been here long?"

"Since last ni… last night." Drat.

"I hope you didn't pick him up somewhere."

Did a graveyard count? "No, I've known him… seems like forever."

"Is he staying at the house?"

"Yes. No. I mean, he's leaving."

"Does Jared know he's here?"

"Not exactly. Do you think you could not mention him to Jared… or anyone?"

One eyebrow lifted. "One horse at a time, girl," he whispered as Faelan approached.

Bree introduced the two men and maneuvered a hurried conversation in which Peter briefly explained the incident again, scrutinizing Faelan as he spoke. "I've got to get back to the office. Just stopped to get coffee. Call if you need me, Bree. Faelan, nice meeting you."

Faelan muttered a reply, staring at the street outside, his eyes narrowed, body stilled. A tingle tiptoed across Bree's arms. She followed his gaze, subconsciously looking for Russell's dark-blond head.

"Let's go home. We have enough food for now." She took the ice cream from the second cart and hurried Faelan to the checkout. His jaw dropped as he watched the items being scanned. He asked the lusty-eyed cashier to charge him for the half a pound of grapes he'd eaten, and she simpered and sighed, paying more attention to him than the groceries sliding past. Bree was certain at least two items made it into the bag without being scanned. When the third item missed the scanner, she started to mention it, but alas, it was a box of extra large condoms.

The tall man reached inside the coffin and removed the metal object hidden under the corpse's hand. He stared at it, stunned. God in heaven, it was true.

This was far beyond what he'd expected. He needed help.

"You did this?" Faelan asked, looking at the newly sanded floor in one of Bree's second-floor bedrooms. Sweeping and scrubbing floors was a woman's work. Refinishing them was not.

"I'm doing the smaller stuff myself. Grandma's dream was to restore this house to its former glory. I'm going to finish it for her. And the chapel, too. There's still a lot of work to be done. My sander broke. I'll have to finish this room by hand, but it keeps me occupied until I go back to my job."

"You work outside your home?" He'd assumed her grandmother had left her provided for, since she had no husband to take care of her.

"If I don't have a job, I don't eat. Come on, I'll show you where you can sleep."

It wasn't enough that he'd brought hell to her door. He was a burden on her purse as well.

Bree led him to the room across from where he'd slept last night. "You can sleep here." There was a dresser, one table, a chair, and a small bed frame without a mattress. He wasn't sure if he'd fit on the bed, but was pleased to see a window facing the graveyard so he could keep an eye on the crypt. No point in sending the time vault back when he'd need it for Druan, but it wasn't safe to leave unguarded. At least he'd hidden the key.

"We'll have to get a mattress from the attic."

"Are you sure you won't—"

"I told you, I'm not going to stay with Biff. This is my house. I'm not leaving."

If he could drive that confounded thing she called a car, he'd throw her over his shoulder and take off. If he had a horse, he'd do it anyway. "A man's been killed not a mile from your back door. It would be prudent to leave."

"Prudence has never been my forte. I'm sure it was a fight between two campers or a wild animal attack."

It wasn't an animal. He knew that scream. It meant one thing. *They* were here. But did they know he was?

"I don't suppose the trip jogged your memory," she said, stacking the rest of Faelan's new clothes on the chair.

"No." He knew she doubted his story, but he couldn't tell her the truth, not until he knew for sure who she was. "Do your doors and windows lock?" he asked, resuming his inspection of the room.

"Yes."

"Keep them locked. And stay away from the graveyard."

"Why?"

Because something was out there. And it wasn't human. Not fully. "You mentioned your great-great-grandfather was killed out there."

"In the chapel, not the graveyard. A falling stone hit him. And I think I'm perfectly capable of deciding whether or not to visit my graveyard. Somebody has to pull the weeds. I'm going to start dinner." She stalked out of the bedroom and left him staring after her.

He'd never seen anything like her. She was intelligent, beautiful, and he felt some kind of connection to her that scared the hell out of him, but he'd never met a woman who explored caves and searched graveyards for treasure, not to mention let him get away with things that would've had a woman of his time hysterical. He hoped she wasn't touched in the head.

It could be she wasn't scared because she was the one who'd brought *them* here. He looked around the room, relieved it was simple, with no newfangled devices. He'd seen enough modern inventions to make him wish he was still in the time vault. Automobiles and airplanes and buildings that reached the sky. He touched his pocket where he kept the phone she'd insisted he have, claiming someone could talk to him on it from the other side of the world. *If* anyone knew he was alive.

The quest for knowledge and convenience in this time was alarming. Nothing was left unexplored. There was some machine or apparatus to do anything a person might want. It seemed to him people had more need for things now, and less for each other. If this generation knew what evil walked among them, their *technology* wouldn't be so prized. If he didn't find Druan, all the knowledge and all the gadgets in the world wouldn't save them.

Faelan started for the door, when he heard a squeak. One end of the board he stood on had risen. He kneeled and lifted the plank, peering underneath. A piece of paper was tucked next to a small box. He picked the paper up, and a necklace fell to the floor, a tarnished silver cross. The bottom tip was notched, like a key. He turned it over and saw an emblem on the back. It looked familiar, but he couldn't think why. The paper was more disturbing, written in a child's hand. *Dear Shiny Man. Thank you for sending my protector to keep the monster away.* It was unsigned. Was this a child's game, or was the monster real? Demons weren't the only monsters out there. Humans could be evil, as well. There was nothing lower than someone who preyed on a woman or child. A painful memory seeped in. He pushed it back and concentrated on matters at hand.

The letter might not be Bree's. Many children would have lived here over the decades. He examined the small box, and heard something move inside. Did the cross open it? There wasn't a lock, not even a lid. He'd wager Ian could open it. His brother loved puzzles and secrets. Holding the necklace, Faelan went to find Bree.

She was bent over the bed, removing the muddy sheets, her skirt revealing more leg than he'd seen on a woman dressed. In his time, that is. He'd seen things downright scandalous in this one. A rush of heat settled in his loins. She hadn't heard him. She raised the edge of the mattress, and he heard her gasp. Moving quietly, as all warriors learned in their youth, he eased back, watching to see if she'd take the key. He couldn't risk it falling into the wrong hands. She pulled it out, and he reached for his dirk. Pish. She still had it. Muttering to herself, she replaced the key and dropped the mattress. He'd have to find a better hiding place, and he'd have to keep a closer eye on her. That would be hell, he thought, rubbing the ache between his legs.

He started to leave, but she turned and saw him. If he hadn't been so disturbed by her legs and her discovery of the hidden key, he'd have done the decent thing and covered his groin.

"I'm going to take a walk, see if I recognize anything," he said. He needed to find out how he'd gotten here and what part she played in this game.

―――――

Bree slid the apple pie in the oven, then stirred the beef stew simmering on the stove. If this didn't loosen his tongue, nothing would. She glimpsed something outside the window. Faelan was headed toward the dig. This was her chance. She grabbed her camera and ran out the back door. Opening the iron gate, she hurried through the graveyard, stopping just long enough to pick up the piece of broken gravestone she'd used to prop open the crypt door last night. She didn't know who Orenda was or why she'd been buried here, but Bree had used part of her gravestone so many times she felt she owed the woman a debt.

She passed Rosalie Wood and her stillborn baby, resisting the urge to stop and pull a lone weed that dared grow against the aged stone. Her great-great-great-grandfather Samuel had buried his wife and child together. Isabel had been only eleven when her mother and newborn sister died. When Frederick built the house, he put it near the graveyard, so Isabel wouldn't have to walk far to tend the grave.

Bree couldn't tend her sister's grave. She'd been cremated. Perhaps that was why she felt so connected to Isabel. They'd both lost a baby sister. What would it have been like having someone to play with, to share her thoughts and dreams?

Other than her twin, all her family members who'd died were here. Samuel, Isabel, Frederick, her father, grandmother, and Aunt Layla. They would be nothing but bones now and a few scraps of cloth, but Faelan, who'd been buried with them before she was born, was bursting with life, eating all her food, and lusting after her with every glance. He'd been here all her life, every summer she visited. When she was a toddler chasing butterflies. Sixteen and heartbroken because her first love thought she was weird. And a few months ago, when she ran to her grandmother's to escape Russell.

Would Faelan leave when he found his family?

Bree's chest felt tight, like her bra was too small. But wasn't that her plan, to find out who he was and get him back where he belonged?

She set Orenda's stone against the crypt door. "I'll put it back again, I promise." Bree followed Faelan's muddy tracks to the burial vault. She picked up the shovel, placed the square tip against the stone covering, and pushed. Wood cracked as stone scraped against stone, exactly how she'd imagined it sounded when the angels opened Jesus's tomb. Finally the time vault stood uncovered for the second time in more than a century and a half.

Faelan passed the archeologist's holes, continuing until he came to a withered pine. He touched the deformed trunk and remembered standing a few yards away when lightning struck. This was the field where Druan had ridden up, the trees where Faelan had hidden the time vault. They were taller now, some bare, some gone.

The earth had aged, but not him.

He didn't know what happened to Druan's disease. Maybe the other demons played some part in it. And his brothers, what of them? He'd dreamed of Tavis last night. Faelan looked at the sky, tracking the waning sun. He needed to get back. Demons preferred the dead of night, still he wanted Bree safely away before then. Until he knew otherwise, he had to assume she was innocent, but getting her to leave would be a fight. Tomorrow he'd check the place where the body had been found and secure the crypt. If anyone discovered the time vault's secret, human or demon, the clan was doomed. He turned and retraced his steps back to the house. When he neared the graveyard, his stomach dropped. The crypt door stood open.

Chapter 7

In the light of day, the time vault was as breathtaking as when she'd first seen it. Wood inlay adorned metal etched with symbols as far as she could see, like a sarcophagus. A polished gemstone was set in each corner. Green jasper. Was that what she'd glimpsed inside? She was dying to inspect the interior, but opening it would be too dangerous. A streak of dried mud smeared the front edge, and she imagined Faelan being dragged there unconscious. Or worse, awake. Who had stood over him, turning the disk, stealing his family, his life?

Bree raised the camera, and a shadow rose from the floor, obscuring the vault. A low growl came from behind her. She turned. A figure loomed in the door of the crypt, blocking the light. The darkness lengthened and grew as it came closer. She opened her mouth to scream.

"What the hell are you doing?"

"Faelan! You scared the stuffing out of me." She glanced guiltily at the time vault, then at Faelan's face, and almost wet her pants.

His eyes were obsidian slits. "What are you doing here?"

The low rumble of his voice made the hair on her neck stand. She backed against the burial vault, clutching the camera to her chest to keep her heart in place. "I lost an earring last night."

"Why is the time vault uncovered?"

"I thought while I was here, I would get a couple of pic—" She yelped as he ripped the camera away.

"Why?" The word dripped with venom.

"Why? Because it's incredible, that's why."

His hands clamped around the camera with so much force she thought he'd crush it. "No photographs." He tugged the heavy cover of the burial vault into place with one hand, grabbed Bree's arm, and pulled her outside, eyes scanning the graveyard and woods.

"Wait," she said, wrenching free. "I promised Orenda I'd put this back." She picked up the piece of headstone, cradling it in both hands.

Faelan's expression was hostile and wary, as if he expected her to bash him in the head. If she could lift the headstone high enough, she would. She left him standing there and started toward Orenda's grave.

Faelan caught up, planting himself in front of Bree. He opened his mouth to speak, looked past her, and his jaw dropped. He walked to the back of the crypt.

Bree turned. From this angle, she could see a pile of dirt behind the crypt. She followed him, still lugging Orenda's stone. Outrage rumbled through her as she stared at the gaping hole. Was this what he'd been doing out here? "What did you do? This is my favorite grave."

"I didn't do it—" his head snapped up. "We have to go. Now."

"Orenda's headstone—"

Faelan snatched it up as if it were a marble and dropped it on the ground. "Put it back later." He pushed her past Layla's and her dad's graves and out the gate.

"Wait. We can't leave the grave uncovered."

"I'll come back."

Had he seen something? She expected gunshots or screams as he dragged her into the house. As soon as they were inside, she wheeled around to blast him for being so rude, and the phone rang. Frustrated and angry, she answered without thinking.

The voice caught her off guard. She gripped the table to steady herself, leveling her voice to hide her dread. "What do you want, Russell?"

"You've been avoiding my calls."

She wrapped her hand around her shoulder to stop the shaking. "I have nothing to say to you." He'd stolen her money, her dignity, and peace of mind. What more could he want? Her blood? "I've asked you not to call."

"I miss you, Bree. Don't do this to us—"

He sounded sincere, like the old Russell from college, and for two seconds she remembered how charming and sweet he'd been. After she moved to Florida, the relationship died a long-distance death. A year and a half ago, she ran into him in an antique shop while visiting her grandmother; the same shop where she'd bought the Highland warrior painting. Bree had reached for an old book, only to find Russell's hand there too. They'd both laughed, and he bought the book for her. She couldn't remember which one now, she had so many. They went to lunch and a friendship renewed, blooming into a relationship, followed by an engagement. But little by little, he'd changed, turning into something dark and ugly. When she finally escaped him, it took her months to feel like herself again.

"There is no *us*, not anymore."

"Just meet me, please. I have something to tell you." His voice grew raspy, like it did when he was desperate. "Something important."

"It's all been said before."

There was a pause on the other end that chilled her blood. "This hasn't."

"Leave me alone, Russell." Bree hung up and threw the phone on the table, swiping at tears threatening to spill over her cheeks, angry she'd let him get to her again. Someone moved behind her. Faelan. She'd forgotten he was here. He stood a few feet away, watching her, his eyes stormy.

Men. Sometimes she wished she were a nun.

Letting Russell make her cry was bad enough, without witnesses. She couldn't deal with Faelan's lies right now.

He didn't know who Russell was, but Faelan wanted to crush the man's skull for making Bree afraid. Yet he'd acted no better in the crypt. "Are you okay?" he asked, following her out the front door, onto the porch.

She jumped and turned away, but not before he saw her damp cheeks. "I'm fine."

"I don't think so," he said softly, moving close behind her. He put his hand out, wanting to touch her, to take away the tears, but he doubted she trusted him any more than the bastard who'd put them there.

Her knuckles tightened on the railing and her shoulders began to shake. This was a new side of her, a dangerous one. It made him want to dismiss the suspicion and fear still coiled around his mind like a poisonous snake.

"Who's Russell?" He moved closer, daring to put a hand on her shoulder.

She flinched. "An old boyfriend."

"Wasn't he a good one?"

"What?"

"You said you couldn't find a good one." The problem wasn't lack of male interest. They'd all but leered at her in town. If she belonged to him, he would have put his fist upside a couple of heads. He'd wanted to anyway.

"No, he wasn't good. He was slime. Most men are." She turned, leveling him with a condemning glare.

Faelan pulled his hand away. He didn't deserve to touch her after acting as he had. "I apologize if I was too rough out there. I might have overreacted."

"Might have?" she said, her damp eyes shooting sparks. "You're acting like Russell, trying to scare me, dragging me out of the crypt. *My* crypt. I was just trying to take a picture."

"Why?" She was too smart to still believe it was a treasure chest. Did she have more devious reasons?

"Someday I'll want to show my children."

"You can't."

"Why not? If you can't remember anything, why are you protecting the time vault?"

He couldn't answer without giving away more secrets. He'd already made a dire mistake by calling it a time vault. "It's just a feeling." She should understand that. Women always acted on their feelings. "Who's buried in that grave?" he asked, hoping to distract her. "There was no name."

"I tried to find out, but kept running into dead ends. I don't think it was ever marked. The stone's too uniform. No indentions or discolorations. I can't imagine why someone would dig it up."

"Maybe the archeologist got bored."

"He wouldn't do that. He's out of town, anyway."

"Could be the killer was going to bury his victim there. Who'd think to look for a body in a grave?" Even demons had to hide their carnage. Secrecy was as important to them as the warriors they fought. "Or someone else is looking for McGowan's treasure. Who knew about the map?"

"Anyone in the family could have found it. Cousin Reggie was always nosey."

The trait must run in the family. "Did he ever mention it?"

"No. He didn't visit Grandma much after he grew up." Her forehead did that pretty puckered thing it did when she was thinking. "If I didn't know better, I'd think someone was playing a prank."

"Nasty prank. Who'd want to frighten you?"

She let out a string of curses that scorched Faelan's ears. "That jackass. I bet he's trying to scare me away so I'll run back to him. He's probably been watching the house, waiting for me to find the grave. That's why he called."

"Russell?" Something had been watching, but Faelan doubted it was human. "How far would he go to scare you?"

"I don't know if he'd kill someone, but if he heard about the dead man, I could see him trying to freak me out. I should tell Peter—"

"No." Faelan's voice was sharp. "Not yet. Please."

Bree studied him so intently he feared she was rethinking her decision to let him stay. He wouldn't blame her. He'd frightened her, nearly beheaded her, was eating all her food, and he'd almost ravished her. She knew he was hiding the truth. If he didn't do something to make up for his actions, he'd end up sleeping under a tree. "You said you lost an earring. I'd like to help you find it."

"Thanks." She sniffed, arms stiff across her body. "It was my great-great-grandmother's." She rubbed her ear, and he noticed the tiny hole.

At least it was in her ear. He'd held the door for a lass in town with enough metal in her face to make a small sword, and she was covered head to toe in black, right down to her fingernails and lips. Better than some he'd seen wearing what Bree called shorts that barely covered their arses.

She still looked uncertain, so he tried a different approach, one that would appeal to her curiosity. "I've remembered something," he said. He despised having to depend on someone and didn't like having to lie, but until he found his clan, he needed Bree's help.

Her eyes flashed, and she pulled in a quick breath. "You have?"

"A name. Connor. I think it might be a surname." He hoped it was enough to lure her inside to her research machine and off this porch. He wanted to believe the shadow he'd seen in the woods out back a few minutes ago was one of her lost campers. Or even a vicious murderer who'd tried to dispose of a body in an old grave. But he wouldn't wager they were so lucky. He desperately needed to find his clan. He'd see if her modern machine could do that.

Connor. The clan named in the *Book of Battles*. Proof he was connected to the legend. So why all the pretense? He couldn't be that desperate for a meal.

He didn't look angry now, he looked worried and ashamed. He probably expected her to toss him out. She should, but she supposed she'd be upset too, if she found someone poking around at the thing that had stolen a lifetime from her. Still, it was no excuse for acting like a caveman. "The computer's in the bedroom." Connor could be a Scottish or Irish surname, but he had a bit of Scottish brogue, and he'd been wearing a kilt. They had a starting point.

Bree fired up the computer while Faelan inspected the artifacts and treasures she'd collected over the years. "What are these?" he asked, running a hand over one of the wooden boxes.

"Puzzle boxes," she said, as the image of a face blinked across the screen, fading to black. She rubbed her eyes. She had to get more sleep. "They were my Aunt Layla's. My dad's youngest sister. She was only twenty-five when she died." No one in the family talked about Layla. The topic was as taboo as Bree's twin. "I always loved the boxes, so Grandma gave them to me."

Faelan moved behind Bree, so close she smelled the warmth of his skin. She pushed her chair back and jumped to her feet. "I think this computer's possessed." She felt like tossing it in the yard.

Faelan glanced out the window and frowned. "It's getting late. We should leave."

"We haven't even had dinner. Are you that afraid?"

His muscles bulged. "I'm not afraid, but there's a killer out there, Russell or someone else. It's not safe for you to stay."

"I'll take you to a hotel, but I'm not running away."

She was tired of running. Russell always found her. Besides, what would he do against a big, bad warrior? Or a big bad demon, for that matter.

"I'm trying to protect you, and you're making it bloody hard." He scowled at her and left the room. A second later, she heard his door slam.

Male chauvinist. She'd never asked him to protect her in the first place. After his behavior in the crypt, she wondered if he was the threat.

Bree studied the names until her eyes blurred. She'd seen hundreds, but no Faelan. The oven timer dinged. His apple pie. She should let it burn. She put the *Book of Battles* back in the box. Tonight, after he was asleep, she'd find his name. The aroma of apples and cinnamon filled the house. She opened the oven. "Ouch." She blew on her burned finger and pulled out the apple pie. Perfect. The crust was golden brown, the smell delicious. She started to dump it in the trash, when it occurred to her there was food cooking and Faelan was nowhere in sight. Maybe he'd left without her. She set the pie on the counter, fighting off a wave of panic.

A thump sounded outside, followed by a crash. Alarmed, she hurried to the back door. Faelan stood near the orchard, beside a pile of wood almost as tall as he was, holding an ax. Her eyes smarted with relief. He'd changed into his kilt again. His hair was loose, his shirt hanging over the shed door. Muscles bunched and released as he raised the ax, sinking the blade into a piece of wood. He tossed it on the pile and reached for another, splitting it clean in half. He looked up, and his eyes met hers. Something quivered inside her, terrifying in its force.

He grinned. If she hadn't dodged it, Cupid's arrow would've nailed her right there on her back porch. After all the inconsiderate jerks she'd dated, one mention of needing the wood split, and he'd done it for her. Even though he was upset.

She swallowed the ball of emotion and called out, "Dinner's ready. I made a pie."

"Give me a minute to stack this, and I'll be in," he yelled back, picking up an armload.

She walked inside, oddly disturbed for someone who'd avoided having to split a load of wood. She'd never had this strong a reaction to a man, and she'd sought out handsome men like a plant seeks light. This was bad. No matter what secrets he held, he had the power to destroy everything she'd worked for, normalcy, peace of mind. Maybe she should let Jared give Faelan a bed. That thought gurgled and died when Faelan stepped in the back door. His damp shirt hung from one hand, and in the other, he held a clump of wildflowers. He stretched out his hand. "I'm sorry."

Her throat clogged, and she focused on the sweat trickling down his chest to keep from crying. No one had ever given her wildflowers. She swallowed and took them from his dusty hand.

"I know I've been… difficult," he said. "I don't find it easy to trust people. And I'm too protective. I don't know any other way to be. Can you forgive me?" He stepped closer and touched her arm. His pheromones shot straight up her nose. She knew all she had to do was take half a step, and she'd be in his arms.

She nodded and stepped back. "Thank you. For the flowers. And the apology."

"I know it's not much, but I do appreciate all you've done for me." He sniffed. "Is that apple pie?"

She nodded. "Are you hungry?" He was always hungry.

"Starving." He glanced at her mouth and quickly looked away. "I probably should wash up first. I'm sure I don't smell as good as the pie." He grinned and wiped his forehead and chest with his shirt, leaving her hotter than the bubbling stew.

"Eat first. Just wash your hands at the sink there. After dinner you can take a long soak in the tub. Your muscles must be sore from splitting all that wood," she said, watching them ripple as he walked toward the sink. She filled a vase and put the flowers on the table.

Dinner was awkward. Every time she looked at him, he was watching her. It wasn't just him. She was battling her own demons. All she could think about was that kiss in the dressing room, sitting astride his leg.

"Leave the dishes," she said when they'd finished. "I'll clean them up while you try the Jacuzzi."

"Jacuzzi?"

"A big tub. Come with me."

He followed her to the master bath. "A lot fancier than what we had," he said, touching the marble sink. "My mom—" He paused, and Bree saw pain flash in his eyes. She pretended not to notice the slip. It was becoming a strain to keep up this charade, but he was softening toward her. She hoped he was close to telling her the truth. "This shower is nicer than the one in the hall bathroom. Or you can use the Jacuzzi." She pointed to the jetted tub. "A massage would probably feel nice."

"Massage?" he said, giving her a look that made her knees wobble.

"The tub... the water massages you. I don't know why Grandma went all out on the bathroom, when the rest of the house needed work, but I'm not complaining. Would you like to try it?"

"Aye. I would."

Bree found an extra toothbrush, one of her disposable razors, and some antiperspirant that claimed it was strong enough for a man. She hoped so. The condoms had rattled her so badly she'd forgotten several things on her grocery list. She gave him the toiletries, pretending she didn't notice his surprise, then quickly left. She closed the door behind her and heard two thuds that sounded like boots against tile. She was still trying to banish the image of him in his kilt, swinging that ax, when he called her name. She eased down the hall and poked her head in the bedroom. The bathroom door was open, water running. His kilt and boots were on the floor.

"Can you help me?" he asked, gripping a white towel around his waist.

"Help you?" she squawked, remembering the old westerns she and her father had watched, with someone scrubbing the cowboy's back while he sat in a big copper tub. Surely he didn't—

"How do you make the tub work?"

Relieved, she showed him how to turn on the jets and escaped into the hall. What was she going to do with him? He was hiding the truth, mysterious, scary as heck at times, but he was also protective and kind. And though he took pains to hide it, he was grieving. If he was as old as she thought, he had reason to grieve. Everyone he knew would be dead.

Turning, she caught her reflection in the antique mirror and rubbed the chill bumps on her arms. Sometimes she could swear the mirror had eyes.

—∿—

Bree stared at the closed door. What was he doing in there? Cleaning? He'd agreed to take bathroom duty, since she didn't have fields to be plowed and cows to be milked. A woman couldn't argue with that. He could be trying to avoid the sparks flying between them. The look he'd given her in the bathroom had darn near incinerated her. Bree put her ear against the door. All she could hear were the jets. What if he passed out? A person could drown in her Jacuzzi. She tapped on the door. "Faelan? Are you okay?" He didn't answer. She turned the knob and peeked inside. His head was against the back of the tub, his eyes closed.

He was unconscious.

Bree burst into the bathroom and tripped over his discarded kilt. As she lurched toward the bathtub, she registered several things at once. His brow furrowed in concentration, lips parted, his left hand gripping the tub. The other…

Oh my.

Chapter 8

SHE FLUNG HER HANDS OUT TO BREAK HER FALL AND crashed on her knees next to the tub. Faelan's eyes flew open, the surprise gone before it settled, replaced by something so hot and dark she wanted to run. She started to stand, but his arm snaked around her neck, and he hauled her forward, his mouth covering hers. No playful teasing, no testing the waters, this was kissing, hard core. Her heart pounded like hundreds of River Dancers stomping out a beat. She didn't care that the side of the tub was digging into her ribs or that she was more in the water than out. She'd been kissing men from the wrong century.

Or were they just human?

The shock of that almost made her pull away, but Faelan guided her hand where he wanted it, trapping it under his. To her astonishment, she left it there. How long they kissed, she didn't know. Seconds, hours. His hand tensed in her hair, gripping hard. His lips stopped moving, open on hers, and he groaned as his body released. Shuddering, he held her close, his forehead buried in the crook of her neck as her heart cried, *Romeo*.

She knew if she searched another gazillion years, she'd never feel this connection with anyone else. But she'd been wrong before. Terribly wrong.

"I'm sorry," he said, drying her hand with the towel lying on the edge of the tub. He turned off the Jacuzzi, letting his head thump softly against the tile. Wet, dark hair clung to his shoulders, and Bree glimpsed the edge of a tattoo behind his ear. How had she missed one?

She rose to her feet and tried to think of something to say. What had possessed her? Historians didn't do things like this. Of course, she'd never had a man like Faelan naked in her bathtub, either.

Without warning, he stood. Water streamed off his body as he reached for another towel. He swiped it across his face and chest, then stepped out of the tub. For a man from the 1800s, he didn't possess much modesty, or maybe he figured she'd already seen everything he had. She, on the other hand, might take a shot at swooning.

He wrapped the towel around his waist and stepped closer. "I don't know what to say. I was trying to get it out of my system. I didn't want to take advantage of you."

"It's my fault for barging in on you. You didn't answer, and I thought you'd passed out… or something."

"Or something." A wolfish grin curved one side of his mouth. "I got you wet," he said, stretching out a hand, following a strand of hair from root to end. "'Thank you' doesn't seem the right thing to say." Another step, and the towel brushed her stomach. His hand moved lower, down her neck, past her ticking pulse. His eyes darkened and nostrils flared, as if he could smell her attraction. "Do you want me to take care of you?" he asked, lowering his head.

"No, I'm good." Bree scooted back, in case his Superman ears could hear her body begging. She tripped over his kilt again and sat hard on the floor.

Faelan blinked, bent, and pulled her to her feet, the passion on his face giving way to self-disgust. "I'm sorry. You should ask me to leave. I would, you know."

She was torn between desire to bolt out the door and desire to comfort his tortured soul, rip that towel off, and throw him on the floor. "I wish there was something I could do."

His eyes flared.

"I mean, you could see a doctor."

"A doctor? What would I tell him? That I crave you—like a starving man craves food? That I'm afraid to get within arm's reach of the only woman in the universe who knows I'm alive, because I might lose control and rape her?" A muscle jumped in his jaw.

It wouldn't be rape. "There are medicines that can affect the sex drive. Herbal supplements. They're always promising to increase things. Maybe they can decrease as well."

"Increase things?"

"You know… enhance."

"Enhance?"

She glanced at his groin, ineffectively covered by the towel. "The feeling. The parts."

"The parts?" His brows climbed higher. "Make it bigger?"

How did she get into these conversations? "Maybe we should…" she hesitated.

"What?" His eyes radiated hope and dread.

"Would it help if you could… if you could get it out of your system?"

"What do you think I've been trying to do?"

"I mean *really* get it out of your system. With a woman."

He took a step forward. "Are you offering?"

Faelan licked the edges, swirling his tongue closer to the center, so smooth, so slick, and the taste! He would slaughter ten demons for one taste. He slid the Caramel Delight container into the freezer and moved into the hall, ice cream cone in his hand; sustenance for his battle with Bree. She was leaving, she just didn't know it yet. He would carry her down the driveway on foot if he had to. Her determination to stay was admirable, but there was a time to fight and a time to leave. This was the latter.

The air stirred against his skin. His warrior senses kicked in. Hardheaded woman, she'd left a window open. It'd be a miracle if he managed to keep her alive until dark. He followed the breeze to the family room, stepping over boxes she'd been unpacking as he headed for the window. He was alarmed to see daylight nearly gone. He heard her voice and looked outside. She stood near the toolshed, her shirt loaded down with—he sniffed—apples. In the twilight, she looked pregnant. He puzzled over the odd warmth in his gut that wasn't hunger. Then, he heard another voice. Male. He reached for his sword, cursed, and grabbed his talisman instead, ready to climb out the window, when he remembered her brother. He must have heard about the dead body. The man was an idiot to leave Bree unchaperoned. If he knew half the thoughts in Faelan's head…

Maybe her brother could persuade her to leave.

"You know Jared," the brother said, moving into view. "He was worried after the message you left."

Who in tarnation was Jared?

"You split most of the wood," the brother continued. "I'm impressed."

"Uh, thanks," Bree glanced toward the house, shifting nervously from foot to foot.

"You should have called. I would've done it for you. I'll finish it up after we get back on site." He leaned in and pressed a kiss next to Bree's mouth, then drew her into a hug so tight Faelan's dirk, wherever in blazes she'd hidden it, wouldn't have fit between them.

The cone in Faelan's hand cracked. This was no brother. Was she courting someone? She didn't act like a woman who belonged to a man, but clearly moral values had changed while he slept. Only a wife would have done what she had in the bathroom. Or someone who expected payment in return.

Whoever the man was, he'd better get his hands and mouth off Bree. Faelan spun toward the door. His shoulder banged into a candlestick on the mantel, sending it and a loose photograph tumbling from the edge. His hands shot out to catch them. The cone went one way, the ice cream another, hitting the wall with a sloppy thump. He wedged the candlestick back into a hole he hoped it'd occupied and started to put the fallen photograph back. It was covered in ice cream. He wiped it on his shirt, and a face appeared, a dark-haired woman, her hairstyle and dress from another time. His time. Faelan's head felt thick, and the first two ice cream cones he'd eaten lay in his stomach like a rock. He stared at the picture, knowing if the image wasn't black and white, he'd see eyes as green as moss.

As green as the first time he'd seen them.

One hundred and fifty-one years ago.

Chapter 9

Faelan waited until Greg left the tavern before slipping outside. To his right, a carriage was unloading. A man with a limp climbed out, followed by a well-dressed young couple, newly married, judging by their intimate smiles. The woman wore a long green dress that matched her eyes. Faelan felt a strange pull, and it disturbed him. He didn't lust after other men's wives.

The older man nodded to Faelan. "Fine day today."

"Not bad," Faelan said, too distracted for pleasantries. He tipped his hat as the couple approached, and darned if the woman didn't trip over the hem of her dress and drop her satchel at his feet. Good manners demanded he help. He and her husband gathered the scattered items, waiting as she crammed them back inside her bag.

She flashed a grateful smile as Faelan handed her the last item, a heavy book engraved with a rose. Large, green eyes met his, and the smile slid from her face. She blanched, pulled her satchel close, and then turned away, hands shaking. The men nodded thanks, not noticing her reaction, and the three strangers walked inside.

Faelan stared at the picture, his chest aching. Only a being with demon blood could remain nearly unchanged for more than a century. She must be a halfling. Was the man outside really a man? He wasn't Druan; the form and hair coloring were wrong. But he could be working for Druan. Faelan raced for the door, still gripping the photograph. He ran into Bree, already on the porch. Her shirt was doubled up into a bumpy pouch. "Who was that?" he demanded, yanking her inside and slamming the door. Apples tumbled from her shirt and rolled across the floor.

"That was Erik," she said. "What's wrong?"

"Who's Erik?" He put his hand on the door, in case she tried to run.

"One of Jared's men."

Erik, Jared. Was she surrounded by men? "Who's Jared?"

"My friend, the archeologist I told you about. What's the matter with you?"

What was the matter with him? He was stuck in a time he knew nothing about, dependent on a woman who was pretending to be human. "Tell me who you are and who sent you." His hand tightened, crumpling the corner of the photograph.

Her breath came fast, and he could smell her fear. "I don't know what happened while I was outside, but you're scaring me," she said, shrinking against the door.

"You'd do well to be scared. Explain this." He thrust the photograph at her, but the phone rang. They both jumped, and the photograph fell. Bree tried to move, but Faelan put his hands on each side of the door, trapping her. The phone rang six more times as they stared at each other, neither one moving. He saw the fear drain from her eyes and fury take its place.

"How dare you accuse me of anything when you're the one walking around telling lies? Acting like Dr.

Jekyll and Mr. Hyde. If you were a real man, you wouldn't be afraid to admit who you are."

He felt like Nandor had kicked him in the face. His honor had never been challenged by a human. The phone rang again. She stomped on his foot and did a quick squat, ducking under his arm so fast he would have been mortified if his brothers had seen. She grabbed the phone, her fiery gaze never leaving his. He was beginning to seriously dislike telephones.

"Hello? Hi, Mom."

Mom? If she hadn't stolen the clan's book, then someone in her family must have. He eased closer to listen. His foot kicked an apple, rolling it under a chair.

"Tell me, darling, is the house a disaster?" a woman said.

"Actually, it's coming along pretty well."

"You said your men won't be back until next week. I was thinking I would come and help—"

"No."

"Are you all right, Briana? You sound strange."

"I'm just out of breath. I've been gathering apples to make *another* pie." She blasted Faelan with a withering glare, and he felt the last of his anger drain. She'd freed him from the time vault, offered him a bed and food, even baked him an apple pie, and he was acting worse than that Russell bastard. He'd witnessed her distress over his call. Halflings lied easily, but they were awkward with false emotions. And he'd never heard of one baking an apple pie and falling in holes. It was possible she only resembled the woman in the photograph or was related to her. According to her, the place had been in her family for generations. His gut told him she was innocent. His gut had said the same thing about Grog, though, and look where that had gotten him.

"Now's not a good time," Bree said. "You know, your allergies. I've been sanding floors. The place is a dust mite motel."

"I'm glad you're staying busy. You needed something to focus on, and I know how much you loved summers there. Maybe this will get those foolish ideas out of your head."

—⁓—

Bree watched Faelan, standing there, arms folded across his chest, eavesdropping. His eyes were intense, but his glower had softened. Bree decided that while he had no regard for her privacy, he did have a soft spot for mothers. Of course he would. He'd lost his.

"I almost forgot," her mother said. "Russell called."

"Russell called you?" Bree's throat constricted.

Faelan moved next to her, head tilted, probably listening to both ends of the conversation. He looked contrite now, as if he hadn't just gone berserk.

"He says you won't take his calls," her mother said.

"Of course I won't take his calls."

"So he's not Romeo. We're not getting any younger, dear. I want to play with my grandchildren, not bequeath them my belongings."

Faelan's brow did its half-lift thing, proving he was indeed listening to her mother's side of the conversation.

"Don't hold your breath," Bree muttered, wondering what her mother would say if she saw Faelan. He made Romeo look like a girl. Heck, he made Rambo look like a girl.

Disaster averted, Bree hung up, wondering which Faelan she'd see. Fierce warrior, wounded hero, smoldering lover. Or Mr. Hyde.

"So you have men here?" he said, making her wish she'd never found McGowan's blasted map.

"It's not a male harem. They're helping me with the house. I don't know what's wrong with you, but you'd better get your act together, or I'll call Peter and have you arrested. See how you like jail food." She turned her back on him. "I'm going to bed. Make your own damn pie." She kicked an apple at him and stomped down the hall toward her bedroom, not caring whether he was gone in the morning or not. The mirror rippled as she tromped past. She blinked and stared at the thing, but it just hung there like mirrors do. First the computer screen, now the mirror. It was Faelan. He was driving her insane. Kissing her one second, scaring the living crap out of her the next, and accusing her of God knows what.

She slammed her bedroom door and locked it, ranting as she threw on pajamas. What had gotten into him? Was he jealous? Erik was a flirt, and Faelan had that whole he-man thing going, not to mention his appetite troubles. She was the only female around. That meant all his pent-up hunger had one outlet. Her. Of course he'd see any other male as a threat.

She had to find his name before one of them ended up dead. She considered going after the book, when a creak sounded outside her door. It could wait until tomorrow. She couldn't face Faelan again tonight. The footsteps moved on, and Bree settled into bed with Isabel's journal. After McGowan's murder, Isabel's journal entries slowed. Bree flipped to an entry dated a few days before Frederick died.

> I dreamed of the chapel again. When I woke, Frederick was gone. I would suspect he had a mistress, but I know he sneaks out there at night. All those years he forbade the children to go because of loose stones, and now he spends hours there himself. Perhaps he goes to pray. I fear that like me, he worries over what to do about the secrets we were told. I suppose we'll have to choose one of the children soon.

Choose one of the children for what? An heir? A sacrifice? What secrets? A noise sounded somewhere in the house, but Bree figured it was Faelan preparing for bed.

> Frederick mumbles in his sleep about a book, but says he doesn't recall it. I should warn him about the chapel, but he will just smile and pat my hand. In all our years of marriage, my disturbing dreams are the only thing I have kept from him, but men expect women to be proper and refined. I was afraid he would think me unladylike, or worse, a witch.

Bree yawned and closed the journal. Had Frederick found the *Book of Battles* in the chapel? Was that why a few nights later he was found dead outside the door? Who could have put the book there? Someone in her family must be a thief. Did Grandma know something about it? Was that what she'd been so eager to talk about before she died? Trying to clear her conscience? Bree wrestled with possibilities until her eyelids drooped.

—₥₥—

Faelan reached for Bree's door then pulled back. Nothing he said would get past her anger tonight. She was furious, and rightly so. He'd bloody well botched this up. He was either accosting or accusing the only woman who knew he was alive. He'd apologize in the morning. If they were still alive. He blew out a sigh and headed to the second floor. Perhaps he could earn back her trust. It was a bit early for demons yet; they preferred the dead of night.

Two hours later, he wiped the sweat and dust from his face and surveyed the sanded floor. That should please her.

He put aside his tools and left the room, aching for his bed. He couldn't sleep, but he could grab a few minutes' rest. Damnation. He'd forgotten to get a mattress. He climbed the narrow stairs, his brain muddled with exhaustion, suspicion, and lust. Regrets at what he'd done in the bathroom. More regrets that he hadn't pulled her into the tub and finished it properly. But that wasn't the way to treat a woman he'd known less than a day. She wasn't a prostitute, but it didn't mean she was fully human.

He stepped onto the dusty floor of the attic, gazing at what remained of the people who'd lived and died here. A stack of boxes was piled in one corner with bed frames, mattresses, and a child's rocking horse. Hers? Tables and other bits of furniture were on the far side. He followed a trail of footprints to an old trunk, similar to one he'd owned. She claimed to have found the map in a trunk. Someone had been here, that much was true. He could smell a flowery scent, like a woman's perfume. Lavender. He hadn't noticed it on Bree. The mattress could wait a bit. If her story was real, he needed to find out why this McGowan had been crawling around the graveyard and if he was connected to Druan.

Faelan opened the trunk, raking through musty clothes, ribbons, and a stack of small boxes. One had McGowan's name on the front, barely visible. She hadn't lied about that. Unless she'd written it. There was no treasure map inside, only a couple of straight razors. It neither proved nor disproved her story, but he still found it hard to believe she just happened to find a map to the crypt where he had been buried, and she just happened to live here in this house where the key just happened to hang on the mantel. In his experience, coincidences usually required careful planning.

He'd have to keep his head clear and his kilt on until he figured it out. Many a warrior had been sent to his grave by a filthy halfling hiding behind a lovely female form. He looked at the trunk again. Why would anyone in her family need one of *these*? Faelan removed the contents and ran his finger along the lower edge until it brushed the familiar slit in the bottom corner. He sorted through the things he'd removed, but there was no key. He tilted the trunk on its side and heard a thump. Something was hidden inside. He was beginning to think this house held nothing but secrets.

It wasn't likely Bree knew about the compartment. Any woman who went around opening burial vaults in the middle of the night wouldn't stop at a locked trunk.

Faelan replaced the items, wondering what had happened to the few belongings he'd brought to America. As he closed the lid, he saw the footprints continued to a stack of boxes. Following the trail, he found books.

He didn't need books. He needed answers. He lifted the top of the nearest box and saw a leather journal with thick bindings. Was this the one she'd read from at breakfast? Why put it in here? He picked it up and opened the cover.

The breath whooshed out of him like it did when Tavis punched him in the stomach.

Chapter 10

HIS CLAN'S SACRED *BOOK OF BATTLES*. WHAT, BY ALL that was holy, was it doing in America? In Bree's attic? Faelan slammed the book shut and put it on the trunk, staring at it as if it were a coiled snake. He'd never seen the book, much less held it. No warrior had. It was forbidden, kept under lock and key in a place known only to the Keeper of the Book. Not even the Watchers were allowed to see it. Inside was a hand-written list of five centuries of battles between warriors of the Connor clan and their assigned demons. It was even rumored to hold future assignments not yet issued by Michael.

If a demon got his—or her—hands on one, the entire clan could be wiped out. Faelan paced the floor, running his hands through his hair. Had Bree stolen it? Was she working with Druan?

He thought about her eyes, the softness of her mouth, how it fit under his, how clumsy she was, how alive. And that pie. The best he'd tasted. She'd saved his life. Probably saved the world. Would a halfling or minion do that?

There must be another explanation, but if not her, then someone in her family was a thief. How else could the book be here, in the place they had lived for genera-tions? Was someone in her family a minion? Or all of them? It would make sense that Druan would put the time vault somewhere it could be guarded. Demons often had a family of minions serve them for generations.

Faelan looked at the book lying there, holding so many answers. All he had to do was look inside, and he'd know if he would destroy Druan. If his brothers had died trying to help him. His suspension and awakening wasn't normal. Would he be forgiven for such a transgression?

Faelan's hands shook as he opened the book again, but he couldn't make himself look at the words. He wasn't beyond breaking an insignificant rule or two, but he'd followed the important ones far too long to cast them aside now. He flipped through the pages quickly to make sure the book was intact. The ink was faded and there were some stains, but it seemed fine until the end. The last few pages had been ripped out.

Someone had taken part of the *Book of Battles*. Bree? She'd admitted to being here. It must be her footprints marking the dust. Years of fighting demons had taught him to look beyond the obvious. If she'd lived here less than three months, it was possible she didn't know about the book. He had no proof she had taken it. It wasn't fair to hold her responsible for something someone in her family could have done.

He started to close the book and saw the last page, half torn, was written in a strange language. He'd heard rumors of secrets hidden deep within the clan. Was this one of them? Closing the book, he left the attic and approached her room. If he confronted her, she'd lie about it anyway. No. Better to watch her. Catch her in a mistake. He hid the book under the floorboard with the time vault key and then climbed into the shower, leaning against the tile in exhaustion. He was certain of one thing. Whether she did or didn't steal the book, he would find his answers here.

———·w·———

A ringing phone woke Bree. She shot up in bed, staring at it, afraid to answer, afraid not to. What if something was wrong with her mother? "Hello?"

"Bree, it's Peter. Sorry to call so late, but it's urgent that I catch your friend before he leaves."

This was her chance to get rid of Faelan, get him out of her hair. But then she'd never find out who he was and how he'd gotten inside the time vault, and she'd never rest knowing she'd walked away from the greatest mystery of her life. "Sorry, you missed him."

"Damn it. Any way to reach him?"

"It'd be difficult. Is he in trouble?"

"No. Just wanted to ask him some questions. Where did you say he lived?"

"Uh… Scotland."

"Scotland? Don't suppose you have his phone number?"

"I don't think so."

"What did you say his last name was? I'll find him."

She hadn't given Faelan's last name when she introduced the two men. "Vault."

"Faelan Vault. Got it. I thought about swinging by your place in the morning. I wanted to look in on you. You could always rustle up some French toast."

"You can't. I've got the flu."

"The flu? I just saw you this morning."

"It hit fast."

"You need anything?"

"Rest. Did you identify the victim?"

"Not yet. Kind of hard, with his body ripped to shreds and his fingers and head missing. Sorry. I'm frustrated. A mutilated body and no leads."

"What about the campers?"

"They don't know anything, or not saying, if they do."

"What about the ones who saw something strange?"

"They hightailed it out of here as soon as we questioned them. Didn't even come back for their gear."

"Did they actually witness the murder?"

"No. Just saw something in the woods near where it happened."

"You think they were involved?"

"I doubt it. I've never seen two people so scared."

"What did they see exactly?"

Peter gave a frustrated sigh. "An orc. Their words, not mine."

"An orc?"

"Like in *Lord of the Rings*. Those monsters with the ugly heads. They were probably on drugs, but keep your doors and windows locked. Whatever did it was either incredibly strong or incredibly insane."

Like Dr. Jekyll and Mr. Hyde. Bree glanced at her locked door. "You sure it wasn't an animal?"

"You can't repeat this, but we found some strands of hair. They look human. They're testing them now."

"What color?" she squeaked.

"Dark. Like your friend's. If you happen to find a number for him, or if you change your mind about staying there alone, call me. Emily had my cell phone number in the kitchen. Bree… be careful."

After he hung up, Bree touched the short piece of hair, remembering how terrifying Faelan had looked lunging at her with his dagger, how angry he'd been when she followed him outside after the scream, the footprint he'd hidden, the blood. His fury in the crypt when he'd found her taking a picture of the time vault. His bizarre behavior over Erik.

Was Faelan the demon? Was that his secret? He was with her when they heard the scream, but maybe he had a partner. Maybe her grandmother hadn't meant for Bree to help Faelan, but to help someone lock him away. Bree threw back the covers. This time she'd find his name in the book no matter how long it took. Demon or warrior. It was time for show and tell.

—◦◦◦—

It was gone.

Bree searched the floor, behind the boxes, in the boxes, but the *Book of Battles* was missing. He must have taken it. A thump sounded outside the window, and she jumped. Dead limbs were always falling from the old oak, but after finding Faelan, Bree didn't chalk anything up to normal. She went to the small window, clouded with age, and lifted the hem of her pajama top to clear a circle. The full moon was surrounded by clouds, throwing shadows on the chapel and graveyard. Trees began to look like skeletons and the chapel windows like empty sockets in a skull. The window facing her darkened as if something stood there. It wasn't Faelan. She'd heard him snoring softly as she crept past his door. The shadow shifted again, and two yellow spots materialized, then vanished and reappeared in the blink of an eye.

She was halfway to Faelan's room before she realized she'd turned to him for protection, when he could very well be the threat. His door was still ajar. Invitation or chivalry? She stepped inside. He lay on his back, one arm flung over his head, the edge of a towel covering his groin. He wasn't wearing the sleeping pants she'd bought. He wasn't wearing anything, from what she could tell.

His face was relaxed. Dark hair fell across his forehead, spilling over his outstretched arm, blending with the fine hair dusting his armpit. Her soul ached, and for a second, she didn't care what he was or where he'd hidden the book. Then her sanity returned. She had to know which side he was on. The book must be here somewhere. She'd hidden her treasures under the loose floorboard when she was a child. Had he found her hiding place?

She tapped her foot softly until she heard the squeak and then removed the plank. A glint of metal shone in the dark. She pulled out a necklace, a tarnished silver cross. Her dad's. Her grandmother had given it to her the night he died, the night she told Bree the story of warriors and demons to distract her from her grief and keep the nightmares away. Before they left for the funeral, her grandmother had asked for the necklace back. It was valuable, she'd said. She shouldn't have given it to Bree yet. Bree knew it was valuable. It kept the nightmares away like her grandmother said it would, so Bree hid it under the floor and said she'd lost it. That was the only time in her life she'd lied to her grandmother. The necklace had lain there in the dark for nearly two decades. How could she have forgotten hiding it here?

Caught up in her thoughts, she didn't hear the noise until too late. Faelan stood next to the bed wearing nothing but his talisman and tattoos, his face set like the Grim Reaper. Bree jumped to her feet, heart racing, the necklace clenched in her hand.

"What are you doing?" he said, advancing on her.

She backed away. "I'm… my… the…" A kind of serenity enveloped her, in the middle of her guest room, facing the most frightening, most naked man she'd ever seen, a man who should be dead, who might have murdered someone behind her house, and who could even be a demon. She stiffened her shoulders, straightened her spine, and gave him her meanest glare. She was sick of it. Sick of the lies, the secrecy, the pretense. On both sides. If he was a demon, she'd rather fight him now.

"You know darned well I'm looking for the *Book of Battles*, and I hope to God you have it, because otherwise, it's disappeared."

"I have it," he said, after a long, hard stare.

Bree put her hands on her hips. "Why did you steal it?"

"Steal it?" His face went from menacing to incredulous. "Steal it? Ye daft woman." The brogue was thicker now and loud enough to wake the dead. "You're the one who stole it!"

"Me? My grandmother had this book when I was a child." Had he lost his mind, along with his pajamas? She waved her hand at his groin. "If you can't keep that thing down, put on some clothes."

He grabbed his jeans from the floor and jammed muscular legs into them, then jerked a shirt over his head. "Tell. Me. Now," he said, forming each word loud and harsh, "how you have my clan's *Book of Battles* and what you did with the missing pages."

"I told you, it belonged to my grandma, and I didn't take the pages. I found it that way."

"The book belongs to the Connor clan."

"Well, I guess they lost it. Like you've lost your amnesia."

Faelan's jaw clenched, his fists clenched, she bet even his butt clenched. She was sure if she wasn't a woman, he would've hit her. And she sure as heck would've hit him back.

"It wasn't lost. It was stolen." His lips thinned and his eyes blazed. "And now it ends up in your house. While you're at it, explain who this is." He jerked open the drawer next to his bed with enough force to turn it into toothpicks and thrust a sticky picture in her face.

"What did you do to my picture?"

"So you admit it's you?"

"It's not me, you arrogant dolt. It's Isabel. My great-great-grandmother."

He didn't say anything, just stood there, glowering at her.

"I've fed you, clothed you, given you a bed, and you're pretending you can't remember who you are or where you came from, while I'm agonizing over whether I've rescued a warrior or a demon." She balled her fists, digging the cross into her palm, and she wished she could punch him in the face. "I was starting to think you were a warrior, but now I'm not so sure."

"How do you know about warriors?" he asked, his voice accusing.

"Grandma told me the story when I was a girl. I thought it was just make-believe."

"Your grandmother?" He looked puzzled, but some of the anger left his face.

"I didn't even remember the story until after I found you, then I discovered the book in the attic while you slept." Bree didn't mention the bizarre dream and her grandmother telling her to find the book, to help him, or how she'd smelled her grandmother's lavender perfume when she woke. "The book's amazing, and that last page, did you notice it's in another language or some kind of code? I could make out only a word or two, but I'd give my entire Civil War collection to know what it says," she said, forgetting for the moment how disgusted she was with him. "There are even dates of battles from the *future*."

He stared at her like she'd channeled Satan. "You read the book?"

"Not all of it… yet."

He scrubbed his hands over his faintly bearded chin. "This must be a test."

"A test? What are you talking about?"

"None of this makes sense. How you found me. How your grandmother got my clan's book, a book so sacred no one but the Keeper is allowed to read it."

"You have a Keeper. Wait… you mean you haven't read the book? Are you kidding?" He didn't look like he was kidding. "I have no idea how Grandma got it. I saw her with it once. I thought it was her journal. That's what I was searching for when I found Isabel's. All the women in our family kept journals." On her father's side anyway.

Faelan looked from the picture to her and frowned. "I have to find out how she got it."

"Does it matter? It's safe now."

"It matters. The book is life and death to our clan."

That explained why he was so uptight. "You can have it if you'll drop the amnesia crap and tell me who you are and how you got inside the time vault."

Faelan opened his mouth to speak, and the window behind him shattered. Before she could scream, Faelan had his arms around her and dove, flinging both of them onto the bed. His body covered hers, her head tucked safely against his chest, from accuser to protector in a second. He looked at the window, drew in a harsh breath, and lurched to his feet, pulling her with him. Bree heard an ungodly growl and glimpsed something tall and gray with yellow eyes as more pieces of the glass broke.

"Get to the attic. Now!" Faelan pushed her into the hall. "Lock the door and stay away from the windows."

"Come with me," she pleaded, gripping his arm.

His face looked like a relic carved from stone. He glanced back at the thing trying to get inside. "I can't. Now go!"

~m~

The minute Bree was out of the room, Faelan leapt toward the window, but the creature had already withdrawn. He reached for his dirk. Damnation. She still had it. It wouldn't be the first time he'd fought empty handed. He climbed out the window and took off after the monster, but the thing was gone. The familiar hum flowed through his body, anticipating a battle, but this fear was new. He looked back at the broken glass. He couldn't go after the creature *and* protect Bree. What if there were others? If he was outnumbered or needed to use his talisman and wasn't strong enough to stop them all, eventually they'd get inside.

He'd lost his touch. He'd meant to rest his eyes, not fall asleep. He should have forced her to leave, angry or not, or at least warned her what might be hiding in her backyard.

After he killed this monster, he'd tell her as much as he could. Soften it up, try not to scare her. She might be braver than most women, but they were all gentle at heart. Finding him alive in a graveyard was nothing compared to the horror waiting out there. Only one kind of creature walked on two legs and had eyes like a snake.

Bree locked the attic door behind her and watched from the window as Faelan vanished like a phantom between the graves. Shadows lengthened and danced until she couldn't tell if they were men or ghosts or trees. What was that thing? Why was it trying to get inside the house?

Unclenching her hand, she slipped the tarnished cross over her head. The smell of lavender hung in the air. Grandma had dried the flowers here to make sachets. Bree let the scent calm her, focus her thoughts. Faelan's instinct to protect told her he couldn't have killed the man in the woods. He'd shielded her. Again. She'd never seen anyone move as fast as he had to get her clear of the breaking glass, and now he was out there defending her while she had his dagger hidden in a boot in her closet. Forget this.

She unlocked the door and hurried down the stairs to her bedroom before she lost her nerve. She dug Faelan's dagger out of the boot, shoved her foot inside, and headed out the back door. There was no sound, not even the lonely hoot of the owl that had kept her company for several nights. Part of her wanted to run back inside and hide, but she couldn't let Faelan face this thing unarmed. She grabbed the broom she'd left on the porch and moved toward the graveyard.

Quieting her demons and better judgment, she tucked the dagger in her boot and put her hand to the metal gate, rough with weather and age. It creaked open as she stepped inside. She crept between the graves, expecting a monster to pop out from behind a headstone.

"Faelan?" she called softly as she neared the crypt. "Where are you?"

She heard a noise from the other side of the graveyard, and she saw something drop to the ground near the fence. She turned and ran past the gnarled oak tree to the back of the crypt. The ground disappeared. Throwing her arms up to protect her head, she landed hard, face down in the dirt. When she could breathe again, she crawled to her knees. She'd fallen into the open grave. Her ankle ached, but nothing was broken.

Another cry came from the chapel, like the one this morning. Faelan? Using the broom for leverage, Bree climbed out of the grave. A figure glided across the yard. Not Faelan. She started to jump back into the grave and hide, but Faelan could be hurt. Why hadn't she listened to him when he wanted to leave? Too late now. She hobbled from the graveyard, not stopping until she stood inside the door of the ruins.

The darkness was thick, broken only by a shaft of moonlight through an arched window. She found the nearest corner and hid until her vision adjusted enough to make out shapes. A pillar—or was it a man? Something moved near the front of the old church. There was a shuffling noise, and another shadow darted off to her side. How many people were here?

"Faelan?" she whispered, creeping behind the pillar.

A hand clamped tight over her mouth, as an arm pulled her against a hard body. Her broom dropped. She kicked back with one foot—the sore one—and heard a grunt echo her own.

"It's me." Faelan's voice was little more than a warm breath against her ear. Her body sagged into his. "Keep quiet. We're not alone."

"Who's in here?" she whispered. Except for the campers, they'd never had trespassers. Now people were sneaking around everywhere, and she was afraid they weren't people.

"Stay here, and don't make a sound," was his only answer.

"Don't leave."

"I'll be back." He squeezed her arm, and something brushed the top of her head. A spider? A kiss? She didn't see him again until he passed in front of the window. A broad shape leapt at him, and Bree stifled a cry. His dagger! She still had it. Silhouetted in the moonlight, the two forms lunged and dodged, moving impossibly fast. She smelled the thing behind her before she heard the hiss. Her spine chilled, like cubes of ice had replaced bone. She slowly turned. Sharp teeth flashed as yellow eyes glittered in the dark.

Chapter 11

IT STOOD AS TALL AS A MAN, BUT EVEN IN THE DARKNESS she could see it wasn't human. Bree backed away until her shoulders dug into the worn pillar. Lips drew back over pointed teeth as it stretched a claw toward her face. Trembling, she scooted sideways, moving out of its reach. The creature hissed and tilted its head, its snake eyes tracking her. If she didn't run now, she would be dead.

Drawing on memories from childhood, she turned and ran. Her ankle throbbed. She could hear the creature coming behind her. Could it see her? Smell her? If she screamed, Faelan would be distracted, which could get him killed. The remnants of a fallen pew caught her foot, sending her headlong into a wall. Her fingers scraped the rough surface as she pulled herself upright.

She looked back and saw the hulking shadow still coming, its movements awkward, as if bones weren't connected in the right places. She had to hide. A memory came from nowhere. The small alcove near the front of the chapel where she'd played hide and seek with her cousins. Hurrying toward the niche, she slipped inside, pressing her body against the wall. The darkness closed around her like a blanket, and she saw in her mind a little girl huddled under the covers. Bree could feel the girl's terror, feel the softness of the stuffed animal that hid her face, blocking the monster with thick, gray skin, sharp nails and teeth, watching by her bed.

The shuffling sounded closer. Bree peeked out. It was almost here. She crouched lower and felt the wall behind her give. A rain of stones hit her. When the creature was so close she could touch it, she lunged past its legs. It swiped at her, claws biting into her shoulder. Her skin burned like she'd been hit with a branding iron.

"Faelan!" She rushed toward the window where she'd last seen him fighting. She heard an inhuman scream, and then Faelan was there, gripping her arms.

"I told you to stay over there."

"I couldn't—"

The thing hissed, and Faelan stepped in front of her. "How did that get in here?"

The ugly one looked from Faelan to Bree as seven others slunk in behind it. The two on the outside appeared normal, from the outline of their bodies, but those in the middle had shapes that were all wrong. Long arms, deformed heads. They pulled out swords, and Faelan tensed beside her.

"We can't outrun them," he whispered. "I'll distract them. You run for the door."

"Wait, I have your—"

He put a hand against her waist and pushed. One of the creatures charged, swinging his sword at Faelan's neck. Bree bit back a scream as Faelan leapt clear and extended his leg, sending his opponent's sword clanging into a wall. Two moved in from behind. Faelan whirled to meet the attack, his body now visible in the dim moonlight at the window. Both creatures lunged, and Faelan leaned backward, his hair brushing the floor as the blades skimmed the air above his nose. There were too many. He would never escape. Claws dug into

Bree's arm. She screamed as the ugly creature yanked her close. Its skin was rough, cold, the smell nauseating. She kicked and punched. Faelan's fist shot past her head, slamming into the creature's face. Faelan pulled her free and planted his foot in the beast's chest, knocking it backwards. It opened its mouth and let loose a sound between a scream and a howl. Like this morning.

"Quick," Faelan yelled, shoving her behind the pillar again.

A voice called from the back of the chapel. "Leave the woman alone, or the master will be angry." Every head turned toward the figure standing outside the door.

Faelan spat out a name. The man cursed then quickly ran. The ugly creature lumbered toward Faelan as the others closed in. He moved back, drawing them away from where Bree hid.

The nearest one spun to look at her, but only his head turned. He rotated his body to match his head, took a step forward, and hesitated, looking at the door where the man had disappeared. Turning back to join Faelan's attackers, he opened his mouth and let out a wail, as the others picked up the terrible cry. They rushed Faelan, forming a circle around him, voices rising in unison, like a pack of howling wolves. One of the creatures flew backwards, opening a hole in the group, and she could see Faelan's arms were trapped, but his feet were vicious. She couldn't make out any details of the one who held Faelan, except the creature had a face that was too wide, body thick as a bull, and sharp teeth closing in on Faelan's throat. She had to get his dagger to him.

Her breathing slowed. A calm settled over her. She smelled the stone crumbling under her fingers, tasted the mustiness of the chapel on her tongue, the stale air of dust and decay. The creatures were clearer now, as if someone had turned on a soft light. As she'd suspected, they weren't human.

Destroy it! The thought punched her mind. She pulled Faelan's dagger from her boot and drew her arm back as if she'd done it a hundred times. She hurled the dagger at the one holding him. It whizzed past Faelan's ear and sank into the monster's chest. It howled and disappeared as the dagger clattered to the floor.

One minute the thing was there, the next, it wasn't.

Faelan's stunned gaze met hers. Before Bree could absorb what had happened, he snatched the dagger, and moving so fast he was a blur, slit the throat of the one next to him. It gurgled and disappeared. He leaped into the air and did some kind of fancy flip, landing several feet outside the circle. Maybe he *was* Superman.

"Bree, cover your eyes!"

She could taste fear, but nothing this side of heaven could make her shut her eyes or leave Faelan to fight the creatures alone. The chapel dimmed again, except for the faint moonlight behind Faelan. He raised one hand to the heavens, clasping his talisman with the other, and in a steady voice, a torrent of strange words flowed from his mouth like the thunder of a waterfall. The air thickened and hummed. A stream of light flashed from his chest.

Bree shielded her eyes against the brilliant light, and she clearly saw the hideous thing that had grabbed her. No wonder those campers had fled. Its skin was thick and gray, the head rounded, with coarse black hair, hideous yellow slit eyes, and pointed teeth bared in a scream. It disappeared in the flash of light, taking the remaining creatures with it.

Faelan stood with one hand still raised, the other holding the talisman. His face glowed, as if carved out of a brilliant stone. Time stood still. She'd never forget it, for as long as she lived. Where the creatures had stood seconds before, there was nothing but fallen weapons. Not even dust remained, like in the vampire stories. The light retracted, leaving the chapel dark again.

Faelan *was* the warrior.

He turned, and even through the darkness she felt his eyes searching out hers. Her champion. Her legs went numb, thinking how close they'd come to dying, how close she'd come to killing him with his own dagger. A few inches nearer…

Faelan sprinted to her. "Are you okay?" he asked, pulling her tight to his chest. The beat of his heart was strong against her cheek, the talisman warm. "Bree, talk to me."

"I thought they were going to kill you. Where did they go? What was that light? I've never seen anything so brilliant."

"You saw the light?" His voice was raw, hands trembling as he cradled her face.

"It was incredible. Why did you tell me not to look?" A rush of energy shook her to the core. She'd killed that evil thing. She, Bree Kirkland, had made it disappear. How? She didn't know, but she wasn't crazy. She wasn't a freak. She'd always known there was more to life, something bigger, something more. Now she had proof.

"You looked at an open talisman?" The words sounded like a death sentence on his lips.

"It was incredible. Amazing. Astonishing. Hey, what's that man doing out there?"

Faelan whirled and faced the open door. A short, skinny man scurried out from behind a tree, slipped a cell phone into his pocket, and ran across the yard. It was the man who'd told the creatures to leave her alone.

A rumble rolled up from Faelan's throat. "Stay here. Don't move." He took off across the yard like a hunter stalking his prey.

Bree scooped up the broom she'd dropped and ran to the door. "Hurry, he's getting away!"

The intruder looked back at Bree's cry and saw Faelan advancing on him, dagger drawn. "Greg," Faelan said through clenched teeth. "Or should I call you Grog? Seems like yesterday I saw you."

The man threw his head back, hunched his shoulders, and groaned. His body contorted, skin rippling, growing thick, as his face stretched, sprouting long teeth and bulging eyes, like in a werewolf movie, but it wasn't a werewolf. It was another of those things from the chapel.

Faelan cursed.

Bree gaped as the thing he'd called Grog drew a knife. She didn't know where it came from. He didn't have any pockets... or clothes.

Grog took advantage of Faelan's surprise and slashed at his throat. Faelan dodged the knife, kicking Grog in the thigh. Grog staggered, regained his balance, and came at Faelan again, swiping at his face with a clawed hand. The two hit the ground rolling, a grunting tangle of arms and legs and claws and blades. Someone cried out, and Bree flew into the fight, swinging her broom.

She went for Grog, but missed and hit Faelan when he spun Grog around.

"Get back," Faelan said, swatting at the broom.

She yelled out a *kiap* she'd learned in first-year tae kwon do and brought the handle down on Grog's leathery wrist. It made a loud cracking sound. She hoped it was his arm and not her broom. Grog cursed and dropped the knife, snatching it up again while Faelan gawked at Bree in shock. Grog lunged, knocking Faelan off his feet, and raised the knife over his chest. Bree jabbed the broom at Grog's face, poking his protruding eyes with the bristles. He sputtered and jumped to his feet, then shifted into a human again, clothes and all. Arms pumping, he sprinted toward the driveway like the devil was at his heels.

Faelan gave Bree a glare that would've quelled an avalanche and leaped to his feet. Bree moved out of his way, but Grog was too far ahead, and barefoot, Faelan was at a disadvantage. He stopped, drew back his arm, and the dagger winged through the air, faster than when she'd thrown it. Grog stumbled and cried out but kept running.

An engine revved, and a black SUV hurtled up the driveway in reverse. The back door opened, and Grog yanked Faelan's dagger from his shoulder, dropping it as he jumped in. Faelan caught up and latched onto Grog's arm, pulling him partially out of the vehicle. Grog swung his knife at Faelan's throat as a black mist materialized overhead. Faelan was thrown back, and the knife caught his arm instead.

Bree sprinted to reach him as the SUV sped away. The mysterious cloud had disappeared, and a stain was darkening Faelan's shirt. "You're bleeding," she panted, reaching for his arm.

He turned on her, his face distorted with fury. "What the bloody hell were you doing?" he bellowed, veins bulging in his neck. "Don't ever interfere when I'm in battle."

She stepped back, shocked, before anger overrode her fear. Rising to her full height, almost a foot shorter than him, she glared back. "Interfere? I saved your butt in there, and you're still playing male chauvinist? I don't know what women were like in your day, but this is my house, my property." She jabbed her finger into his chest. "I don't take orders from you. I'm going back to get those swords before any more of those things come to kill us."

Faelan opened his mouth, but Bree stalked off. Let him bleed to death. He caught up to her a few steps away. His hand touched her shoulder, and she cried out.

"What's wrong?" he asked, his voice softer. The dark stain spreading across the torn cotton of his brown T-shirt, dripping down his arm, drained her anger like air escaping a punctured tire. She'd almost lost him tonight. If he hadn't fallen back, his throat would've been slit instead of his arm.

"You startled me," she fibbed. No need to tell him that thing had clawed her, or she'd hurt her ankle, which seemed fine now. He already thought she was dying from looking at a light. "Is this why you wanted to leave?"

"You have no idea what we're dealing with." He held his arm stiff against his side.

"Then stop pretending you can't remember anything, and tell me what's happening." She lifted his sleeve.

Blood ran from a gash above the scar on his left bicep. She pulled her dust-covered pajama top over her head, thankful she'd worn a bra. Turning it inside out, she pressed it against the cut. "You need stitches."

"I just need a bandage," Faelan said, staring at her breasts. "I've had worse injuries." His gaze hesitated on the cross she wore, before lifting to her eyes. "I didn't know you could throw a dirk."

"I didn't either. It's like something was controlling my arm. I can't believe I killed it."

A muscle twitched erratically in his jaw. "That makes two of us."

"All those cousins who thought I was crazy, even my mother. I knew there was more to life than just… life. Hold my shirt against your arm," she said. "After I get those swords out of the chapel, I'll bandage your wound. No need to leave all those weapons for them to kill us with."

"They don't need swords. They could kill you with their fingernails. I'll get the weapons tomorrow."

"What *were* those things? What were they doing in my chapel, and what the heck did Grog do? One minute he was human then he… wasn't."

Faelan still watched her as if she'd swallowed a hand grenade. "They were halflings, and they were looking for me."

"Halflings? Like in the movies?"

"I don't know about your movies. These aren't full-blooded demons, but they have some demon blood. Full demons can't step on holy ground. That's why Grog couldn't come through the door."

"Why didn't he disappear like the ones in the chapel?"

"I only wounded him. Are you sure you're okay?"

"Good grief. I just looked at a light. You saw it too, and you're fine."

"It's *my* talisman. What are you doing out here, anyway? I told you to stay inside."

"I was bringing your dagger," she said, checking his wound. "You have control issues, and you're a chauvinist. A nice one, but a chauvinist. You should work on that."

"You could've been killed."

"I know. That thing had claws an inch—"

"No. My talisman could've killed you. It should have killed you. That's why I told you to close your eyes."

"How could I not look? It was glorious—"

He shook his head and rubbed his hand over his face. "You're the most exasperating woman I've ever known. Nobody looks at an engaged talisman and lives."

"Then I guess I'm lucky I'm seeing only shadows and black spots. But if we don't get inside and bandage this cut, you'll likely bleed to death right here in the driveway, and I'll have to kill Grog myself."

Faelan said something not very gallant as he retrieved the dagger Grog dropped.

Bree ushered Faelan into her bathroom, since the first-aid kit was there, and remembered too late, so was the Jacuzzi. "Don't move." She wasn't about to keep hovering over him half naked. Even wounded, he hadn't stopped staring at her breasts. She put on the first thing she saw, an old T-shirt of Russell's she'd planned to burn in a cleansing ceremony, and walked back to the bathroom where Faelan sat on the toilet lid holding her shirt against his wound. His fingers were long and lean, strong. He'd thrown that dagger like he'd been doing it forever. She could think of other things those fingers would probably do well, but until she found a way to keep her Prince Charmings from morphing into frogs, she couldn't get romantically involved.

"Raise your arms." She reached for the hem of his T-shirt, helping him pull it over his head. Her irritation was forgotten at the sight of all those muscles inches away and the bloody cut on his bicep.

She took a calming breath, which didn't help at all, since all she could smell was him, and bent to get the first-aid kit from under the sink. When she looked back, she caught him staring at her butt. She scrubbed her hands and examined his wound. It was deep, still bleeding.

"You should get this stitched," she said, after she'd cleaned it.

"No."

"It'd be a shame to die of an infection because you were scared to go to the doctor."

"I'm not scared… ouch! What did you do?"

"It's antiseptic."

"That hurt more than the knife. Well, do it then."

"I'm done. Hold this gauze against it until it stops bleeding. I've got some pain reliever and sleeping pills, if you need them."

"You need pills to sleep?"

"Not anymore." Although she wouldn't rule out tonight. "I hope this heals as fast as your palm."

"That was a small cut, but I heal fast, unless I'm weak."

"Good, because hospitals want ID, and you don't exist."

"ID?"

"Identification. Proof of who you are. We're big on

that in this century. If we go to the hospital, I'll have to tell them you're homeless." If he stayed long, she'd have to get him a fake ID.

"I *am* homeless."

"Be glad you're sleeping in a bed and not a crypt."

He gave her a wry smile. "What happened to your shoulder?"

"A wall collapsed in the chapel. A stone hit me."

"That's how your great-great-grandfather died," he said, looking like a knight who'd failed to slay his damsel's dragon. "I can take a look at it for you."

"It's fine." The last thing she needed was those hands on her. She was already dying from his scent. It must be the rush that came from cheating death. Nothing like sexual energy to prove you were alive. "You've had a cut on this arm before. Another demon?"

Pain flickered over his face. "A long time ago."

"Peter called. He wants to ask you some questions. I think he suspects you were involved in that man's death."

"What did you tell him?"

"That you were gone. He wants your phone number and address."

"Do you think I killed that man?" Faelan asked quietly.

"I think those things in the chapel did. But I think it's time you told me who you are and why you were buried in my crypt."

Chapter 12

FAELAN LOOKED AT BREE, EXPECTANTLY WAITING, face smudged with dirt, hair a mess, like she'd been rolling on the ground. She deserved some answers after all she'd done for him, and he was bloody tired of lying.

"I'm Faelan Connor, warrior of the Connor Clan of Scotland, as my brothers were, and my father before us, and his father before him. Since the beginning of time our assignment has been the same... to protect humanity from demons."

"Scotland... since the beginning of time..." Her eyes danced.

Any other woman would have been sniffing smelling salts.

"This is incredible. I thought you had a bit of a brogue. Are there many warriors? Where do they come from? How come the world doesn't know about this?"

He groaned. "You need answers like everybody else needs air."

"You can't expect me to see what I did and not have questions."

She already knew too much. She'd read part of his clan's *Book of Battles*, something no one was permitted to do except the Keeper. Faelan considered asking if she'd seen his name, or his brothers. Had they survived their duty to have families, find love? Or had they arrived and faced four ancient demons alone? Certain death. But even asking would've broken the rules, and rules had to be protected, although Bree didn't seem governed by them. Like making a halfling disappear, something only a warrior could do. Michael must have intervened.

"There were many warriors before. I don't know about now." He didn't understand why the world hadn't been destroyed, but if there were humans, there must be warriors. Humans couldn't exist without them. "The world doesn't know about us because we've bled and died to keep it that way. The secret must be protected at all costs."

She took a step back, clutching the roll of gauze. "Don't tell me you have to kill me."

He gave her his warrior stare. "Not yet." But there was a time when she would have been killed because of the knowledge she held. If she wasn't who she claimed to be, it would still have to be done.

"Just remember, if not for me you'd still be in the time vault. How did you get inside?"

"Druan—"

"You mentioned his name in your sleep. Was he the one in the chapel?"

"He makes the one in the chapel look like an angel. Druan's been around for a long time."

"You think he locked you in there?"

"I know he did." Faelan sighed, knowing he'd have to tell her the whole tale. Most of it anyway. "I was sent to America to suspend Druan, but I couldn't find him. I knew he had a lair nearby, but it was well hidden. Demons are cunning, especially the ancient ones. They don't live to be the age they do by being dim-witted. I met Grog in a tavern. Called himself Greg. He'd heard I was looking for Jeremiah, that's the name Druan was using. Grog claimed he held a grudge against Jeremiah; said he could take me to him. Bastard. I should've realized Grog was a demon."

"You went after this demon alone?"

"I brought warriors with me, but I sent them to track down Druan's minions. My brothers were supposed to be coming behind me, but I couldn't wait any longer."

"Your brothers were warriors?"

"Aye. Strong warriors." And loyal. Unless they lay dying, nothing could've kept his brothers from coming to his aid. By sending the other warriors away, he'd likely sent his brothers into a death trap. "When Grog and I got to where Druan was supposed to be, he wasn't alone. There were a dozen more with him. I was hit from behind. When I woke, I saw you."

"No wonder you tried to cut off my head. So the amnesia was always a lie?"

"I couldn't tell you who I was until I knew who you were."

"Who else could I be?"

Ah, but there were so many choices.

"Did all this happen near here?"

"Aye. By the old burnt-out farmhouse."

"Samuel's farmhouse? That's just through the woods. Did you meet Samuel?"

"No. The house had already burned down."

"Where did you stay? You had to sleep."

"I got work on a horse farm a few miles away, so Druan wouldn't notice me."

"Not notice you? Wearing a kilt on a farm in America?"

"I didn't wear the kilt here, only on the ship."

"You had it on in the time vault."

"I'd ripped my trousers the night before, tracking those halflings. The kilt was all I had clean. By then, it didn't matter. I was going to suspend Druan and go home."

"Suspend? Put him in the time vault?"

"It's easier said than done, but aye."

"What do you do with the time vault then?"

"It's complicated."

She stared at him, but let it go. "Is everyone in your clan a warrior?"

"Not all. The duty is handed down from father to son, on the son's eighteenth birthday, but we're always preparing, even as lads. At eighteen we enter formal training. After a year we go into battle. An older warrior fights alongside us for the first year. We're released from duty at twenty-eight, unless we choose to remain."

"How old are you?"

"Twenty-seven." Or a hundred and seventy-eight. "I was put in the time vault in 1860. August 1860."

"Just before the war," she mumbled.

The war. His stomach twisted.

"That's one hundred and fifty-one years. The book said one hundred and fifty. Why didn't someone wake you last year?"

"My clan probably thinks I'm dead."

"What about the women? Do they hunt demons?"

"You can't be serious. Females don't fight demons." They kept the home fires burning.

"So if I wanted to hunt demons, I couldn't, because I'm a girl?" Bree scowled and crossed her arms, covering her breasts.

"Why would a lass want to hunt demons?" The

notion was laughable, but he didn't dare do it with her scowling like that.

"For the same reason a man would. You act like women aren't as good as men."

"If anything, they're better. That's why they need to be protected—"

"I don't want your protection. I want your respect."

"You remind me of Alana." Except she was perfectly content not hunting demons.

"Alana? Your wife?"

"My sister."

"Your sister?" Bree sounded relieved, then sad. "How old was she?"

"Thirteen."

A wistful look clouded her face. "I had a sister. A twin. She died."

"I'm sorry." Would she have been as reckless as Bree if she'd lived? As beautiful?

"You weren't married?"

"No. We don't usually marry until we're finished with our duty. Females are a distraction. We've enough to worry about as is."

"How old were your brothers?"

"Ian was twenty-five. Tavis was twenty-six."

"Why do you think they didn't come?"

"A battle, the weather. I'll never know."

Her eyes filled with sympathy. "It must have been terrible for your family, wondering what happened to you, where you were."

He clenched his jaw, recalling the fear in his mother's eyes when she heard he'd been assigned another ancient demon, the horror when she discovered his brothers were coming with him, and his reassurance that all would end well. "Aye. All I can do now is rid the world of Druan."

"How do we find him?"

We? There was no *we* here. He was the warrior. She was the female. "I'd hoped to question Grog." Which he might have managed, if Bree hadn't gotten in the way.

"Is that why you didn't use your talisman on Grog?" she asked, sorting through her little white box, pulling out tubes of ointment and other things he didn't recognize, muttering to herself.

"That, and I was too weak to use it again."

"You said those things in the chapel were part demon, what's the other part?"

"Human."

"Why would a human…"

"Mate with a demon? The human might not know. Demons can shift into much nicer forms."

She leaned back. "Are you completely human?"

"I am," he said, insulted. He could easily ask her the same.

"Can they choose any form? Animal? Human?"

"Aye, but most prefer human forms. They can do the most harm that way. They usually stick with one form. It takes them a while to get comfortable in new skin."

"And to think I was worried about cellulite."

"What's that? Some newfangled weapon?"

She smiled. "It's nothing you'd have to worry about. It's more of a modern problem. Why didn't those half-lings shift like Grog?"

"Halflings don't shift. A few learn how to project an illusion. Their natural form is still there." So was the smell, but most humans weren't sensitive enough to notice.

She wrinkled her nose. "Do they all stink like the one that grabbed me?"

Was there anything normal about this woman? "Only in their natural form, but the smell varies, depending on how much demon blood they have. A halfling that's mostly human might not smell at all or need an illusion. Some of them look like you and me."

"That's frightening," she said.

Bloody frightening.

"Where did Grog get that knife? He didn't have any pockets or clothes."

"They can summon their weapons at will, manifest them, like the clothes."

"Anything they want?"

"Natural things from the earth. Metals, fibers, temporary things that leave with the demon."

"What about those swords in the chapel?"

"Those were real. Only full demons can manifest material things."

"Where do these demons come from?"

"Hell. But it takes a lot of power to get here."

"Do you get to decide whether to zap them with your talisman or suspend them?"

"We destroy them if there's no other choice. If they're destroyed, they cease to exist, and they can't be held accountable for their evil." The young ones were the exception. They were always destroyed.

"So that thing I killed will never pay for the evil it's done?"

"But it'll never hurt anyone again." He didn't tell her the thing shouldn't have disappeared at all. When anyone other than a warrior killed a demon or halfling, the dead body stayed on earth while the spirit went back to hell, powerless, to start the journey all over, whereas death by a warrior was judgment in itself. Even if the thing couldn't be held accountable for its evil, it was destroyed forever. But nothing about Bree seemed to work the way it should.

"At least you wounded Grog. That might make him think twice about coming back. Your dagger must be powerful, since it made that halfling disappear when I hit it."

The dirk had no special powers, but he didn't tell her that, either. "How much longer is this gonna take?" There were times when a warrior's senses were a curse. Like now. Every move she made drove her scent deeper inside him. It didn't help that she was standing so close he could kiss her without even moving.

"Not long. Stop squirming. I need to add more gauze."

He was squirming because her breast was two inches from his face. "Just put a bandage on it."

"You're still bleeding. Be patient," she said, adding another layer of gauze. "It's a virtue."

Much more patience on his part, and she might lose her virtue.

"Now we know time vaults can suspend humans as well as demons. Imagine all the things we could do. Revolutionize medicine, keep people from dying, from aging—"

"No. Time vaults were made for demons." If humans found out about the time vaults, they could pose as big a threat to the clan as the demons. If he thought she'd tell someone… he swallowed, not wanting to think about what he might have to do. No matter how much she'd done to help him, he couldn't allow her to endanger his clan.

"Why won't they open for so long?"

Was there no end to her questions? If he wasn't careful, she'd uncover every secret his clan had hidden since the world began. "After a hundred and fifty years in suspension, demons lose their power. If someone opened the time vault afterwards, say a historian who thought she'd found a chest filled with treasure, the demon would be powerless."

She rolled her eyes and grabbed another piece of gauze. "I guess the time vault doesn't have the same effect on warriors and talismans."

"Some things seem… different." Like this cursed ache for a woman who'd watched an engaged talisman and lived to tell it. The tip of her tongue appeared. It was pink and wet, and he could think of so many places he'd like to see it besides in her mouth. "Are you finished?" He had to get out of this bathroom so he could breathe without inhaling her.

"Almost. The bleeding is slowing. I was reading Isabel's journal last night. Remember, I told you how Frederick was killed near the chapel? I found the entry in Isabel's journal. She said he was acting strange, wouldn't stay away from the chapel, and he kept talking in his sleep about a book. He died a few nights later. I bet he found the *Book of Battles* inside."

"Who put it there?"

"That's what I'd like to know. Let's start with finding out who that car is registered to. It might give us some answers."

"How do I do that?" Nothing here was familiar to him.

He glanced at her breasts. Well, some things were. He was tired of relying on her for everything. He wished he had his horse and his sword. In Scotland, he'd had the finest stallion. People had admired him. There wasn't a warrior more respected. Now he hadn't even a halfpenny to his name, dependent on a woman for every morsel of food and for shelter, transportation, and a bed. His brothers would give him the devil if they saw him. He could almost see Tavis, his chest puffed out, arms held wide, a mischievous grin. "*Lads and lasses, here in the flesh, the Mighty Faelan, famous throughout Scotland, admired by lasses the world over, and his magnificent stallion, Nandor,*" Tavis would bellow, as Ian rolled on the ground laughing. That was usually as far as Tavis got before Faelan leaped off his horse, pinning his brother until he stopped. Until the next time. God, he missed his brothers.

"I memorized the tag number. Cars have to be registered with the Division of Motor Vehicles. They keep track of who owns what. My friend Janie's boyfriend works there. I'll try to sweet-talk him into telling us who owns the car."

"Can't Janie do the sweet-talking?"

"If we can find out who owns the car, we can go after them. Figure out what they want."

"We?"

"You think I'm going to sit around on my backside and do nothing, with demons and halflings running around my yard?"

That's exactly what he thought she was going to do.

"The bleeding stopped." She glanced toward the window as she covered the wound with fresh gauze. "Do you think they'll come back tonight?"

"I doubt it. Grog will be afraid to tell Druan what happened. That could give us some time."

"I still think we should get those swords from the chapel. I'd like that big one with the curved blade."

He was beginning to understand why she wasn't married. "That big bag you carry could do damage enough."

She tore off a piece of tape and secured one edge of the thick bandage. "For what it's worth, you threw that dagger like a pro."

He felt a rush of pride until he remembered she had thrown it like a bloody warrior herself. "You've got dirt on your face." And everywhere else. He wiped a smudge from her chin.

"I fell into a grave."

"A grave? Damnation. I forgot to cover it."

"That's cute," she said with a lopsided, dirt-smudged smile.

"What?"

"The way you say damnation all the time."

He'd had a lot of compliments in his lifetime, on how he handled a horse, a sword, a pistol, and his fists, and a few compliments on other things from a pretty lass or two, but no one had ever complimented him on cursing. He grinned. Only Bree.

She added another piece of tape to the bandage, her warm fingers brushing his skin. "There, that's the best I can do. You're going to have another scar, and this shirt's history." They both reached for the ruined shirt, fingers touching. She dropped her hand and turned to gather the first-aid supplies.

Faelan threw the shirt in the trash and stood. "You sure you don't want me to look at your shoulder?" He was doing a lousy job of protecting her, though to be honest, she fell a lot on her own. Her feet had a mind of their own, and they seemed partial to holes. The scrape on her cheek had healed quickly, but her shoulder was cut, and the knees of the trousers she slept in were torn. Who knew what other scratches he'd find under there? That started him thinking about her naked again.

"No. It's fine."

Probably for the best. He might end up doing more than bandage her. "Whose shirt is that?"

"Russell's." She pressed her lips together and put away the first-aid kit.

"Why would you wear his shirt? He made you cry."

"I grabbed the first thing I saw."

"Did he hurt you?"

"Mostly my dishes and walls."

She wasn't telling him everything. "How often does he call?"

"Every day. I've tried changing my phone number, moving. But he always finds me. He's the reason I'm off men."

"Off men?" Surely she wasn't one of *those* women, not after what she'd done with him in the bathroom. In his day, there weren't many gays, as they called them now. Whoever came up with that name was one wheel short of a wagon. A man with a man, there was nothing happy about that.

"I'm avoiding men for a while." She glanced at the big tub. Her cheeks turned pink, and she looked away. "I've made a lot of mistakes. I need to figure out what I want in a man before I let another one in my life."

What about him? He was in her life. She hadn't

avoided him in the bathroom. Would she brush him off, brush off what they'd done like it was dirt? What did it matter? Nothing could come of it anyway.

She covered a yawn.

"We need to rest." Maybe a good night's sleep would help him remember he was a warrior, not a wronged lover. "I should sleep close by, in case they come back."

She nodded but still avoided looking at him. "We can sleep in my room. There's glass on your floor. I'm going to take a shower."

Just what he didn't need, another image of her naked. "I'll block the broken window and then shower in the hall bathroom." This would be his fourth cleaning today, more than he usually had in a fortnight or more. In the wilds he wouldn't have bothered, but he couldn't sleep in the same room with her when he was sweaty from battling demons. He shouldn't stay in the same room with her anyway, but in truth he wasn't confident more demons wouldn't show up tonight.

He cleaned up the broken glass and shoved the dresser and mirror in front of the broken window. It wouldn't stop a demon, but it might slow him down or give warning. He checked the floorboard. Only the necklace was missing.

After a quick, tormented shower, thinking about her doing the same, he took a blanket and pillow to her bedroom. The bathroom door was closed. He heard the water shut off, and he cleared his mind, focusing on making a bed on the floor. The door opened. Bree stood there wrapped in a towel, eyes wide, skin damp. "I… need my gown."

Faelan tried not to stare at her long legs, dainty feet,

and the swell of breasts he'd take a beating to kiss. He could see all of her but the bits under the towel, and his brain immediately started imagining the rest. He stepped closer, knowing it was a mistake. Her mouth parted, and her tongue darted out to wet her lips.

He followed the damp trail with his thumb. "What you said earlier, what did you mean?"

"What… what did I say?" she asked, taking a step back, staring at his mouth.

He moved closer. "You mentioned my getting this," he brushed the front of his body against hers, "out of my system. With a woman."

"I was curious if it would help or make it worse." She took another step backwards, looking like a trussed rabbit.

Faelan followed, bringing their bodies close again. "Were you offering?" A stupid question after her declaration that she was avoiding men, but his brain wasn't in charge now.

"I… I don't know." Her eyes said she did.

"I need to know," he whispered. "Badly."

Knowing how close he'd come to losing her, the torture of sitting next to that tub while she hovered over him and her soft skin covered by only a towel was too much. One kiss, then he'd focus on Druan. Faelan lowered his head. A wisp of a sigh escaped lips already opening for him, and all thoughts of demons and battles fled. Nothing mattered but her. Her lips, her body pressed against his, her stomach soft against his groin. She moaned and sank into him. He pushed against her, aching, as her tongue touched his. He put his arms around her shoulders to draw her closer, and she winced.

Faelan tore his mouth away, disgusted he'd let lust make him forget her injury. And his mission. How could he protect anyone when all he thought about was getting Bree to the nearest bed? Those halflings weren't the last Druan would send or the worst. "I can't do this to you." Faelan looked at Bree's lips, still open and moist from his kiss. "It's not fair. And it's late. We both need rest. Tomorrow we'll have to find a place to stay. Would your brother let us stay with him a day or two?" He didn't want to endanger anyone else, but he wanted Bree away from this. He was surprised Biff hadn't stopped by already.

"I don't have a brother."

"What?"

"I lied."

Chapter 13

"You lied?"

"I didn't want you to think I was alone," Bree said. "But I am, except for Peter and Jared. Jared's out of town, and I didn't think you'd want to stay with a cop. He already suspects you're involved. So there's nowhere for me to go."

It was smart reasoning on her part, but a lie was a lie. Of course, he'd done nothing but lie since he'd met her, but he'd had no other choice. "You feel safe with me now?"

"Yes."

"Good. Then turn around and let me see your shoulder."

"It's fine."

"It wasn't fine when I touched it. Let me see for myself."

She sighed and turned.

He brushed her hair aside. Three claw marks ran down the top of her shoulder. "What the… I thought you said it was a rock."

"I knew you'd make a big deal, like when I saw your talisman light."

He leaned forward and sniffed. Sulfur. The smell was faint. A human wouldn't even notice it. "You've been marked by a demon."

She whirled around to face him, clutching her towel. "What does that mean?"

"They like marking their prey. Their claws are like poison."

"Poison?"

"Not deadly, but it can make you sick." So sick she'd wish it had been deadly.

"I'm sure you've had them before, and you're fine."

"I'm a warrior." His body had been built to withstand things that would kill an ordinary person. "Does it burn?"

"Only when you touch it."

It should be stinging.

"I didn't expect we'd spend the night bandaging each other's wounds," Bree said, when he was done.

"If you'd left, like I asked…"

"If you'd told me why you wanted to leave, I would have." She glanced at the blanket and pillow on the floor. "You take the bed."

"No." He'd never sleep, anyway, knowing she was so near.

Her chin lifted. "We'll both take the bed. It's big. And we both need sleep." Her words held more conviction than her eyes. She opened a drawer and pulled out something white. "Choose a side of the bed while I put on a gown." She went back into the bathroom, closing the door.

He grabbed his pillow, sighed, and lay down, awk-wardly waiting for her to join him. No good wishing this was something it could never be. Clan law had to be followed. They were too tired to do more than sleep anyway, and if he needed a distraction from his lust, he'd think about what other lies she might have told, like pic-tures on mantels and keys and books that shouldn't be.

~~~

"Are you asleep?"

Faelan rolled over. The mattress shifted under his

weight. "No." His throbbing arm didn't help, but mostly he was dying from the warm scent drifting across the bed.

Bree lay on her side facing him, her hand curled under her chin. "I can't sleep, either."

"Does your shoulder hurt?" It should be on fire by now.

"Not really, but I'm too tense to relax."

He had a solution, but it wouldn't be wise. "Sometimes I have trouble sleeping after a battle." Especially if a warrior died.

"I've been thinking about all this. I think Isabel's visitor, McGowan, was searching for you. I told you about the riddle on the map, but there was also a name at the bottom. *F VAULT*. That's one of the reasons I thought the treasure was inside the vault." She gave him a saucy smile. "Until I opened it and a screaming man popped out, swinging a dagger."

"I don't scream. It's a known fact." Tavis had considered it a personal challenge.

"Pardon me. Your manly roar scared ten years off my life."

That cooled his loins. She was lucky she'd only gotten a fright. He rarely missed with his dirk. Never at close range.

"He could've been hiding the time vault," Faelan said. "Demons can't go into graveyards. Druan would've had a minion or halfling do it for him."

"Isabel said McGowan acted peculiar. Would Druan kill his minion or halfling?"

"Druan kills as easily as you and I breathe."

"Another possibility is that McGowan was looking for the book."

"Or hiding it. McGowan could've stolen it for Druan.

There was some concern over its safety before I left Scotland." Druan might have planned to steal it, which would explain why Michael had warned Faelan, and not the Keeper, that the book was in danger. That meant the responsibility for the *Book of Battles* being stolen lay squarely at his feet, along with Druan's disease and the war.

"And Druan would get rid of any witnesses."

"For a human, you understand the demon mind very well."

"Thank Russell. He introduced me to the dark side."

She didn't say more, so they lay in silence as Faelan wondered exactly what Russell had done to her. When this was over, he'd see how brave Russell was against a man.

She moved her arm, baring the creamy slope of her breasts, adorned by the necklace. Had she written the letter he'd found with it? Tomorrow he'd ask her. If someone had hurt her, he would track him down after he finished with Druan and Russell.

"What do you think Grog meant about his master being upset if I was hurt?" Bree asked. "Why would a demon care if a human got hurt?"

He wouldn't, unless the human was his minion or he wanted her for breeding. Had Druan seen Bree and become infatuated with her? She was beautiful, and Druan was obsessed with beauty. "Some demons take humans to breed halflings."

"Take?"

"Kidnap. Then they kill the mothers."

"Okay, I could've done without hearing that."

"Demons need halflings to help hide their evil plots. Demons live a long time."

"How old is Druan?"

"Around eight hundred years."

"Good grief! Do they all live that long?"

"It depends on the order. The first order is the created demons. They're eternal. They operate on a spiritual plane." Warriors didn't battle them. Michael handled that part. "The second order is born, like humans, but both parents are full demons. They live anywhere from a few hundred years to a millennium. The older ones can become very powerful, like Druan. We call them the demons of old or the ancient ones. They're the strongest demons a human will encounter. There's only a handful left." Faelan had destroyed one in his seventh year as a warrior. It was the first time since the seventeenth century that one of the ancient demons had been assigned.

"What about halflings?"

"The third order, the lowest. They're earthbound, live a couple hundred years or so. Demons like using halflings to do their bidding because they're more loyal than minions, and halflings don't live long enough to become a threat, which sometimes happens with lesser demons. They've been known to steal from each other, though it's against their rules."

"They have rules?"

"Of a sort."

"So Druan's got another couple hundred years to wreak havoc on earth?"

"Unless he's gained years. They can extend their lifespan if they serve their master well, even become eternal, like the first order."

"Their master? Like in Satan?"

"They call him the Dark One, but he goes by many names. Satan, Lucifer, the Devil. If it stinks, he's behind it. Each demon has a purpose. Addiction, cruelty, deception, greed."

Bree shuddered. "I'm tired of demons. Tell me about your family. Faelan sounds Irish."

His family. He relaxed his mind, and the memories rushed in, smiles and laughter, battle cries and swords. A tiny casket being lowered into the ground. He pushed that one away. He couldn't deal with it now.

"My mother was Irish. She named me after her grandfather."

"What did you do when you weren't hunting demons?"

"We raised horses. Clydesdales, some Highland ponies, a few Arabian mixes, like Nandor."

"Nandor?"

"My horse. He was more like a friend than a horse. Sounds daft, aye? But there were times when he was the only living thing I saw for weeks. You grow fond of an animal when he's the only one around to listen to you talk."

"Do you miss him?"

He sighed. "Aye, I do. In my day a warrior valued his horse as much as his sword. I reckon Nandor must have thought I left him. My father would have taken care of him. Now there's a man who loved horses, almost as much as he loved fighting demons, and Alana spent most of her time riding or in the stable when she wasn't painting. She was the youngest. My parents didn't expect another bairn." Not after the first tragedy. "We all coddled her. She should have been a wee devil, but she had a heart as big as the Highlands. My brothers and me, we spent most of our time training, or with the horses. Until it was time to hunt."

"You don't use many Scottish words for a man in a kilt," Bree said, her voice growing thicker.

"I'm a Highlander," he said, thumping his knuckles over his chest, "always will be, but I've spent so much time in different parts of the world, surrounded by other warriors who've done the same, it messes with the speech." Part of the reason warriors were sent so far from home and dressed and talked as natives in the lands where they fought was to keep demons from identifying the clan.

"Have you been to America before?"

"When I was seven, a demon came after my father, after our family… we came to Philadelphia, stayed until I was eight, then moved back to Scotland. My brothers didn't like it here."

"Your brothers, were you close?"

He saw the wee casket again and his mother's grief-stricken face and felt guilty for brushing the memory aside. But having Bree as a distraction was bad enough. If he let past mistakes make him weak, he'd fail again. "Aye. Most people thought Tavis and me were twins. Twins are common in our clan."

"What were your brothers like?"

"Tavis was quiet, when he wasn't mad or teasing us. Hot-headed, but loyal to a fault. Usually acted before he thought. Ian was full of mischief. Both of them were always getting into trouble." Much like Bree. Faelan had saved his brothers' arses from getting strapped many a time.

"And your mother?"

"She was cook, storyteller, and nurse. She had an elderberry bush she used to treat us for ailments. The stuff tasted bloody awful. Ian ran away every time he got sick." Faelan and Tavis had dragged him home more times than Faelan could remember. "And she made the best shortbread in Scotland." He smiled, almost hearing the tinkle of her laugh as she handed him the plate. His smile faded. She couldn't laugh anymore. She was gone. Everything he knew was gone. No one knew he was alive, except Grog and Bree.

"Did she tell you stories about fairies and kelpies when you were a boy?" Bree's voice was only a whisper now.

"Aye," he said softly, touching the section of hair his dirk had sheared. But he'd always known the stories weren't true. The real monsters were out there roaming the earth. And one day it would be his job to destroy them.

<center>~~~</center>

Shrouded forms circled the time vault, chanting, "Liar. Demon. Demon." Faelan lay inside, his body like stone, unable to move. The crowd parted, and Faelan saw his father. He tried to call out, but his lips were numb. His father leaned closer, his face harsh with disappointment and disgust. The others dropped their hoods, and Faelan saw his executioners. His mom, Ian, and Tavis pointing accusing fingers at him.

Then he saw the woman, her eyes green as moss—Bree—holding a little boy, his skin and clothing wet. Liam. A dainty hand reached for the lid, and Faelan's brain seized with fear. He saw the pale arm and then her sweet face. Alana smiled sadly and started to lower the lid. Another face came into focus. A smile started slowly, spreading wide, revealing sharp teeth as the man melted into Druan. Faelan watched in horror as darkness descended. Then there was nothing but silence as the key turned in the lock.

Faelan jerked upright, chest heaving, muscles taut as bowstrings. Bree lay with her back to him. He could see the curve of her cheek, her face as bonny as an angel. It was just a dream. He lay down beside her, watching her sleep as his nightmare faded. He touched her hair, wishing he dared pull her closer. He'd never felt anything like this for a woman. She set his body on fire, but it was more than that. He wanted to right the world for her, hold her and tell her every dream he'd had, every mistake he'd made—Druan, his deadly disease, the war… wee Liam. That was scary as hell. Not only was she not his, he also didn't know what she was. She'd destroyed a halfling with his dirk and looked at the light from his talisman and lived.

Bree moaned and moved in her sleep. Her dreams were unsettled too. No wonder, after what she'd seen tonight.

"Russell, no."

What had the bastard done to her? She'd faced half demons, killed one, yet her nightmare was about Russell? Faelan stroked Bree's hair. There was a small birthmark at the top of her back, near the demon's scratch. He dropped a kiss there, and she seemed to calm. Moving closer, he slid his good arm under her head, the other around her waist, and pulled her against him, careful of her injury. He told himself it was to comfort her, but he knew he needed to feel her breathe, to know he wasn't alone. A century and a half had passed. Even if he could locate his clan, had they forgotten him?

Bree nestled her back against his chest, her backside snug against his groin, and Faelan was glad he'd worn a T-shirt and the sleeping pants she'd bought him. He should've put on his Levi's for an added layer, and his kilt, if he could find it. He wasn't just worried about Druan and his evil, Faelan worried he'd lose control and do something unforgivable to Bree.

—◦◦◦—

The ache spread low in his groin. He rolled over, searching for warmth. A noise intruded, her voice. He was dreaming of her again. His body burned as he rubbed against the softness and found the place he craved. He shoved the barrier away and freed himself. He pushed, and pleasure poured over him like honey. Home. He was home.

The noise came again, and he felt pressure against his back, pulling him deeper into the dream. His nose tickled against something soft. Hair. The grogginess faded, and he had a feeling he shouldn't be here, but something dug into his thighs, keeping him close. He heard a whispered plea and felt hips moving against his. He groaned as he thrust, burying his face in her hair. The fire grew hotter. A soft moan sounded at his ear, and something sharp pierced his back, jerking him from the dream. Fingernails.

Faelan opened his eyes. Bree was under him, her lips parted, both of them panting for the same air. Her nightgown was pushed above her breasts, and his hand crushed between their locked bodies, holding aside a scrap of material she wore underneath. This was no dream.

He pulled out and leaped from the bed, heart in his throat, body aching with near release. The front of his pants gaped open. He adjusted them, afraid he'd spill it on the floor.

"I'm sorry." His mouth opened and closed, but he didn't know what to say. Had he raped her?

Bree pulled her nightgown and strange undergarment over her breasts. "Faelan—"

He struggled again for words, shaking inside. "I don't know what happened. I'm sorry." How could he guard her if he could do this? He would have to leave. He would take her to her archeologist, or Peter.

"You don't have to apologize," she said. Her face was still flushed. "You were dreaming at first." Her fingers clutched the hem of her gown. "I think I was too."

He'd done a lot of unforgivable things to her, but this…

She stood and moved next to him. "You didn't force me, Faelan. I could've stopped you… if I'd wanted to. This has been building since I opened the time vault. We both know it."

For half a second he was tempted to drag her back to bed, beg her to let him finish, so he could rid himself of this burning in his loins just once, but he'd already crossed the boundaries of acceptable behavior. He rubbed at the knot of tension in his neck as the throbbing in his body gave way to disgust. "The sun will be up in a few hours, then we should be safe until nightfall."

―――∾∾――

Bree watched Faelan leave the room, his shoulders stiff. Hers still tingled. She wasn't sure what had just happened, but when she'd realized it wasn't another sizzling dream, that it was really Faelan lifting her gown above her thighs, it was too late to care. How they'd managed it without even removing her panties, she didn't know, but she'd never felt anything like it. How he fit inside her, the sheer beauty of male and female joining, had been pure magic. If that was his sleepy version of love-making, she'd never survive him wide awake.

She felt guilty. He must be ready to pop. He was the one with the appetite problem, and he hadn't even finished. He was off tormenting himself thinking he'd raped her, while she was bathing in the afterglow. She couldn't leave it like this.

She found him in the family room, staring out at the moon, his body still. She was sure he heard her, but he didn't move. The sight of him standing so stoic, so full of guilt, made her want to comfort him. She slipped behind him and touched his back. He tensed, but still didn't turn. His skin was so warm through his shirt, she wondered if he had a fever. She checked his neck, his arm, and before she could question the wisdom of it, slipped her hands around his waist and laid her head against his back. The feel of his body, so big and strong, so protective, stirred more than a desire to comfort. She ran her hands over his chest, exploring the hard muscles encased in the soft T-shirt.

"What are you doing?" he whispered.

"Finishing." She let her hands slide down his rib cage, along the outside of his hips.

He pulled in a sharp breath. "Don't."

She kissed his back through the T-shirt, and her fingers drifted inside his thighs.

He groaned and turned, pulling her into his arms. His lips were on hers, on her neck, her face, like a man desperate for a drink of water. His hands roved her body, almost too rough, but she accepted it, knowing his need for her was stronger than chivalry. He lifted her gown over her head, letting it fall, then struggled with her bra clasp, his fingers clumsy with need. And he'd probably never seen a bra before tonight. She helped with the snap, releasing her breasts. In a flash, he was naked, tugging at her panties. She tried to help wriggle out of them. Their movements were quick, desperate, and she felt the fabric tear. He ran a hand between her legs, gave her a hard kiss, then put one arm around her waist, the other beneath a thigh. He picked her up and planted her against the wall. Her legs lifted, latching around his hips.

"Are ye sure?" he asked, his brogue thick, eyes locked on hers, dark as night.

She couldn't speak, only nod. He'd barely touched her, and she felt like a she was ready to explode again. He rubbed himself against her and then slipped inside. She moaned as he filled her. He stopped, staring at her, and stroked her face. "I'm sorry… we should do this in bed."

"No," she gasped. "Don't stop." She clutched his shoulders and pushed down harder on him. He pulled out and thrust in again, and again, each stroke bringing her closer to the edge. They panted, trying to kiss, but the movements of their bodies were too rough.

His breathing grew faster with each thrust. "*Mo*," he whispered in her ear. "*Mo*."

Gaelic? She couldn't think anymore, with her body

erupting into a million fragments of shimmering light. He groaned and shuddered as his body released. Limp, she clung to his shoulders. He touched his forehead to hers, then rested his head against the wall. They stayed that way for several minutes before he eased out and lowered her to the floor. Her legs trembled. Faelan swung her into his arms and carried her back to bed. He put her gently down, grabbed an old T-shirt off the floor—Russell's, and wiped off the semen running down her thighs. She had no words, so she didn't speak. He crawled in beside her and pulled her against his chest. Her heart soared, but a small voice whispered doom. What had she done? Had unprotected sex with a man from another time, a man she barely knew, who, until tonight, had told her nothing but lies.

The tall man stood over the open grave, surprised they'd left it uncovered. God forgive him, there was no time to cover it himself. He had to hurry. He looked at the house once more, making sure he hadn't been seen and made his way to the chapel. The outer walls and roof still stood, along with some pillars, but the place was littered with fallen stones. At one time it would have held the locals who'd come to pay their respects to God, but now the place was like a tomb. His foot struck something, and he started at the sound. It was a sword. There were half a dozen of them.

His curiosity piqued, but he had more important things to worry about. He took out the piece of paper he'd brought from Scotland. Studying it, he made his way to the front. Stones were scattered from a small interior wall that had collapsed. Behind them, he found the hidden steps. His pulse quickened. This was it.

Chapter 14

BREE WOKE SNUG AND WARM, COMPLETELY AT PEACE. A ringing sound broke through her haze of tranquility. She heard a grunt, lifted her head, and found herself face to face with Faelan. She was draped over him, both of them naked, her leg between his, his between hers, breasts pressed to his stomach, a spot of drool on his chest where she'd used it as a pillow. They stared at each other, eyes bleary from sleep.

The ring sounded again. "What is it?" Faelan asked, looking around the room.

"The doorbell," she whispered. "Someone's outside." She wasn't expecting anyone. Would Russell come right up to the house? Or the killer? Bree scooted off the bed, grabbing her robe, but Faelan was already at the bedroom door.

"Stay here," he ordered.

"No." She belted the robe. "You can't let anyone see you." Especially like that. "It's probably Peter." And she was getting tired of being told what to do. She hurried to the living room. Faelan lingered in the hallway as she eased the curtain aside and peeked at the man on the porch. "It's okay," she whispered, "but you should—"

"Aye, I know," he muttered. "Go hide in the other room."

Bree gave Jared a weak smile as he kissed her cheek. If she'd been in the market for romance, Jared would've been the mother lode, good-looking, charming, kind, with a love of old things that rivaled her own. Not to mention a fabulous library she hadn't yet seen. That he was an archeologist, and all lean, sexy muscle, didn't hurt either. A match made in heaven, but Bree wasn't looking for romance, not even from a man with a fabulous library. Certainly not one from a time vault.

"Did I catch you at a bad time?" Jared asked, eyeing her robe and her hair. "You don't look so good. Sorry. That didn't come out right." He smiled, and the dimple in his cheek warmed his face. "I mean you look tired and your hair's…" He made a sticking-out motion with his hands, and his grin widened.

His smile was infectious. She longed to throw open the door and bare her soul. "I have a headache," she lied. "I was in bed."

"You having trouble sleeping again? Your message the other night sounded strange." Jared glanced behind her at the open door. Had he overheard Faelan whispering when he rang the doorbell?

"I called to see if you'd heard about the guy who was murdered."

Jared frowned. "Murdered?"

"Out in the woods. They don't know who he is or who did it." If it was one of those things in the chapel, they'd need more than good luck and a gun.

"I just got back. I hadn't heard. I go away for a few days, and all hell breaks loose. You shouldn't stay here."

"It's okay. I keep the doors locked, and I've got my grandpa's old gun."

"If there's a killer out there, it's not safe for a woman to be here alone."

Another overprotective male—it was like a disease. "I'll be fine. Peter has the cops driving by every few hours. It was probably a wild animal anyway. How was your trip?"

"Not good. Some locals are raising a stink."

"Why? It's not like you're digging up graves."

"My backers are threatening to pull the funding. If I don't find something soon, this project's over. Have you thought any more about my proposal?"

He wanted to expand the dig closer to the house. She'd planned to tell him yes. That was before she'd found Faelan. "I haven't decided. I'll have an answer for you soon, I promise."

"Thanks for considering it. You need anything before I go?" he asked, tucking her hair behind her ears.

"Thanks, but I'm good."

"Maybe I should stay—"

"I'm fine. Really. You have your dig to worry about."

His calloused palm touched her cheek as he brushed her forehead with a kiss. "Keep your doors locked. That's an order. I'll call you tomorrow."

Guilt set in the minute he left. Jared was her closest friend. She'd told him things she hadn't told another living soul. He'd listened without judging, comforted her when she was sad, and restored her faith in humanity. The male side.

How could he forgive her when he found out she'd hidden the biggest secret of all?

She turned and found Faelan watching her, holding a pillow over his groin.

"Who was that?"

"Jared."

"The archeologist? What's he doing here?" And how did he know she had trouble sleeping? "Is he your lover?" Faelan was certain he'd heard a kiss.

"Jared? No, he's just a friend. We have a lot in common. We both love old things."

Her eyes glowed with a warmth that made him want to pound the archeologist into one of the holes he'd dug. *I'm old*, he wanted to shout. "He proposed marriage to you?" Would he still want her if he knew she'd had Faelan's body in places only a husband should be?

"No. He proposed moving the dig. I'm not looking for marriage."

Weren't all women looking for a husband? It was the goal mothers drilled into a lassie's head from the time she could talk. Of course, for him, relationships with women could be only a dalliance, and highly frowned upon, at that.

His mate had been decided before he was even born.

"Jared's just looking for friendship."

No man could know Bree and not want more than friendship. "He insulted you. Doesn't sound like much of a friend?"

"He didn't insult me, and he is a friend. My best friend. He was there to pick up the pieces after Russell almost destroyed me." She scowled. "I have to go out for a while. I won't be long."

"You can't leave. Not alone."

"I'm going out to meet a friend."

"Him? The archeologist?"

"Does it matter?" Bree glared at him. "I don't need a bodyguard."

Of course it mattered. He'd just made love to her. He had a right to know where she was rushing off to. "I'm trying to protect you. A man's been murdered, and there's an eight-hundred-year-old demon who's spent centuries perfecting ways to destroy humans like you. If that's not reason enough for a bodyguard, there were twelve half-demons in the chapel last night. One of them tried to capture you."

"I counted ten."

"I killed two before you got there. I'm trying to keep you alive, but you're making it bloody hard."

Bree sighed. "I'm going to see Janie. If her boyfriend can trace the tag number on that vehicle from last night, we'll know where to start looking for Druan. And I think he knows some people who might be able to get you a passport and fake driver's license."

"It's not safe to go alone."

"You can't go with me. If Janie sees you in person, you can forget protecting clan secrets. You think I ask questions. I'll be back in a few hours. You can raid the fridge and flip through the TV channels to your heart's desire. Your sex likes that."

"My sex?" Faelan readjusted the pillow.

Bree picked up a camera and pointed it at him. "I need a photo in case he can get you an ID," she said stiffly, and clicked a button. She rushed from the room, leaving him wondering who he wanted to kill first, Druan or Jared. Faelan had held her, made love to her, and here she was, defending another man. She obviously regretted last night. He heard the shower turn on and wondered if she was trying to wash him off her skin. He showered in the hall bathroom, and when he came out, she was gone. A note on the kitchen counter said she'd be back in a few hours. What kind of society allowed women to go rushing off into danger without a thought for their safety?

Enlightened? Advanced? Hell, they were insane.

He stormed through the house looking for his kilt. She must have thrown it away. His body thrummed with tension. He needed exercise. He needed to ride Nandor, and he needed his sword. Except for the battle in the chapel and chopping wood, he'd been still for too long, hiding inside like a lass. Some fresh air and sunshine might clear his head. Maybe he'd run into a demon. A fight would relieve some of his frustration.

He pulled on his boots and heard a car turn onto the driveway. Bree must have forgotten something. He'd talk some sense into her if he had to tie her to a chair. He hurried outside and moved around toward the driveway, when he noticed this car sounded different. It didn't rumble. A strange vehicle rolled up to the house, and Faelan dove behind an apple tree, slamming his arm into the ground. He felt fresh blood soak the bandage and trickle down his arm. A man got out. Her friend, Peter. He went to the door, knocked, and when no one answered, he wrote something on a piece of paper, stuck it on her door, and left.

Faelan read the paper. "Call me. Having trouble tracing your friend's name. Urgent." It wasn't enough that demons were hunting him, now the authorities were after him, too. He went inside, still dripping blood, and fixed his bandage. The cut would've been nearly healed if he hadn't used so much energy with the talisman while he still hadn't regained full strength from the time vault. He crossed the backyard and started running along the old trail. In Scotland, he'd raced against Nandor to keep ready for battle. The last time Faelan had seen the stallion, Nandor had followed along the fence, neighing softly, as if he'd known Faelan was never coming back.

Everything Faelan knew was dead, even his horse.

God wasn't dead. Michael wasn't dead. Did Michael even know he was awake?

There was no going back. He couldn't change what was done. He started running again, slowly at first, then picking up speed, until his thoughts were banished and all that touched him was the wind. He could feel Nandor running beside him, could hear the whinny of excitement as the stallion surged ahead. For miles he ran, feeling nothing but the life pumping through his veins, his feet pounding the earth, the talisman slapping his chest as Nandor urged him on.

———

Bree ran her finger across the drop of blood on Faelan's bedroom floor, stark fear erasing her earlier worries of pregnancy and disease. Druan's demons must have come back for Faelan. She shouldn't have left. He was still weak from using his talisman. The car must belong to one of his minions. They'd probably taken Faelan there. She grabbed the DMV report and hurried to the computer, working for once. She printed the directions from MapQuest, snatched her tote bag, and raced out of the house to rescue Faelan yet again.

Foot to the floor, she flew past familiar streets, onto a small road she didn't know existed, and another so isolated she doubted God knew it was there. She'd have been less surprised to see Disney World than the stone castle outlined against the sky. At either end, towers stretched toward the heavens, dark and forbidding. Thick forests surrounded the castle, blocking out the fading sun. This wasn't the home of a minion. This was a demon's lair, and it felt familiar.

Faelan had told her the demon would have a base nearby, but she hadn't expected a castle or an iron fence like the Great Wall. A dungeon. The castle probably had a dungeon. That's where they'd keep him. If he was alive. *Don't even think it. He's alive. He has to be.* The problem was getting him out. She couldn't march up and knock on the door. She should've called Peter. What could the police do against demons? What could she do? She didn't even have a weapon.

Something moved in front of the massive structure. She slowed the car as two huge vultures took flight, then continued past the heavy gates until she found an opening in the trees where she could hide her car. Across the road, a large tree grew next to the fence bordering the castle, a good place to climb and jump the fence.

After hiding the car, she whispered a prayer, tossed her sandals over the fence, and hiked up her skirt. She got a firm grip on the lower branch of the tree and started climbing barefoot. At the top of the fence, she slipped a foot between the iron bars and swung over. That scumbag rock climber she'd dated hadn't been a complete waste after all. She dropped to the other side and bent over, hands on her knees, as she caught her breath. How would she get Faelan back over the wall if he couldn't walk? First, she'd have to find him.

The first-floor windows were covered with bars. She'd have to find another way in. She darted from tree to bush until she was a hundred feet from the castle and then ran. Pressing her back flat against the wall, she dried her sweaty palms on her denim skirt and switched her cell phone to vibrate, in case it rang. Russell had wrecked everything else. It'd be just like him to spoil the only covert mission of her entire life. Keeping to the shadows, she slipped around to the back of the castle and found a door unlocked. It opened to a pantry behind a large kitchen. Empty. She peeked out into a corridor wide enough for her Mustang.

The walls and floors were made of stone, and draperies covered windows taller than a house. Statues stood in the corners, and ancient weaponry decorated every space. A battle-ax and a war club hung next to a lance. Even without examining them, she was certain they were authentic. There were a few pieces that didn't resemble anything she'd seen, and she was an expert. After Faelan destroyed Druan, she would come back, but now, she had to find the dungeon. There must be stairs somewhere.

Holding a shoe in each hand, she darted from statue to statue, hiding behind each one until she was sure the way was clear. Footsteps rang on the stone. There was no place to hide. She squatted behind a fat statue of a hellhound and stopped breathing as the footsteps drew near. A tall, well-dressed man with a shocking streak of silver in his auburn hair passed by. Was that Druan?

The man stopped outside a door, peered up and down the hall, then fiddled with a lock. The door opened, and he darted inside. Why would Druan break into a room in his castle? A crash sounded, followed by a raised voice.

Bree hurried inside an arched doorway and almost dropped to her knees. The room was two stories tall with bookshelves lining the walls from floor to ceiling. The castle library. She gazed in awe imagining the stories, the history held there. But this was a demon's castle, and Faelan's life was in danger. She didn't have time to look at old books. Bree started to leave, when she felt the air shift and pressure against her back, like a hand. She bumped into a tall table and grabbed it to steady herself, dislodging a book. *Castle Druan.*

It couldn't be. Just like that? She'd always been fascinated with castles, studied them, visited several, gotten lost in a few. Most had a written history, often including a map. If she could find one, she'd get to Faelan far faster than stumbling around looking for stairs. She opened the book to the back. There it was, a meticulous diagram, like an answer to a prayer. Someone was watching out for her.

She ripped the fragile page from the book and started to leave, when she saw a glass case in the center of the room. A broadsword lay inside on a black velvet cloth. She moved closer, her head spinning, noting the length, the polish of the metal, the ornate hilt, like the one her Highland warrior held in the painting. Here in the demon's castle. Her stomach rolled as she remembered the old painting that looked like Faelan, the same sword. She'd rescued him from a time vault made for demons. Could Faelan be the demon? Why hadn't he hurt her? Why kill those halflings? Halflings! She touched her stomach. Oh God. She'd slept with him.

A door slammed outside, and she heard male voices. She peeked down the hall. Two men stood outside a door, so immersed in conversation they didn't see her. One was older, shoulders bent, his hair white, and the other tall and muscular, dark blond.

Russell.

—⁂—

Faelan stepped out of the shower, slipping in his haste. He didn't want Bree to come home and find him in her bathroom. Well, part of him did, but it wouldn't be wise. He'd stayed out longer than he planned, exploring the area. He'd found the yellow tape in the woods and the blood-stained earth. He'd picked up an odd scent. Sweet. Not animal, not demon. Not that a demon wasn't responsible. Too much time had passed to tell. A demon's scent was terrible but faded quickly. The incident left him with an unsettled feeling as he blocked the crypt and covered the grave.

The run had helped, connected both parts of him, the one that was one hundred and seventy-eight and the one that was twenty-seven. He'd reconciled himself to the fact that his family was gone. He wouldn't see them again in this lifetime. The only thing he could give them now was a safe world for their descendents. The run hadn't done a thing to ease his hunger for Bree, but he was beginning to think nothing would. Making love to her had made it worse. He couldn't allow it to happen again. There weren't just bairns and disease to worry about. The box he'd slipped into the cart would take care of that, but distraction from his mission could mean the end of humanity.

He dried off and inspected his arm. Looked better than it had before. He bandaged the wound, lifted his arms, and smeared the stuff on his oxters that kept a man from sweating. It hadn't stopped this generation from bathing every day. With these fancy showers and Jacuzzis, having hot water at the touch of a hand, he couldn't blame them. Wiping the steam from the mirror, he lathered his face with something that smelled like flowers and ran a tiny razor over his chin. Even his father couldn't have cut himself with one of these. A man who'd wielded a sword all his life shouldn't have had so much trouble removing whiskers.

Swords! Damnation. He had to get rid of those in the chapel before Bree found them. He'd never seen a woman so interested in weapons. It wasn't natural. He tucked the towel around his waist and padded across the hall to his bedroom. After dressing in jeans and a T-shirt, he grabbed a bottle of water from the refrigerator. His mother would have loved this kitchen. With freezers and ovens and microwaves, she could've baked for an army. At times, she did, with help from their grumpy old cook, Nan.

Faelan drained the bottle, set it on the counter, and headed out to the chapel. Enough daylight remained to see the interior of the chapel was a mess. Crumbling stones, pillars toppled. It was a wonder the roof held. He gathered the fallen swords and one small knife, looking for a place to hide them until they could be cleansed. There was a large pile of debris near the front. Must be the collapsed wall Bree mentioned. Perhaps he could hide the swords behind the stones. He entered a small recess and saw rubble piled in front of a gaping hole. She could've been killed. Then he noticed the rough-hewn steps. It was a hidden doorway. Bree hadn't mentioned a secret cellar. She must not know, or she'd have knocked the wall down long ago. It would suffice. After he piled up the stones, she'd never know there'd been an entrance here.

Carrying the swords, he carefully descended the worn steps. It was black as Hades down here. The entire thing was underground, no windows. He tuned his vision, trying to make out the shapes. Against the far wall, he saw a coffin. Was this a catacomb? He hid the weapons in the corner and went to examine his find. When he was close enough to make out the details, he saw it wasn't a coffin at all.

It was a time vault.

Chapter 15

BREE'S BREATH PIERCED HER LUNGS LIKE ICICLES. What was Russell doing in the demon's castle? Was he working with Druan? Why else would he be here? Had the whole relationship been an evil scheme? The chance meeting in the antique store. The reconnection of kindred souls.

A darker picture formed in her mind, one that made her stomach revolt. Had she been seduced by Druan himself? And how had the sword from her picture gotten into the demon's castle? Was Faelan involved, too, or had Druan stolen it?

The men walked away, heads close, their strained whispers carrying to where she hid. She could tell from Russell's posture that he wasn't happy. The old man glanced over his shoulder, and Bree jumped back, her fingers digging into the wall. If she gave in to the shock, she'd have dropped to the floor and bawled, but she didn't have time to cry. She had to move fast.

The map showed a staircase to the dungeon on the opposite side of the castle. She ran past several doors, stopping when she heard a woman's voice. Bree cautiously looked inside. It was a sitting area filled with antiques and more medieval weapons. A woman lounged on a low sofa that must have dated back to the eighteenth century. She was slender but full-bodied, her hair jet black, lips red, with fingernails to match. Bree had never seen anyone so beautiful. She was drawn to the woman. Was this a premonition? Did the woman need help? Maybe she was a prisoner here, one of those females demons used for breeding. Bree debated approaching her, when the woman flowed to her feet, sinuously running her hands up her body, through her long, silky hair. The hands that emerged didn't have red polish. They each had four hoof-like fingers tipped with long claws. A female demon. The woman laughed, her voice seductive, as her forearms began to ripple. Shaken, Bree covered her mouth and backed away.

She had to find Faelan. Which way to go? Druan on one side, this creature on the other.

A door closed inside the room. Bree held her breath and hurried past. Using the same hide-and-peek method as before, she located the stairs. Voices echoed off the stone. Someone was coming up. There was no place to hide, so she moved up to the next landing and waited for them to pass. Her skin tingled, as if she were being watched. When it was quiet, she started back down and saw two men still there. Their heads were lowered as they studied a piece of paper. One of them spoke, and they started to climb.

She didn't remember moving, but before she could blink, she found herself on the second floor, as if an unseen force had propelled her up the stairs. This floor was decorated in the same theme as the first, dark ages meets darker ages. All the doors were closed, and she had no choice but go higher. Two stairs at a time, still holding her shoes, she silently huffed to the top floor. It was dark here. No sconces hung on the walls. She waited a moment, but the voices still came.

Using the dim light from her cell phone, she navigated a narrow staircase she found tucked at the end of the hall. She climbed her third set of stairs and came to small door with a lock on the outside. She was in the tower. The darkness was as thick as smoke, and she felt like someone was breathing on her neck. "Faelan?"

The voices sounded closer. Were they following her? Bree put her shoulder to the door and pushed, but it was stuck. A breeze brushed her cheek, and her hair lifted. The door slid open like it was greased, and she toppled inside. The room reeked of decay, and from the dim light on her phone, she could see a metal cot with blankets in the corner and a table with tubes and vials. "Faelan?" The door closed behind her, hanging on the same spot, leaving a sliver of light in the dark. The voices were near the door now. Something scuttled in the far corner of the room. The sliver of light blacked out, then reappeared.

"Hey, where did you come—" The voice outside gurgled, a wet, choking sound, then was silent.

Bree dropped to the floor and hid behind a table, breath coming hard. She pushed a button on the phone, clutching the faint light close for comfort. What was out there? She scooted over, trying to see around the edge, and stubbed her toe. She cradled her foot, trembling. She could call the police, but what could they do? Anyway, she had only one bar of signal, and it kept fading. The sliver of light went black as the door scraped shut, and she heard the clink of a lock. Was this how her life would end, trapped in a demon's tower after stumbling onto the biggest mystery of her life? Her mother would grieve, speaking fondly of her reckless nature at the funeral, but there'd be no body, because no one would ever find her.

It wouldn't matter anyway. Faelan wouldn't be rescued, and the world would die with her.

The air stirred beside her, and she heard a soft footstep. She stopped breathing, easing her phone shut as she shrank lower to the floor. Something was in here with her.

<center>~~~</center>

Faelan lifted the lid of the time vault and stared at what little of the inside he could see. How long had it been here? Who brought it? Where was the key? He closed the lid, disturbed. Had Michael reassigned Druan? How could he, without Faelan's talisman? There must be another entrance to the cellar besides the old hidden door. Faelan poked around for clues, but even with his sharpened vision, he needed more light. He hurried up the steps, climbed over the debris, and ran outside. Twilight. They had to get out of here. Where was Bree?

He checked inside and out. She wasn't there. A piece of paper lay on the counter. Division of Motor Vehicles. This was the paper she'd gone to get. Had she come home while he was out? According to the paper, the car belonged to a man outside Albany, probably one of Druan's minions.

Surely Bree wouldn't go there alone. He remembered watching in disbelief as she threw his dirk at that halfling, how fiercely she'd attacked Grog, how she'd insisted on going back inside the chapel for the swords. Damnation. That's just what she'd do.

His talisman heated, growing uncomfortably warm. She was in danger. He could feel it. Why hadn't she called him on that fancy phone? Shite. He'd forgotten to take it with him. He punched in her number from the house phone, but it went straight to voice mail. He wasn't comfortable talking to a machine, so he hung up. He needed a horse. No, he needed one of those yellow cars. He called 411, like she'd showed him, and used his fiercest warrior voice to order a taxi. He found his cell phone in his bedroom, turned off. Bree had tried to call him earlier. By the time he slipped on a shirt and boots and dug through drawers looking for money, a horn honked outside. A dark-skinned man drummed his fingers on the steering wheel.

"You're sure this is a taxi?" Faelan asked him. "It isn't yellow."

"Says so right there on the side. See? Taxi."

"No. It says, 'ax.'"

"The *T* and the *i* fell off. You getting in or not?"

Faelan got in, but he didn't like it one bit. Before he'd been suspended, he could have walked this area blindfolded. He'd scouted every mountain, every valley and hill hunting Druan. But now there were houses stacked on top of houses and highways that stretched for miles. He gave the man the address from the report and hoped the pile of coins from her junk drawer would cover the cost. It was enough to destroy a man's sense of pride. How could he save Bree, much less the world, when he couldn't buy himself a loaf of bread?

He highlighted Bree's number and pushed Send again. On the third ring, she answered.

"Faelan?" she whispered. "Thank God… escaped… dungeon…"

"You've escaped from a dungeon!"

"No, did… you…"

"Where are you?"

"…castle… trapped…"

"Castle?" His heart thundered in his chest like a race-horse running for the finish line.

"…blood…"

"Blood? Are you injured? I can't understand you."

"Piece of crap cell phones," the taxi driver said.

"Blood on your floor… kidnapped… rescue." Bree's voice faded.

Blood on his floor? "I hit my arm."

"…thought you were… kidnapped."

"Kidnapped? Me? You mean you went to…" the words stuck in his throat. "You went to rescue me?" Faelan squeezed the phone so tight he heard it crack. "Are you bloody mad?"

"Women," the driver said, his gaze darting from Faelan to the road.

"I've been fighting demons since 1850—"

There was a squeal, and the car slammed to a stop. Faelan's face bounced off the back of the seat and the phone flew out of his hand. He grabbed it and rose, meeting the driver's round eyes in the rearview mirror.

"I don't think—" the man started.

"Drive," Faelan ordered, rubbing his nose. The driver's head bobbed nervously and the taxi leapt forward. "But don't kill us getting there."

"Exactly where are you?" Faelan asked Bree.

"…right tower… Druan's castle." Her voice dropped so low, he wouldn't have heard it if not for his warrior senses. "Hurry. Something's… here… with me." The connection went dead.

The taxi drove past it twice before Faelan saw the back of Bree's car hidden in the trees. Where was the castle? Deeper in the woods? He paid the driver, and as the car sped away, Faelan crossed the small road and headed for the field. His skin started to prickle a second before he smacked into something hard. He caught a glimpse of trees, iron, and stone before he stumbled back. Warily, he stretched his hand in front of him. The air parted like a curtain, and a picture unfolded before him. A high stone wall, and behind it, a castle.

His clan's castle. Here in America.

Chapter 16

WHAT SORCERY WAS THIS? FAELAN TOOK TWO STEPS back, and the castle disappeared. Two steps forward, and it appeared again. An invisible cloak. Druan had hidden a castle in the middle of a field, a castle that looked exactly like the Connor Castle in Scotland. The illusion was only from outside the cloak. From inside, he could see the road and the trees where Bree had parked. No time to ponder it. He had to get Bree out before Druan discovered he had a guest. Faelan had seen what the demon did to his enemies.

His arm throbbed as he dropped over the iron fence. He sniffed. No demons close by, and no dogs, he hoped. It wasn't likely. Demons hated animals. An animal could sense a demonic presence long before a human could. Faelan headed toward the north side of the castle, keeping to the shadows. A man with long, raven hair appeared near a narrow door. Faelan jumped behind a tree, his hand on his dirk. The man's movements were graceful, almost elegant, but powerful. He was too far away to scent for demon blood, but he wasn't someone Faelan wanted to meet until his strength returned.

Faelan glanced over his shoulder to make sure he hadn't been spotted. When he turned around again, the man had disappeared.

―⚡―

Tristol perched on a branch high in the tree and watched as the warrior dropped and ran the few remaining feet to the castle. He tried the side door, and when it wouldn't open, he stepped back, surveying the second-story balcony far above his head. He tested a thick vine, seemed satisfied, and began to climb. Muscles bulged as the warrior inched his way up the wall. He'd just reached the top when his dagger caught on the vine. He tugged it free, and the vine started to pull away. Leaping, the warrior grasped the edge of the balcony, dangled for a moment, then threw his legs over and stood.

Impressive.

He peered over the side and quickly turned away.

Tristol smirked. So the Mighty Faelan didn't like heights, but he had strength and power. If it matched his reputation, he might be worth more than a way to eliminate Druan. He would have to bide his time and wait. Not only the fate of the living depended on the outcome of this fight.

———

Faelan leaned against the cold stone and touched his burning arm. He hated heights.

A chill worked up his spine. He glanced over his shoulder, then tested the small door to his left. It was locked. Next to it was a small, dark window. This would be a bedroom in his clan's castle. He pushed against the glass, and it moved enough to get his head and injured arm through. He pushed hard, and his right shoulder scraped through, followed by his hips and legs. The room was dark. He pulled his cell phone from his pocket, using the faint light to get his bearings. He was dismayed that the room looked just as he'd expected.

He opened the door and peered into the dimly lit hallway. The sight was disturbing. The second floor was a replica of Connor Castle. A staircase stood at the end of the wide hallway, like the one he and his brothers had played on. He heard voices approaching and ducked back inside the room, leaving the door cracked so he could hear.

"If Druan doesn't find the key and the time vault soon, there won't be any of us left."

"You'd think he would've guarded it."

The other voice shushed. "Don't say that. If one of those half-demons hears, it'll tell, and Druan will do to you what he did to Onca for losing the key. You know Druan's been on edge, always looking over his shoulder. Can't say I blame him. Lately, this place feels like it has eyes."

"You're working for demons, and you're worried about ghosts?"

"You know what I mean. You almost jumped out of your skin when that ugly demon woke us this morning. Sometimes I wish we'd never…" the voices faded, and Faelan moved into the hallway, trying to listen. There was no doubt this was Druan's castle. Faelan was so busy examining the similarities of this castle to the one he'd called home that he didn't notice the white-haired old man until it was too late. The man—at least he looked like a man—ambled by, his head buried in a book, talking to himself. Faelan's hand went to his dirk. He'd have to kill the man quietly, so he didn't raise an alarm. The old man looked up, nodded, and continued toward the stairs, paying Faelan no mind, as if he belonged here. Like a bloody demon.

If Druan was still looking for the vault and the key, then he didn't know Faelan was awake. Not surprising that Grog would be too scared to tell him. Faelan moved to the third floor. It was dark—no lights in the hall. He didn't need the glow from his cell phone to find the last set of stairs, exactly the same as Connor Castle's, small and winding, barely wide enough for a man's shoulders. At the top was a small iron door. In Scotland, Alana had used the room to store her paint supplies.

"Bree?" he whispered.

"Faelan?" Her voice came back small and frightened. He wanted to hold her, comfort her, and then tie her to a chair. Or a bed. "Hurry, please."

Faelan tried the door. It wasn't locked, but it wouldn't move. "Stand back." He put his shoulder to the metal and pushed, feeling a rush of fresh blood. He pushed again, but it wouldn't move. Odd, it wasn't locked. Kicking it in would make too much noise. "Stand back."

He put his shoulder to the iron and pushed. It opened enough for Bree to squeeze her body through. She rushed into his arms. "Are you okay?"

"I thought… just get me out of here." She looked over her shoulder. "There's something inside. I heard it move."

If one of Druan's horde was in there, Bree would be dead. Faelan gave it a quick look from the doorway, but even with his heightened senses, it was too dark to see much of the room. He didn't hear any breathing besides hers and his own. If there was something inside, it wasn't alive. "We have to leave before we're discovered."

"There are secret passages, but I don't know if they lead outside. I came in through a pantry off the kitchen. I can show you."

"I don't think I'll have any trouble finding it." He could walk it blindfolded. With one hand on his talisman and the other holding his dirk, Faelan led the way to the dark kitchen.

"I came in through there." She pointed to the pantry, and her hand hit a bowl, sending it crashing to the floor. "Darn it."

He pushed her inside the small room as the lights came on.

"What was that?" a man asked.

"There's a bowl on the floor," the second man said.

"I can see that. It didn't just leap off the counter."

It was the two from before.

"No one's supposed to be over here, but I've had this feeling all day, like someone's watching me. You ever get that feeling?"

"In this place, I do. Check it out."

Faelan pressed Bree against the wall, as he'd done last night. He could feel her heart pounding against his… as he had last night. He couldn't be thinking about that now.

"You check it out. I don't take orders from you."

"Come on. There's nothing here," the first man said. "This whole plan is hopeless."

"If you don't stop talking like that, you're gonna be hanging up there with Onca." The voices faded away, and Faelan felt Bree exhale.

They moved outside and across the castle grounds as fast as they could, keeping to the shadows and hiding behind trees. When they reached the wall, he offered his hands to lift her up. She hesitated a second before pulling her skirt up to her hips. Hunger hit him hard, but he pushed it aside and concentrated on getting her over the top. Climbing the wall himself wasn't easy, with his arm screaming in pain and his thoughts locked on her thighs.

"How'd you get here so fast?" she asked once they were in the car.

"I saw the paper on the counter. I thought someone had taken you. Or you'd done something… reckless."

"I was so sure they had you," she said, starting the car. "I knew the police wouldn't believe me, and if they did show up, Druan would kill you and them too. Then I'd have to find your family and tell them they'd lost you, even before they knew you were alive."

"What kind of woman goes around invading a demon's castle?" An invisible one. How'd she even find it? What had happened to the meek, gentle women of his time? She was bold, with a temper to match, and with too much curiosity for anyone's health. He felt a surge of something, but didn't dwell on it. He was afraid it might be respect. He'd done unforgivable things to her; still, she'd put her life on the line because she thought he was in trouble. And she'd climbed over that fence like a warrior. Most women he'd known would have expected a man to carry them across. 'Course they wouldn't have broken into the demon's castle in the first place.

"Don't yell at me. I was trying to help."

"I'm not yelling."

"You look like you want to. Besides, you thought the same thing. Weren't you coming to rescue me?"

"I'm a warrior." Not a damsel in distress. "I was fighting demons before you were born."

"A warrior who just slept for one hundred fifty-one years and would've slept for eternity if a woman hadn't interfered." She looked across the road and shivered. "Let's say we're even and get out of here," she said, putting the car in gear.

"What do you see there?" Faelan asked, nodding toward the empty field and trees hiding the castle.

She frowned. "A castle. Big iron fence."

Damnation. How could she see it when he couldn't?

"Why?" she asked, pulling out so fast he had to pry his head from the headrest.

"No reason." He checked his bandage. The fresh blood hadn't reached his sleeve.

"I thought you would've healed by now."

"I reopened the wound earlier."

"I'm sorry. I guess climbing over that wall twice didn't do it any good. Sometimes I do things without thinking."

That went without saying.

"We have another problem," she said. "It gets worse."

He didn't see how. The demon was living in a replica of Connor Castle that was invisible to Faelan but visible to Bree? And now there was a time vault hidden under her chapel, and he had no idea if Druan had been reassigned.

"Russell is the demon."

"I beg your pardon?" He must have misheard.

"Russell's the demon. I saw him in the castle." Her voice was strained, her fingers tight on the steering wheel.

"You've been under stress. The mind can play tricks when one is frightened—"

"No. It was him."

Faelan's insides knotted. It couldn't be Russell. "What does he look like?" Demons rarely switched human forms. It took too long to get comfortable.

"Tall, muscular, dark blond hair, blue eyes. Handsome. Dresses well."

Like Jeremiah. Damnation. Bree and Druan? His stomach knotted. There had to be another explanation. "Does Russell have any distinguishing marks?"

"Not that can be seen with clothes…" Bree trailed off, looking embarrassed.

A growl rolled from Faelan's throat. He'd seen Druan without human skin, but never without clothes, and it irritated him knowing Bree had. How many other men had she seen naked? "Do you have a photograph of him?"

"I think I burned them all. I can't believe that I… that he… but he was standing right there. It was him. Remember, I thought I saw him in town. I think he's been watching me."

"Maybe he followed you to the castle."

"No. He didn't even see me there. He was talking to an old man."

Faelan's knots twisted and formed new knots. Russell, the bastard who'd made Bree cry, was Druan. "How close were you?"

"We were engaged. Betrothed."

"You were going to marry him?" Faelan's knots grew claws.

"The whole thing must have been a setup. He used me to get to the time vault."

That would explain why Grog told the halfling not to

hurt her. Druan still needed access to the place, since he didn't know Faelan was awake. Faelan rubbed his hand over his face. A demon of old had tried to marry Bree to get to him. Faelan knew he would have to ask her some brutal questions, but not now. "How did you meet him?"

"In college. We were both majoring in history. We dated a few times, then I moved to Florida. About a year and a half ago, I was visiting Grandma, and I stopped by this antique store. I reached for a book at the same time he did. We laughed about what a coincidence—"

"Coincidences rarely are."

She gave him a startled glance, likely thinking how they were drowning in the damned things.

"He invited me to dinner in his tiny apartment in Albany. The jackass probably had a castle the whole time."

"They're all infatuated with castles, every last one of them."

"One thing led to another, and we got engaged. He moved to Florida to be with me, but after a few months I saw another side of him, not so handsome. Demonic bastard."

The tremble was in her voice again, and it made Faelan want to kill Russell, whether he was Druan or not. "What did he do?"

"He started hanging out with weird people. They'd call the house late at night, and he'd go off for days without any word. He was like a stranger when he got back, hateful and jealous, like a shell of himself. I know he stole money my dad left me. And there were other things." Her lips thinned.

"Why didn't you leave?"

"I kept making excuses for him. Then one day… one

day when he was out doing whatever it was that he did, I packed and went to Grandma's, and I got a restraining order, a legal document that says he has to stay away. Fat lot of good it did against a demon. As soon as I left, he started begging for another chance. I guess he was desperate to find you."

"Did he hurt you?" He'd asked the question before, but he suspected he hadn't gotten the correct answer.

She met his gaze then looked away. "Once." Her chin tilted. "Only once."

"What did he do?" he asked, dreading her answer.

"He hit me."

"Why didn't you tell me?"

"It's embarrassing that I stayed long enough to let him."

"He'll pay," Faelan said. "I'll make him pay." But he had to find him to kill him, and if Druan had been reassigned, Faelan would die too. "Did anyone see you in the castle?"

"I don't think so. Where were you when I came home earlier?"

"I went for a run to clear my head."

"Did it?" She cast a sideways glance at him.

"Up until an hour ago." He wouldn't mention the time vault in the cellar or that the castle was invisible to him, until he could sort it out.

"None of this would've happened if you'd taken the cell phone with you."

None of this would've happened if she'd taken a minute to think things through instead of leaping to conclusions. The woman was a magnet for danger.

He saw a quick movement in the side mirror. He spun around and looked out the back window.

"What's wrong?"

"Something's back there."

"Behind us?"

"In the air."

"A bird?"

"Bigger."

"Can demons fly?"

"Not that I know. They can choose an animal form, but I've never seen one as a bird."

"I saw two huge vultures at the castle. We'd better move faster, just in case." For ten minutes she drove like a horse running from flies.

"I think we'd be safer back at the castle fighting demons."

"You're not used to riding in a car. After Janie's boyfriend gets you a driver's license, I'll give you some lessons. You can practice in the driveway until you get the hang of it."

A woman giving him lessons, like a bairn learning to walk. A man didn't need a license to ride a horse. Then again, horses didn't have that rumbling sound that gave him chill bumps. "You need a GPS," he said, after she'd taken so many turns he figured they must be lost.

Bree frowned at him. "You're from 1860. What could you possibly know about GPS?"

"I saw it on a commercial. We'll have to find somewhere to stay."

"I guess it's not safe to go back to the house."

"Not tonight."

"There's a hotel up ahead."

"And food?" His stomach rumbled. "You must be hungry." He hadn't eaten in two whole hours.

"We'll hit a McDonald's."

He started to ask what the MacDonalds were doing in America and what they had to do with food, when she pulled up to a store with that name. She ordered food at a talking sign, then went to a little window and gave a plastic card to a lad with tattoos covering his arms from the wrist up. The next window slid open, and a lass with metal wires on her teeth smiled and handed Bree a bag of food. It was remarkable, but distressing. He didn't belong here, but he couldn't go back. Did he belong anywhere?

"What's wrong?"

"I can't keep living like this. I had to take money from your kitchen drawer to get a taxi."

"You've got a demon to kill and a world to save," she said quietly. "You'll feel better after you find your family. It'll be proof you exist. You can figure out money and all the other stuff later. You could always write a book. You could keep the clan stuff secret and write about the people of that time. Better yet, write a novel about your battles. Nobody would believe it, and they'd probably make a movie of it. You'd be rich." She looked him over, head to feet. "You could always model. They'd probably pay double if you wore the kilt."

"Model?"

"Pose."

"Pose? Doing what?"

"Just stand there, smile, look good holding some product."

"You mean people in this time will pay a person to just stand and smile? That's daft."

"It's complicated. Do warriors get paid?"

"We live modestly, but our needs are met. The clan has someone who handles those things."

"I'll cover your expenses for now, and you can pay me back." She took a drink of her soda. "You could always work with horses. I don't imagine they've changed."

"Horses." He gave her a quick look. "I know horses." He was good with horses. He picked up his food, took a bite, and almost moaned. "What is this?"

"A Big Mac. Welcome to fast food." While he downed two Big Macs, a large order of french fries, and a vanilla milkshake, Bree made some phone calls and found lodging. Seemed there was a conference in the area that had all the hotels full. "It's an old bed and breakfast," she whispered, covering the phone. "This should make you feel right at home."

He wasn't worried about feeling at home. He was worried about keeping his hands off her. If necessary, he could sleep in the car.

"We'll take two rooms," she said into the phone, and Faelan gave a sigh of relief. Bree put the phone away and rummaged in her big bag, took out a tissue, and dabbed at his chin.

"What are you doing?" he asked, pulling away.

"You've got dirt on your face. They'll think you're an escaped convict."

"Do you want to know how many cobwebs are in your hair?"

Bracing her knees against the steering wheel, she brushed at her hair with both hands.

Faelan stared at the cars approaching them. "I'd feel more comfortable if you weren't driving with your knees." He leaned over, running his hand through her hair, helping her clean up the worst of the mess. She grew unusually quiet. Had she finally realized how much danger she'd been in? It was a wonder she wasn't swooning. Women were sensitive creatures, with delicate natures.

"I should've taken that sword and chopped him into little bitty bloody pieces."

Damnation, but the woman was obsessed with swords. "You can't fight him. He's spent centuries preying on humans, figuring out their weaknesses, using deception, lies, any tricks he can to destroy them."

"You're right. Even as Russell, he got scary. How could I have not known he was a demon?"

"Deceiving is what they do best, especially the ancient demons. They give off an aura that draws people to them. Even warriors get fooled sometimes."

"But I let him get close… oh, God." Her face went white as alabaster. "Our children."

Chapter 17

"CHILDREN?" FAELAN'S LUNGS BURNED. HE REALIZED he'd stopped breathing.

Bree let the car roll to a stop on the side of the road and turned off the engine, looking as sick as he felt. She covered her face with her hands. Her shoulders started shaking, slight trembles growing into deep, silent sobs.

Faelan pulled her into his arms, mindful of her scratches, refusing to think how Druan had likely held her the same. The position was awkward, making his arm throb, but he held her close and let her cry. He rubbed her back, whispering soft words he hoped were of some comfort as he fought his own dread. Bree's flesh and blood mixed with a demon's?

"I'm sorry," she said, when the tears were finished. "I guess the shock wore off." She leaned back and wiped her face with the bottom of her shirt. "About five months ago, I thought I was pregnant. Russell went berserk. That's when he hit me, and I knew I had to get out."

"The bairn—"

"It was a false alarm. But if there had been a child, it would've been half... I can't even say it."

Half demon. A halfling. One of the things he was honor-bound to destroy, no matter who the mother was. And she could've gone years without discovering its true nature. Some didn't reveal their evil side until puberty. He had no qualms about suspending and destroying demons. It was what he was born to do. They were tormentors, created for evil. But aiming a talisman at a nine-year-old trying to rip your throat out wasn't an easy thing to do, and impossible to forget.

Thinking that Bree could be mother to one…

She sniffed. "I'm scared. If Druan doesn't already know you're awake, he will soon, and he's going to come after us."

Faelan reached for her again. "I won't let him hurt you. I'll destroy him if I have to." Even if it meant his own death. His lips brushed her temple, then the side of her mouth. She made a soft sound that thickened his blood, and she moved her lips to meet his.

"What you do to me," he whispered against her lips and then eased his tongue inside. Her hand, already resting on his thigh, brushed his groin, and he remembered slipping inside her, the desperate ache, the warmth, the belonging. He put his hand over hers, pressing it harder against him, then moved to her breast. His body cried *mine*, though his head knew she wasn't. He moved to her thighs, then slid his hand under her skirt, encountering a frilly piece of cloth. His fingers tugged at the lace. "What's this?"

"Panties," she gasped, when he touched what lay beneath.

That hadn't changed, but he didn't remember it having this effect on him. The flicker of lights from an approaching car hit the windshield, breaking the spell. "I'm sorry," he said, his voice thick as he slid the lace back in place and smoothed down her skirt. Bree pulled her hand from his lap and settled back in the seat, her face flushed. He couldn't do this to her again. Not without his ring on her finger.

And bound by clan rules as he was, that could never be.

———◦∿◦———

"Fix your sleeve," Bree whispered. "I can see blood—" She broke off as a gray-haired woman opened the door of the white Victorian bed and breakfast. "Mrs. Edwards? I called earlier. You're holding two rooms for us."

"You're lucky," Mrs. Edwards said. "This conference has every hotel filled. Some new-world-order thing. I had a few of them staying here, but they went to a friend's house. Can't say I'm sorry. They were strange. I have two guests besides the two of you, but they keep to themselves. Haven't seen hide nor hair of them since they arrived. Haven't seen the one at all. Where's your luggage?"

"We didn't bring any."

Mrs. Edwards peered over the rim of her glasses with a look that made both Bree and Faelan blush.

"We were on the way home and got too tired to drive. I have trouble seeing at night, and he gets migraines."

"Poor thing," she said to Faelan. "I do too. I have medicine, if you need it." After checking them in, she led them up a wide staircase to a landing and pointed out a large room to the left, with walls painted green and a canopied bed. "The other one is right next to it. Fresh toothbrushes are in the bathrooms. If you need anything, I'll be downstairs for another hour. Breakfast is at eight."

"Any preference on rooms?" Bree asked, feeling awkward after making out in the car.

Faelan wasn't listening. He'd walked inside the green room and was staring at an old painting hanging over an antique dresser. Bree followed and stood beside him. The dark-haired girl in the painting was feeding her horse an apple.

"She looks like Alana," he said, his eyes so haunted Bree wanted to kill Russell with her bare hands.

"She must have been lovely."

"Aye. She was full of life. Loved people, animals, especially horses. And painting. She painted anything that would sit still. Tormented me and my brothers." A smile touched his lips. "She hid a portrait of me in my trunk before I left Scotland. Her note said it was so I wouldn't forget her. I could never forget."

Bree touched his arm, wishing she could erase his pain. He pulled her close and buried his mouth in her hair.

"I'm so sorry." She couldn't imagine what it would be like to lose everything she loved, everything she knew, in one instant. "You may get to meet Alana's descendants. Won't that be amazing?"

"Aye, that will be amazing," he said, his words muffled. When he stepped back, there was sadness on his face. "I apologize for what happened in the car, and before. You shouldn't have to put up with me." Before she could speak, he touched her cheek and walked away.

———

"Eek! " Mrs. Edwards's plump hand flew to her equally ample bosom as she stared at the tall, raven-haired man who'd entered. "Oh my word, I didn't even hear you come in."

"My apologies. I know it's late, but the sign out front

did say welcome." His eyes flashed, then he smiled, and something she couldn't name wound its way up her body. "I'd hoped you might have a room for the night."

"Well, you're in luck," she said, fanning her face. "Most of my guests checked out already. Thank God. They were part of that strange conference in town."

He smiled again, and she glimpsed strong, white teeth. She was no spring chicken, but looking at him made her insides all gushy, like she hadn't felt for thirty years or more. Or was it thirty minutes, she thought, remembering the other man who'd just arrived. This one looked almost too pretty with his long, glossy hair, like one of those male models, but bigger. Odd that she'd get two such handsome men in one night. Three, if you counted the other one. Made her wonder what the guest she hadn't seen looked like. She glanced out the window. "Where's your car?"

"I didn't drive."

"You're lucky you found a taxi. This darned conference has taken over everything." Then again, he probably didn't have trouble getting taxis or anything else. With that smile, he could sell Bibles to atheists. "No luggage for you either, I suppose," she said, looking at the floor. "Nobody has luggage tonight."

"I think my brother's friends might be staying here. Young couple, both dark-haired, attractive."

"What are their names?" Mrs. Edwards asked, handing him his invoice.

"I don't recall. I only met them once."

"I can't give out guests' names. Policy, you know. I'm sure you'll see them at breakfast."

"I doubt it. I'm not much of a morning person."

Bree scrubbed herself raw with the vanilla soap Mrs. Edwards provided, but the horror of the castle, and Russell, still coated her skin. There was a knock on the door. Bree turned off the shower, wrapped herself in a towel, and went to the door. "Yes?"

"It's Mrs. Edwards, dear. I brought some toiletries you might need, and I think you dropped something downstairs."

Bree opened the door, and Mrs. Edwards handed her a notebook. "It's not mine."

"I found it on the stairs. I thought… well I suppose I should look inside for a name—oh, Mr. Smith. Did you drop this?" Mrs. Edwards took off toward a tall, light-haired man who'd started up the steps. He stood with one foot on the landing, staring at Bree as the color drained from his face.

She grabbed hold of the door, her head spinning. The man took the notebook and thanked Mrs. Edwards, his eyes never leaving Bree. Instead of going to his room, he turned and started downstairs. With one quick glance at Bree over his shoulder, he hurried out the door. Unless Bree was mistaken, his hand had been trembling.

"Did he just check in?" she asked Mrs. Edwards, when she gave Bree the toiletries.

"No. He arrived several hours ago. That's the first I've seen of him since he got here. Haven't seen his *friend* at all. They didn't want to be disturbed," Mrs. Edwards said, wiggling her eyebrows. She left, but Bree couldn't shake her queasiness. Was the man in danger? Usually her premonitions were about family or friends, not strangers. Exhausted, she lay on the bed, her finger tracing circles on the chintz spread. She was too wound up to sleep. Sighing, she threw back the covers, wishing she had the nerve to go to Faelan's room for company, but neither of them could afford the temptation. She couldn't let her guard down again, for either of their sakes. After Russell was out of the way, then she and Faelan could see what this thing was between them. She dressed in her old clothes and stood in front of the portrait that looked like Alana, wondering what else Faelan had left behind. A woman? Friends? Sighing, she moved to the window and pulled back the lace curtains.

Across the street, an engine revved. A car pulled out of a driveway, headlights sweeping the small courtyard under Bree's window to the edge of the woods. Two men stood near the trees, bodies locked in an embrace. The taller one turned, shielding the shorter man as the lights swept past. Bree searched the tree line again, but the men were gone. A quick movement below the window caught her attention, a flash of black hair and a face looking up at her from the courtyard. She jumped behind the curtain. When she looked again, he wasn't there. She bolted out of her room and ran into a wall. Male. "Faelan, I think someone followed us—"

"Pardon me." The unfamiliar voice rolled over her like thick caramel. Bree looked up into the darkest eyes she'd ever seen, even darker than Faelan's. Long, raven hair framed a pale face so compelling, so beautiful, so incredible… she stared at him, mesmerized, like a bug caught in a spider web, waiting to be sucked dry.

"Sorry. I thought you were someone else."

"My loss," he said, a seductive smile on his lips.

Something danced in his eyes—knowledge, wisdom, sex—and she felt like she'd been thoroughly seduced. "I'll try not to disturb you. I don't sleep well at night."

She blinked, and he was across the hall, opening his door.

Too late. She was already disturbed.

Chapter 18

BREE STOOD, FEET ROOTED TO THE FLOOR, UNTIL HIS door closed. He couldn't be the man from the courtyard. That had been seconds ago. Had he followed them? He didn't look like a demon, but neither did Russell. Bree ran to Faelan's door and burst inside without knocking. There was a bump and a muttered curse.

She shut the door, speechless, the strange neighbor forgotten. Faelan wore jeans and nothing else. His chest was bare, except for his talisman and tattoos, damp hair held back with the leather strap she'd seen in his sporran, exposing a jaw line that made her knees tremble. Behind his ear, she could see the small tattoo she'd glimpsed in the Jacuzzi. A fresh white bandage added a vulnerable touch, making the combination deadly.

"I heard voices," he said, holding his nose.

"I ran into one of the other guests. Did the door hit your nose?"

He nodded.

"Sorry. It's not bleeding."

He rubbed his finger under it and frowned. "Are you okay?"

"Fine. I ran into the guy across the hall. I'd just seen someone outside my window, and it startled me."

Faelan picked up his dagger from the bed. "Wait here," he said, and eased into the hall, his steps as soft as a panther's. He paused outside the stranger's door, sniffing the air. Moving to the next door, he ran his hands over it and lingered there, a faraway look on his face. Frowning, he entered Bree's room, emerging minutes later. "I didn't see anyone," he said, after shutting his door. "Or smell anything, though I'm not sure I could after hitting my nose." He touched it gingerly.

"Sorry. I'm just jumpy. It's not every day you find out you almost married a demon."

Faelan put his dagger on the table. "Do you want to stay awhile?" He cleared his throat and studied his toes. "Sleep here, if you want."

Staying with him was a bad idea, but hanging out with a warrior who had a talisman capable of blasting a demon into nonexistence was preferable to going back to her room with only her imagination for company. She nodded. "I was coming to see you anyway. I figured we could talk."

"Talk?"

"It might help to talk about your sister. Talking helps. Men don't usually know that. They have to be prodded into these cleansing conversations."

"Then prod away. We have much to discuss anyway. Please, sit down."

His room was similar to hers, but painted a soft blue with a queen-sized four-poster bed, mahogany tallboy, chest of drawers, and an old roll-top desk. Antique pictures covered the walls, but no little dark-haired girls to remind him of the sister he'd lost. The lamp beside the bed cast a warm soothing glow.

Then, she did a stupid thing. She moved past the only chair in the room, a wingback, and sat on the end of the bed with her legs folded under her, in a skirt that didn't reach her knees when she was standing.

Faelan glanced at the chair before joining her, settling at the top of the bed. He crossed his ankles and leaned against black and cream toile pillows, his bare feet almost touching hers. Bree swallowed and gave him a quick once-over, thighs stretching the fabric of his jeans, the faint trail of hair low on his stomach, hard abs, and finally the tattoos on his chest, dancing under the lamp's glow. This was a mistake, but it was too late to leave.

"I see Mrs. Edwards gave you a bandage." Other than opening his old wound, he appeared unscathed.

"Told her I'd bumped into a tree. Not quite a lie," he said, dragging his gaze from Bree's legs.

Bree tugged at her skirt, wishing she'd sat in the chair.

"I won't take advantage of you," he said, watching her squirm. "Not that I blame you. I wouldn't trust me either."

"You didn't take advantage of me before." If he apologized again, she'd hit him over the head.

"Maybe I'm trying to convince myself." He folded his arms against his chest, biceps bulging. "I'll keep my hands right here," he said, tucking them under his armpits, eyes twinkling. "We could ask Mrs. Edwards for a brush."

"A brush?" Had she forgotten to comb her hair? She ran her hands over her head, feeling her damp ponytail.

"If I get out of line, you can hit me with it like you hit Grog."

"Oh, a broom." He didn't use many Scottish words, but when he did, it was utterly charming.

"That's a sight I'll never forget, no matter how hard I try. I don't know who was more surprised, Grog or me." He shook his head. "Having a woman try to rescue me is an experience I don't relish. And not one I'd care to repeat. You live up to your name, I'll say that. You are a disturbance."

"I'm disturbing?"

"You disturb me." He grinned, and she felt lava pulse through her veins.

They were treading dangerous waters. "These are modern times. You need to be man enough to let a woman do some rescuing too," she said, which resulted in a dubious scowl. "Do you think Druan knows we were there? Could he smell us?"

"I doubt it. They stink like the devil, but their sense of smell isn't strong. Couldn't live with themselves if it were." His hands dropped to his talisman. "He must be desperate by now. We've got to find my clan. Druan's disease—" Faelan stopped.

"Disease? What disease?"

Faelan blew out a breath and closed his eyes.

"You're *still* hiding things." She started to get up, but he caught her arm. He moved closer and sat with his legs crossed so that their knees almost touched.

"I didn't see any reason to worry you further. It's not your fight."

"Not my fight? I almost married Druan, and you wouldn't be sitting here if I hadn't opened the time vault. That makes it my fight. Where do you get this idea you're Superman?"

"Who's Superman?"

"He thought he was a one-man show, too."

"Druan created a disease. I found out the night before I went to suspend him."

"What kind of disease? Like the flu? The plague?"

"The plague was Druan's father's creation. Druan's disease will make the plague look like a runny nose. It'll destroy all human life."

"Cripes. That's why you were mumbling about war and disease." It sounded like Druan had created a deadly virus.

"Those halflings I tracked said Druan was ready to release the disease. I couldn't suspend Druan until I knew what the disease was, how he planned to use it, and there wasn't time to wait for help, whether I wanted it or not. My only choice was to capture Druan, put him in shackles, and force him to tell me where it was before I suspended him." Faelan's jaw tightened. "If I hadn't been so preoccupied, I might have realized Grog was a demon."

"Do you think the halflings lied? I mean, humans are still here."

"No. When I mentioned it, Druan was scared. I don't think he wanted the other demons to know. Maybe Tristol destroyed it. He looked pissed enough."

"Who's Tristol?"

"Another ancient demon. Probably the most powerful. He's supposed to be the closest to the Dark One."

"This demon was with Druan?"

"He was, and two more ancient demons. Malek and Voltar."

"Are they as powerful as Druan?"

"Aye."

"That's why you're worried. I wondered why you'd

be bothered over a few demons after what you did to those things in the chapel."

"Those were halflings. Most of the demons with Druan were full. But the ancient demons, well, you know that FBI's Most Wanted List you told me about? If our clan had a list, they'd be on it. They're powerful, fast, and clever. It would be nigh impossible for anyone to get close enough to hurt Druan, even a warrior, unless he was assigned."

Bree shuddered. She'd held hands with one, touched its face... slept with it.

"What were these ancient demons doing with Druan?"

"I didn't have time to find out. They must have been helping him with the war."

"War?"

"That's why I was sent to America, to stop a war."

"In 1860? You don't... you can't mean the Civil War."

"That's the name you've given it."

"You were supposed to stop the Civil War? *My* Civil War?" The war she'd spent her life studying? Weekends she'd spent metal detecting with her dad. The Civil War collection they'd built. "You mean Russell was responsible for it?"

"He was."

Talk about coincidences. "This is... beyond bizarre. How could one man stop a war?"

"The warriors who came with me were helping. I had them hunting Druan's demons and halflings, but destroying him was my responsibility. I'd hoped getting rid of him would collapse his efforts. I didn't expect the other ancient demons to be helping him."

"Why a Scottish warrior? Didn't America have warriors?"

"America was still a bairn, as far as countries go. All the warriors in this country came from Scotland."

"If Druan is so powerful, why didn't you keep some of the warriors with you? Was it because you thought your brothers were coming?"

"I didn't want anyone else with me. It was too dangerous. Only my talisman can destroy Druan or his evil. If another warrior accidentally aimed his talisman at Druan, the warrior would be dead."

"So these warriors and your brothers risked everything to help you fight Druan?"

"Aye. They trusted me with their lives, and I let them down. I sent the warriors away, which means that when my brothers arrived, they would have faced Druan, and maybe the other demons of old, alone."

Druan was alive, so that meant his brothers hadn't succeeded, probably hadn't survived.

Faelan focused on a spot over her head, a muscle working in his jaw. "I failed at all of it. Druan, his disease, the war."

Bree touched his hand. "It's Druan's fault, not yours. The war started a year after you were suspended. You couldn't have stopped it even if you had destroyed Druan. The trouble had been brewing for too long. Those other three demons were probably helping him for months, even years. You're a good man, Faelan. Don't carry Druan's blame."

"I betrayed the clan, the entire human race, when I sent the other warriors away."

"If they'd stayed, or your brothers had arrived, could you have killed all of the demons?"

"I don't know." He looked doubtful.

"You may have saved the warriors' lives. Druan might have been gone when they arrived. They could've lived long, full lives."

"Perhaps." He turned his hand over and captured hers, linking their fingers.

"Did anyone else know about the disease?"

"I sent word to the clan and the other warriors in America before I went to meet Druan. I doubt my brothers knew. They were likely already on the way."

His brothers must have been desperate when they couldn't find him. "Did they know where to look for you? Where had you planned to meet?"

"They would have brought a Seeker. Seekers can locate a warrior's talisman. It's the only way to find a warrior when he's hunting or lost... or dead. I don't know if they could find a talisman inside a time vault. They couldn't have opened it, anyway."

"What happens when a warrior dies?"

"His talisman is reassigned to another warrior."

"But your talisman was locked in the vault with you. Cripes! Do the demons know a warrior's talisman can destroy them?"

"No. None live to warn the others. If they found out, our greatest weapon would be compromised, one of the reasons secrecy is so important."

"Can I see yours?" she asked. Her body tingled, as if she'd asked to see something far more private.

Faelan held the talisman out so she could take a closer look. She ran her fingers across the metal, brushing his. "How does it work?"

"It's hard to explain. I guess you could say it's like holy light." He gripped her chin softly, raising her eyes to his. "Don't ever look at it again. You can yell or hit me if you think I'm belittling you, but if you're around and I aim this thing, you'd better close your eyes."

"Yes, warrior."

"I think the time vault weakened it. Otherwise, you'd be dead. We're lucky it destroyed those halflings."

"It didn't look damaged to me. Does it do anything beside destroy demons?"

"It transports the shackles and time vaults. We have shackles that paralyze the demons so we can get them inside the time vaults."

"What do you do with the time vaults? Bury them?"

"They're sent to a holding place, not on earth."

"Another dimension?"

"Aye."

"Good heavens. Can you take the talisman off?"

"No. We don't take off our talismans. Ever."

Not even when they bathed or made love? "You were almost finished with your duty. You could've married soon. Did you have anyone special? Were you ever in love?"

He studied an old scar on his hand for too long before he shook his head. There had been a woman. Bree was sure of it. The thought gnawed at her, but there was no point in asking him. Whoever she was, the woman would be dead now.

"You must have dated?" He'd put every other lover she'd had to shame. He had acquired the skill somewhere.

"Dated?"

"Courted women."

"A warrior needs his head in the battle, not worrying over a lass or a mate," he said, not answering her question.

"Many remain virgins until they take a mate. There are always demons trying to find weaknesses to use against us. The female demons take on exceptional forms."

"I saw one in the castle. She was incredibly beautiful, then she turned into this thing with hooves."

"Be glad she didn't see you. They can be very nasty."

"So a female demon uses her beauty to distract you, then ka-bam. It must be tough going into training while your hormones are raging."

"It teaches us to focus. Makes us stronger. What about you and all these men?"

He still acted like she had a male harem. "I've dated some… well, a lot."

There was a slight narrowing of his eyes. "Define a lot."

She cleared her throat, not wanting to explain her disastrous love life to a man from the nineteenth century. "Ten boyfriends… more or less. Most of them didn't make it past the first good-night kiss."

"Most?" He stared at her knees. "How many did you…" his jaw worked, as if he was clenching his teeth.

"Four." She blushed and looked away. Including him… and Druan. The unspoken words lay between them like a ticking bomb.

Faelan didn't say anything, just studied her, so she didn't know if he was horrified or relieved.

She touched his talisman again, the warmth of the metal soothing. "So no one else can use your talisman?" she asked quickly, changing the subject.

"Not unless it's reassigned. It would kill him… or her."

"These symbols," she said, running her fingers over the markings, "look like writing."

"They are."

"I don't recognize the language."

"No one does. It's a heavenly language."

"Like *heaven* heaven?"

"There's only one."

"Is that what you were speaking when you destroyed the halflings in the chapel?"

He nodded.

"At first I thought it was Gaelic. You do speak Gaelic?" She was sure he'd spoken it when they'd made love.

"Aye."

"Say something."

"What?"

"Anything."

A gleam lit his eyes. "*Tha thu as do chiall.*"

"What does that mean?"

He smiled but refused to tell her, and she finally gave up. She'd look it up on the computer, if she could ever get the thing to work.

"Where do the talismans come from?"

"Michael—" Faelan pressed his lips together.

"Who's Michael?"

"It's a long story. Why don't you tell me about this instead?" He slipped one finger underneath her shirt collar, pulling out the silver cross.

"It was my dad's."

"What was it doing under the floor?"

A barrage of memories assaulted her. A young girl in tears, bloody fingernails, a glowing crypt. Her dad before he died, fear in his eyes, hugging Bree so tight it scared her. "It's a long story," she said, throwing his words back at him.

He met her gaze, then gave a brief nod and released the necklace.

"What about your tattoos? What do they mean?" She stroked one of the curved symbols on his chest, and his skin quivered under her touch.

"They're battle marks. They appear after our training, when we accept our calling."

"You have a choice whether to be a warrior?"

"A warrior can refuse his mission. He wouldn't do much good if his heart weren't in it."

"Are all battle marks the same?"

"Each warrior is marked according to his strengths and weaknesses. Same with the symbols on the talismans. They protect and bless."

"There's writing on the side of your talisman, too. I didn't see it before."

"Before?"

"The night you passed out, your shirt was off. I saw the talisman and your marks then."

Faelan's look turned mischievous. "I remember waking with far less than my shirt. What else did you notice?"

"Very little. And I didn't take your clothes off. You did."

"Little? You think I need some of those supplements you were talking about?" His gaze flickered over her breasts and legs.

She grabbed a pillow and clutched it to her lap, cheeks burning. No, he didn't need them.

"I remember a dream. But it didn't feel like a dream. I was kissing you." He brushed a knuckle across her lips. "And you were kissing me back."

Danger, Bree Kirkland. Danger. "Do I need to get a broom from Mrs. Edwards?"

He grinned and tucked his hands back under his arms, making the muscles in his shoulders and chest ripple. "Better?"

No. "Is this another battle mark?" she asked, touching the small circle behind his ear. She felt a jolt run up her fingers.

"I don't have…" He stood and walked to the mirror. The color drained from his face.

Chapter 19

FAELAN SCRUBBED HIS FINGERS ACROSS THE SMALL circle with jagged edges. A mate mark. How? Bree stared at him, puzzled. Her hair was pulled back. He could see she didn't have a mark, at least not behind her ear. A woman often got her mark later than her mate, and it wasn't always in the same place, but Bree wasn't his mate. She wasn't even from his time or his clan. Was his mark for a dead woman he'd never known?

He wanted to sleep, to forget about coincidences and questions without answers and things that couldn't be. Just for a few hours.

"Is everything okay?"

"I'm tired. It's been a long day." He sat on the bed with a weary sigh and lay crossways on the soft mattress.

"I should get back to my room." She glanced at the door but didn't move.

"Don't go."

She watched him, her eyes wide. Her hair was damp, and her skin, scrubbed clean, was as smooth as porcelain, cheeks with a hint of blush, growing deeper as he stared at her. Clear green eyes he knew he'd see in his dreams, whether he was alive or dead. And red, juicy lips, like an apple waiting to be tasted. She'd broken into a demon's castle and escaped, but she looked like a princess. His bonny princess, he thought, like the stories Alana had begged him to tell. He touched his neck again and patted the bed next to him. "Sleep next to me." He didn't want to be alone. Not tonight. "Please."

———※———

The man eased across the landing, unaware he was being watched. The air thickened, forming a black mist. The man turned. It was Faelan. The mist swirled like a great, dark cloud, and when it was gone, Faelan had vanished.

Bree's eyes flew open, and it took her a minute to figure out where she was. Faelan's body was curved around her, keeping her warm and safe. He moved his head, mumbled a name she couldn't make out, and tightened his arms around her. Was this a premonition or another dream? She let the steady beat of his heart soothe her to sleep.

———※———

Faelan woke to a warm scent as familiar as his talisman, but he felt unsettled, maybe because Bree was sleeping half on top of him. Her head rested on his chest, one leg nestled between his thighs, and her hand curled close to his belt.

He shifted, and the arm holding her prickled with numbness. He needed to see the mark on his neck again, to make sure. It must be the time vault throwing things off kilter. He didn't know everything Bree was, but he knew what she wasn't. His mate. And lying here any longer would be a bad idea. He didn't need the entanglement. He couldn't let his guard down again, and she'd said she didn't want a man in her life, but having her draped over him made it hard to remember what was best. He tried to lift her head so he could move, but she sighed and rubbed her face against his chest. He repositioned his arm, and blood flowed into the starved limb. Both of them.

He made the mistake of sniffing her hair, which had worked loose from its clasp. He pressed his lips to it and inhaled. Hunger stirred, making him hard. He suspected she wouldn't say no if he persisted, but it wouldn't be right. Last night he'd wanted her next to him for comfort. It would add insult to injury to ravish her after what he'd already done. Even as he tried to talk himself out of it, her scent roared into every part of his body. Now that he'd had a taste of her, it was harder to hold back.

He felt her wake and heard a soft gasp. Her fingers twitched, far too close to his groin. He reached down to pull the covers across his lap, to spare them both further embarrassment, but her hand moved quicker. He held back a groan as she grazed one fingertip over him. Did she have any idea what she was doing? She made the trail a few more times while he held his breath. Unbuttoning his pants, she tugged on the zipper, and slipped her hand inside.

He nearly lost it as her fingers wrapped around him. He remembered how it felt being inside her. Did he dare beg her to let him do it again? She stroked him twice, moved her hand lower, and he shifted to make room, gritting his teeth to keep from exploding as she cupped him. His lack of control was shameful. Not that any respectable woman in his time would've had her hand wrapped around his balls.

If she didn't move away soon, he'd make a mess all over both of them. He didn't want that. He wanted her, to join their bodies the way nature intended. Married would be better, but he couldn't marry her; it wasn't allowed. He eased her hand out of his pants, trapping it against his stomach. "I can't let you do this."

"Yes, you can." She pulled free and continued caressing. His resolve fled as quickly as a hungry child tempted with sweets.

He touched her thigh, bare underneath her skirt, the skin silky and soft. He wanted her so badly it hurt. Other than a few mistakes, he'd tried to follow the rules, but he'd never felt anything like this burning, beautiful ache. Rolling over, he settled his thigh between hers and slipped his hands under her shirt, touching the warm skin of her stomach before moving higher. He pulled at her. "What is this thing?" It was much smaller than the undergarments lasses wore in his day.

"A bra." With a flip of her fingers, she opened the front, spilling her breasts out for him. If he wasn't awake before, he was now. He filled both hands with warm flesh, sure he'd die if she stopped him now, but the soft sounds she made told him she was enjoying it too. He was glad. He wanted her to feel good, but partly he was relieved he wouldn't have to stop. He tried to be gentle, but all he could think about was getting inside her. He removed her shirt and started to push her skirt up, but he wanted to see all of her. He moved over, far enough to pull off her skirt and the thing she called panties. He threw them on the floor and feasted on the sight of her bare body as his hands stroked the inside of her thighs, caressing the rough scrapes—already healing— moving closer and closer to his prize. He wanted to taste her, to drown in her scent, but he couldn't wait that long.

He shrugged out of his jeans and underwear, wishing he'd worn his kilt. Easier access. With one quick look at her, to be sure she was sure, he lowered his body to hers and entered, working in deeper and deeper until her breath caught as he slid home.

He withdrew, thrust in again and held, burying his face in her hair. He felt her tongue on his neck, against his throbbing pulse. She wrapped her legs around his hips, clinging to his shoulders as he drove into her.

"Stop," she said, her voice muffled.

Damnation. He didn't know if he could. "Am I hurting you?" he asked, forcing himself to hold still.

"No," she gasped. "The bed. It's shaking." In spite of her words, she tilted her hips and gave a little moan.

To hell with the bed. He thrust in again, and from the sounds she made, she must have stopped worrying about the noise too. He wanted to make it last, but any chance of that was lost when her hands dropped to his arse, fingers digging into his flesh. Her body tightened around him, telling him she was already there. Her mouth, still open in a moan, reminded him he'd neglected to kiss her. Too late now. One more thrust, and he erupted, the pleasure so intense it hurt. He collapsed on top of her, shivering, and he knew for certain why warriors weren't supposed to take a mate. She wasn't even his, but she held the power to destroy him. If a demon came now, he'd be done.

He feared he was crushing her, but he didn't want to leave. He wanted to lie here forever, locked in her arms. He eased a bit of his weight, but stayed inside her. Realization slowly seeped in. He'd done it again, a fast, hard tumble, without even a kiss. He hadn't cleaned his teeth yet, so she was likely glad he hadn't kissed her. But what kind of love was that for a woman? Even if she enjoyed it, that was no way to treat her, rough, without tenderness.

"I'm sorry," he mumbled, but he didn't sound sorry, even to his own ears. He lifted himself on shaky elbows, wanting, yet dreading, to look at her. "Are you okay?"

She blinked twice and focused on him. "I've never felt anything like it."

And he'd barely tried. He smiled and wished to God she could be his. He pulled out and rolled next to her, his body sated with pleasure, but questions were starting to fill his head. How did a man thank a woman for such a gift? Yet again. He should offer to help her clean up.

He reached for her, but she scooted away, moved off the bed, and stood, holding the pillow over her body like a shield. *Not good.* Brushing her tangled hair from her eyes, she searched the floor, still not looking at him. *Definitely not good.* She backed toward the bathroom, pillow in place, clothes dangling from her hand. If he hadn't been so dismayed, he'd have found the sight amusing.

He leaned on one elbow and watched the bathroom door shut. Once again he'd taken advantage of the only human being who knew he existed. He slammed his head against the pillow. He was an arse. Not to mention, he could've made a bairn with a woman he couldn't marry.

—⁓—

Cleaned and dressed, Bree sat on the side of the claw-foot tub still holding the pillow. What was wrong with her? It wasn't bad enough that she'd almost entered into holy matrimony with a demon, that she could've been the mother of a halfling. No, she had to go and make love, unprotected, yet again, to a man who at best should be dead, who believed women were helpless creatures to be coddled and protected, and at worst, could be another demon pretending to be a warrior who was more than a century and a half old.

Then there was the sheer embarrassment of it. Had everyone heard the bed shaking?

There was a soft rap at the door. "Bree?"

"Yes?"

"Are you okay?"

Bree opened the door a few inches and peeked out.

"I'm sorry," Faelan muttered, looking not sorry at all. His eyes were already darkening, roving over what parts of her he could see.

She lowered her gaze to his bare feet. He had nice feet. Strong, solid, sexy—

"Bree." He slid his arm through the crack in the door, fingers tipping her chin. "Look at me. We need to talk. I was out of control. I shouldn't have taken you like that. Again. A woman deserves more than what I gave you."

"More?" She'd not have lived to dream about it.

"Gentleness and caresses." He wedged the door open and pushed his head inside. His fingertips moved lightly up her arm. "Sweet words and kisses," he said, eyeing her mouth. "Lots of kisses." His head lowered, and Bree stepped back. "Damnation. I can't even get close enough for an apology, and I want to make love to you again—" A knock sounded outside. Faelan glanced at Bree, and she watched through the crack as he went to answer it.

He checked once more to be sure she was out of sight, then turned the knob. Bree couldn't see who stood there, but she could see the red fingernail marks she'd left on his back. Cripes.

"Good morning—oh, my. What interesting tattoos. My goodness me."

"Good morning, Mrs. Edwards." Faelan put his hand on the door, preventing it from opening too wide.

"When you didn't come to breakfast, I got worried. And Ms. Kirkland isn't answering. If you *see* her, would you tell her about breakfast?"

Bree rolled her eyes. Mrs. Edwards had probably heard the bed shaking.

"I'm sure she overslept, like me," he said, tugging his ear. "Uh, we'll be down in fifteen minutes… if I find her, that is."

"The other guests have up and disappeared, including your friend's brother, so there's plenty of food."

"My friend's brother?"

"I had a migraine last night. I got up for my medicine and saw you two on the landing. I'm glad you met. He asked for your name, but I can't give out that kind of information. Policy, you know."

Faelan's shoulders went rigid. "It wasn't me."

"I could've sworn I saw… it must have been the other two guests. It was dark, and I didn't have my glasses on. Then you didn't meet him? Too bad. He thought he recognized you. Ms. Kirkland, too. Said you looked like his brother's friends. Described you both, and everything. I wonder why he didn't stay."

Faelan's knuckles whitened against the door. "Did he have dark blond hair?" His voice was all warrior now.

"Why, no. It was black, black as sin. Had these dark eyes, like they could see right through you."

"He's gone?"

"Must have been early, before all the policemen arrived—oh dear."

"Policemen?"

"I shouldn't have mentioned it. A homeless man was found dead in the woods."

Bree's brain whirled. Another dead body?

Chapter 20

THAT'S WHERE SHE'D SEEN THE TWO MEN. MAYBE they weren't embracing.

"How did he die?" Faelan asked.

Mrs. Edwards's voice took on a conspiratorial hush. "Well, I called Mrs. Rutherford, down at the post office. She knows everything anybody's ever thought about doing. Her son works for the coroner. He said there wasn't any trauma to the body, no bleeding, like the man just dropped dead. And he was white as a ghost."

Definitely different from the man behind her house, Bree thought.

"Who found him?" Faelan asked.

"Another homeless man, before daylight. I didn't hear a thing. No sirens, nothing. I guess on account of the police knew he was already dead. I thought they'd want to talk to me, and my guests of course, but nobody called. Come, now, let's not ruin your appetite."

Nothing could ruin Faelan's appetite.

"Hurry down before the food gets cold. I have French toast, scrambled eggs, and bacon. And lots of it."

Faelan rubbed his stomach. "We'll be there in five minutes."

Five? She couldn't get the knots out of her hair and the smell of Faelan off her skin in five minutes. Bree finger-combed her head, wondering if he'd even wait for her.

Mrs. Edwards left, and Bree stepped out of the bathroom.

"You heard?" Faelan asked, pulling his shirt over his head.

"If he was asking about us, he must have seen us leave the castle."

"I don't know how else he would have known we were here."

"I saw two men in the woods last night. I thought it was a tryst, but I probably witnessed a murder. Maybe we should skip breakfast and get out of here in case they decide to question us."

His face fell. "Skip breakfast?"

"Never mind."

"We'll leave as soon as we eat. Then, if we can't locate my clan, we've got to find someplace else to go."

Faelan slid the board back into place. The book and the key were safe. Now, if he could find his kilt and sporran. Bree was still on the phone trying to get a hotel. He'd spent a good part of the day in the chapel, searching for another entrance a warrior might have used to gain access to the cellar, then a couple of hours driving her car up and down the driveway, anything to stay away from her. He didn't trust himself within smelling distance. He'd even spilled a bottle of perfume, trying to block her scent.

He made sure she was still on the phone and slipped inside her room. Maybe she'd put his kilt in here. He checked her closet, under her bed, and then opened a drawer in the table. He stared at the painting in disbelief.

"How in tarnation?" Was it more proof of what he didn't have the courage to admit? There were too many coincidences already. Now this? Faelan heard Bree enter the room, and he swung around to confront her.

"What are you doing?" Bree's gaze darted to the bed, as if he'd come to seduce her.

"Oh," she said, noticing the painting he held. "I meant to show you that. Doesn't it look like you?"

"It *is* me."

"What?"

"It is me. My sister painted it."

"Your sister?" Bree's mouth dropped open. "This is the painting you lost?"

"Aye. Where did you get it?"

"An antique shop in Albany. How is it possible?"

"I was wondering the same thing."

"Certainly explains why you looked so familiar when I first saw you."

Faelan felt a prickle behind his ear, the one with the mark that couldn't be. "I looked familiar?"

"It was kind of alarming, until I remembered the painting. I knew you looked like the warrior, but I thought it had to be a coincidence."

Damnation, he hated that word.

"The man at the shop didn't know anything about it, since it wasn't signed; there's just this little smudge."

"It's a four-leaf clover. She signed all her paintings that way. So you end up with my sister's painting, and you own the property where I was buried, and you found the map that led to the crypt, and you had the key to the time vault on your mantel, and my clan's *Book of Battles* was in your attic. Did I forget anything?"

She scowled. "Are you going to do this again?"

"What are the chances—"

"I don't care what the chances are. I'm tired of trying to prove I'm on your side. I rescued you from the time vault, fed you, tried to help you find your family, saved your life in the chapel, and blast it, I even slept with you. More than once. You should be happy the painting isn't lost." She turned on her heel.

Faelan caught her arm and pulled her closer. "I am. It's just a shock to find it here. I apologize."

Her scowl softened, and she stood beside him as he turned the portrait to catch the last rays of evening light. His thumb brushed the smudged clover on the bottom. He remembered Alana begging him to let her paint this. She'd do anything, she'd pleaded. He'd stood for what felt like hours as she painted, while his thoughts drifted, searching for—Faelan's gaze swung to Bree. It was impossible.

"You look so lost in the painting. What were you thinking?"

She wouldn't believe him if he told her. "It's hard to say." Even harder to believe, himself.

She leaned closer and softly gasped. "That sword, I saw it in the castle."

"This sword? My sword?"

"It's in Druan's library, in a glass case."

He gripped her arm. "You're sure?"

"Unless there's another one like it."

No, there was only one. His father had made it special for him. "I was surprised Druan didn't take my dirk. He took everything else. Probably didn't see it tucked in my boot."

"We can steal the sword back."

"*I'll* get it." His painting and now his sword. It felt like bits of him were coming back. He glanced out the window. "We need to leave soon. Any luck with hotels?" After she was safely settled, he would slip back here.

"No, everything's full, but I have an idea," she said, twisting her ring.

"What kind of idea?" He doubted he'd like any idea that made Bree nervous.

"I was thinking we could spend one more night here. We need to know what Russell—Druan—is up to. You've got your dagger and your talisman. I have my grandfather's old shotgun. There's some rust on the barrel, but I'm pretty certain it'll fire. Maybe one of them will get close and we can capture him."

"Have ye lost yer mind?" If Druan wasn't the death of him, she would be.

She crossed her arms and looked offended. "I'll stay inside," she said, glaring. "I promise."

Setting a trap was a good idea, *after* he got her away from this place.

"I won't do anything stupid," she said, as if she hadn't just broken into a demon's castle and barely escaped with her life.

She was a walking calamity, but Faelan knew she'd never leave unless he forced her, and then she'd most likely sneak back. It was safer to have her where he could watch her. He gave her a pained nod.

"What were you doing in my room, anyway?" she asked.

"Looking for my sporran. I can't find any of my things."

"I'll help you look for them later," she said, nudging

him toward the door. She glanced at her rocking chair, and he saw the edge of his kilt sticking out from under a blanket.

"That's my kilt." He moved to the chair and pulled the blanket aside. All his things were there. The kilt, sporran, shirt, belt, and hose. "Are you hiding my clothes?"

She hurried after him. "I was just taking pictures. This is an authentic Highland outfit, worn by a real Highlander. From the 1800s. Do you know how incredible this is?" She picked up his kilt and pressed it to her chest, stroking it softly, like a woman would stroke her lover's face.

He shook his head. "You and your photographs."

"What are you doing?"

"Taking my things."

"But, but," she sputtered. "Do you have to?"

"You want to keep my clothes?"

Her eyes grew brighter. "Could I?"

"Suit yourself," he said, discreetly removing the white stone from his sporran and slipping it into his pocket. He put the sporran back on the chair. Maybe she'd be so busy photographing his kilt that she'd forget about those swords he'd hidden in the chapel.

"The kilt looks like it's been dyed using plants. I did some research, and I believe the red comes from the madder plant. If I'd known for certain they were authentic I wouldn't have used Spray 'n Wash…" She put the kilt down as gently as she would a new bairn. "Did all the warriors in your time wear a kilt?" she asked, following him to the door.

"At home we did. Otherwise, we dressed as natives of the land where we traveled."

"Isn't a kilt awkward for climbing over things, like fences and castle walls?"

"No, it's comfortable. 'Course, someone standing below would likely get an eyeful. Though, there was the time Ian almost castrated himself."

———

Faelan crept toward the parlor in his underwear. He'd just taken off his jeans when he heard the car. This one was brave, driving right up to the house. Faelan stood behind the door and waited. The handle jiggled, and the door opened. He sniffed, but he couldn't smell a bloody thing except Bree's perfume. The whole house smelled like her. He heard a thump and seized the man from behind, wrapping his arm in a stranglehold around his neck. He was short. Faelan pressed his dirk against the man's jugular vein, and a feminine shriek pierced his eardrums.

Faelan was shocked, but he held on. In this new century, he couldn't afford a female the courtesies he'd been accustomed to giving before. He tightened his grip, lifting the intruder off the floor. "Who are you?" he demanded.

Light flooded the room. Bree stood in her soft sleeping pants, like the ones she'd bought him, and a shirt that left most of her shoulders bare. Her mouth hung open. The thing in his arms sputtered, and Bree shot forward.

"Mom? Oh my gosh."

Mom?

"Put her down."

He lowered the dirk and set the woman on the floor. "I'm sorry. I thought she was…" he stopped, not sure how much Bree wanted revealed about their nocturnal visitors.

———※———

"What is the meaning of this, Briana? Who is this man? And what is that smell?" Bree's mother stepped away from Faelan, rubbing her neck but maintaining her composure. Orla Kirkland always maintained her composure, even when she was being strangled. She turned to face Faelan. Her eyes widened.

He did make a spectacular sight in his boxer briefs, dark hair hanging to his shoulders, and muscles no gym could endow, sporting tattoos, a dagger, and bare, sexy feet.

"Oh my." Orla looked him over, head to toe. "He's in his underwear, Briana. Why is he in his underwear?" Her eyes grew even rounder. "That's why you aren't taking Russell's calls." She smiled and gave him a look Bree knew too well, the kind that was sizing him for a tux and wondering where to order the wedding cake. "Hello, I'm Orla Kirkland, Briana's mother, and you are…?"

"This is Faelan." It wouldn't do any good to deny the conclusion to which her mother had joyfully leapt.

"Faelan Connor, ma'am," he said, gallantly tipping his head, a rather absurd-looking gesture with him in his underwear, holding a dagger. "I apologize. I thought you were a burglar."

"Protective. How nice," she said, glancing at his underwear again. "Are you staying here?"

"Uh…" Faelan threw a panicked look at Bree.

"For the moment. Why didn't you tell me you were coming?" Bree asked.

"I mentioned it on the phone, dear. I'd planned to get a hotel, but there's not a vacancy to be had. Some sort of conference in town." She glanced at the house. "Not too bad." She crinkled her nose. "But I think you went a bit heavy on the perfume."

"The bottle spilled. What about your allergies and all this dust?"

"I'll be here for only a day or two. I'm on my way to meet Sandy. You remember my friend. She's coming to Florida for a visit, but she hates to drive alone, and she refuses to fly. Can you believe someone in this day and age afraid of airplanes?" she asked Faelan. "I'm going to pick her up. You have clean sheets, don't you, Briana?"

"I, uh… yes." The problem was, she didn't have a bed to put them on, and Bree was certain her mother had never slept on a sofa. "You can have my room."

"Where will you sleep, darling?" She tossed a loaded glance from Faelan to Bree.

"Uh, the couch."

She held her arm out to Faelan. "Well then, that's settled. Faelan, would you be a dear and bring my suitcase? In the morning, we'll have a little chat, get to know one another, and I'll tell you some of the cutest stories about Briana."

Faelan handed Bree his dagger and took the suitcase in one hand, her mother's arm in the other, and the two of them walked down the hall to the bedroom.

"She was an adorable child, but had the wildest imagination. She was terrified of the graveyard. Had horrible nightmares until that nasty Reggie locked her inside the crypt. After that, we couldn't keep her away. She had picnics right there next to the headstones, with her little tea set and blanket and her ragged old panda bear, talking to thin air. She had an *imaginary* friend," Orla stage-whispered.

An imaginary friend. That might explain why she sometimes felt like someone else was living inside her, had thoughts she knew weren't her own.

For someone who'd never seen a ghost, she damned well felt haunted.

"And when she was twelve she wanted to be a deep-sea treasure hunter," her mother told Faelan as they toured the house the next morning.

They were lucky no demons showed up during the night. The perfume probably kept them away. Bree had caught Faelan in the kitchen, staring out into the back-yard, his hand clasped to his talisman. Standing guard.

"She was certain Atlantis was down there some-where. Remember that, dear?" Bree's mother asked as they entered the room where Bree had been sanding the floor.

"How could I forget?" *When you keep reminding me.* How she could've been born to Orla Kirkland was as much a mystery as how Faelan was alive and breathing when he should be nothing but bones. Her mother never pumped her own gas. She got her nails done every week and a half on the dot, and she wouldn't dream of charging out to rescue a man for any reason whatsoever. This apple not only fell far from the tree, but it rolled down the hill and bounced into another town. Bree couldn't imagine her mother giving birth to one baby, much less twins.

"You finished the floor, Briana. I thought your sander broke."

"It did." Bree stared at the finished floor. Her mouth dropped. She looked at Faelan's eager smile, and her eyes stung. "You finished it for me? By hand?"

"Oh, my." Orla beamed and dabbed at one eye.

"Thank you," Bree whispered, squeezing his arm. They headed to the living room where her mother continued her embarrassing stories, and Faelan listened with rapt attention while Bree dug through a box of her old things her mother had brought. She picked up Emmy, the stuffed panda she'd had since she was a child. It was missing one eye and its black and white body was worn and ratty from being held through too many bad dreams.

"But she suffers from sea sickness, like Layla—" Her mother pressed her lips together and brushed at invisible lint on her skirt.

"Aunt Layla got seasick, too?" Bree asked.

"Lots of Kirklands do, dear. Even your grandmother did. Remember how sick she got on that cruise? I've been meaning to ask, did you find out what she wanted to talk to you about before she died? She called the house the day before, trying to find you, but I wasn't there. Her message sounded strange. I tried to call her back, but… I haven't asked before now, because I didn't want to upset you, with everything going on."

Her mother was almost rambling. Bree rambled when she was nervous. Orla Kirkland never rambled. It must be the wedding bells clanging in her head.

"She left a message, but by the time I got it, it was too late."

"Perhaps she wanted to say good-bye. I think she

knew she was nearing the end. She seemed troubled the last time I talked to her. Maybe she mentioned something in her journal. I don't suppose you've found it," she added, picking at her skirt again. As if lint would dare attach itself to Orla Kirkland's clothing.

"No." Why did her mother care? She'd never been interested in anyone's journal before. "Besides working on the renovations, I've been busy cleaning up the graveyard and watching the archeologists dig." Bree hadn't mentioned finding Isabel's journal. She hadn't wanted to share her secret, not even with her mother and her best friend. Why had she shared it with Faelan?

"Archeology digs and graveyards. You should be thinking about marriage and children," she said, casting a desperate glance at Faelan.

Dead people weren't so bad. At least they didn't judge.

"Her grandmother's side of the family, that's where she gets her adventurous spirit," Orla said to Faelan. "Even in kindergarten. Oh, the drawings she brought home. Aliens one day, monsters and angels the next. Your old sketchbook is in there, Briana. I thought you might want it."

Bree spotted the book at the bottom of the box. A chill slid over her body as her mother's voice faded. She stared at the cover, hands heavy with dread. Slowly she opened it. The first sketch was of the house and graveyard with its leaning headstones. The crypt sat in the center, larger than everything else. The tree hovered over it, its blackened branches stretching out like claws. She shivered and slammed the book shut. She shoved it back in the box and looked up to see Faelan watching her. Bree realized she had Emmy gripped tight against her chest. She put the panda back in the box as her mother droned on about her recklessness.

"Thank God the nightmares stopped after the crypt. I wish the recklessness had. The migraines she gave me. All through middle school and high school, she was always looking for some relic or treasure. You'd have thought she was on a quest. There was the gold-panning fiasco in college... I don't know what she was thinking, traveling alone out in the middle of nowhere looking for gold that didn't exist. But Lord, were there snakes."

Faelan cocked one brow. "Snakes?"

"Her grandmother and I thought she would die. The doctor said she should have died. He'd never seen anyone recover from so many poisonous bites at once. She fell into a den of them. Cobras." Orla gave an elegant shudder. "But she always heals fast. Her cousin Reggie used to say she was indestructible. She fell a lot, you know."

"Aye," Faelan said, the edge of a grin peeking out of his sexy mouth. "She still does."

"They were copperheads, Mother. They don't have cobras in Colorado. And if the medevac helicopter hadn't flown in to get me, they wouldn't have found Todd."

"Who's Todd?" Faelan asked, grin disappearing as his eyebrows gathered into a glare.

"Your disasters usually do end well." Orla sighed. "For someone else. The poor child was hiking with his uncle," she told Faelan. "They got caught in a rockslide, and the uncle died. The boy had a broken leg. The cell phone was buried with the uncle, and there wasn't a soul around for thirty miles. He took shelter in a cave. He'd been there two days without food or water. When he heard the rescue helicopter, he crawled out and waved his shirt. The pilot saw him. Sweet boy. Bree visits him every year."

"Was that the cave where she broke her ankle?"

"*The cave*," her mother drawled in horror, wrapping a manicured hand around Faelan's arm. "That was a different time. They had to cut the bat out of her hair. Have you ever heard of a bat strangling in someone's hair? It's a wonder she didn't fall off the cliff. There she was, hanging from a tiny branch with a dead bat in her hair."

"Damnation."

"It was a small cliff," Bree mumbled, glad her mother didn't know half of her adventures. Too bad her sixth sense didn't work in her own life.

"Her father, rest his soul, should've put his foot down. He bought her the most beautiful dolls, but all she wanted to do was hunt for treasure and explore caves, so he trekked around the countryside after her, metal detecting, bringing home twisted bits of metal they called coins. And the Civil War reenactments, egad! All those men lying on the ground pretending to be dead. Just not healthy for an eight-year-old. It's her specialty now, the Civil War."

The laughter left Faelan's eyes like a candle doused by a wave.

"Mother, you're going to make Faelan think I'm unstable." She gave her mother a *you're-not-helping* stare.

"Oh, but she's not nearly as impulsive now," her mother said, tightening her grip on Faelan's arm. "She has quite a reputation as an antiquities expert. Her knowledge is very much in demand. She authenticated a dagger last year for a prince. And since most of her work is consulting, it won't interfere with having children. You do like children?"

Bree suspected her mother had the wedding half planned. "Aren't you going to be late meeting Sandy, mother?"

Her mother glanced at her watch. "Oh, where did the time go? I'm going to miss seeing her granddaughter. I'm beginning to think I'll never have one." She gave a dramatic sigh.

If they weren't careful, her mother might get one, wedding or not.

Bree set the box behind the couch. "I need to leave too. I'm supposed to meet Janie—"

"Not alone," Faelan said, scowling.

Bree's hands balled into fists. "Are you going to do this again?"

"It's too dangerous. I don't trust Janie's boyfriend," he added, when Orla raised a perfectly plucked eyebrow.

"So protective, Briana. Just like your father."

Bree gave Faelan a defiant glare. She didn't need another man protecting her.

"Give me a hug, darling. I'm so glad I got to see you. And Faelan, it was wonderful meeting you. I hope this won't be our last visit. Oh, what's this?" she asked, leaning back to look at Bree's necklace. "A gift?" She blasted Faelan with a blinding smile, like the necklace was a three-carat engagement ring.

"Don't you recognize it?" Bree asked.

"Should I?"

"It was Daddy's. Grandma gave it to me after he died. I… lost it. Faelan found it for me."

Orla's smile collapsed. She looked blank. "Your

father's. Of course. How silly of me. I must have forgotten. It's been so long since I've seen it. Well, I have to run. I'll probably sleep at Sandy's. I almost suffocated last night from the dust and perfume. Faelan, dear, would you start the car and load my luggage? It's so nice to have a man around. You need to bring him to Florida for a visit, Briana."

"What are we going to do about her?" Bree asked, when her mother drove off.

"I was thinking she could give you lessons in proper female behavior."

She turned to glare at him and saw his grin. He'd seemed delighted to meet her mother. He probably missed his own.

"But I'll have to talk to her about embarrassing you," he said.

Bree felt as gushy as when she'd seen the sanded floor. She started to hug him, but decided against it. They'd hardly touched since the bed and breakfast. Neither seemed sure which direction to go after making love again. Faelan acted worried, like he'd taken advantage of her, and Bree was feeling the aftershocks of discovering she'd almost married an eight-hundred-year-old demon.

"Why'd your cousin lock you in the crypt?"

"He was a brat. We thought it was haunted. We called it the Tomb of the Unnamed." She could still remember the terror as Reggie closed the door and his wicked nine-year-old laugh, as he'd taunted that she was locked inside with a thing so evil it couldn't be named. That was all she could remember about the event.

"What made you think it was haunted?"

She smiled. "Maybe I knew you were in there," she said and shivered. She thought he paled, but it might have been a trick of the light. "There've always been stories about lights moving at night, shadows near the graves. Forget Cousin Reggie. I've been dying to show you something I found this morning." Faelan followed her to the computer and stood behind her chair. "See there? Faelan Connor, born 1833."

Chapter 21

"IT'S ME." FAELAN LEANED CLOSER, EYES SOAKING UP the words on the screen. "Aiden there, that's my father."

"Duncan Connor. He must be your brother's what, great-great-grandson? He was born in 1983, so he should have a year or so left as a warrior."

"You've done it. You've found my clan." Wrapping both arms around her shoulders, he kissed her cheek.

"And there's a Sean Connor. There's a phone number listed for him."

"We can call."

"We shouldn't drop the news over the phone. I know it seems like days for you, but it's been over a century and a half. The stories may have been lost."

A muscle ticked at the corner of his mouth, and he nodded.

Bree knew his greatest worry wasn't that there wouldn't be warriors to help him, but that his clan had forgotten him. "I'll call and say I have news of a relative, and we'll fly there tonight. We need to get out of here anyway. Between the archeologists, the demons, and Peter, it'll be impossible to keep you hidden."

"What about your mother?"

"I'll tell her something's come up, and I'm going to meet your family. She'll think we're… well, it can't be helped." She'd be so excited about her misconceptions she wouldn't mind.

"She'll think we're considering marriage."

Bree enjoyed a brief daydream; her in a wedding dress, gliding down the aisle to join a dark-haired man…

"Does she like me, or is she desperate?"

Her daydream screeched to a halt. "Desperate? Don't you think I can get a husband?"

"It's just that a lot of people are trying to marry you off. I guess they figure you need a husband to keep you out of trouble."

"That's a chauvinistic thing to say."

He grinned. "It'd bloody well take a jailer, not a husband." The phone rang before she could throw out a sarcastic comment. "You're going to answer it?" he asked, as she picked it up.

"It's probably Peter. If I don't answer, he's going to show up at the door again." Faelan had given her the note Peter left. Bree scrambled for an excuse to give him, but it was Jared.

"Can I come by? I need to talk to you."

"I was just leaving. What's wrong?"

"My backers are pulling out. Any chance you've made a decision about moving the dig? It's probably too late anyway," he said, voice weary.

She hated seeing Jared distressed after all he'd done for her. Maybe he was the one her grandmother wanted her to help, not Faelan. It was her idea to let Jared dig. Bree had met him here. She'd showed up at her grandmother's, on the run from Russell, and interrupted Jared and her grandmother discussing excavating. Both of them had taken one look at Bree and known she was in trouble. Jared offered to track Russell down and tell him to leave Bree alone. She refused, but she and Jared had been friends ever since.

"I'll let you move the dig if you can wait until I get back. I'm leaving town for a few days." She couldn't have Jared and his men here until Druan was no longer a threat. "You think it might help keep your funding?"

Faelan stood with his arms crossed over his chest, listening. With him, there was no such thing as a private conversation.

"It'll have to do," Jared said. "Thank you. This is a sudden trip. Where are you going?"

"I have some friends in Scotland who want me to look over some old documents." Faelan lifted one sexy brow, and Bree tugged at her necklace, distressed at how easily lies were dripping off her tongue. "I've always wanted to visit Scotland," she said, diluting the lie with truth. "We… I'm leaving tonight." The chain snapped, and the necklace fell to the floor.

"After that murder, I'd feel better if you weren't there. I caught one of my new guys snooping around. And someone broke into the trailer and stole a shovel and some clothes."

She hoped Druan hadn't planted one of his henchmen on Jared's crew. She could warn him, but that might put him in more danger. Jared would barge out and confront the man.

"I won't be around for a couple of days myself," Jared said, "but I'll check on the house when I get back."

"You're leaving, too?" She hoped he was. This place was too dangerous.

"My uncle is taking me to meet the backers, to see if I can get them to change their minds. The possibility of expanding the dig might do the trick."

"What was that about?" Faelan demanded after she hung up.

"He wants to move the dig closer to the house."

"I heard. He's already too close."

"I'm trying to hold him off until Druan is out of the way."

"I should meet Jared," Faelan said, frowning.

"He's leaving for a couple of days. I'll introduce you when we get back. I can say you're Cousin Reggie." She picked up the necklace, looking at the broken clasp. She hoped there'd be an earth left to dig in.

The trembling man watched as skin stretched and thickened, nose flattening, forehead bulging. The stench of sulfur filled the air as the man transformed into a monster.

"What did he look like?" the monster snarled.

The man shrank back. "T-tall. It was too dark to see anything," he lied, not knowing why the monster cared.

"Did you hear his name?" Long teeth gnashed inches from his face.

"No," he lied again, afraid to say more.

The monster turned to the skinny man beside him. Or was he another monster hiding under human skin? There was a bulge under his shirt, like a bandage, and the man looked as terrified as he felt.

"You didn't tell me anyone was with her, Grog. Two centuries I've kept you, helped you increase in power, and you hide this from me? You've seen the man. Was it him?"

The skinny man's skin rippled. "Master, I didn't see anyone—"

"Liar." The monster swiped with one of his claws, and Grog smashed into the wall. Half his face was gone. "If it's the warrior, the plan will have to be altered. Keep looking, and find out the man's name, or you'll be keeping Grog company."

The man ran from the room, sick with fear. He wiped his clammy forehead and tried to think. He was almost certain he had what the monster wanted. He'd found it by sheer luck when he'd stepped on a loose floorboard. If he gave it to him now, though, the monster would have no reason to keep him alive.

The hair rose on his neck. A stranger with long, raven hair stood in a dark doorway with a smug look on a face that was startlingly handsome after the earlier nightmare. The stranger watched from the shadows as two men talked farther down the corridor, one not fully human, the other immaculate, his hair streaked with silver.

When he looked back, the raven-haired stranger had vanished. This place was rife with secrets as well as horrors. He had to warn her. It was too late for him, but she shouldn't have to pay for his sins.

⁓

Faelan gripped the arms of the seat, trying not to look at the earth disappearing below. His stomach dropped as the plane rose higher. He couldn't remember what he'd eaten last, but he'd be lucky if it stayed down. Hot air balloons were one thing; this was madness. A big metal bird hurtling through the sky. He hadn't stopped sweating since he stepped into the airport terminal carrying his fake birth certificate, driver's license, and passport.

In his time, a man's name and his reputation were all the proof he needed.

At least the documents bore his real name. He didn't know how he'd repay Bree. She'd given the man a wad of money that would have fed a family for a year, in his day. He was going to owe her his first bairn. If he ever had one.

"Can we change seats?" he asked Bree, averting his gaze from the clouds rolling past his window.

Her lips twitched. She patted his hand and stood in the aisle while he unbuckled and slid over. He didn't dare try to stand, so she was forced to climb over him, her backside in his face as she took her seat. It was the only time his stomach had stopped rolling since he boarded this death trap. He wondered if the flight attendant would let her sit in his lap so he wouldn't have to think about how long it would take for them to plummet from the sky.

Bree sat down and slid a cover over the window. Damnation. He wished he'd known the thing closed. He could've pretended he was in a car and worried instead about what he'd find when they arrived in Scotland. He started feeling almost normal until she said, "You'll be fine. These things hardly ever crash."

The plane landed none too soon, and he had to do it all over again. If he wasn't afraid the disease would be released, he'd take a ship back to New York. Or did Bree expect him to stay in Scotland?

They rented a car at the airport, and after Bree finished chattering about having to drive on the wrong side of the road, Faelan got his first view of his homeland in more than a hundred and fifty years. This wasn't the

Scotland he remembered. Quaint villages had been replaced with crowds and buildings and cars, but outside the towns, the place was much the same. Homesickness gripped him as the scenery rolled by, flowers and sheep dotting hills and glens, farmhouses with curls of smoke drifting from stone chimneys.

"Look at those border collies. And sheep. I think there are more sheep here than people." She turned her head as they passed a flock, and the car veered into the path of an oncoming vehicle.

"Watch out!" he yelled, grabbing for the wheel. They'd be lucky if they lived to meet his family, with Bree talking and driving and looking all at the same time.

"I see it," she said, wrestling the car into the lane.

Trouble was, she wanted to see everything. At once.

"Look at that field of heather, and beyond it, the mist hanging over the valley. Can't you picture the men in their kilts, raising their swords for battle? Oh my gosh, you experienced it, for real."

He hadn't battled other clans, but he'd battled many a demon on this soil.

"And the sky, it's so… Scotlandy."

"Scotlandy?"

"Just like I pictured Scotland. But better. I should have traveled here years ago."

He was glad she was so enthralled with the land where he'd spent most of his youth. There was a kind of rightness about it all. It helped ease his worry over what he'd find when he arrived. He leaned his head back as she prattled on about fairies and kelpie, letting the gentle motion of the car and the scenery soothe his nerves. He wished he could show her the fields where he'd run and played with his brothers, the cold river where he'd caught fish and cooked them over a fire and frozen his arse off when the water was deep enough for swimming. The hidden cave where he'd camped, pretending to be a warrior long before he was. No matter where he roamed, the Highlands would always be home. Home. He closed his eyes.

"Faelan?"

Faelan woke with a start. Bree was shaking him.

"We're almost there."

"Why didn't you wake me?"

"You needed the rest. According to the GPS, this is it. Oh, my." She turned onto a paved driveway and pulled up to a large stone and iron gate.

Faelan wiped his bleary eyes and looked at the fence-lined fields rolling into green hills and copses of trees already showing red and gold. A dozen horses grazed, tails flicking. He leaned forward, gazing at the driveway that disappeared into the woods. A few feet beyond, it would cross a wooden bridge, spanning the gentle burn that in hard rain could reach Nandor's head. The road had been dirt then. Home.

———

Duncan Connor surveyed the monitors covering the perimeter of the castle and grounds. Five hundred acres wasn't easy to protect. In olden days, they'd relied on warriors stationed around the boundary. His father still talked of those days. Things were different now. In modern times, man had to use modern weapons, not that a demon couldn't get through if he really tried, but he'd have hell to pay when he got over the fence. Shane moved into sight on monitor B, his sword strapped to his back, a Glock at his waist. He wouldn't need the Glock. He was one of the fastest with a sword. Duncan glanced at the other monitors, checking the warriors' positions. There were more on guard than usual today.

A beep sounded, announcing a visitor. Duncan turned to the gate monitor. A rental car sat at the entrance. This must be her. He pushed the button. "Yes?"

"Hello," a female voice said. "I'm Bree Kirkland. I spoke to Duncan Connor about a relative. I believe he's expecting me."

Duncan couldn't imagine what news she could have about a relative, but she'd sounded nervous, making him suspect a trick. He saw movement in the passenger seat. Almost surely a trick. She was supposed to be alone. Two warriors entered the room behind him.

"Gate's open. Follow the drive and pull around back." He pushed the button opening the gate, and the car rolled forward at a snail's pace past the cameras mounted along the long road.

"Keep your weapons close," he told the men flanking him.

"You think this has something to do with Angus?" Brodie asked.

"Aye. I'm starting to think so." Her suspicious call, coming so soon after the one from Angus, made Duncan leery. Reinforcements had been called in, just in case she had something deadly up her sleeve. Duncan slipped his dirk into its sheath and listened for the car to roll to a stop. When he touched the doorknob, a shiver rippled up his arm. He'd been restless all week. Sorcha wasn't helping, disappearing for days at a time, and when she deigned to resurface, she never revealed where she'd been. Did she have a serious boyfriend this time? The question stung like a hook in his gut. She flaunted her men like a fisherman flaunted trout.

He hoped her lies were as big.

———

"It's a castle." Bree stared at the large, stone structure and turned to gape at Faelan. "Druan's castle. Why didn't you tell me his castle looked like this one?"

"What was there to say? I don't understand it either." Connor Castle was almost the same as the last time he'd seen it. The stone appeared more weathered, and there were boxes mounted along the walls. Cameras, if his twenty-first century knowledge was correct. He'd seen them at the gate and on poles and trees along the drive as well. It would be interesting to see how time had changed the battle.

The castle sat in the middle of five hundred acres, encircled by a thick stand of woods blocking it from the prying eyes and the curious townsfolk of his day. Warriors had been posted at the boundaries, rotating every six months. Anyone who got past them—almost none did—found a horse farm, which it was, in part. It was also the seat of Clan Connor. Faelan had spent more than his share of time watching for busybodies and demons. When he wasn't hunting, he stayed in one of the cottages along the boundary, to his mother's delight and his. Her cooking beat his by far.

Bree turned off the engine. Faelan opened the car door and stepped out. A gust swirled at his knees, lifting the edge of his kilt. He pulled in the crisp highland air, filling his lungs with memories. The trees were thicker, taller, but the lay of the land was the same. The stable was larger, and he could see horses in the back fields. There'd always been horses. They hadn't had Mustangs with powerful engines back then. There was a large building close to the castle, with several trucks parked outside and other buildings beyond it. He went around to open Bree's door, but as usual, she'd already jumped out.

"It's beautiful," Bree said, her head turning in all directions.

"My great-great-great-grandfather built it to house all the warriors who came through." In Faelan's day, the grounds had been astir with young boys training. From the time a lad could walk, he was groomed to be a warrior. From birth until death, the warrior blood flowed, but the responsibilities changed to make room for families, for a new generation to be bred. The retired warriors handled most of the training, some specializing in weapons, others fighting, and some instructing in spiritual matters, so a lad understood the importance of his mission, why he was required to make such a sacrifice. All areas had to be mastered before warriors could do battle.

The active warriors, when time allowed, took pride in demonstrating special skills, how to fight, using their weapons and minds. Faelan remembered the first time he'd seen Kieran, how big and powerful he seemed to a lad of fourteen years. Kieran had done more than teach Faelan what it meant to be a warrior. The mentor had become a trusted friend, fighting by Faelan's side, and in the end, Kieran had given his life so Faelan could live. A debt Faelan could never repay.

"Do you think Druan saw this place before he built his?"

"I think if Druan had seen this place he would've tried to destroy it." Maybe his clan would know how such a thing could be. Faelan's stomach knotted like twine. How would his family take meeting an ancestor who should be rotting in a grave? He glanced at Bree for reassurance, thinking how strange to be in his own land, standing in front of his home, finding comfort and familiarity in the face of someone he'd met only days before.

What would she do if his family didn't believe him? Would she abandon him? Eventually, she would. She'd fall in love, maybe with the archeologist, marry, and have bairns. Jealousy took the edge off his nerves.

"Is it always this windy?" she asked, eyeing his flapping kilt.

"Aye. Much of the time." He'd warned her to pack warmer clothes, and they purchased thick shirts and a coat for him when they went to get his identification.

"You realize we've just set foot in Scotland and you already sound more like a Scot?"

"That's the way of it. Always has been." When he became a warrior, he went wherever his assigned demon went, which was often and far. He'd mingled and hidden, whichever was necessary, picking up customs and languages from many lands. But this was home.

She smiled and reached for his hand. "Let's go meet your descendents."

Faelan nodded. "We can fetch our things if they invite us to stay."

"They will." Bree squeezed his fingers, and they started for the entrance. The door opened, and his brother Tavis stepped out.

Chapter 22

OR HIS BROTHER'S SPITTING IMAGE. DARK HAIR HUNG TO his shoulders. He wore a white shirt and a kilt, the same tartan as Faelan's, and a leather strap around his neck. Faelan struggled to control the rush of emotion. It wouldn't be good to disgrace himself before he was introduced.

"I'm Bree Kirkland." Bree stepped forward and put out her hand. Faelan could see two shadows lurking inside the open door. They were being watched, of course. No warrior would trust her story without proof.

"Duncan Connor," Tavis's image said, shaking Bree's hand, but watching Faelan. "You said you had news of an ancestor. I thought you'd be alone." He looked at Faelan's kilt and frowned, his face so like Tavis, he could have been his ghost.

"I have more than news. I've brought him. This is… this is Faelan Connor," Bree said motioning to him. They'd decided it best to spill it all up front and see where it landed.

"Faelan Connor?" Duncan's baffled gaze searched Faelan's face. Faelan's dread deepened with each added line in Duncan's forehead. "We don't have any Faelans in the family, except The Mighty—"

"I'm Faelan Connor," he said, holding out his talisman. "Your ancestor."

Duncan's eyes narrowed. "Is this a joke?"

"Out of my way," a crusty voice said, and Duncan

was pushed aside. An old man stepped out, followed by two younger men—one reddish-haired, one blond—clad in kilts, hands hanging deceptively loose over their dirks. The old man ran his hands through his hair, eyes lit with wonder. "I was starting to think I wouldn't live to see it." He studied Faelan's talisman, then his face. He ran his hands over Faelan's forehead and cheeks like a blind man would. The old man turned to Duncan, his eyes glistening. "You're looking at the Mighty Faelan, put in the vault by the demon Druan a century and a half ago."

Duncan stared at the old man as if he suffered from madness. "There are legends, but…"

"I'm Sean Connor." The man patted Faelan on the arm. "By my recollections, I'd be your great-great-nephew, and Duncan here would be your great-great-great-nephew. Welcome home, lad. Welcome home. You can't know how glad we are that you're here." A crooked smile split his face, and Faelan's burden slipped away.

He cleared his throat. "Dust," he mumbled, blinking.

"Aye, it's getting to me, too. Coira, come quick," the old man yelled, his movements so agitated Faelan thought the man might break out in dance.

"It could be a trick," Duncan said.

"Can't you see the family resemblance?"

"It might be a shell."

"No, that talisman belongs to none other than Faelan Connor. It's in one of the portraits inside. Besides, he looks just like you, any fool can see that." To Faelan, Sean said, "We've been expecting you, but not like this. Come on inside, and we'll get it all sorted out, right enough. Coira! Blimey, where's that woman when you need her?"

Home. He was home. Faelan glanced at Bree's damp eyes and fought the swell of emotions. There were times it wasn't good to be a man.

"It's really him?" Duncan stared as the other two warriors moved closer, eyes wide, jaws slack.

"It's the Mighty Faelan," the red-haired one whispered in awe.

"You must be my brother Tavis's great-grandson," Faelan said to Duncan.

"No. Tavis was my great-great-great-uncle. I'm a descendent of… of your brother, Ian," Duncan said, looking dazed. "I've heard the legend since I was a lad. We all have, but most believed you'd died."

"I have to say I was starting to have a wee doubt myself. We've had a swarm of warriors and Seekers looking for that key this past year. We were getting a bit desperate, what with the Watchers being so troubled these last few weeks, and knowing it was long past time for you to awake." He moved deeper into the foyer.

"What are Watchers?" Bree asked.

"They have dreams, warn us of trouble," Sean said. "Like guards. They've been worried about Druan. We've searched for him for decades, but he was spotted only once or twice in all the years since I was born."

"We found him," Faelan said. "In New York. We found his lair."

Sean stopped, bushy eyebrows lifted. "Blessed be. Now that we have you and your talisman, we'll send him to hell."

"Are there many warriors now?" Faelan asked the old man.

"Aye, as many as you need. There's Duncan here,

Tomas, Brodie, and a whole parcel of others. Some are here, some out hunting, and others are on the way. We weren't sure... well, about the lass's reason for coming. Wait until you see how things have changed, lad. Tomas, Brodie," Sean said to the two tall, lean warriors lurking in the background, "one of you find Coira for me. Hurry now, you can talk to him after we let everyone know." Sean rubbed his hands together. "We've got celebrating to do." He scuttled forward, and Faelan followed his great-great-nephew into the home where Faelan had been born and played as a child.

The portrait on the wall stopped him as if his boots were mired in stable muck. He reached out and touched the painting, afraid it would disintegrate. His mother and father, Tavis, Ian, Alana, all staring back at him from a lifetime ago. Two years, in his time.

The day was still etched in his memory, his mother nearly in tears because his father complained his shirt was choking him, and Faelan and his brothers wouldn't stop squirming. They were already late for the games. Ian was sweet on a lass there, and Tavis was nursing a grudge against the warrior he'd let beat him in the caber toss the year before. The warriors were too strong to truly compete with local clans, but if they hadn't participated, it would have drawn too much attention, so they tempered their strength. Although, Tavis had to be reminded from time to time.

Bree touched Faelan's hand. "He looks like you," she said, pointing at Tavis. "And that must be Alana. She does resemble the painting we saw. Is that you?" She pointed at a small laddie with mussed dark hair and an inquisitive face.

Faelan's jaw tightened. "No, Liam."

"Liam? He's adorable—oh, look at this one. It has the four-leaf clover," Bree said, distracted by another of Alana's paintings, and Faelan was relieved he didn't have to explain.

There were several paintings of his brothers, his parents, Nandor, many of them done by Alana.

"Why did she use a four-leaf clover?"

"One leaf for each of us. She said, as far as brothers went, she could've done worse."

"You had a beautiful family."

Had.

"You're welcome to anything you see," Sean said. He and Duncan had stopped as well. "The whole place is rightfully yours."

Faelan would take the portrait. It was all he had left of his family. He looked at the old man waiting anxiously, eyes shining, and Duncan still looking suspicious, exactly how Tavis would, if he were alive. No, it wasn't all. The portrait was paper and paint. Sean and Duncan and the others he hadn't met, they were what remained of his family. Spirit, flesh, and blood.

Within the hour, there was a celebration fit for a king. Faelan met more relatives than he could remember names, and they were all talking at once, asking questions about how Bree found him and what would happen now. Children rushed to and fro, laughing, hiding under tables as young lassies giggled and the older ones sighed. Food appeared from nowhere, modern and traditional. He hoped the haggis and blood pudding hadn't been prepared in his honor, since he'd never had a taste for either. He had gotten a good laugh when Brodie sneaked some onto Bree's plate, and she'd turned white as sheep's wool.

"Well, now, it appears I'm too late," a sultry voice drawled. "The legend has already arrived."

Faelan turned and saw a woman standing near the door. She was a bonny thing, if you liked redheads. Dressed all in black. Black shirt, black skirt—short skirt. Faelan could see the hilt of a *sgian dubh* at the top of a black boot that reached her knees. She stared at him until heat rose up his neck. Unable to help himself, and irritated because of it, he glanced at Bree to see if she'd noticed.

She had.

"Come in, lass. Don't linger in the doorway." Sean motioned for her to come forward. "Faelan, Bree, this is Sorcha, a cousin." He leaned close to Faelan and whispered, "Gird your loins, lad."

Sorcha gave him a long, slow look from top to bottom, and Faelan felt like he was being fondled from afar. She slinked across the room and stood motionless, staring at him, one eyebrow arched. "The Mighty Faelan, so I didn't have to come get you after all?" She turned her head and gave an assessing, then dismissive, glance at Bree, who took a long sip of wine before setting it aside. A hand appeared from behind a bookcase, refilling her glass.

"What do you mean?" Faelan asked. When had women become so bold?

"I was coming to wake you," Sorcha replied.

"You?" Duncan blurted out.

Sean stroked his chin. "The Council decided Sorcha should join Angus."

"Why wasn't I told?" Duncan asked, frowning.

"You were busy with that demon in Belfast," Sean said.

"You would've gotten in the way, cousin." Sorcha waved her hand as if Duncan was of no consequence.

"Why her?" he demanded.

"She's dreamed of the key."

"We've all dreamed of the key." Duncan gave Sorcha a black glare, but she turned her back on Duncan, focusing on Faelan, who wished she'd look elsewhere. She was making him jittery.

"You should've told me it was her," Duncan said, under his breath.

"Who's Angus?" Faelan asked.

"The last one sent to look for the key."

"A Seeker?" Bree asked, her words friendlier than her expression.

"No, a warrior," Sean said.

"How could you wake me without the key?" Faelan asked Sorcha.

"I was going to find it, assuming Angus hadn't already done so," she said, a shadow crossing her face. "Like Sean said, I've dreamt of it."

Another woman coming to rescue him.

"And I've dreamt of *you*."

Sorcha smiled, and again he felt like he should apologize to Bree. This wouldn't do. He'd done nothing wrong. He had no ties on Bree and she had none on him, regardless what his body screamed. Just lust, he thought, then wondered why he didn't feel the same pull for this attractive woman standing too close to him, looking like she wanted to make him her next meal.

"What kind of dreams?" he asked, immediately regretting his question.

Sorcha's eyes flashed and her lips tilted.

"Stop with your silly grins and tell him what he wants to know," Duncan said.

He was a good foot taller, but Sorcha managed to look down her nose at him. "I've had them for weeks now," she told Faelan. "Dreams of destruction and mayhem. And a key. *The* key." She frowned. "There's danger in that key yet. Keep it safe." She started to tremble, then gave him a coy smile, and he decided she must have been wiggling her body at him. "Then, there were the handsome men."

Duncan ground his teeth together.

What kind of woman behaved so brazen in a crowd?

"Russell is handsome," Bree said, giving her wine glass a puzzled look before she took another sip.

Faelan's hands clenched. Russell was a demon, for God's sake. She ought to stop talking about him like he was a man.

"Good grief." Bree giggled, looking from Faelan to Duncan, who stood next to him, still glowering at the audacious redhead. "Look at those frowns. You two could be brothers." She set her glass down, and Faelan saw Brodie slip around and refill it, wearing a sly grin. Faelan would've been worried the warrior was trying to get her drunk and take advantage of her, but he'd seen Brodie doing it to several others as well, female and male. A prankster. Probably descended from Ian.

"There, even the lass sees the resemblance," Sean told his son.

Like Isabel and Bree, Faelan thought, who looked the same but were a century apart.

"Who's Russell?" Sorcha asked.

"That's the human name we think Druan is using now," Faelan said. "We're not sure if he knows I've been freed, so we might have the element of surprise. But there's not much time. He's trying to find the key. I don't know why the disease hasn't been released."

"I may know something about that," Sean said, and the room fell quiet.

Faelan looked around the room. "Is it safe to speak of such things?"

"We're all family. Bound by blood and oath, and Bree brought you to us, so I think that makes it acceptable for her to be here."

Family. Not Tavis, Ian, Alana, or his parents, but born of them, carrying their blood. He wasn't completely lost.

"We all knew the legend," Sean said, "but most believed it a myth, like dragons and such, but I heard stories from my father and my grandfather when I was a wee lad, when they thought I was fast asleep. Your brothers, they went to help you." He paused, and not a sound could be heard in the room. "And they found you."

Faelan's breath felt like a gust of wind trying to squeeze through a hole too small. "My brothers found the time vault? They came?"

"Aye. A storm had delayed them. The Seeker who traveled with them found the time vault, but it was buried in a field. They didn't know if you were alive or dead. They had to hide you, but the time vault couldn't be moved far. My grandfather spoke of a graveyard nearby and how Tavis secured an empty crypt from a man named Belville."

"Belville? That was my great-great-grandfather's last name," Bree said, her face flushed from her wine.

"Frederick Belville?"

"Yes."

"Blimey. Then you must be Emily's granddaughter."

"You knew my grandmother?"

"Met her once. Last year Coira and I went to look for the key. The time vault was ready to be opened, and the Council was anxious. We suspected Druan had something planned, but without the key there was no way to bring Faelan and his talisman back. Your grandmother invited us to stay, but Coira got ill, and we had to leave. To think we were so close to the key." Earlier, Bree had told them about finding it on the mantel. "No use fretting about it now. Things usually work out as they're meant to. How is your grandmother?"

"She died a few months ago. Cancer."

"I'm sorry lass. I am. She was a kind soul."

"Did she know why you were there?" Bree asked.

"No. We couldn't share that."

"If my brothers put me in the crypt, then they didn't battle Druan."

"No." Sean paused. "They didn't battle Druan. But they couldn't find the key. Tavis captured one of the demon's minions, and he told them who'd held the key that night. They found the halfling, but he said he lost it when he left the place. He was hoping Druan would forget about it over the years. He offered to show them the trail if they wouldn't tell Druan he lost it. They agreed, but the key couldn't be found. It had vanished. Even the Seeker couldn't find it. Your brothers didn't know about the virus—that's what Druan had created—until they ran into one of the other warriors who'd gotten your message. Your brothers used their wits. They couldn't destroy Druan or his virus, since your talisman was locked in the time vault, but they did the next best thing. They decided to kill the demon's sorcerer, hoping the virus would be ruined. They claimed a stranger came forward and told them where to find the sorcerer. They killed him right under the demon's nose."

"Brilliant," Bree said, looking a bit glassy-eyed though her wine glass was still full. "Who was the stranger?"

"They never knew. He disappeared. According to my grandfather, Tavis and Ian figured it'd take Druan another century or two to make another virus, and by then you'd be awake. Your brothers made a map of where you lay, so when the time came, you'd be found." Sean walked to the cabinet where Faelan's father had kept his important papers. He took out a key and opened a small drawer, pulled out a thin box, and set it on a table. Opening it, he lifted out a piece of paper and placed it in Faelan's hand.

Faelan could feel the heat of bodies crowding close. The paper was old, thick, with shapes like rectangles and squares. The graveyard. His brothers had come. They hadn't faced the demons of old. They'd tried to save him. The brothers he'd always protected had taken care of him and made sure he wouldn't be lost forever.

His brothers had saved the world when he failed.

"Your brothers made the map," Bree said, her voice awed. "It's like the one I found. Except it's dated last year."

"The clan sent many warriors and Seekers over the decades, but this past year the search has been a fair frenzy."

"McGowan," Bree blurted out. "Was he a Seeker?"

"How do you know about McGowan?" Sorcha and Sean asked in unison, staring at Bree as if she'd shifted into a demon.

"I found a journal."

"McGowan left a journal?" Sorcha asked, shocked, her seductress side nowhere in sight.

"No, my great-great-grandmother's journal. She said McGowan visited. She thought he was searching for treasure."

"Indeed," Sean said. "McGowan and others were sent."

"All those lost campers," Bree said.

"McGowan and another man were murdered," Faelan said. "Druan must've killed them."

"He did," Sorcha said. "Druan will not only face you, he'll answer to me."

A woman against a demon? Faelan wisely kept his mouth shut. "You were related to McGowan?"

Sorcha gave him a peculiar look, but he paid no attention. She'd given him a lot of peculiar looks since she'd arrived. "No, but the man with him was my great-great-grandfather. Quinn Douglass."

"Why did they send the Keeper of the Book to look for a key?" Faelan asked, surprised.

"He didn't go for the key. He went for the *Book of Battles*, at least we think that's why he was there," Sean said. Another look passed between him and Sorcha.

"I, for one," Sorcha said, staring at Faelan, "would give my sword arm to know why you stole it."

Chapter 23

"You think I stole the *Book of Battles*?" Faelan asked, appalled.

"Now Sorcha, stole is a harsh word." Sean's blunted fingers knotted in his lap. "The stories say it disappeared around the time you went to America."

"Why would I take it? Warriors weren't even allowed to see the book then, much less touch it."

"They still aren't, but the clan figured you had a reason," Sean said. "It's caused a bit of worry over the decades, not knowing if it was locked inside the time vault with you or if a demon had stolen it. Since it never turned up, they assumed it was with you. The Seeker couldn't tell if it was there."

"I'd never even seen the book until now."

"Until now? So you do have it?" Sorcha asked.

"Bree found it in her attic. It's safely hidden, but I didn't steal it." He would've brought it, but he hadn't been certain of his welcome, and it was too valuable to be dragged across the sky in a metal bird that could crash and burn.

"It's safe. Thank God." Sean's shoulders slumped. "That's one less thing to fret about."

"But if Faelan didn't take it, who did?" Duncan asked. "And how did it end up halfway around the world?"

"Would Quinn have taken the book?" Sean asked of no one in particular. "The clan always assumed he went to find it."

Sorcha looked affronted. "Why would he do that?"

"Because he was charged with keeping it safe," Faelan told them. "Michael warned me the book was in danger before I left for America. I told Quinn, and he said he'd move the book."

"But why take it to America?" Sorcha asked.

"Faelan's brothers were going there anyway, to meet him. Perhaps Quinn thought it was best away from Scotland," Sean said.

"Wouldn't he have informed the Council?" Duncan asked.

"Not if he didn't know where the threat came from," Faelan said.

"You think the danger came from inside the clan?" Sorcha asked.

"I don't know, but some of the pages are missing."

Sean gripped the arms of his chair. "Which ones?"

Faelan hated to tell them, because they would know he'd looked inside. "Near the end. I didn't read the book, just checked to see that it wasn't damaged."

"Ah, those. Don't fret. They've been missing for centuries, according to the Keepers. No one even remembers what they were. It's our clan mystery."

"A clan mystery," Bree said in awe.

"At least you have the book," Sean said. "Most of the knowledge has been passed down orally, but there's no measuring the damage exposing those names could do."

"You're the Keeper of the Book," Bree blurted.

"I am," Sean said. "Not that there's a book to keep, since it disappeared. The Keepers have tried to put together as much information as they could from other documents." Each clan had its own book. Every half a millennium, a new one was given.

"Since Michael warned Faelan the book was in danger, it would make sense that Druan was involved," Tomas said.

"That was my thought," Faelan said. "Druan could have stolen it."

"Quinn was probably tracking it," Sorcha said.

"Who's Michael?" Bree asked.

"He's a warrior," Faelan said.

Sorcha toyed with the hilt of her *sgian dubh*, and Faelan wondered why she carried it. "Before you put Druan in the time vault," she said to Faelan, "I want a piece of him. He'll pay for my great-great-grandfather's life."

"That's suicide. You may be a warrior," Duncan said, "but Faelan is the only one who can touch Druan."

Faelan had grown adept at hiding emotions, but his mouth dropped. "You're a warrior?"

"Times have changed while you slumbered," Sorcha said. "We have many female warriors and Watchers."

Faelan closed his mouth. Had the world gone mad? What next? Would they send children into battle?

"But some don't know when to back off," Duncan muttered.

"And some don't know when to mind their own business," Sorcha fired back.

It seemed Bree's penchant for boldness wasn't unique. "In my day, women were to be cherished and protected," Faelan said.

"You can protect our backs while we fight alongside you and cherish us when we defeat the enemy."

Damnation. What had happened to the sane world he'd left behind where women minded hearth and home?

"So women can be warriors and Watchers now?" Bree asked with a smug look.

Like a female warrior wasn't ludicrous enough.

"Aye, but only one or the other. Never both," Sean said.

"Isn't Sorcha a Watcher?" Bree asked. "She has dreams."

"Warriors often have dreams as well."

"Would Angus have brought a time vault?" Faelan asked. "I found one in the cellar of the chapel next to the graveyard."

Bree choked on her wine. "My chapel? There's a time vault in *my* chapel? And you didn't tell me?"

"I didn't want—"

"I know. You didn't want to worry me. There are demons running around my backyard trying to kill me. After all that's happened, I can't believe you would keep this from me. It's *my* chapel." Her eyes were sharp as dirks, making him long for the days when the women would've been in the kitchen cooking. "Wait. The chapel doesn't have a cellar."

"Aye, it does. The steps were behind the wall that collapsed."

"I have a hidden cellar?" Her eyes sparkled with excitement, momentarily dousing her anger.

"The wall that hid the entrance was old, but I figured there might be another way into the cellar, something a warrior could've used recently."

"I don't think so," Bree said. "But I didn't know about the hidden door, either. Grandma never mentioned it. Isabel did say something in the journal about someone hiding slaves. I wonder if someone was using the cellar as part of the Underground Railroad."

"If so, there could be a tunnel. Would your mother know?" Faelan asked.

"I'll check with her."

"A warrior from Canada was supposed to arrive a few days ago to help Sorcha and Angus," Sean said, "but we haven't heard from him yet. I suppose he or Angus could have brought a time vault and hid it after the wall collapsed."

"Is this Austin the one who *helped* Sorcha last year?" Duncan asked, frowning.

Sorcha bristled. "Stop acting like a Neanderthal, cousin. You're not my bloody bodyguard."

Duncan cursed and stormed out, letting the door slam behind him. A few in the room chuckled, but most paid no attention.

Faelan hid a grin and wondered if Tavis had also risen from his grave.

"I think Angus would have told us if he needed a time vault," Sean mused. "Same for Austin."

"If Druan's been reassigned, another warrior could have brought it for him."

Sean shook his head. "I think we would have heard if an ancient demon had been assigned. Was there a key to this time vault?"

"No key. And no sign of another warrior." Could it be the archeologist? How long had Bree known him?

"Maybe the time vault was for Tristol, Malek, or Voltar," Bree said.

Sean looked puzzled. "The demons of old?"

"They rode with Druan that night," Faelan said.

A pall fell over the room. "You're sure, lad?" Sean asked, alarmed.

"I'm sure." Other than Druan, Faelan hadn't seen the ancient demons' human forms. They protected that knowledge like the warriors protected their talismans and time vaults. But there wasn't a warrior alive, at least in Faelan's day, who hadn't heard the stories from his father and seen clan sketches of the demons of old in their natural forms.

"That's disturbing, it is," Sean said, the wrinkles in his forehead growing deeper.

"I think they were helping Druan with the war. I don't think they knew about the disease, Druan's virus. Tristol was angry when I confronted Druan about it."

"Too bad Tristol didn't kill Druan for us. I'd have paid to see that fight." Sorcha lifted her glass to blood-red lips.

"There've been rumors about the horror those four have wrought in the past, but they haven't been spotted this century," Sean said. "We'd hoped some of them had died."

"I'm afraid we have more to worry about than ancient demons," Faelan said. "Druan's castle is an exact duplicate of this one."

The room fell silent again, then everyone began to whisper.

Sean's voice rose out of the din. "You've seen it?"

"We both have," Faelan said, motioning to Bree. "In fact, we have a map of the inside. The only differences are some of the secret passages."

"Could Druan have seen this place?" Brodie asked.

"Not likely, or he would've tried to destroy it," Faelan said.

"Maybe there was a traitor," Sorcha said, holding Faelan's gaze.

"Even more puzzling, the castle is cloaked by some sort of spell."

Tomas frowned. "Cloaked?"

"It's invisible. That must be how he's stayed hidden. I searched the area before. There was no sign of his lair."

"What do you mean it's invisible?" Bree asked. "The castle was right there."

"You saw it, lass?" Sean asked, shocked.

"Of course. You didn't?" she asked Faelan.

He shook his head. "All I saw was a field and trees. I found where you'd hidden your car, and I walked across the road, right into a tree."

"But how—"

Further speculation was interrupted as Coira announced another group of warriors arriving. For hours the festivities continued, everyone smiling and hugging, bombarding Faelan with questions, comparing the current world with the one he'd known, whispering about ancient demons, invisible castles, and the American Civil War until he ached for quiet.

"Would you mind if I spoke to Bree?" he asked, interrupting her conversation with Sean.

"What do you want?" She was still upset.

"I want to apologize for not telling you about the other time vault and the cloaking spell. I didn't want to—"

She held her hand up, her face darkening. "Don't say it."

"Sorry. This is a different world from the one I knew. In my time we took care of women, tried to make things easier for them. I don't know what to do with you," he said, studying her face. "I didn't mean to insult you."

Her expression softened, though her body still looked stiff as a corset. "I know you mean well, but I'm not a child. Don't treat me like one. I don't need another father."

Like a child? That was nowhere near how he wanted to treat her. After he made sure Brodie had grown bored with his wine tricks, Faelan slipped away from the noise and commotion. Alone, he wandered through the house reliving memories far older than they felt. The library still smelled like a warm fire on a cool night. He could close his eyes and see his family gathered around the hearth listening to one of his father's wild tales of his warrior days, while Tavis and Ian poked at each other when no one was looking. The furniture had changed, and the kitchen had modern appliances like in Bree's house, but even bigger, to feed all the warriors coming through. The solid oak table was still there, with Ian's initials carved under the edge.

Several bedrooms had been converted into fancy bathrooms like Bree's. His mother would've loved it. His father too, who'd love to sing in the tub, his voice booming so loud they could hear him outside. In Faelan's time, most of the bedrooms had tubs for bathing, but the water had to be carried by hand. One room had a basin and a water closet of sorts, but most of the time they used the privy out back.

He paused when he reached the bedroom he'd shared with his brothers, running a hand over the gouge in the wooden door. Tavis had thrown a knife at Ian for teasing him about Marna, the blacksmith's daughter, who always gave Tavis extra sweeties. When their father saw the gouge, Faelan claimed he'd used the door for target practice, but his father wasn't fooled, and all three of them had gotten their hides tanned.

Faelan opened the door, wondering if any of his things had survived. His mom had kept the room unchanged, even after he and his brothers moved out. It was painted yellow now. The curtains and quilt were different, but his old iron bed was the same. He opened the closet. None of his belongings were here. Slipping off his boots, he lay on the bed that was too small. He pulled the smooth stone from his pocket, rubbing his thumb over it as the distant sounds of laughter faded and exhaustion brought sleep.

The wind whipped his hair against his face as Faelan galloped ahead of the storm. He glanced over his shoulder and saw Tavis on the hill closing in, but Ian hadn't caught up. Faelan nudged Nandor to go faster. The lucky stone would be his. A tree branch smacked his chest, wiping the triumph from his face. He righted himself as Tavis sped ahead with a victory cry.

"The stone's mine," Tavis shouted over the wind.

Faelan jumped to the ground outside the stables, leading Nandor inside, while Tavis held the door.

"Where's Ian?" Faelan asked, looking into the storm.

"I thought he'd catch up by the burn." Tavis put his horse in the stall as Faelan watched from the open door for a sign of their brother. Two more crashes sounded. Faelan swung onto Nandor's back. "You're not going back out there," Tavis said, glancing at the sky.

The next flash brought an image of a tiny casket being lowered into the ground. "I have to."

"You're daft. It's lightning like the devil out there. We'll get Father. Ian probably saw the storm coming and went to the cabin."

"I can't leave him out there. He's my responsibility. I'm the oldest."

"It's not your fault, Faelan," Tavis said, and they both knew he wasn't talking about Ian. "You tried to save him. I'm the one who didn't get there in time. I'm getting Father—"

"No," Faelan shouted. "I'll take care of it." He rode out the open door into the storm, leaving Tavis frowning after him.

Nandor's hoofs splattered mud as they raced across the back field. Faelan wished he'd never suggested this game. He wasn't a kid anymore. In two years, he would start training. He should've known better, read the weather beforehand. Faelan rounded the corner of the orchard and stopped.

Ian lay face down in the dirt, his horse nowhere to be seen. Faelan jumped off Nandor and sprinted to his brother. "Ian?" He crouched over him, but Ian didn't move. Faelan pulled Ian's kilt over his backside and rolled him over, putting his ear to Ian's chest. His heartbeat was strong. "Come on, Ian." Faelan shook his brother, but he didn't move. A horse whinnied behind him. He turned and saw Tavis jump from his horse and run toward them. He should have known Tavis would never stay behind. "His horse must have thrown him," Faelan said.

Tavis nodded.

Together they carried Ian to where Nandor stood. Faelan whistled, and the young stallion straightened *his forelegs and leaned down. They laid Ian across Nandor's back, and Faelan jumped on behind him, adjusting Ian so he was leaning back in Faelan's arms. Tavis mounted, and they hurried home. Faelan gripped his brother's lanky body as he urged Nandor to go faster.*

Ian roused in sight of the house. He tried to move, but Faelan held him still.

"Hold on. We're almost home." His father ran across the field toward them, his face black as the sky.

"What happened?" he yelled as they lifted a grumbling Ian off the horse.

"He fell."

"You should've come for me. Why do you try to do everything yourself? There's no shame in asking for help, lad. You're not God. All we need is for your mother to lose another son."

Faelan opened his eyes and looked at his bedroom. Loneliness settled like a heavy fog. He squeezed the stone he held. He should've given it to Tavis. He'd won it fair and square.

Faelan stuck the stone in his pocket and shoved his feet into his boots. Crossing to the small balcony, he climbed over and dropped to the ground, landing lightly, like a cat, almost hitting a huge elderberry bush in the same place where he'd helped his mother plant hers. He sprang up and ran. Whoever was watching the cameras would see him, but he needed space to think. He filled his lungs with the night air, thick with memories, and felt the breath of others who'd walked here and gone.

He moved forward without thinking, letting his feet lead the way. He passed the stables, the trees he'd climbed as a lad, fields where he'd raced with Nandor, and he headed for the knoll. The crumbling wall stood as it had for centuries. Faelan swallowed the lump in his throat as he stepped inside. The markers stood in silence, their occupants undisturbed by evil or wind or cold.

He moved between the headstones, past grandparents and great-grandparents, generations of Connors who slept here. There hadn't been so many graves then. In the corner, he found them, their markers stained with age. Ian dead in 1863. Beside him were his wife and three sons, two of them born on the same day. Twins. Then Alana, who'd lived until 1925, and her husband. A small headstone lay alongside them.

Faelan, beloved son of Alana and Robert Nottingham, eleven months old.

Alana had named a son after him. Faelan's throat tightened. Beside the tiny grave were two more sons and three daughters born to his sister. Next was Tavis's marker. Dead in 1860, buried at sea, the year Faelan had been locked in the time vault. Why hadn't they told him? Behind his brothers' and sister's graves, sheltered under an old tree, Faelan found his father and mother. Aiden and Lena Connor. His mother had lived until age fifty-three. His father had died the same year as Tavis. Between his parents lay Liam's small grave.

Memories welled like a dam and broke free. A giggling Alana, smelling of apples and sunshine. His brothers in swordplay as their father corrected their form. Dirt smudges on his mother's cheery face as he helped her plant the elderberry bush. Liam, his limp body drenched with water when they pulled him from the well. Gone. They were all gone.

He thought about how many others had grieved for a father or brother or son who'd died in a war he failed to stop. A wife mourning a husband who'd never return. A mother weeping over a son who'd died far too young. Another who'd killed his brother for a cause that was nothing more than a distraction for Druan. Families destroyed, lives ruined, because he hadn't stopped Druan in time. The lonely wail of a dog pulled Faelan's pain inside out. He moved back to where his brothers lay and placed the white stone on Tavis's grave.

Chapter 24

BREE REACHED FOR THE TELEPHONE AND LET OUT A delicate belch. The haggis. Her stomach rolled. She'd been too distracted watching Faelan's reunion with his family—and all those men wearing kilts—to notice what was on the plate Brodie handed her. Maybe she just dreaded the thought of facing all those warriors and admitting she'd almost married an ancient demon. Or it could have been the wine. She'd had only one glass, but it felt like four. Faelan had disappeared earlier. It was some consolation that she'd seen Sorcha wrapped around another man downstairs, but with Sorcha's flirting and Faelan's out-of-control lust, it was a matter of time. If Duncan didn't kill Sorcha first. He obviously saw something in the witch that no one else did.

Laughter drifted from below as Bree dialed her mother's number. Coira had told Bree to make use of the house phone. Her mother didn't answer. She must be out with Sandy. Bree checked her voice mail next. There was one message.

"Bree, this is Peter. Thanks for letting me know you're out of town. Call me as soon as you get this. I'm having trouble tracing your friend's name. I don't know how long you plan to be away, but longer might be better. We still haven't caught the killer. This case is getting stranger by the minute."

She'd call him when she got back. Bree went upstairs to the room they'd given her, a few doors down from Faelan's. She stepped onto the balcony overlooking the fields and stables at the back of the castle, her thoughts on Sorcha and Faelan and dead bodies and how she could get Peter off Faelan's tail. The night was cool, the moon bright, but not full. A hill rose in the distance, and Bree saw a stone wall enclosing a graveyard.

Her aching stomach forgotten, she left the room and hurried downstairs, smiling at two men in kilts she passed in the hall. She'd met them earlier but couldn't remember their names. Outside, she wove her way through the cars parked in the driveway and made her way up the hill. Hugging her arms against the night air, she approached the crumbling wall. She loved cemeteries. She was some distance away when she spotted a figure near the back of the graveyard. Her heart lurched for a second, then she saw it was a man standing underneath an old tree. He moved from grave to grave, head bowed, stopping to touch each one. She watched as he dropped to his knees and leaned his head against a stone. Faelan had found his family.

Her eyes stung. She wanted to go to him, but was afraid to intrude on his grief. Instead, she turned away, hurrying back to the castle, her face wet for him. She crawled into bed and cried for his pain. Then she cried for herself, her father, her grandmother, her twin, and her poor Aunt Layla, who died too young.

Bree woke when the covers lifted and the mattress dipped. Her nose told her who it was before a masculine leg brushed hers. Faelan. She lay still as he slid closer and slipped both arms around her, cradling her against his warm body. He didn't speak, just held her. Did he want to sleep next to her again? She wasn't sure it would be enough for her tonight. Several heartbeats later, she felt a prod against her backside and started to turn, but he held her in place. He slid his hand under the soft cotton of her top, filling his hand with her breast.

"I need you," he whispered, nudging her hair aside, touching his lips to her neck. His hand moved to the other breast and then lower, dipping inside her pajamas, until with an impatient sigh, he made them disappear.

With her back still facing him, he slid a hand under her thigh and pulled her leg up. She bent one knee, giving his fingers the access they desired. For minutes she hovered between two worlds, then she felt the tip of him nudging for entry.

She reached back, clutching his thigh as he slipped inside, one slow inch at a time, until their bodies were joined. He pulled her against his chest, holding them both still. His teeth scraped her ear. Steadying her hip with one hand, he pulled out slowly, and then slid in again. Two strokes, three, and she was ready to fall.

His fingers dug into her hip as he moved faster, driving in, pulling out… then nothing. He was gone. She turned, but he was already pushing her onto her back. He lowered his body between her thighs, and locking eyes with hers, he entered again. His mouth covered hers, and on the second stroke she exploded, lips open against his, her heart crying words she had no right to feel.

Still inside her, he rose to his knees and wrapped both hands high around her thighs, eyes glittering as he watched their joining. He groaned and dropped back down to her, body against body, still, except for the throbbing inside as he emptied himself into her.

They lay quietly, the only movement the fast rise and fall of chest against breasts, and Faelan's breath warm at her ear. He dropped a gentle kiss on her brow, her cheek, and finally her lips. He slipped out and gathered her in his arms, snug against him. She lay with her head on his chest, her leg resting on his hip, listening to the beat of his heart, and she knew it was where she belonged. She'd met him only days ago, yet she trusted him more than anyone she'd ever known. If the world was ending, which it might well be, he would be the one she'd run to.

But what about him and her? Would he want to stay here? Would she have to leave?

"Are you okay?" Faelan asked.

She nodded, too sated to move, even to clean up.

"You're quiet," he said, gently stroking her arm.

It was hard to speak, with her heart so overwhelmed. "I'm worried," she said, deciding to share the lesser of her concerns.

"About what?"

"Tomorrow I'm going to have to tell everyone about Russell. How he deceived me."

"You needn't worry about that. They've all faced deception, in one manner or another."

She felt his even breathing and thought he was asleep, until he spoke again.

"I had a brother. Liam. He was two. Tavis, Ian, and I were keeping an eye on him while my father was having a sword repaired. We were in the village playing marbles outside the blacksmith's shop. We got busy and didn't realize Liam had wandered off. Then we saw a man leading him away. I chased them. Tavis followed me. Ian went to get my father. The man grabbed Liam and ran. When he turned, I could see he wasn't a man. He was a demon. He let me get close enough to taunt me, then he dangled Liam over an old well. I was the closest, just on the other side of the well. Tavis was a few steps behind me. The demon laughed and dropped Liam. I grabbed for him. Caught his hand. I tried… but I couldn't hold him. He was screaming and wiggling, and my hands were sweaty. My father came running, but it was too late. He climbed down, but Liam was already dead."

"Oh, Faelan." Now she understood why he was so protective. Bree turned and wrapped her arms tighter around him, resting her head on his chest. Her face tingled where it pressed against his battle marks. "I'm so sorry. How old were you?"

"Seven. That's why we moved to Philadelphia. We didn't come back until my father thought it was safe."

"What happened to the demon?"

"He ran as soon as he dropped Liam. We never found him. Never knew who he was. I dream about it sometimes. There was something about the demon…" Faelan sighed. "But I can't rightly place it. I can't see his face. All I can see is Liam screaming." Faelan ran his hand hard across his eyes. "It was my fault. If I'd been watching him…"

"It wasn't your fault." But that was like telling the waves to stop crashing. At least he had memories of his brother. She hadn't even had a chance to know her sister.

He pulled her closer, holding her too tight, and in minutes, he was asleep. His hold on her relaxed, and Bree lay there, aching inside for the little boy who'd watched his brother die, believing it was his fault, and grown into a man who carried the weight of the world on his shoulders. And now he was trying to save the entire human race. Whether he knew it or not, he needed her. She couldn't fight her feelings anymore.

He'd hidden things from her, but he hadn't outright lied. He'd had to be certain she could be trusted. So what if he was a warrior born in another century? Did it matter in the long run? He was here now. There was no way back. He was honorable, and he loved his family. That was a plus. Except for his lovely cousin. And there was something about him that made her feel as though she'd found the one thing she had searched for all her life.

She would accept whatever he would give, make the most of the time they had. After her heartbeat calmed, she slept. In the early hours of morning, she woke, still snuggled close to him. She'd dreamt of making love to him again. She wiggled closer, and he murmured her name, tightening his arms around her. Bree ran her hand over his chest, and the muscles quivered in his sleep. She worked her way down his flat stomach, dragging her fingers through the arrow of hair until she met firm, hard flesh. His body tensed as he woke.

"Mmmm."

Her hand slid lower, detouring over his thighs before coming back to the parts that made him groan. He started to turn, but before he could move, she climbed on top, sitting astride him, knees digging into the mattress. She rubbed against him until his breath grew ragged. He clutched her hips and tried to lift her, but she snared his hands and planted them on her breasts. He groaned again, hands kneading, hips thrusting. "Have a care, lass. I'm dying here."

She smiled and let go of his hands. He lifted her hips, impaling her body on his.

━━◦◦◦━━

"They died the year I was suspended?"

Sean sighed and folded his hands. "I didn't want to ruin your homecoming with sadness."

"How did they die?" Faelan asked. "Tavis's grave-stone said he was buried at sea."

"There was a shipwreck on the way home."

"From America? From coming to help me?"

Sean nodded.

Tavis had died trying to save him. Faelan had to swallow before he could speak. "Ian?"

"He survived, but your father died around the time Tavis did."

"How?"

Sean lowered his gaze. "There was heavy fighting after Druan's virus was destroyed. The Underworld was in chaos. Even retired warriors were caught in the battle."

His whole family had paid for his failure. His whole clan. The whole world. He wouldn't let her suffer, too. She wasn't even his.

━━◦◦◦━━

Bree hid behind a rosebush, watching Faelan race across the field beside a huge black stallion, a descendent of Nandor. The horse must be holding back, because they ran neck and neck for the length of the field. At the end, they slowed. Faelan swung onto the stallion's back, and the horse reared, front paws dancing in the air. Faelan threw back his head and gave a fierce shout that sent shivers through Bree's body. The stallion lunged forward, and horse and rider galloped like the wind, hair and mane flying, melded together, man and beast, an image she'd take to her grave.

She watched as he brought the horse toward the stable, shading her eyes from the midday sun. "Hi," she said, stepping onto the path. She blushed, thinking about last night. He hadn't talked to her all day. If there hadn't been so much activity at the castle, warriors arriving every few minutes, she would have thought he was avoiding her.

He frowned and jumped off the horse, affording her a good look at his kilt-clad legs. He led the horse past her without a glance.

"That was amazing," Bree said to the back of his head.

"I have to take care of the horse." He picked up a bucket of brushes and kept walking, leaving her gaping after him. Not even a hello, how are you, did you sleep well after I spent my body in yours? Mr. Hyde was back.

Had she been too bold last night? Was he just preoccupied? Confused, she turned and trudged toward the house. She looked back once and saw him staring at her. She knew that frown. She'd worn it many times herself. It wasn't preoccupation. It was regret.

Sean's wife, Coira, was in the kitchen, trying to pull a man away from her stove.

"Come join us, Bree," she said, voice tinkling with laughter. "Rescue me from this rogue." She swatted the man with her dish towel, and he turned. He was stunning—weren't they all? Tall, muscular, dark hair a little lighter than Faelan's, and he was wearing a kilt. "This is Ronan. He's Faelan's... let's see...

great-great-great-nephew on his brother Ian's side. Is that right? Oh, well, Ronan, meet Bree. She's the one who brought Faelan home to us."

"Bree, huh? You've caused quite a *bree*."

"In Gaelic, that means *a great disturbance*," Coira explained.

Ronan moved forward, lithe as a tiger, and took her hand. "Nice to meet you, Bree. Ah, sorry," he said pulling back. "Bacon grease. Coira's kindly fixing me breakfast for lunch." He snagged Coira's towel and wiped Bree's hand first, then his own, leaving her breathless.

"Nice to meet you too."

"We'll be forever grateful for what you've done. In fact, I'd say the entire planet is indebted to you. Not that they'll ever know."

"I have to admit it was an accident," she said politely, her thoughts still with Faelan.

"So you were searching for treasure and found the Mighty Faelan instead?" He smiled. "I hope you're ready for fame. They'll be telling this story for generations to come."

Fame? She'd always been obsessed with legends, now she would become part of Faelan's. Her story would be told and passed down, and someday, maybe a hundred and fifty years from now, someone would stumble across it and wonder if such a thing could happen.

"Ronan just got back from Ireland." Coira turned the bacon sizzling in the pan.

"You're a warrior?" Bree asked.

Something dark flashed behind his eyes, fading just as fast. "Until something persuades me otherwise." He grinned mischievously and leaned closer.

"If he stares into your eyes, ignore him. He knows it's too soon."

"Too soon for what?" Bree asked.

"To find his mate."

"You think you'll find her by looking into a woman's eyes?" Bree smiled, their frivolous banter soothing her gloomy mood.

"They know their mates at first sight." Coira pinched Ronan's arm lightly as she passed. "She must be from one of the clans, Ronan, you know that. It's an excuse for him to look at bonny lasses," she told Bree. "If he actually saw the sign, he'd run so fast there'd be no catching him. There was that one cousin from England. He stared at that lass every time he saw her, even knowing he wouldn't see anything." She gave Ronan a mild disapproving look. "I doubt it stopped him."

Ronan's grin turned wicked, and Bree doubted it had either. "At first sight?" she asked, confused.

"Aye," Coira said. "They know their mates as soon as they see them, in most cases, usually after their duty is finished, when they go on a different kind of hunt altogether, for a mate, not a demon. It's always a distant cousin or someone from another clan."

"Why?"

"Warriors can't marry outsiders," Coira said. "It's clan law. We have to keep the lines pure. There's too much at stake."

Ronan smiled. "We don't have to worry about divorce."

Bree's head rattled as if she'd head-butted Coira's iron skillet. She struggled to keep her voice light. Faelan had known all along nothing could come of this thing between them and never once bothered to mention it.

Ronan grinned and leaned closer. "But one never knows where a distant cousin might turn up."

Faelan came in and found them that way, Ronan's hands on either side of Bree's face, noses so close they were almost touching. Faelan's face looked as volatile as a thundercloud. Served him right, with Sorcha hanging all over him like a cat in heat, when he wouldn't give Bree the time of day.

"You must be Faelan." Ronan reached for Faelan's hand and then clapped him on both shoulders. "Welcome home, brother. You're a legend here, you know. Not one that most believed, but a legend, nevertheless. I've just got back from Ireland. I can help you battle Druan. We'd wondered where he was lurking these days. If you have the time, I want to hear this fantastic tale."

Tension filled the air as warriors gathered from near and far. The friendly homecoming was over. It was time to focus on the mission the clan had carried out since the beginning of time, protecting the world. A world most people—including Bree, until a few days ago—didn't know needed saving. Keeping their normal, unenlightened lives safe from demons running around disguised as their neighbors, co-workers, and friends. Bree had learned demons were responsible for most of the diseases and viruses she'd always considered an ugly part of life. Wars, famine, natural disasters, all orchestrated from hell. It was as if her entire existence until now had been lived in a vacuum.

Ronan fell in step as she walked toward the library. "You look a bit nervous."

"Are you kidding? I have to walk in there and tell them what I know about Russell. How many people can say they've been engaged to a demon?"

"More than you'd think." He stepped aside and allowed her to enter first, then whispered close to her ear, "Don't they say you should picture people in their underwear?" He glanced around the room, where most of the warriors, including Ronan, wore kilts. "Guess you'll have to picture them without…" He gave her a devilish wink. Bree ignored Faelan's brooding stare and politely refused Ronan's offer to find her a place to sit. He squeezed her shoulder and moved to the back of the room. Still smiling, her gaze connected with Faelan's. Something akin to despair crossed his face before he glanced away. What had happened? If she hadn't seen him in the darkened room and smelled his intoxicating scent, she'd have thought someone else had slipped into her bed and ravished her.

Several times now he'd made love to her without protection, although she initiated the last. It seemed out of character for him, with his sense of propriety, to risk having a child with a woman he could never marry.

The room had already filled with warriors, all male, except for Sorcha. Bree hadn't met any other female warriors yet. She'd learned they were far fewer than male warriors. The house had been bustling all day with arrivals, some coming after news of Faelan, but others already en route because of Bree's call so soon after Angus's message.

She took one of the few empty seats near the blazing fire, settling between Tomas and Brodie, the warriors she and Faelan had met when they first arrived. Brodie glanced over, and his sheepish grin confirmed a man's suspicion that he was the one who'd gotten her drunk. Both warriors were tall and strong, with ready smiles, but underneath the charm lay deadly skill.

Faelan sat on a large leather sofa between Shane and Niall, warriors descended from Faelan's sister, Alana. Niall, with a golden buzz cut and arms as big as a man's thighs, looked like he could take on an army by himself. Shane was tall and slim, quiet but alert.

There must be some unwritten code that warriors be gorgeous or beautiful, Bree thought, looking at Sorcha lounging on an oversized leather love seat, flirting with Jamie, a warrior who'd just arrived. Maybe the warriors' beauty was part of their defense, luring the demons until they could get close enough to grab them.

They all wore talismans, some Bree could see, some hidden by their shirts. The talismans were all similar, made out of the same metal, held on a thin leather cord, except Sorcha's, which she wore on a chain. And they were all armed, despite being in a castle in the middle of hundreds of acres, surrounded by well-trained guards.

Bree was included in the meeting, since she was the one who'd known Druan best in his human form and the one who freed Faelan. Sean introduced Faelan and Bree to the warriors they hadn't met then turned the meeting over to Faelan, who explained to those who hadn't heard, how he discovered the war Druan was trying to incite was a cover for his virus. He told of the night he'd planned to put Druan in the time vault, pausing to clear his throat when he spoke about the urgency, not having time to wait for his brothers.

Bree would have thought these warriors had seen almost everything, but not a sound was uttered. Even the ones honing and polishing weapons sat spellbound as Faelan described seeing the other three demons of old riding with Druan, how he'd felt the blow to his head, then awoke what he thought was a moment later to Bree's shocked gaze and found himself in another time.

Curious faces turned to her, and she saw almost everyone in the house, even those who weren't warriors, had crowded around the door listening to his story. There must have been a dozen questions at once, everyone wanting to know about the legendary demons, why Faelan hadn't been killed, why he'd been sent alone.

Conall, a young warrior who couldn't be a day over twenty, asked her with a gentle smile, "How did you know where Faelan was hidden?"

Bree faced the room of warriors and opened her mouth, but nothing came out. Ronan coughed once, and when she looked at him, he waggled the bottom of his kilt and winked. Bree couldn't help smiling. From the corner of her eye, she saw Faelan glance at Ronan and frown. She wouldn't dare think of Faelan's kilt. She knew all too well what was under there.

"I found my great-great-grandmother's journal. She wrote about a visitor who thought there was a lost treasure hidden nearby. We know now he was someone the clan sent. I'd also found the map he drew. When I saw the crypt was missing on the map, I knew it was important. I think I've always known that crypt was special. It's haunted me since I was a child."

"Has it now?" Sean asked, watching her.

"I've always found it... disturbing." An image

formed in her mind, a little girl reaching for the burial vault with bloody hands. Bree pushed the thought away and focused, describing how she'd believed the missing treasure was hidden inside the burial vault and discovered the locked chest. The three days she spent trying to open it, and the shock of finding Faelan. She then talked about the dreaded part. Russell. How charming he'd been, how dark and disturbing he became at the end. It was embarrassing to admit to these brave warriors that she'd been engaged to a demon, but they needed to know if they were going to fight this battle.

"How do you know Russell is Druan?" Duncan asked.

"Druan sent halflings to the house. We traced their vehicle to his castle. I thought he'd captured Faelan, so I sneaked in and saw Russell talking to an old man."

Niall, in the process of taking a drink of water, spewed it all down his shirt. "*You* sneaked into the demon's castle to rescue the Mighty Faelan?" He turned to Faelan. "Sounds like you got yourself a warrior." He chuckled as he wiped his mouth. Most of the others joined him, except Faelan. Even Sorcha wore a look of respect.

"Maybe the old man was the demon, or someone else inside," Tomas said, next to Bree.

"Russell's description matches how Druan looked as Jeremiah," Faelan said. "And Druan's too vain to take on an old body."

"Most of them are," Duncan muttered. "Makes sense he would target Bree. He'd need access to the place."

Sorcha crossed one booted leg. "Were you and Druan lovers? If you mated, you could've had halflings. I assume Faelan filled you in on what an unpleasant quandary that would have presented."

Bree's bitch alarm went off. There was some relevance, but she doubted it was the reason for the question. Sorcha was a bitch on the surface, but Bree had a feeling her behavior was a cover for something else. "There were no children," Bree said, holding Sorcha's gaze until the female warrior blushed and squirmed in her seat.

Duncan watched Sorcha's cheeks warm, and he leaned back with a satisfied smirk. Faelan looked like he might throw up.

The uncomfortable moment was averted when Ronan walked into the room wearing jeans, apologizing that he'd arrived late. Bree looked at the back of the room where Ronan sat in his kilt, polishing his sword. There were two of them? Faelan had told her twins ran in the clan. God help the female population.

"Faelan, Bree, this is Declan, Ronan's twin," Sean said. He asked Declan, "How did the battle go?"

"I got him in the vault," the handsome warrior said, "but he was a whiner."

"I hate the whiners," Niall agreed. "I'd rather have one fight to the death."

Including Bree in his welcome, Declan walked over to Faelan and clasped his hand. "The legend lives." He searched Faelan's face with wonder. "Welcome home. I've heard stories about your suspension since I was a lad, and I have to admit, I believed they were fables the trainers made up to keep us in line. 'Pay attention. Don't underestimate the demons. Remember what happened to the Mighty Faelan,'" Declan said, his voice theatrically gruff.

There were chuckles and commiserating nods from the others as Faelan grimaced.

"Soon the legend will be the Mighty Faelan on wheels," Brodie said. "You think he's good with a sword? You should see him drive. Left Tomas in the dust."

"Like you weren't right beside me," Tomas grumbled.

Bree had watched them racing their vehicles over the fields like little boys playing with toy cars. Faelan learned fast.

"I would be honored to help you fight Druan," Declan said, "but now I want to hear this story. I've heard at least five versions in the last twenty-four hours. My cell phone hasn't stopped ringing. A warrior in Sweden said he heard Faelan had found the virus and had it in the time vault with him all along."

"You've just missed it, but it wouldn't hurt us all to hear it again, so we're clear on the facts." Sean waited for Bree to agree. She pulled out a smile and nodded at the grand opportunity to relive her stupidity before an audience of superheroes.

"Wait up. Anna's right behind me, and Cody MacBain's with us. I know they'll want to hear this too," Declan said.

"Cody MacBain's the one who suspended that demon of old last year," Tomas whispered to Brodie, his voice hushed with admiration.

"Two legends in one room. It's enough to give a man an inferiority complex," Brodie replied.

A woman with black hair and the most incredible turquoise eyes Bree had ever seen stepped into the room. She was followed by a dark-haired man that made Bree's jaw drop. His eyes were intense, radiating danger. He scanned the room, gaze settling on Faelan before moving to her. The room faded, and Bree saw a wispy image of a woman standing next to the man. Not Anna. This woman was blond, her green eyes dull with pain and loss and fear, and she bore a scar. A letter carved into her skin.

The room resurfaced as the vision faded. Bree was slumped against Brodie, who stared at her, his expression puzzled. Only he and Tomas had noticed.

"Sorry," she whispered. "Too much wine last night."

"I told you that you were overdoing it, but do you ever listen to me?" Tomas quipped.

Brodie blushed as red as his hair but continued to watch Bree.

"I think most of you know Cody MacBain from America," Declan said. "He's here looking for Angus."

Cody nodded to everyone, then to Faelan, the intensity in his eyes replaced with curiosity and respect. "There isn't a warrior alive who hasn't heard of the Mighty Faelan. Can't say I believed you were real." He shook Faelan's hand and nodded to Jamie, whom he seemed to know. Sorcha scooted closer to Jamie, offering Cody a seat.

Anna greeted the warriors and approached Faelan. Before he could jump up, she leaned down and shook his hand. Her white T-shirt lifted as she bent. Bree could see symbols on Anna's back, similar to Faelan's, but starting above her hips and opening to a vee below her waist.

She rose, and every male eye followed as she moved to sit cross-legged on the floor in front of Bree. Every male except Faelan, still staring at Bree, his face a maze of secrets, and Duncan, glaring at Sorcha, who preened between Jamie and Cody like a cat who'd stolen the cream.

Brodie tapped Anna's shoulder, and when she turned, he gazed hard into her eyes.

"Not in this lifetime, Brodie."

"Humph. You never know."

"I'd dive into a volcano first."

"Spoilsport. The snake wasn't real."

"Put another one in my bed, and you won't be, either."

"What'd I tell you?" Tomas muttered, nudging Brodie.

"Watch out for this trickster," Anna said to Bree, then glanced around the room as Brodie mumbled about people not having a sense of humor. "Where's Angus?"

Duncan dragged his gaze from Sorcha. "He's not here. Last time he checked in, he was looking for you. Said he'd see you back here. He was upset, wouldn't say what it was about."

"He tried to call me, but I'd didn't have my phone."

"You? With no phone?" Brodie said.

"The demon I was battling ate it."

"That's two phones you've had eaten in the past six months," Brodie said. "What are you doing, trying to choke the demons to death?"

Anna rolled her eyes and ignored him. "Angus's message said he needed to meet me. It was urgent. I thought he'd be here."

"So did I," Cody said. "Angus contacted us and said he'd discovered something unbelievable. Something that would affect all the clans, but he'd blown his cover. He needed us to hide it."

"What did he find?" Shane asked. "We know it wasn't the key. Bree had that."

Cody shook his head. "He didn't say. Anna thinks it might've had something to do with the *Book of Battles*."

"Several months ago we started looking into the disappearance, but I got busy with my next demon and had to put the search aside. When I went to Angus for an update, he said he'd discovered some things, but didn't want to say anything until he was sure. You know Angus."

"That lad could find a mystery in thin air," Sean said. "But we've already found the *Book of Battles*."

"You have it here?" Anna asked, her turquoise eyes so brilliant they seemed to glow.

"No. Faelan found it in Bree's attic."

"It's hidden safely away," Faelan said, but he looked uneasy.

"What was it doing in America?" Declan asked.

"I have no idea, unless McGowan or Quinn brought it," Bree said.

"Who's McGowan?" Declan frowned, making him look even more like Ronan.

"Uh, he was the Seeker who went to America with Quinn," Sean explained.

"I thought… ah, I see," Declan said.

"Angus didn't say what he found, but he mentioned a gathering," Cody said. "Since I was the closest, I was supposed to meet him before he left for Scotland. He didn't show up and I figured he was headed here. I ran into Declan and Anna on the way."

"Coira, see if you can get Angus on his cell phone," Sean said, rubbing his forehead.

"Where was this gathering?" Bree asked.

"I'm not sure, but I was supposed to meet Angus in Albany."

"Albany? Maybe Angus did bring the time vault."

Faelan explained to the newcomers about the time vault he found hidden in the chapel cellar.

"He was acting weird lately," Tomas said. "Kept hiding his notebook every time anyone came near. I got a glimpse. He'd written something about a league."

"This is getting more troubling all the time," Sean said, drumming his finger against his kilted knee.

"There was a conference in Albany a couple of days ago," Bree said. "Some kind of new-world-order thing that had all the hotels booked. The woman at the bed and breakfast where we stayed said the people were strange. And a lot of suicides and crimes have taken place in the last few days. We know Druan's castle is near there. The conference must have had something to do with the gathering Angus was watching."

"New world order, my ass," Niall said, earning a glare from Coira, who was standing by the door. "All the demons want is chaos."

"I suspect Bree's right. The one I just suspended mentioned Druan by name," Declan said. "Yelled something about retribution, then clammed up."

Ronan laid his sword across his lap. "A few months ago I suspended a demon in Prague. He said something about a reckoning. Didn't make sense at the time."

"He may be referring to Druan's virus. How badly was the first virus damaged?" Faelan asked Sean.

"My memory isn't what it was, but I got the impression the virus was useless."

"It's been more than a century since then," Faelan said. "I'm guessing it's ready."

"Why didn't he kill you and be done with it?" Anna

asked. "Why miss an opportunity to kill the Mighty Faelan? Could he have had some other use for you?"

"If he somehow found out about the talisman's power, he would've known he'd be home free with Faelan and his talisman imprisoned in the time vault," Cody said. "But if he'd killed Faelan, the talisman would've been reassigned."

"That's a bloody scary thought," Niall said. "If the demons know the secrets of our time vaults and talismans, we're in a world of hurt."

"Blimey, I hope not," Sean said.

"Could be he's like our Brodie here and likes to pull pranks," Coira said, giving the warrior a mild, reproving glance. Bree wasn't the only one complaining about being too drunk for the amount of wine consumed.

"You think Druan did it as a joke?" Conall asked.

"We were thinking it was his way of getting revenge," Faelan said, glancing at Bree.

Two glances and a few glares since she'd given him her body and soul. At least he'd acknowledged her existence.

"It'd have to be one hell of a vengeance to wait that long." Cody moved his thumb over the outline of the talisman showing under his cotton shirt.

"He's vain enough to want me to witness him release the virus," Faelan said. "His final triumph."

"I'd like to think he doesn't know about time vaults or how long before they'll open," Duncan said. "But it's possible his virus has been ready for years, and he's been waiting for you, which would make him pretty pissed off by now."

Faelan glanced at Bree, his eyes dark with worry.

Jamie folded his arms over his chest. "Wish I could be there for this battle, but I'll be in Virginia."

"No problem," Duncan said. "We have several warriors, and Cody's offered to stay and fight."

"I hope someone has an extra pair of jeans. I'm a little short on luggage," the dangerous-looking warrior said. Most of them wore T-shirts and jeans when they weren't wearing a kilt.

After Bree and Faelan had told the story again for Declan, Anna, and Cody, Bree escaped to the kitchen to help Coira, unable to bear Faelan ignoring her any longer.

The warriors spent the rest of the day locked in the library, strategizing battle plans. They didn't come out until Coira announced dinner. Most of them left to get ready for the trip they'd make in a couple of days. Those remaining moved to the large dining room, complaining loudly of empty stomachs.

"You should've stopped to eat," Coira scolded. "You've been doing this long enough to know you can't save the world on an empty belly."

Bree had helped Coira prepare the huge pots of mutton stew, with toffee pudding for dessert, but all she could manage was a few bites. Faelan seemed relieved to take a seat at the other end of the table, far away from her, nestled between Sorcha and Anna.

"So you're from New York?" a deep voice asked at her elbow.

Bree turned to Cody, who'd settled next to her, his polite smile not covering the pain in his intense, hazel eyes.

"Near Albany," she said, troubled, because she knew he had more pain to come.

"I live in Virginia, but I have a... friend who used to

live not far from there." His voice held no emotion, as if he'd trained himself to feel none.

She wanted to ask if his friend had blond hair and green eyes, but that would open a can of worms she knew nothing about. "You're part of this clan too?"

"Yes. My family's been in America most of my life. We had a mission there."

What kind of mission lasted a lifetime?

Just then, Sorcha leaned in and whispered something to Faelan. He smiled and turned to include Anna. How could a mere woman compete against modern-day Xenas? Bree had truly believed Faelan was different, but she'd done it again. The curse of the frogs.

"Everything okay?" Cody followed her gaze.

"Just overwhelmed."

"I can see that you would be." Cody took a bite of stew, chewed it slowly, and swallowed. "You've probably saved the world, you know. Keep that in mind if things get too bad," he said, glancing at Faelan again. "I've found distractions don't get rid of the problem, but if you think on your troubles too much, they'll eat you alive."

Bree saw Ronan watching her, his expression one of sympathy and concern. Was she a blasted open book? She stood to excuse herself, when a commotion sounded in the hallway.

A man burst through the door. Blood ran from his face, soaking his clothes. He swayed on his feet and looked around the table, staring at each one of them. He stopped at Sorcha. "Traitor." When he saw Faelan, his eyes widened, the whites garish against his blood-covered face. "You!" he gasped, and then collapsed.

Chapter 25

THE SILENCE WAS DEAFENING, SWALLOWED BY mayhem as chairs flew backward and everyone ran toward the fallen man. He lay on his side, with deep gashes running across his face and chest. It was impossible to tell his age because of the wounds.

"Angus... Oh, Angus," Coira wailed as everyone crowded closer, blocking Bree's view. "Get him to the infirmary. Where's Niall? Never mind, Duncan, Faelan carry him. Gently. Sean, call Doctor Gillum." The injured man was unusually tall, but the warriors lifted him as if he weighed nothing. At Coira's direction, everyone went into a kind of ordered pandemonium.

Bree didn't know how to help, so she started cleaning up the trail of blood. When she finished, she followed Coira's voice to a large infirmary. Coira and Anna hovered over Angus while the others watched in silence. He lay still as death.

Faelan moved next to Bree, watching as blood was cleaned from the warrior's face. "Coira's a nurse," he said, slipping his warm hand into Bree's. Her fingers closed around his, grateful for the comfort. Immediately Faelan looked down at their linked hands in surprise. "Pardon me." He pulled free, moving away to where Sorcha motioned by the door. She whispered something in Faelan's ear, and they slipped from the room.

Bree's desire to scream fled as her attention came

back to the wounded man. The floor slid under her feet, and she grabbed for the nearest solid object. With the blood cleaned from his face, she recognized Angus—Mr. Smith from the bed and breakfast. No wonder she'd sensed danger surrounding him. He was a warrior trying to save the world. She'd sensed he was in trouble, washed her hands of it, and walked away. She pried her fingers from the back of Cody's shirt, but he hadn't noticed. His face was drawn with guilt. She wanted to tell him about her vision, but he turned and left.

Angus moaned, and his eyes fluttered open. He stared at Bree, lips moving as he struggled to speak. His bloodied hands clenched the table as he tried to rise. Two warriors stepped forward to help Coira settle him, blocking Bree's view. Anna leaned closer, putting her ear close to his mouth. When Bree could see him again, Angus's eyes were closed, and he lay unmoving. Had he recognized her? Why did he look so alarmed?

The worried crowd dispersed as Dr. Gillum arrived. Bree headed for her bedroom wondering if she could have saved Angus and still seething with jealousy, despite the fact that Faelan had chosen her bed last night and not Sorcha's.

If a warrior's mate was destined, Bree's resentment should be toward a woman long dead, a woman who had lost her mate without ever knowing he lived. Who was this woman buried in the cold ground, who'd never even met her mate, who should've been the mother of Faelan's children? Where did that leave him? Or had a mate been chosen from the time he would awake in, like Sorcha?

His family seemed to think so, from the way Bree had

seen them whispering over the pair of warriors. She had to face the truth. Her time with Faelan was over. It was probably best. She wasn't ready for a relationship, much less an intense one, and there would be no other kind with him.

She rounded the corner, stopping short. Faelan stood with his back to her, outside Sorcha's room. Long, red-tipped fingernails moved up his arm as Sorcha drew him closer to her door. How could a woman kill demons and still look like she'd just gotten a manicure? The door opened, and Faelan put a hand on Sorcha's back, ushering her inside.

Bree's heart felt like a wrung-out sponge. She had a sudden longing for home and Jared. Maybe he'd gotten back from his trip. She walked to the phone and punched in the number. "Is Jared there?" she asked, when a man's shaky voice answered.

"Who's this?"

"Bree Kirkland. Is this Jared's uncle?"

There was silence and then a whisper. "You shouldn't…" A noise sounded in the background, and he spoke louder. "Here he is."

"Bree." Jared's voice slid over her like a warm hug. "Hey. How's your trip?"

"Great. But I miss home. How's everything there?"

"Fine," he said. He didn't sound fine. He sounded worried. "I met with my backers. They're on hold for the moment."

"I'll be home in a day or so."

"That soon? I wish you'd stay longer. At least until they catch the killer. Peter's not eager for you to come back either. Besides, Scotland is nice this time of year."

"You've been here?"

"Years ago. Seems like another lifetime. Are you making progress with the documents?"

"Yes… they're old family papers." It wasn't a complete lie. There was the map Faelan's brothers made, but she hated not telling Jared the whole truth.

"Sounds interesting. Wish I were there with you. Enjoy the job and the scenery. The house, and me, we'll be here when you get back."

Thoughts of Sorcha and Faelan, destined mates, and Angus's bloodied body made her want to bawl. "I miss you, Jared."

A noise sounded behind her, and she turned. Faelan stood there, his face tight. He'd changed to jeans. He must've given Sorcha a quickie. Bree turned her back to him. "I should go," she told Jared. "You're sure everything is okay?" There were so many things that could go wrong. Dead bodies, demons, and halflings.

"It's all good. I'll take care of things here, and we'll talk when you get back."

"Jared, be careful." She hung up and turned to blast Faelan, but she was alone.

Bree grabbed her coat and walked outside, following the stone path to the flower garden Coira had shown her earlier. She sat on the bench and tried to let the fragrant scents wash away images of Faelan naked in Sorcha's bed. Footsteps shuffled behind her.

"Couldn't sleep?" Sean asked, dropping next to her on the bench.

"I had a lot on my mind."

"I come here when I'm troubled. Helps me put things to right. Could be the scent of Coira's roses or maybe the night air. Gets a mite chilly in these parts."

"That's for sure." Bree shivered and pulled her light-weight wool coat closer. "Don't your legs get cold?" she asked, looking at his kilt.

"A bit. I usually wear trousers. Most warriors wear jeans when they're not here. The kilt draws too much attention. We have to protect the clan, protect what we do, and we don't want to announce our presence to the demons. But as soon as the lads come back, they put on the kilt."

"I'm not complaining," Bree said, smiling. She sobered. "How's Angus?"

Sean sighed. "Not good. Blessed idiot drove himself here."

"How did he get through the front gate?"

"He didn't. There's a hidden entrance, a tunnel that leads to the secret passages. Angus left his car there and walked."

"Why didn't he call someone?"

"His cell phone's missing."

"What do you think he meant about a traitor?"

"I don't know, but I fear there's something bad brewing. Cody said he'd felt it too. Even before Angus called him."

"What do you know about Cody?" Bree asked. She still needed to talk to him.

Sean watched her for a minute, and Bree knew he was judging what to tell her. "Fierce warrior. His brothers, too, from what I hear. They're private. I've heard their secrets run deep. Cody finished his duty a few weeks ago. Besides Faelan, Cody's the only warrior in recent times who's been assigned one of the ancient demons."

Bree remembered the danger emanating from him. She guessed the demons were happy he was retired. "But he offered to help fight?"

"Warriors can fight as long as they can hold a sword. They're encouraged to marry and have families after their duty is over, but some choose to serve for life."

"Do the talismans still work, even if a warrior is retired?"

"That they do. Why this interest in Cody?"

"I had a premonition, a vision, something about him. There was a woman with him. I think she's in trouble. I should warn him. Like I should've warned Angus."

"Angus?"

"I've seen him before. In New York, at the bed and breakfast where Faelan and I stayed. I sensed danger surrounding him, but I brushed it off. I didn't recognize him until Coira cleaned off the blood. I think he recognized me."

Sean grew quiet. "Have you had these feelings, these visions, before?"

"Since I was little. Usually about family or friends." When she was younger, after she'd learned about her sister, she'd believed it was her twin helping her from the other side.

"Anyone else in your family have these abilities?"

"I think my great-great-grandmother did. Are you thinking about Druan's castle and how I could see it?"

"It is peculiar."

"Maybe only warriors can't see it. It was right there, plain as day."

"Perhaps. There are many things we don't understand."

"That's a problem for me. I have to know things."

Sean chuckled. "So Faelan says."

At least Faelan was saying something to someone. It sure wasn't her. But her problems paled next to Angus's fight for life. Bree sighed. "Will you let me know how Angus is doing? If I'd said something, warned him, maybe this wouldn't have happened."

"Angus is hard-headed as a mule. Who's to say he would've believed you, anyway? You were a stranger to him. He's strong. Dr. Gillum is with him, and Coira. She's a fine nurse."

"It must be tough on the women."

"That's part of the reason warriors aren't to marry until their duty is over. Not to mention they don't need the distraction of a demon targeting a mate."

"What about the female warriors? Can they marry before their duty is up?"

He shook his head. "Same rules apply. It's frowned on, because of the danger involved, but there's plenty of time for raising a family after a warrior is done. It's not uncommon for a warrior to live well beyond a hundred years. We almost never get sick. Something in the genes. It's getting past the battles that's tricky." Sean patted her hand. "This has been a whirlwind for you, finding Faelan, getting thrown into the middle of all this. Most women wouldn't have taken it so well. You're strong, Bree Kirkland. It was good that you found him."

"I don't know. Maybe Sorcha should have…" Bree trailed off.

"No, I think it was best this way. Destiny. That's what it was, destiny," he repeated, almost to himself.

"Well, I thank you for your hospitality. I wish I had more time to see the sights, since this is my first trip to Scotland."

"Ah, there'll be plenty of time for that later. You're welcome back here anytime you want, lass. You see the size of this house. We've got plenty of bedrooms, and they're always ready. Warriors come and go like it's a train station. I hope we'll be seeing more of you." He studied her again, as if trying to decipher a code. "In fact, Coira will likely come fetch you if you stay away too long. She's taken a liking to you, as we all have. Now I'd best check on Angus and get these old bones off to bed."

"Good night, Sean. Oh, can I ask you something?"

"Aye, lass."

"You speak Gaelic?"

"I do, though we don't use the language much now."

"What does... let me see, I'm not sure I have this right. *Tha thu as do chiall*. What does it mean?"

Sean smiled. "Why don't you ask Faelan?"

"He won't tell me. He's the one who said it."

"Then I can't say as I blame him," he said, chuckling, with a twinkle in his eyes, "but I think I'll leave that telling to him."

Bree waited a minute before leaving the garden. The house was quiet. At the top of the steps, she turned the corner and saw Faelan enter her bedroom and close the door behind him. When she got over the shock, she began to seethe. Did he honestly think he could go from Sorcha's bed to hers?

Bree turned and headed back downstairs, wandering aimlessly for a while, trying to distance herself from anger and hurt. She ended up in the library, every bit as grand as Druan's. She sat at a table, staring at the pile of books Sean had given her to study, but her mind was too troubled to concentrate. She sank into an overstuffed leather chair near the low-burning fire and settled in for the night.

—∿—

A noise pulled Bree from her restless dreams. She opened heavy lids and saw Ronan leaning against the door, arms crossed over his chest, watching her. Or was it Declan? He wore Levi's and a black T-shirt. "Oh," she said, sitting up from her awkward position. Had she snored or drooled in her sleep?

"Ah, Sleeping Beauty awakes."

Ronan. There was that sexy lilt to his voice.

"How long have you been standing there?"

"Long enough to know you don't snore."

Thank God for small favors. "I fell asleep."

"Must have been a good book." He glanced from her bookless lap to the floor, but didn't comment. "I'd wager you're stiff as a board."

"More like a steel beam." She liked Ronan. He was easy to talk to, if you didn't get distracted by his body and face.

"It's not yet dawn. You could stretch out on a real bed."

Bree's stomach rumbled softly.

"Or we could raid the kitchen. I was headed there when I heard the moan."

"Moan?"

"You must have been dreaming." He gave her a grin that should've been outlawed.

"Do all warriors have Superman hearing?"

"Afraid so. The caped hero has nothing on us."

"He can fly."

"Well, there is that."

Bree rubbed her tummy. "I *am* hungry."

"Then let's see what treats Coira's hiding from me."

"She hides food from you?" Bree followed him out of the library.

"From all of us. Warrioring works up a hearty appetite."

She knew a warrior with a hearty appetite, she thought sadly. "Then lead on, and I'll blame it all on you."

He led her into the kitchen and flipped on a light. "I'd bet my dirk she's got cookies hidden somewhere." Looking around the big, cozy kitchen, he went straight to the refrigerator, where he reached up and grabbed a cookie jar hidden behind some boxes. It sounded like he groaned. "Shortbread. Coira makes the best." He took one, bit it, and held the rest to Bree's mouth. "Try it. Don't worry. I don't have cooties, and my hands are clean. I haven't scratched my ass all day."

She smiled and took a nibble. "That is good."

He took another and handed her the jar. "Coira says it's Faelan's mother's recipe."

Bree stopped chewing, but Faelan had already ruined her sleep; she wouldn't let him ruin her appetite too.

Ronan pointed to a cabinet. "Grab a couple of glasses, and I'll get the milk."

"You must spend a lot of time here."

He patted his flat stomach. "Does it show?"

Bree laughed. "I meant here at the house."

"This is a second home, like base camp, for all of us. Warriors from the clan travel all over the world, wherever we're sent, but we're always welcome here."

"I guess it's all the traveling that makes the accents so

hard to place. I can hear a hint of brogue, but no two are alike. Faelan sounds more like a Scot since he's gotten here. He'd started to sound modern."

"We pick up languages and dialects fast. It's part of our disguise, but the tongue knows when it's home." Ronan poured two glasses of milk and took a long drink of his.

"I suppose not having a definite accent makes it harder for a demon to find out where you live."

"Aye. We've gone to great lengths to protect our clan's location. It wouldn't be good if we were found out."

"Druan's castle is a duplicate of this one. Someone must know."

"Let's hope whoever it is, is dead."

They chewed for a few moments in silence. Bree reached for another cookie. "Ronan and Declan sound like Irish names, not Scottish."

"Celtic," Ronan said, wiping his mouth. "Mostly used in Ireland. My mother was Irish, like Faelan's. Many Scottish warriors find their mates in Ireland. My father named the first son…" His eyes shadowed. "My mother got to name the second. She didn't know she'd get two."

"You have an older brother? Is he a warrior?"

Ronan stared into his glass. "He died."

"I'm sorry." Bree dropped the subject, since he seemed uncomfortable discussing it. "Cody said he's from the Connor clan, but he lives in America."

"His family's been there a long time. Some secret mission. There are other warriors in America besides the Connor clan, but they all originated from Scotland. Warriors were sent to guard the new country. I've lived there the last few years myself, when I'm not hunting."

"In America?"

"Montana. I was in Alaska for a while. We had a warrior who went rogue. I needed some time to clear my head, so I volunteered. I chased him to Montana. Liked it there, so I stayed, as much as any warrior stays put. Last month I was given a demon in Ireland, so here I am."

"A warrior went rogue? They can do that?"

"Just like angels can fall. It's a choice."

"Like being a traitor?" she asked, and they both grew silent. Was he thinking of Angus's pronouncement?

"Like being a traitor," Ronan agreed.

"So what did you do with this rogue warrior?"

He studied a cookie then met Bree's gaze. "That's nothing for a bonny lass to worry about."

Bree traced the circle on her glass. "Then tell me something else. What's with Sorcha and Duncan?"

"Don't tell me you can feel the tension." He rested his elbows on the counter. A look of pain crossed his face. Did he have a thing for Sorcha too? "Duncan's always been protective of her, but protecting Sorcha's like protecting a porcupine. She makes it hard for him. Hmmm, I think that was a pun."

Bree's face warmed. "Are they together?" she asked. "I mean this whole mate thing?"

"Duncan's never said anything, but for his sake, I hope not. I'd shoot myself first." Ronan handed Bree another cookie.

"Do you think Faelan and Sorcha could be..." Bree's voice hitched.

"Mates?" Ronan finished, watching her closely. "Does it matter?"

"I don't know. She seems attracted to him."

"Sorcha acts like that with all men. She does it to piss Duncan off."

"Why?"

"Who knows why Sorcha does anything. I don't know how he puts up with her. I'd throw her in Loch Ness and be done with her. As for Sorcha and Faelan being mates, there's been some speculation since she was to come and wake him, but that's about it. Speculation." He popped another cookie. "So life threw you for a loop, waking a warrior from another century. Not just any warrior, but the Mighty Faelan."

"It's been interesting."

"You two get along? I mean, he's living in your house, sleeping there…" His tone was deceptively casual. She suspected everything about Ronan was deceptively casual.

"I guess so. He didn't have much choice but stay, waking after a century with only the clothes on his back. Well, that and his dagger and talisman."

"That'll change soon enough. His money's been invested all this time."

"You're kidding."

"That's what Sean said. A century and a half. Not bad, huh?"

"Does Faelan know?"

"Don't know if Sean or Duncan mentioned it yet, with all the excitement."

"He'll be relieved. He hates depending on someone else. After this is over, he was going to get a job working with horses."

"He could buy a hundred horse farms. Half the stock here came from Nandor's line. Do you ride?"

"Me, on a horse? I have balance issues." Bree smiled.

"The cutest little boy offered to teach me to ride earlier. I've never seen so many happy kids."

"We breed like rabbits. When a warrior finds his mate, he can't think of anything else." Ronan grinned. "Keeps the clan supplied with plenty of warriors."

They munched in silence as Bree puzzled over Ronan's words. Was that what Faelan's appetite was about? Not a side effect from the time vault, but he'd met his mate? He was almost finished with his duty. Had he left behind a mate? He seemed guarded when she asked him about it earlier.

"Faelan speaks highly of you."

"He does?"

"That surprises you?"

"He's different lately."

"Stands to reason. He's got the world to save, demons to chase. And now we have mysterious time vaults popping up in cellars and castles vanishing into thin air." He rubbed his chest and winced. A dark spot on his shirt seemed to be growing.

"Are you bleeding?"

He glanced down. "It's just a scratch."

"Scratches don't bleed like that." She put her cookie down, moved closer, and reached for his shirt collar to peek at the wound. It was about two inches long, above his battle marks. "This is way more than a scratch."

"It's nothing. I'll throw a Band-Aid on it."

"Warriors heal fast, but it'll take more than a Band-Aid to cover that. I saw Coira put a first aid kit under the sink."

"Aye, nurse, but don't get too close. I haven't showered yet. I'd hate to overpower you with my manly scent."

Bree gathered the first aid kit and turned to find Ronan easing his T-shirt over his head. Jiminy Christmas! His chest was a work of art. His battle marks looked similar to Faelan's, but they ran in two rows down the center of his chest.

Bree examined the wound. "Don't tell me one of your girlfriends did this."

He lifted a dark brow. "Somebody's been telling tales. Just taking care of some unfinished business. It got a little messy."

"Angus?"

He nodded. "I tracked down the demons that attacked him. Three of them. They wouldn't say who ordered the attack. I'd say someone thought Angus knew something important."

"You went after them alone?"

"I fight solo." Ronan's jaw was hard. Guilt flashed in his eyes. He watched her clean his wound, and when he spoke, his voice was soft, as if the words came from a sacred place. "My older brother was killed by a demon. I was there but I couldn't save him."

Like Faelan and Liam. Did all warriors feel responsible for everyone around them? "I'm sorry." Bree wiped a drop of blood that ran down one of his marks, and her head started to buzz. "But you shouldn't go out alone." She covered the wound with antibacterial cream. "Getting yourself killed won't bring Cam back."

Ronan's whole body tensed. "How did you know about Cam?"

"Who?"

"Cam. My brother."

"You just told me."

"Not his name."

"I said his name? Are you sure?"

"Maybe I imagined it." He rubbed his eyes. "Old ghosts."

"Do you think those demons followed Angus here? He said something about a traitor. If they know where the house is—"

"I don't think they got that far. If they did, they won't be talking now. I have a hard time believing there was a traitor in the clan." But like Sean, Ronan looked more worried about the matter than he sounded.

"There you go," Bree said, smoothing the last piece of tape. "Next time, take someone with you."

"Thank you. Faelan's a lucky man. I am too, to have such a bonny nurse," he said, inspecting his new bandage, almost touching his talisman.

"Are all talismans different?"

"Aye. Some look similar, but no two are alike."

"I can't imagine wearing something so powerful around your neck. I mean one flash of Faelan's and those halflings were gone, right before my eyes."

Ronan's mouth dropped. "You saw the light from his talisman?"

"It was the most beautiful thing I've ever seen."

"You watched an engaged talisman? Bloody…" He stared at her, frowned, and shook his head. "The time vault must have messed it up. If you'd looked at the Mighty Faelan's talisman full strength, we wouldn't be sitting here swiping cookies. You, my bonny lass, would be dead."

"That's what Faelan said."

"His talisman has probably killed more demons than any warrior who's lived. He was the first warrior in two hundred years to be assigned one of the ancient demons, the only one to be assigned two of them."

"Why aren't they usually assigned?"

"They're too powerful. Cody MacBain's the only one who's been assigned one since Faelan."

"Who does the assigning?"

"Michael."

"This warrior? Where is he?"

"Oh, here and there." Ronan rubbed his stomach. "I think that last cookie was one too many."

"I should have stopped after the third." Bree replaced the first aid kit while Ronan put the cookie jar back. They rinsed the glasses and loaded them in the dishwasher.

"I know nothing about this." Holding his shirt in one hand, Ronan took her arm and led her from the kitchen. "Fairies," he whispered.

Bree giggled. "Or bogles."

"We'll blame it on Brodie."

"I think I'll try to sleep for a couple of hours," Bree said. "It's only six o'clock."

"I'll walk you up. I need some rest, myself." Ronan put an arm around her back as they walked up the stairs past Sorcha's door. Had Faelan gone back for another round after he'd found Bree's bed empty? "You speak Gaelic?"

"A bit."

"What does *Tha thu as do chiall* mean?"

"You're out of your mind."

"What?"

"That's what it means… *You're out of your mind.* Can't imagine where you heard that," he said, grinning.

She was out of her mind. For feeding Faelan, giving

him a bed, sleeping with him, when all he did was hide the truth. Before she and Ronan could say good night, her door flew open. Faelan stood in his underwear, glaring at them, mouth so tight she was afraid he'd grind his teeth to powder. His eyes blazed from Ronan's bare chest to his arm at Bree's back.

"You good here?" Ronan asked Bree.

"Fine," she grated. If he hadn't been there, she would've told Faelan what he could do with his glare.

"Good night then. Faelan," Ronan kept a straight face until he turned away. Bree saw him grin.

"Where've you been all night?" Faelan demanded before Ronan was out of hearing. "And why's he half naked?"

"Go ask him." She shoved past Faelan. If this was how things were in his day, treating a girl like he owned her one minute, like a leper the next, and bouncing from bed to bed, then he could go back.

Faelan shut the door, his arms stiff, hair mussed like he'd been sleeping. "What were you doing with him?"

Bree whirled on him. "Faelan, there were plenty of times in my own home when I would've been justified in saying this, but I didn't." She walked around him and opened the door. "I'm saying it now. Get out!" She put a hand on his chest and pushed him into the hall. He scowled and blinked as if she were the one being rude. He started to say something, but she shut the door in his face and locked it.

He was like the rest, a toad in a Prince Charming shell.

She stepped over his discarded jeans and T-shirt, changed her mind, picked them up, jerked open the door, and dumped his clothes at his feet. He was still standing there when she relocked the door. She crawled into bed without undressing. It was warm, and it smelled like him. He'd slept here. She buried her face in the dent his head had made, and soaked the pillow with tears, swelling her eyes, making her temples throb. When she finished crying, she got out of bed and rummaged in the side pocket of her suitcase for one of the sleeping pills she'd brought, since Faelan seemed nervous about flying. The sketchbook was there. She'd brought it on a whim, thinking she'd face her ghosts while Faelan faced his.

Bree's hands trembled as she opened the first page. An abyss of shadows and gloom rushed at her, and blocked memories loosed with each turn of the page. There were sketches of the graveyard and the crypt beneath the overhang of trees that looked more human than wood. Of a castle. This castle, or was it Druan's? A face looked out of a window, a monster with thick skin and sharp teeth, like that thing in the chapel, but worse. Bree as a little girl, reaching for the burial vault with bloody hands as a light glowed behind her.

Memories flashed in her head, like an old movie reel, becoming clear for the first time since that night. She remembered screaming for help, clawing at the blocked door until blood dripped from her nails. Then she'd heard the whispers, soothing her. Her sobs quieted, and she'd fallen asleep. She'd dreamed of the shiny man like she had so many times before. He was tall and beautiful and kind. He'd always told her she was special, that she had something great to find. This time he told her that her father was gone, but he'd sent someone else to protect her. He showed her a man's eyes. Beautiful, dark eyes. She'd awoken to yells and lights and a dozen searchers. After the commotion died down, her grandmother took her inside and explained that her father was dead. She never told her grandmother that she already knew. Bree turned the page and gasped.

Before she'd hidden the book, she'd drawn her protector's eyes.

Chapter 26

BREE AWOKE TO YELLS AND THE CLASH OF METAL. A battle! She bounded out of bed. Had the demons found them? She ran to the window overlooking a fenced area she thought was a riding ring. There were no horses. There were warriors, at least a dozen of them, practicing in the late morning mist hanging over the meadow. Most of the sparring men were dressed in kilts. Some fought with swords, lunging and sidestepping, others hand-to-hand combat.

Ronan stood bare-chested, holding a bow. He pulled an arrow from a quiver belted on his kilt. There was no way he could hit the target. It was a hundred yards away. He nocked the arrow and drew back, held for a second, then released. The arrow hit dead center of the bull's-eye. Cripes. Robin Hood had nothing on this guy.

Her gaze shifted, and she saw Faelan standing off to one side, a sword pointed to the sky. Like the others, he wore no shirt. Even this far away, she could see the muscles in his arms and back tense as the sword lowered and his body began to move in that flowing rhythm of power and grace. Poetry in motion.

She pulled herself from her stupor, gave her teeth a quick brushing, threw her hair into a ponytail, and left wearing wrinkled jeans and a long-sleeved green T-shirt. Over the cries and clash of metal, Bree heard more familiar sounds. The clink of dishes and pans accompanied Coira humming a tune. Breakfast smells filled the hall, stronger as Bree neared the kitchen. Coira was setting a buffet with the usual fare and others Bree didn't recognize.

"Good morning. I hope the noise didn't wake you."

"Do they always do this?"

"They have to stay ready for battle. You get used to it after a while."

"They look… amazing. I saw Ronan with a bow."

"No one can beat him at archery. He's almost a legend, like our Faelan," she added. "Do you want some breakfast? We eat late when they're practicing."

"Maybe in a bit. I think I'll wander outside."

Coira smiled. "It is an impressive display. All those braw lads. Oh, I remember when Sean was young." She patted her heart and sighed. "My, my."

Bree laughed with her and walked outside. The sounds grew louder and the testosterone thicker as she approached the field. Sorcha wasn't there. Faelan must have worn her out. Bree paused to watch Jamie throw Brodie onto his back, relieved to see he wore underwear beneath his kilt. "That'll teach you to fight wearing a skirt," Jamie teased. Brodie shot up and grabbed Jamie around the knees, and they both went down.

Faelan was still in the same spot, sparring now with Cody, who, like Jamie, wore jeans. The men circled each other like big cats, swords extended, movements controlled, precise. Metal clashed as the blades met, muscles shifting with each clang. Then, Faelan whirled and lunged, knocking Cody's sword from his hand.

"The Mighty Faelan lives," Cody said, retrieving his sword.

Faelan grinned and wiped the sweat from his forehead with his arm.

Just a show of teeth, and Bree's knees turned to water. She looked away before she forgot how angry she was.

At the back of the field, Tomas was fighting hand-to-hand with Anna. She flipped him over her head, landed behind him, and kicked out, catching him in the back of the knees. Bree grinned and wandered over to a table holding an assortment of weapons; knives, daggers, the bow Ronan had used, and a wicked-looking crossbow. A target was set up against several bales of hay.

She idly picked up a dagger, testing it in her hand. It felt like a crowbar, not an extension of her arm. She made sure no one was watching, drew back her arm, and let the dagger fly. It sailed over the target, and she heard a curse.

Ronan stepped out, chest glistening above his kilt, hair damp with sweat. He held the dagger in his hand. His bandage was gone and the gash was almost healed. "If you need more practice bandaging wounds, just ask, darlin'. In fact, if you feel the need to practice anything at all…"

"Sorry about the dagger."

"You're holding it wrong." Ronan moved behind her and placed the dagger in her hand.

"You don't have to do that."

"Please," he whispered. "I'm trying to look busy. I had only two hours' sleep. Niall's killing me." He put one hand on hers, pulling it back, slow and smooth. The heat from his body seeped through her, though the morning was cool. "Now, release, with your wrist like this." He demonstrated with his left hand. They practiced the move a few more times, Bree doing exactly as he said. As she released the dagger, she caught sight of Faelan coming toward them, face set like one of Druan's gargoyles. The dagger flew over the target a second time.

Niall stepped from behind it. "You throw like a lass." He turned the dagger sideways, tossing it to Ronan. "You hiding from me?" Niall asked, folding thick arms over his chest. His legs looked like tree trunks sticking out of his kilt. He had to be over six and a half feet tall, the only warrior she'd seen with a hairy chest.

"No." Ronan gave Bree a warning nudge.

"Sorry," Bree said. "I threw the dagger. Ronan's trying to show me how to do it, but it's not working like it did before." She frowned and looked at her hand. "When I killed that halfling, it felt different, like the dagger was part of my arm."

"You killed a halfling?" Ronan said.

"Faelan was fighting off a bunch of them after rescuing me. They had him trapped. I knew he was going to die, and I had his dagger." She shuddered, thinking how close the blade had come to his head. "I threw it at the one holding him. Hit him smack in the chest, and poof, he was gone."

Both warriors went slack-jawed. "The halfling disappeared?" Ronan said.

"Impossible," Niall muttered.

"It is?"

Ronan shook his head. "You said you saw the light from Faelan's talisman, but I didn't know—"

"She watched an engaged talisman?" Niall put his

hand over his massive chest, his expression wavering between horror and shock.

Faelan approached. "I need to talk to Bree," he said, addressing Ronan and Niall.

Still looking dazed, Ronan raised a questioning brow at her. When she nodded, he nudged Niall, and they walked away.

"How the hell could she…" Niall's words faded as they moved toward the fence. She could see their animated gestures and puzzled stares and knew they were talking about her.

"We need to talk," Faelan said, his voice expressionless.

She stared at the trickle of sweat running like a lazy river between his battle marks. She wished he'd worn a shirt with his kilt. She wanted to tell him what she'd discovered in the drawings, but she was too angry. "I don't," she said and turned away. Ronan and Niall pretended to study the warriors still sparring on the field.

Faelan moved in front of her, gripping her arm, his features like his voice, recognizable but fake, as if he wore a mask of himself. "I shouldn't have jumped you like I did."

"Are you referring to last night or the night before?"

"Both."

Now he was going to tell her it shouldn't have happened. She knew it shouldn't, but she didn't want to hear it from him. She pulled her arm back and tried to step around him, but he stopped her again.

"When I saw you with Ronan—no matter, I haven't had much of a chance to talk to you in the last day or so, but—"

"Cut the crap. I woke up alone, cleaned up the sticky

mess *you* left," she said, jabbing his chest, "and you don't even bother to say hello or thank you. Go find Sorcha and leave me alone."

Ronan and Niall weren't even pretending to watch the field now.

Faelan trapped her hand in his. "Bree, listen to me. Angus is dead. I just found out." Faelan's face was real now, somber.

Bree's fingers tightened on his. "Dead? No." She pulled away, walked a few steps, and slumped against a maple tree, watching a dying leaf float to the ground. She'd killed Angus. She hadn't warned him, and now he was dead. She wanted to lean into Faelan, feel his heart pounding, safe. For now.

"I think it would be best if you left."

She looked up. "What?"

"I want you to leave here," he said, the mask back in place.

Leave? The idea made a few passes around her head, looking for a place to land. He was dumping her. Bree was familiar with dumping. She'd dumped and been dumped, but it had never made her feel like her lungs had been pureed. It wasn't that she'd awakened him and helped him fit into his new world or fed and clothed him when she should've had him arrested. Or that she'd lent him money and turned him loose in her Mustang. She'd put her life in his hands. Given him her body, her heart, and he was throwing her out of Scotland. Out of his life.

"You should be away from this. It's too dangerous. Go someplace safe, maybe your mother's."

In male speak it meant he didn't need the guilt of

seeing his folly every time he bumped into her. He'd known all along she wasn't a suitable mate, but now he had Sorcha to quench his lust.

She bit her lip to keep it from trembling, hoping he thought she was upset over Angus. Sorcha walked across the grass carrying her sword, but stopped when she caught sight of them. Bree moved past Faelan, holding her head high, and past Sorcha, who watched with an inscrutable look on her face. Bree had to get away from this place. Away from him. Every man in her life had let her down, even her dad, although dying hadn't been his fault.

No. Not every man.

There was still one she could count on.

<div style="text-align:center">~~~</div>

Faelan stood outside Bree's door, sweat running down his chest. He'd tried sparring with Brodie to work off his frustration, but it hadn't helped. He had to make her understand. He raised his hand to knock and flinched as something crashed inside. It was followed by cursing and a flurry of banging and stomping.

"What time does your flight leave?" a male voice asked. Faelan felt the doorknob dig into his palm. What the hell was Ronan doing in Bree's room?

"Six a.m. I'll get a room for tonight," Bree's muffled voice said.

"You want me to come with you?"

Come with her? Faelan pressed his ear to the wood, straining to hear her response. All he heard was a smacking sound. Was that bastard kissing her?

Faelan flung open the door. It bounced against the wall

and almost smacked him in the face when he charged inside. Ronan was half naked, as usual, and there wasn't an inch between him and Bree. Both of them turned, and Bree's face frosted over. She stood on tiptoe, gave Ronan a kiss on the cheek, and snatched her suitcase.

"Thank you, Ronan, for everything. I'll call you later." She stalked past Faelan, her eyes liquid with pain.

For *everything*? What had he bloody given her? Faelan stared at Bree's retreating back and Ronan with his arms crossed, eyes hard. Faelan wanted her to leave, but not like this. He hurried after her. He'd throw Ronan out a window later.

Faelan raced down the opposite hall, shoving past several warriors who looked up in surprise. Rounding a corner, he ran into Conall, the young warrior he'd practiced with earlier. "I need your help."

After a hurried conversation, Faelan followed Bree outside to where Anna's car was waiting. "Let me carry that." He reached for her suitcase and she whirled, eyes ablaze. The corner of the case grazed his groin, and he grunted, doubling over as she turned and stomped to the car. He hobbled after her. "Wait, we have to talk," he wheezed.

Bree flung her luggage inside Anna's car. "Talk." Her expression was dour, as if she'd been sucking lemons. "You lie to me, treat me like a leper, and now you want to talk? You're just like those demons you hunt. A handsome form hiding a troll. I risked my life for you, fed you, clothed you, tended your wounds. I found your family. I gave you everything I had to offer, and you shoved it all back in my face. There's nothing left to say."

She climbed in the car and slammed the door. Anna,

standing by the driver's door, gave him a cool stare and got in. The car sped down the driveway, leaving Faelan standing there holding his groin. He was still there when Conall's car rolled by.

A troll? She'd called him a troll? He turned and saw the flash of faces disappear from the window behind him and warriors watching from the field. "Mule-headed woman." He started toward the stable. Horses didn't nag or bombard a man with hundreds of questions and look at him with accusing eyes that wrapped his heart in layers of guilt.

"You gonna let her go?" Ronan asked, coming up behind Faelan. He'd put on a shirt, at least.

"Aye." Faelan debated on knocking the scowl off Ronan's face. Instead, he clenched his fists and trudged toward the stall of the black stallion that reminded him of Nandor.

"I could go with her. For protection," Ronan said, his face hard. "Then meet you in Albany."

Faelan turned and moved inches closer to the tall warrior. "She doesn't need any more of your bloody *help*. Or anything else you have to offer." He'd heard about Ronan's exploits with the female sex. It appeared he was trying to add Bree to his list of conquests.

Ronan stepped forward, bringing them nose to nose. "She's sure not getting anything from you. Everything she's done for you, and you throw her out like yesterday's trash. I don't care if you are a legend. She deserves better than that."

The horse skittered away, sensing the tension.

"I'm taking care of her," Faelan said, moving to steady the stallion. Conall would keep an eye on her.

"What you're doing is acting like an ass. She spent last night in a chair because you were in her bed."

"I'll wager you had a solution."

"What if I did? Unless she's your mate, you have no say in the matter. And you sure as hell have no say over where I sleep."

Faelan knew if he didn't leave now, one of them would end up on the floor. He opened the door to the stall. "I'm going for a ride before I do something *you'll* regret." His groin still ached, but it would serve as a reminder that women and warriors didn't mix.

"I liked you better when you were in the time vault." Ronan punched the stable wall and walked away.

Faelan stayed out all day, riding the horses, grooming the horses, complaining to the horses. He watched the moon rise and considered waiting for the sun, anything to keep him away from family members and warriors who kept popping around corners and out from behind trees like jack rabbits, their dark looks heaping on the guilt.

Sorcha was the only one who understood.

The next morning, his stomach forced him to breakfast. The smells of eggs, bacon, beef sausage, potato scones, and kippers were ruined by Ronan's black glare. Anna, Brodie, and Shane didn't look any happier. No one spoke but Coira.

"Faelan, I found this in Bree's room. She must have forgotten it." Coira laid a book beside his plate and patted his shoulder. At least she wasn't glaring at him. "Could you get it to her? Or I could mail it, if you'll give me the address."

It was the sketchbook Bree's mother had brought.

Faelan swallowed a bite of tasteless bacon and opened the first page. There were drawings of the graveyard and a lassie standing inside a glowing crypt, blood dripping from her hands as she reached for the burial vault. The bacon felt like a live pig tromping in his stomach. There was a castle—Druan's or the clan's, he couldn't tell—and a face in the window, drawn by a child. The torment of the tiny artist leapt from the pages, in the evil slant of the eyes and the thick skin on the head and tiny pencil strokes where Faelan knew firsthand there were sharp teeth.

Druan.

Faelan's fork clattered to the table. How could a child draw a picture of an eight-hundred-year-old demon?

He turned the page and stared at the last sketch in shock.

For God's sake. How many coincidences could one person bear?

He shoved back from the table, catching his chair before it crashed. "I have to go..." He left the others staring after him. Holding the sketchbook, he hurried to the phone. Bree didn't answer her cell. He scrubbed his hand over his face, trying to calm the panic. Sorcha had warned him this was somehow connected to Bree, that she was in danger. He'd thought sending her away would fix it.

Faelan tried Bree's mother and found she knew nothing about her daughter coming to visit. Maybe Bree hadn't told Orla. Using the credit card Sean had given him, Faelan called the airline and arranged for the first flight home. Home, where was home? He was stuck between times. He would arrive before the others, but he needed to make sure Druan didn't escape and that he was far away from Bree. And he needed time to settle his thoughts, figure out what he would do after the battle was over. Figure out if he could fix the damage he'd done to Bree.

Faelan grabbed a suitcase and started throwing in clothes. The door opened, and Ronan stepped into the room. "What do you want now?" Faelan asked.

"You look like you saw a ghost."

"Worse. I think Bree's in danger."

"'Bout time you showed some concern for her safety," Ronan said as his gaze fell on the open sketchbook. "What's that?"

"Druan… drawn by Bree when she was not much more than a bairn."

"Bloody hell."

"You have no idea what's happening here."

"Then enlighten me."

~~~

"Hello, Druan."

The fine, human hair on Druan's neck rose. His skin melted, bones cracked and popped as he shifted. He spun and faced the tall, raven-haired demon that women of all species followed like bees after honey. "What are you doing here?" Druan spat, furious at his lack of control, while Tristol remained calm.

"You know I don't need your welcome. How's your little virus?"

Druan's claws lengthened. "How's your mother?" he jeered, using the only weapon he had. Tristol's eyes reddened, the only outward sign of his hatred, and Druan felt a moment of triumph at the flash of fear that crossed

Tristol's face. If the Dark One knew Tristol's secrets, he wouldn't last two seconds, but then neither would Druan, if the Dark One found out he'd created a virus while he was supposed to be focused on that war. The Dark One had to approve all major disasters and diseases, and he didn't tolerate his demons messing with his plans, or each other. The good book some humans embraced had that part right. Demons came to steal, kill, and destroy. From humans, not other demons. Fortunately the Dark One often got caught up in his plans and didn't realize the level of competition in his ranks.

Tristol swaggered about the room, stopping to pick up a particularly nice chalice Druan had taken from a dead king.

What was he doing here? Druan knew Tristol was the one killing the minions. Grog had spotted him near the chapel before twelve of Druan's best guards were slaughtered. Grog alone had returned, with only a shoulder wound.

"I should have listened to the warrior instead of your lies," Tristol said. "You betrayed me. You betrayed us all, even the master, but I'll have my revenge." He fondled the chalice and then replaced it. "I know a secret about your warrior."

Druan tensed. "What secret?" So Tristol did know about the time vault? Had he watched Faelan being buried? "Did you take my time vault?"

"You've lost it?" Tristol grinned, and Druan was shocked that even he felt the pull of Tristol's smile. "The Dark One has requested my presence. Should I tell him about your woes?" Still grinning, Tristol swirled into a black cloud and vanished.

"You won't stop me," Druan yelled to the empty room, but he felt a growing sense of panic. He remembered an apparition of the warrior and the glowing room he'd seen decades earlier. He'd hoped it was some kind of sorcery on Tristol's part, but now he wondered if he'd been searching for something that wasn't there. Had Tristol stolen Druan's warrior?

The gray branches reached out like bony arms, pleading with her to hurry. Whispers filled the air, desperate, as a mist rose from the graves, winding around her legs. She tried to run, dragging one weighted foot, then the other, but the crypt seemed farther away with each step. A large shadow appeared in the doorway then slunk into view. Gray skin and yellow eyes. An evil hiss rolled past sharp teeth, and long talons held up the metal disk. The hiss became a laugh as the specters pulled her down. She clawed at the ground, frantic, lurching forward with one final scream.

Chapter 27

"ARE YOU OKAY?" A NASAL VOICE ASKED BESIDE HER. Bree opened her eyes to curious faces. She was on a plane. The other passengers were staring, even the toddler in front of her, eyes round as her mouth, her orange lollipop stuck to the back of the seat. "Are you okay?" Bree heard again, and she looked at the man seated next to her.

"I'm sorry." She pulled her hand back from his arm and saw the white half-moon prints in his skin. "Nightmares… I have nightmares." She unbuckled her seat belt and climbed over him, ignoring the flight attendant hurrying toward her. She stumbled down the aisle, past the one passenger who wasn't gawking. He sat taller than everyone else, head buried in a newspaper, but it didn't disguise his handsome profile.

The young warrior who'd smiled so politely in the meeting.

Faelan had sent someone to make sure she left. Bree collapsed on the toilet seat before her legs dropped out from under her. The creature in her dream was similar to the one Faelan had destroyed in the chapel, but this face, she'd seen as a child. It was the face she'd sketched. She closed her eyes and remembered hiding under the covers, her face buried in Emmy's fur, as she clutched the cross on her father's necklace.

It wasn't working. The monster was here. It wasn't

*a dream. She could feel him. Smell him. She squeezed
her eyes tight, gripped the necklace harder, and saw
a soft glow like the one she'd seen in the crypt, the
one from the shiny man. She peeked out from underneath the blanket. The monster was still there, but
he looked different. Afraid. He stared at something
behind her.*

*Bree glanced over her shoulder. A man stood there,
his face and body shadowed, but he wasn't the shiny
man. He spoke, but she didn't understand the words.
Then he turned, and she recognized his eyes, the ones
she'd seen in the crypt. Her protector's eyes. Feeling
braver now that he was here, she gripped the cross and
held it out toward the monster, who was still staring
at the man in shock. "Get out, now! Leave, and don't
come back!"*

*The monster jerked as if she'd kicked him. He van-
ished, like a ghost on* Scooby-Doo. *It worked. Bree
looked around, but she was alone. She fell asleep
comforted by the soft glow. When she woke to leave for
Daddy's funeral, the magical light was gone, and she
thought it must have been another dream.*

It wasn't. A real monster had sat by her bed, which
explained the drawings and the nightmares she'd
blocked, how she knew what the thing in the chapel
looked like before she'd clearly seen it. Faelan was
right. None of this was a coincidence. She was meant to
wake Faelan, not Sorcha. There was some satisfaction
in that. It was her destiny to help Faelan save the world,
whether he liked it or not. Afterwards, she'd walk away
with her pride intact, even if her heart wasn't. The shiny
man hadn't said he'd send someone to marry her, only to

protect her, and Faelan had done that. It would take time to wrap her head around how he'd been in her dreams when he was still buried in the crypt and who the shiny man was. A figment of her imagination? Her father's ghost? She welcomed the mystery. It would distract her from the pain.

Bree stood and splashed water on her face. First she had to get off this plane, and she had to lose Conall. An hour later, Bree peeked around the door of the ladies' room in the Atlanta airport. The young warrior had his hair pulled back, a baseball cap on his head, trying to blend in with a group of college students. He was too striking to blend.

How was she going to get rid of him? He might be young, but he was a warrior. She needed a distraction. Bree spotted a young woman washing her hands. Attractive, endowed with more curves than clothing. Bree plastered on a smile she hoped conveyed sisterhood. "Could I ask a favor?"

The girl looked up and smiled. "Sure."

Bree led her to the doorway. "See that man over there? Tall, with the baseball cap?"

"That hottie the girls are staring... oops—"

"Hey, he's just a friend. You're welcome to him." The fringe benefit couldn't hurt.

"What is he? A soldier?"

"Sort of. Anyway, it's his birthday, and I want to get him a present before our flight. Do you think you could uh, distract him while I slip by?"

She eyed Conall again, licking her lips. "How much time do you need?"

"As much as you can give me. He's hard to shop for."

She wiggled her eyebrows at Bree. "You got it," she said, adjusting her pushup bra. "By the way, I'm Sherri."

"Uh, Evelyn. Nice to meet you. I really appreciate this."

The girl slipped around and approached Conall from behind. The minute he turned, Bree bolted, not waiting to see how impressed he was with Sherri's offerings.

"Alb…" she gasped, minutes later, leaning on the counter. "Albany. I need the next flight to Albany."

The ticket agent checked the computer. There was a flight leaving in one hour.

"No good. It's an emergency."

"There's a flight boarding at gate 13B, but I don't think you can make it."

"I'll try."

The agent looked doubtful, but issued the ticket. Luckily the security line was short. As she handed the man her boarding pass, her name was announced over the intercom.

"Ma'am, they're paging you," he said, the slight widening of his eyes the only indication of how bad she must look.

"My boyfriend," she said, panting. She clutched her tote bag and tried to smooth down her hair. "I'll call when I get seated."

Bree didn't rest easy until the plane was several thousand feet in the air. It was a toss-up who would kill her first, Russell, Conall, or Faelan.

The plane landed in darkness. She'd hoped to arrive in daylight, when it was reasonably safe. She'd dart in, grab the *Book of Battles*, the disk, a change of clothes, and some cash.

After a long search for her car—she'd forgotten which lot she parked in—Bree plugged her dead cell phone into the charger and dialed her mother.

"Darling," her mother simpered. "Do you have exciting news?"

You were almost the mother-in-law to an eight-hundred-year-old demon. "I'm on the way home. I wanted to see if you'd gotten back okay."

"Where's Faelan?"

"Still in Scotland."

"Making plans—"

"I don't know what he's doing." *Probably banging Sorcha.* "You got home okay?"

"We had a lovely drive. But you need to call Peter and have him look around. I'm sure I saw someone near the chapel."

"The chapel?"

"I came back to the house and spent the night—"

"You stayed at my house?" Bree screeched.

"Sandy had company, and it was so loud there, I was getting a migraine."

A migraine was nothing. Her mother was lucky she was alive. "The trespasser was probably Russell. I think I spotted him in town."

"No, Russell was inside."

"Russell was there? *In my house?*"

"He stopped by, and I felt sorry for him. He didn't look well. He'd lost weight, and I don't think he'd bathed. We had dinner, and he spent the night. I put him in Faelan's room. I don't remember him being so paranoid. I woke up to go to the bathroom and found him prowling through the house, peeking out the windows, like one of those drug addicts on TV. The next morning, he was gone. Didn't even say good-bye."

A cold sweat formed on Bree's forehead. Russell had spent the night in Faelan's room where the *Book of Battles* and the disk were hidden.

"You sound troubled. You haven't done something foolish, have you, dear?"

"Foolish?" Bree muttered, distracted with her unpleasant thoughts.

"Faelan's a good man. He's like your father. He'd do anything to protect you, even something he hated. Like that silly war. Don't throw it away."

"War?"

"You know, the Civil War and all that treasure hunting."

"What about it?"

"Well, he did it for you. You knew that, right? He hated the war and those caves and digging for buttons and coins."

Bree's head spun. "I thought he liked it."

"Oh, dear. You didn't know? He liked being with you. He hated when you weren't near. Oh, darling, I'm so sorry."

"It's okay, Mom. I'm a big girl." Disappointment wasn't anything new.

"He loved you so much, you know. Like his... he couldn't have loved you any more than he did. He just worried about you. You were his world."

After Bree was sure her mother hadn't been possessed or cursed, she hung up and drove like a zombie, not seeing the road but her father's face; dark eyes crinkled against the sun as father and daughter trudged along on their adventures. His forehead rutted with the lines of someone troubled. Had he known she wasn't normal? Was that why he hated to let her out of his sight?

Bree put the pedal to the floor. She had to make sure the book and the disk were safe. She glanced in the rearview mirror at the dark SUV that had been behind her since the airport. She didn't recognize the car, but she hadn't known Russell had a castle, either.

Bree took a few quick turns, just in case, finally letting the car roll to a stop in front of her house. Fog covered the ground, and the dark windows stared out at her like a lost soul.

What had happened to her life? She'd found a treasure beyond anything she could've imagined, and she'd lost him. Now there were demons roaming her yard, trying to destroy the world, and they could be waiting for her. She pried her fingers from the steering wheel, put her phone in her coat pocket, gathered her tote bag, and climbed out of the car. A light drizzle had begun to fall, as if the sky wept for her.

She started toward the porch and came to a sudden stop. Her backyard was gone. No green grass. No azaleas. Just piles of dirt.

∼∼∼

If the flight to Scotland was bad, the return trip was hell. Faelan kept seeing those sketches and replaying the hurt and anger on Bree's face. She'd never believe why he—Ronan's words—threw her out like yesterday's trash. Would she ever forgive him? He'd had no choice but get her out of out Druan's reach before the demon found out she'd opened the time vault. And if the demon discovered Faelan's feelings for Bree, no one would be able to protect her. Certainly not a young warrior with barely a year's fighting under his belt.

He should've sent a seasoned warrior with her, but he needed someone fast, and Conall had been right there, more than willing to follow her in exchange for a chance to join the battle. The others wouldn't like it, but Conall had strength and determination older than his years, and Faelan remembered being twenty and needing to prove himself. He'd keep Conall out of danger and let the seasoned warriors handle the real fighting.

Faelan looked out the window, turning away from clouds so close he could've touched them. He'd never understand these times. Airplanes, televisions, satellites, rocket ships, computers. You could bank and buy goods from the comfort of your home, even find a wife. He hadn't figured that one out yet, but with everything else he'd seen, he didn't doubt it.

He leaned his head against the seat and let his thoughts drift back to Scotland. Meeting his family's descendents had been bittersweet. Sitting at the table where Ian had carved his initials. The kitchen where his mom had baked shortbread, while his father hovered, and his brothers and Alana argued over who could eat the most, when they all knew he could. The smells of the stable had hit just as hard. Alana wasn't there sneaking apples to the horses, and Nandor wasn't whinnying for his morning ride.

The place had changed in the century and a half since he'd left. It had been modernized, and a security system added. There were cars and garages and weapons he'd never have believed possible. He supposed progress was necessary, but it made him feel like a relic. He missed simple times and his family. He missed Bree.

The plane bumped, and Faelan closed his eyes, remembering the feel of her skin as it slid across his, the sound she made when he slipped inside. He let it soothe the knots, let the remembered scent of her pull him away from his pain. He shouldn't have made love to her again, knowing he'd have to send her away, but after the stress of meeting his clan and the guilt and anguish of seeing his family's graves, when he lay in Bree's arms he'd known he was alive, and for a moment she had been his, even if she could never truly be.

She could never be Ronan's either, but that fact hadn't made it easier seeing them together. Some warriors took lovers, and the rumormongers said Ronan had left a trail of broken hearts. Ronan and Bree and her bloody archeologist. Pish. It shouldn't matter. She wasn't his. His mate would be long dead with everyone else. Even if he were given a second chance, the woman had to be from a warrior clan. That was set in stone. As much as he wished he could sink into Bree night after night, see her face every morning, and have children with her, there was too much at stake. The rules were there for a reason. He'd been a warrior too long to break one this important.

He closed his eyes as the plane tilted. Was he even a warrior still? He was more than a hundred and fifty years past his duty. He hadn't had an order from Michael since 1860. A memory tugged at his mind, or was it a dream? A glowing room and a wee lassie huddled under the covers, terrified. And one last order from Michael.

To protect.

Chapter 28

THE FOG SWIRLED AT HER FEET, AND A MAN MATERIALIZED out of the mist. Russell. His eyes were red rimmed, his face wild. Bree tried to run, but her legs were paralyzed like in her dream. A light moved in the woods, coming closer. Russell wasn't alone. He lunged at her, and she swung her tote bag. It hit his arm and fell to the ground. He grabbed her from behind, one strong arm pinning her against his body, the other hand clamped over her mouth, silencing her scream.

"Do what I say, or you'll die."

She could smell his sweat, feel his beard scratch her cheek as he dragged her across the yard. Digging in with her shoes, she twisted and pulled her upper body. When they reached the woods, Russell lost his grip. Bree yanked free and ran toward the graveyard. She'd be safe there. Footsteps pounded behind her. Russell grabbed her arm, and she fell.

She lay there, face pressed into the fresh dirt. A blanket of calm settled over her. Her heart slowed. She smelled raw earth, the damp wool of her coat, and the stench of Russell's sweat. She tasted the fog on her tongue as she locked eyes with a huge white owl sitting high atop an oak branch. It held her gaze as something sharp dug into her palm. Her fingers curled around a stone. A weapon. She leaped to her feet and smashed the stone against Russell's head. He grunted and fell.

Bree's heart sped again, her breathing came faster. *Run, now*. The words flashed through her head. She had her hand on the graveyard gate when the flashlight cut through the mist, and she heard a familiar voice. "Bree, what are you doing back—"

"Jared! We've got to get inside the graveyard before he wakes up."

"Before who wakes up?"

"Russell. Turn off the flashlight."

"Russell's here? I chased someone through the woods. Did you see your yard?"

"It must have been him. Hurry. He'll kill us."

"Kill us? What're you talking about?"

She looked back at Russell, inert on the ground. Was there enough time to get the book and disk and escape? "I'll explain it in the car. You'll need to be sitting down, anyway." Where could they go? The only person who could stop Russell was still in Scotland, and he believed she was safe in Florida.

"My car's still at the dig," Jared said.

"Start mine. The keys are in it. I have to get something."

She grabbed the tote she'd dropped and hurried to the house. She unlocked the back door, ran to Faelan's room, and pulled up the loose floorboard. The only thing inside was the puzzle box. Had he moved the book and key? She didn't have time to search the house. She hurried to her room and yanked off her damp coat. She pulled out drawers so violently the dresser tilted. She steadied it and flung clothes into her tote bag. She ran back to the kitchen and opened the refrigerator, swiping bottles and jars aside until she reached the mayonnaise at the back. Her head was still in the refrigerator when someone pounded on the back door, rattling the knob. Russell's contorted face pressed against the window beside the door, fists rattling the glass.

"Oh, God." She shoved the mayonnaise jar into her bag and ran outside to the waiting car. Russell came around the side of the house, just steps behind her. She jumped into the passenger side and slammed the locks. "Go! Go!"

Jared spun out of the driveway, throwing her against the seat. She looked back and saw Russell loping after the car, mouth open in a scream. Another man—or creature, considering how it moved—materialized out of the woods behind him.

"What's wrong? What are we running from?" Jared asked, looking through the rearview mirror. "Was that Russell?"

"He's not really Russell. He's a demon. That's just his disguise."

Jared stared at her, his face rippling with shock.

—⁓—

"Keep the change." Faelan got out of the taxi, yawned, and rubbed his gritty eyes. The trip home had been a nightmare, changing planes in London, getting lost in the Newark airport. He'd almost missed his connecting flight. He would have kneeled and kissed the ground if he thought he could get back up.

"I can drop you closer to the house," the driver said, peering down the tree-lined drive.

"This is good." He was already taking a risk coming here at night. He had to make sure the key and the book were safe. Then, he was going to trap a demon and find out what Druan was plotting. A couple hours' sleep first would help in case he had to use his talisman. He longed for his bed, but it would be safer if he slept on protected ground in the crypt.

Faelan dragged his bag out of the taxi and crept up the driveway. He kept close to the trees, eyes and ears tuned for things that didn't belong. He felt naked without his dirk, but Bree had warned him that airport security would scan their luggage. Not only did people fly through the air where only God and birds belonged, but now they could see through walls and inside locked luggage. He couldn't chance having to explain his weapon while he was carrying fake identification.

The top of the house appeared through the trees, and he thought he saw an old woman's face in the attic window, but when he blinked, she was gone. When he broke through the trees, he saw Bree's front door standing wide open. The demons had been here.

Thank God she was in Florida.

He set his suitcase down and eased inside, sniffing the air. He could smell lavender, but no demons. The house was empty. He passed Bree's antique mirror, and it rippled like the surface of a loch. Jumping aside, he waited until it became solid again, then pulled it from the wall, laid it face down on the floor, and put his foot through the back. An enchanted mirror. He'd seen only one before. They weren't used much; they were too unstable, but when working properly, Druan would be able to see inside the house. Did he already know their secrets, already know how Faelan felt about Bree? Damnation. He should have sent her someplace besides her mother's. Russell would know where his future mother-in-law lived.

More warriors would have to be sent to protect Bree and her mother. He'd call Cody, see if he and his brothers could help. Faelan reached for his phone but remembered he'd left it in Scotland. There was one in Bree's bedroom. First he had to get the *Book of Battles* and the key. Faelan hurried to his room. The plank lay next to the gaping hole in the floor. He dropped to his knees, heart drumming against his ribs as he searched every corner of the hole. Empty. If Druan had the *Book of Battles*, the whole clan could be destroyed.

Faelan grabbed his dirk and crossed the hall to Bree's room. Her drawers were open, clothes strewn about the room. Had Druan searched Bree's bedroom for the key? Faelan saw a coat crumpled on the floor, the coat she had worn in Scotland. Fear slithered up his spine.

Bree wasn't in Florida.

Where was she?

He grabbed the phone and dialed her cell. It rang in his ear as a tune played on the floor. The music grew louder as he picked up the coat and pulled her phone from the pocket. She wouldn't leave her cell phone. Had she forgotten it, like he had? Or had she been taken against her will?

With his dirk in one hand, talisman ready, he crept down the hall, searching the rooms. The kitchen was a mess, refrigerator open, bottles strewn across the floor, as if there had been a struggle. After checking the entire house to make sure she wasn't sleeping or unconscious, he opened the back door. Her yard was gone, nothing left but dirt.

A groan came from near the chapel. Bree? He moved

closer. A man lay outside the door. Blood ran from his head, dripping over his face. Faelan made sure it wasn't a trap, then kneeled beside the man. He'd taken a right good thrashing, but he was breathing, and most of the blood was dried, not fresh.

The man stirred. His eyelids opened but didn't focus. "…attacked me. Help…"

"Who are you?" Faelan asked. Was this Jared? As much as he hated thinking about her and the archeologist together, he didn't want to see her friend hurt.

"…got to stop him."

"Stop who? Who did this to you?"

"…took it… hide… chapel… couldn't get in," he rambled, struggling to sit. He gripped Faelan's arms for support, and Faelan felt something thick underneath the man's stained sweater. "Hide it… warn Bree."

"Warn Bree? Who are you?"

The man's blue eyes focused, and he blinked. "You're… him."

"I won't hurt you. Where's Bree?"

He wrapped blood-stained hands around Faelan's wrists.

"…doesn't know about him… have to protect it."

"Tell me your name?"

The man spoke his name, turned, and ran. The blood drained from Faelan's face.

The sorcerer jumped in surprise as Druan entered the room and the heavy box crashed to the floor. He picked it up, flinching at the hot breath on his neck. Next would come the claws.

"If you damage it," Druan said slowly. "I'll hang you beside Onca."

"Yes, Master." If this thing didn't end soon, he would die of terror anyway. He was expendable now. Each hour that ticked by, he waited for Druan to realize it.

"The others are in place. How long before we can deliver the vials?"

"A couple of hours."

Druan glanced at the ancient books spread over the worn table. "Did you find out what went wrong with the mirror?" Druan asked.

"There was a problem with the spell." He wouldn't mention he'd gotten it mixed up with her computer screen. No one used enchanted mirrors anymore.

"I have something I need to do. Then we wait for the warrior." Druan laughed. The sound started out human, but he left the room in his natural form, without so much as a thank you for all the sorcerer's efforts in the endeavor, an endeavor that could raise Druan's status to first rank under the Dark One himself.

Years of perfecting, making and discarding, testing on animals and unsuspecting humans, even some halflings, and finally he'd gotten it right. His formula, his work, but would he get credit? No. He'd be lucky to keep his life another half century, while Druan got all the glory. He wished he'd been someplace else when Druan came looking to replace his dead sorcerer. He looked around, agitated, afraid Druan might have read his thoughts. He hated what was going to happen, but he wanted to live, even if surrounded by monsters.

Faelan snuck into the castle using the same entrance as before. Crawling up that infernal vine was worse the second time, with it half pulled away from the wall and his mind in torment over the clues he'd missed. He should've checked all possibilities, not only the obvious ones. He let attraction get in the way. Instead of being honest with her, he let her play right into Druan's hands.

Faelan kept close to the walls, listening for any sound. He was on the second floor, halfway across the castle, when he heard voices, one of them familiar. Clasping his talisman, he peered around the corner. Two men were talking, the white-haired man Faelan had seen in the castle the first time, and a tall, dark-blond man.

Jeremiah. Druan wore the same human shell.

A burst of adrenaline hit first, then rage. Faelan opened the talisman. He would end this now. At that moment, the old man lowered his head and walked away, leaving Druan a perfect target. Faelan aimed the talisman, lined up the symbols, then clenched his teeth, letting the talisman fall against his chest. Druan was likely the only one who knew where the virus was, and he probably had Bree. If Faelan failed again, if he destroyed Druan and couldn't find the virus, every human would die, including Bree. He had to wait for the other warriors. They'd been alerted and were on the way. It wouldn't be long. They could handle Druan's halflings and minions, while Faelan took care of the demon. In the meantime, he'd find Bree.

Druan opened a thick, wooden door behind him and stepped inside. Faelan waited, hoping the demon would come out and lead him to Bree. After fifteen minutes of hell, the door was still closed. If Druan was asleep, he could be bound with the shackles. Although it would be almost impossible to sneak up on a demon of old. Faelan listened for sounds inside, but all was quiet. He eased the door open, and the scene inside struck him with the force of a blow.

Chapter 29

SHE LAY ON HER SIDE IN AN OPULENT BED, HER ARM curved over her breasts. Long, dark hair spilled across a pale cheek. The demon lay behind her, his human arms holding her close, the woman he'd met outside the tavern. Not Isabel, but Bree. She was a halfling. That's how she was able to draw his eyes. She'd seen them just days before he was locked in the time vault. He remembered how gracefully she'd descended from the carriage, the green of her gown, her smile, then the look of shock. Had she known then who he was? Had they been following him while he followed Grog? The two men with her were probably Druan's minions. Had she watched while they locked him in the time vault and waited to wake him when it was time?

Druan touched Bree's shoulder, running his human hand over her arm and down her hip. With her eyes still closed, she smiled and murmured something, then reached for Druan's hand. Pain roared through Faelan, ravaging everything in its path. Lies. All of it. The passion and kindness, the secret he'd seen in her eyes. All lies. He had no one to blame but himself for being deceived. The signs had been there. The key and the *Book of Battles*. She must have stolen them. Even if he destroyed the virus, with the book and the key, the Underworld would have the power to obliterate not only his clan, but the entire planet.

He gripped his talisman. If he destroyed Druan now, Bree would die with him. No matter what she was, he couldn't do it. Another warrior would have to kill her, which was why warriors were warned to avoid women. He started to move, when Druan turned and looked at him. Fear flashed over Druan's handsome, human face, shifting into a cunning smile as he focused on a spot behind Faelan. The smell came too late for him to react. Not again.

"Faelan, behind you!" Kieran shouted.

Faelan turned from the three demons advancing on him, and a halfling's blade sank deep into his left arm. The pain was fierce, but at least it wasn't his sword arm or his head, where the halfling would've struck if Faelan had turned a second later. Holding his injured arm close to his side, he raised his sword and met the halfling's blade. Metal pinged against metal as the half-human backed into a corner. Faelan's arm tightened as he swung. The evil in the halfling's eyes flashed a second before the head separated from the body, sizzling as it vanished.

"Not bad for a novice," Kieran said, before Faelan had even lowered his sword. He turned, gritting his teeth against the pain. Kieran grinned, but Faelan saw the concern in his mentor's eyes before Kieran moved to help the others with the remaining demons. Faelan added his sword, and they quickly destroyed them.

"You should've called for help," Kieran said.

"I thought I could handle it."

"The others can take care of this. Let's get that arm fixed while there's some blood left in you."

His arm burned like it had been gouged with a hot poker. This was his second battle since he left training and his first real injury. He was lucky he still had his head, and his arm. He never should have let the halfling sneak up on him. He followed Kieran through the corridors, clean except for the blood of warriors. Everything grew hazy.

The battlefield changed. Smoke and sulfur filled the air as swords clashed amid screams of horror.

He saw Kieran again, his face older, pale. He stood outside the circle of demons advancing on Faelan. Onwar, the ancient one, stood farther away, his teeth bared in a triumphant smile. Faelan knew he had to do something fast, or both he and Kieran would die. He couldn't use his talisman on all of them; Onwar was too powerful. If he could kill Onwar by hand, then the talisman might be strong enough to take care of the rest.

"Kieran, get out of here," he yelled.

Kieran's face set. He dropped his sword and pulled his talisman from his shirt.

Faelan's eyes widened. "No!"

"Close your eyes, Faelan," Kieran said, his gaze resolute, sad.

"No! Kieran. I can—"

"Close your eyes, my friend." Kieran didn't give him time to react. He began the chant, and Faelan felt the air churn.

No, *his heart screamed.* No. *He pushed through the deformed bodies, shoving aside claws and swords as he tried to reach Kieran. The blinding light appeared. Faelan squeezed his eyes shut and threw his arms over his head. There were screams and the clatter of*

metal from the halflings' swords. He opened his eyes,
his breath raw. The demons were gone, except Onwar.
The ancient demon let out a howl and leapt at Faelan.
Faelan roared out his own rage and sprang, meeting
Onwar in midair. He swung his sword with a ragged cry
and took the weakened demon's head. Faelan landed in
a crouch, his throat closed, and forced himself to face
the lifeless body on the castle battlement.

A hiss shattered the dream, and Faelan cracked open
one eye. His stomach heaved as the light pierced his
head. He remembered something nasty being forced
down his throat and Bree's intimate smile as she reached
for Druan's hand.

"How was your sleep, warrior?"

Faelan's head jerked. His vision was hazy, but he
could see he was in a dungeon, smell the dank air.
Druan stood by the door, his human lips curled in a
sneer. Faelan flexed his muscles, and cold metal bit into
his wrists.

"Rejuvenating." He tried to swallow, but his mouth
was dry as rawhide. "Michael sends his regards," he
rasped through a split lip.

Druan's skin rippled, bones lengthening, but he
stopped the change. All the Underworld feared Michael,
even the Dark One himself.

"I've waited a long time for this," Druan said, smiling. "You thought the war was the best I could do, but I
had far bigger plans. I always have. This world will be
mine, without the stench of humans."

"Tristol might have something to say about that. He
didn't seem pleased to learn about your virus."

"Tristol." Druan spat the name. "He wasn't supposed

to see you. Grog was supposed to bring you later, after the others had gone, but Tristol won't be a problem for long. I manipulated him and the others as easily as I did you."

"Bree's trap worked. You have me. Now what?"

Druan threw back his head, laughing so hard he almost shifted again. "Ah, it's too good."

Faelan clenched his jaw. It ached like it was broken. "I'm honored that you've been waiting for me all this time," he mocked.

"Your family kept me entertained. Your brothers…" Druan smirked. "Little Alana. She grew into a lovely woman. So… generous."

His family? The fuzz in Faelan's head wove itself into panic. He couldn't let it show. "Still telling lies?"

"I love a good lie, but this beats a fib by far." Druan moved closer. "I couldn't let your brothers get away with killing my sorcerer and ruining my virus. Your mother was quite distraught when I finished."

Faelan yanked at the chains until his right shoulder began to dislocate. He saw Druan's satisfaction and stopped.

"If you think it's a lie, then take a look." Druan slapped his scarred hand on Faelan's forehead. He tried to jerk away, but the chains binding his wrists held fast. An image formed, his mother, her body draped over a coffin covered with flowers, her frail shoulders shaking with silent sobs. She looked so small. A low wail pulled from inside her hunched body, and she called a name. Ian. It was his brother's funeral. There was a young woman, heavily pregnant, and a wee lad barely old enough to walk, clutching at her skirt. The lad's lip quivered as he let go of his mother and touched a tiny hand to the wood coffin. Ian's wife... and son?

Druan pulled his hand away, and Faelan's head fell forward. His surroundings swam into focus, and he saw the demon's twisted gloat.

"Ian was magnificent. Crying out for his wife and son as he died, a week before she bore him twins."

Faelan's blood raged, pumping anger and pain with each surge, like a nail driven inch by inch until it could go no more. "Don't speak their names," Faelan roared. "You're not to speak their names!" He twisted and pulled. If he could reach his talisman. He yanked the chains, and his shoulder popped.

A fist smashed into his face, slamming his head into the wall.

"When you wake, we'll talk about Bree," Druan taunted as everything went black.

Bree heard a soft noise like the wind. Something brushed her face. She opened her eyes, and a shadow disappeared into the high ceiling above her. Her head ached, and she felt like she'd cleaned the carpet with her tongue. She was in a bed. A huge bed. Jared's? After she'd told him everything, he insisted on bringing her to his house. Why didn't she remember getting here? The pills he'd given her for her headache must have been too strong, or she had a serious case of jet lag.

Bree sat up and looked around the room. It was too dark for details, but the bed was king-size, the covers a rich brocade—not what she would've expected of Jared. What disturbed her more was the imprint of a head on the pillow next to hers. Had they slept in the same bed? She couldn't remember anything, other than a dream of Faelan curled at her back. Bree peeked under the covers. She was still dressed, not that she thought Jared would take advantage of her.

She got out of bed and tripped over her shoes. She had to find a phone. She'd slept away precious time. Her tote bag was in a chair that looked like it was made for a king. She slipped on her shoes and checked her watch. Five a.m. They'd left her house around ten last night. She had to find Jared and get out of here. Russell could have followed them. Bree went to the door, turned the knob, and registered three things. A gargoyle, voices, and stone. Everywhere she looked there was stone. She wasn't at Jared's.

She was in Druan's castle.

Where was Jared? She eased back, heart thudding with dread, and peeked through the cracked door. Two men stood talking farther down the hall, except they didn't look like men. They were tall and thick, with skin like leather. Like orcs. Long daggers were sheathed at their sides and swords hung across their backs.

"I'll guard her," the first demon said. "You go to the dungeon and check on the warrior. If he escapes, it'll be our hides."

Warrior? Not Faelan. He couldn't be here.

"You're hoping Druan'll give you a taste of her."

"He'd kill anyone who touches her, and you know it."

"It's unnatural, how he watches her," the second demon agreed. "I'll go in a minute, after the sedative's had more time to work. He almost broke my arm when we chained him to the wall."

It had to be Faelan. Why was he here? It was too soon.

"What about the other one?"

"Probably dead. Throw him on the buzzard," he said with a nasty laugh.

Bree's chest constricted. Jared?

"You'd better hurry before he gets back."

"Where is he?"

"In the tower hiding the key."

Druan had the disk. There were two prisoners in the dungeon, one almost dead. Faelan and Jared? Russell must have followed them. Why couldn't she remember anything? Bree eased the door shut, locked it, and examined her prison. Of course there were no phones. She'd have to rescue Faelan and Jared herself. She went to the window and eased the heavy draperies back. The sky was still dark. The best she could figure, she was on the second floor in the middle of the castle. Too high to jump.

The secret passages. If she remembered correctly, they also led to the dungeon. The map should be in her tote, if Russell hadn't taken it. She found the bag and located her tiny flashlight. Someone had gone through her things. Nothing was where it was supposed to be, except the map. Russell had missed the hidden side pocket.

Bree ran a shaky finger over the faint lines running along several interior walls. According to the map, there was an access in the adjoining room, with a hidden door near the fireplace. Using the mini flashlight she carried after she'd gotten trapped in the tower, she inspected the elaborate fireplace and found the left lion's head on the mantel was loose. She pushed, and a secret door opened.

Stale air hit her in the face. With a death grip on her

flashlight, Bree climbed inside. She had to get to the dungeon before Russell returned or the guards discovered her missing. Something slid across her foot, and she smothered a yelp. All this for a man who'd dumped her. No, not for a man. Bree was doing this for the world. She had to rescue the one who could save it. She'd worry about her heart later.

And she had to free Jared. He didn't deserve this. One more turn, and she found narrow, curved steps that led to the first floor. Several times she heard muffled voices. Stepping softly, as she'd seen Faelan do, she came to a dead end. She searched the wall and found a notch. A section swung open and she saw steps leading down into a dark hole.

The dungeon.

Dank air coated her lungs as she crept down the stairs. Her flashlight cut a beam through the darkness. At the bottom, she stood still and listened. The lack of moaning was a relief, until she considered what the alternative could be. Moving quickly, she peered in the open doors and saw chains and torture instruments, but there was no sign of Faelan or Jared.

Deep in the dungeon, a dim light shone, no brighter than a night-light. Beyond it, she found two doors, both locked. On the wall between, she saw a glint of metal. She swung her flashlight. Two sets of keys. She grabbed them both and pointed her light at the lock. The first set worked. The lock clicked open. She pushed the heavy door, nerves crawling with every creak. Someone would surely hear.

The sight inside ripped all else from her mind. Faelan was half lying on a crude, stone surface, his hands chained so high on the wall his upper body dangled, his arm twisted awkwardly.

"Faelan?" She ran to him and pressed her ear to his heart. She heard the slow, steady thump. A ragged cry wrenched from inside her. "What are you doing here?" Holding the flashlight in her mouth, she ran her hands over him, checking for broken bones. His talisman was still under his shirt. Russell must not know its power. A huge lump marred one side of Faelan's head, and his bottom lip was covered in blood where it had split. His cheek was discolored and raw.

Bree dropped a soft kiss on the side of his mouth and tugged in vain at the heavy chains. She tried the second key, but it took several tries to get the rusty lock open. She released his right wrist, gently lowering his arm onto his chest. His shoulder was dislocated. His head rolled to the side, the weight of his body digging the shackle deeper into the flesh of the wrist still trapped. She struggled to support his weight while she freed his left arm. He sagged against her, his shirt gapping open, his battle marks exposed. Tears trickled down her cheeks and dropped onto his chest as she held him.

God grant this warrior's aim be true as his heart. Bend time and bring forward, his mate beside him, not apart. Bree whipped around, but she was alone. There was no time to figure out where the disembodied voice came from.

"Faelan, wake up. We've got to go." Her efforts to pull him to a sitting position were useless. She wasn't strong enough to move him. And she still had to find Jared. A noise sounded outside, and she stopped breathing. It came again, the brush of a shoe on stone.

Someone was coming, and they didn't want to be heard. She checked that Faelan was lying secure before moving toward the door. A pile of rags lay in the corner, a boot beside it.

Jared?

"I'll come back for you, Jared. I promise." She turned off the light, stuck her head out, and saw a shadow dart into another hallway. Carrying her shoes, she felt her way back toward the secret passage. Her fingers shook as she searched for the notch. The stone wall scraped open. She hurried inside and closed the entrance, agonizing over each lost second.

After a minute of quiet, she slid her finger into the notch. A light tap sounded from outside. Yanking her hand back, she listened to the soft searching sounds on the other side. Easing away, she turned and fled, taking the first turn she saw, and soon found herself lost in a maze of tunnels.

She checked her watch. Fifteen minutes had passed. Too long. Choosing a random direction, she ran into one dead end after another. She opened at least ten secret doors, expecting to be discovered, then she found a small, wooden doorway, surprising in a place made of stone. She eased it open and bumped into a huge tapestry. Pulling back the edge, she saw a room with several men—or creatures—seated at a table. They were discussing something in a language she couldn't understand, but the emotion translated well. Excitement. She had to hurry. She stepped back and tiptoed the other way. One last turn, and she came to a wall that seemed familiar. She opened the door and stumbled onto the dungeon stairs, welcoming the musty air. Praying whoever was there had gone, she aimed her light and rushed toward the room where she'd left Faelan and Jared. She opened the heavy door. Empty chains dangled from the wall.

Faelan was gone.

It couldn't have been him outside the secret passageway. He wasn't even conscious. Bree moved toward Jared, still motionless in the corner. The back of his head was matted with blood, and he lay too still. Tears blurred her eyes as she knelt and rolled him over. She stared at his bloodied face, illuminated by her flashlight. Her body went cold. "No. God, no."

The soft tap of a shoe behind her alerted her that she wasn't alone. "Where have you hidden my warrior?" The voice was quiet. And terribly familiar. Bree slowly turned, her body weak with shock.

Druan.

Chapter 30

Faelan held tight to Conall's shoulders as the fence came into view. "Slow down." His shoulder ached, and his legs wobbled like a new foal's.

"Can't. Not if we want to get out of here alive."

Conall pulled faster, and Faelan fought the churning in his stomach.

"Up you go," Conall said, shoving Faelan over the fence. He teetered and fell to the other side, knocking the breath out of him. A second later, Conall landed beside him. He took Faelan's arm, wrapped it around his shoulders, and dragged him forward. "Sorry about the arm. Your shoulder was dislocated. I had to put it back."

"Bree… here," Faelan said, as his throat struggled between pulling in air and getting rid of the vile stuff in his stomach.

"I'll come back for her." Shouts sounded behind them, and Conall pulled faster. "Hurry."

"No. She's a halfling."

"A halfling? What'd they give you?" Conall pulled Faelan across the road, into the trees.

"…feel sick."

"You'll be better off if you throw up."

Faelan stumbled to the closest tree, held on, and did just that. Conall dragged him away before Faelan could wipe his mouth.

"We've got to keep moving."

"She was in bed with Druan."

"Who?"

"Bree."

"Blimey. They must have given you some kind of hallucinogen. The last place Bree would be is in Druan's bed." Conall parted some branches, uncovering a dark vehicle like the one Druan's minions had driven, but larger. Opening the door, he shoved Faelan inside and buckled his seat belt. Conall jumped in the driver's side and cranked the engine. "Hang on."

Conall stared at the winding road. Faelan leaned back, trying to clear his head.

"I'm sorry I lost Bree. She distracted me. Got on another plane in Atlanta before I could stop her."

"It's not your fault. She's strong-willed." Most half-lings were. "How did you find her?"

"I figured she was trying to get back home. I found the next flight to Albany and saw her boarding."

"You got on the same plane?"

"No. Took an hour to get another flight, but her connecting plane was delayed. Mechanical problems. I got her address from Information, but when I got to her house, she was pulling onto the road. A man was driving. I thought she'd been kidnapped. I tried to follow them, but got lost. Bloody roads. I'm not used to driving on this side. I decided to check out Druan's castle. Took forever to find it, even with the map coordinates. Just like you said, an empty field and woods. That was an eerie thing, watching the air part like a curtain."

"How'd you get inside the castle?"

"I found that hidden door around back and headed

for the dungeon. Figured if she'd been kidnapped, she'd be there."

"Did you see her?"

"No. After I found you, there wasn't time to look. I had to get you out. I've taken the same oath as you. There's more at stake here than one woman, or me. You're the only one who can stop Druan."

So much for his plan to keep Conall out of danger.

"I should've called for help," Conall said. "I thought I had it under control, but I almost cost you your life."

Faelan knew that sentiment well. He remembered his father's words, as the talisman slid over his head. *Warriors need each other. The battle's not meant to be fought alone.* "I would've gone to the castle anyway. I'm the one who should've asked for help. Let's say we've both learned a lesson." He'd learned several. "How'd you get my chains off?" Faelan asked, looking at his scraped wrists.

"I didn't. They were off when I found you."

"Then who…?" Faelan touched his battered lips. "I think somebody kissed me."

Conall's eyebrows rose. "Not me. There was a guy in there with you. Wasn't him either. He was dead. I heard noises behind the wall. Someone must have been in the secret passageway you told us about. Did Bree know about it?"

"She's the one who found the map." Probably drew the bloody thing.

By the time they reached Bree's house, Faelan was feeling closer to alive. They hadn't been followed, as far as they could tell, but it was too dangerous to stay more than a few minutes. He drank water until he couldn't taste the bitterness in his mouth and stood under her shower, watching his blood run down the drain.

He wrapped a towel around his hips and started toward his room to get clothes, when he spotted a small marble cup behind several fallen picture frames on Bree's dresser. The cup held a pocket watch and a diamond earring. A prickling started under his skin. He picked up the pocket watch and turned it over, his hands moving shakily over the silver. He didn't need to read the engraving to know what it said.

To ADC, all my love, always.

He didn't remember bringing it.

Conall poked his head through the door. "Sean says the others should be here by morning. What's that?"

Faelan shook his head. "My father's pocket watch. I don't remember wearing it." He was sure he hadn't worn it. How did Bree get his father's pocket watch?

"Your brothers probably forgot it—" Conall broke off, clamping his mouth shut.

"My brothers?"

"Sorry. I was thinking of something else," Conall said, whirling toward the door.

"You're lying."

Conall stopped, hands on the door frame, and blew out a sigh. He turned, his face glum. "Your father was here. He came with your brothers to help you fight Druan."

"My father? Here?" The air rushed from Faelan's lungs. "McGowan?"

"They used fake names to protect their identities."

Faelan dropped onto the bed, the watch clenched in his hand. "My father was McGowan. Why didn't someone tell me?"

"The clan didn't want you distracted."

"Druan killed my father?" His father had come to help him and died. Had his coffin rested in the crypt, next to the time vault? Father and son. One dead. One sleeping. Side by side.

His father's death was his fault. If he'd let the warriors stay with him, there was at least a chance they would have succeeded, and his father may have lived, but Faelan had taken that chance away. His mother had lost her husband and two of her sons to the demon. Had she died of a broken heart? "We've got to get out of here. I know a place where we can stay. I have some clothes that might fit until yours arrive."

"I'm sorry about all this, about Bree. Maybe there's an explanation. He could have taken her."

Faelan scrubbed his hands across his face. "If she was a prisoner, she would have been in the dungeon, not his bed." And she wouldn't have been smiling. "I fell for her story... the map, the photograph she claimed was her great-great-grandmother, the key hanging on the mantel. She probably killed my father herself."

"No. Please, no."

His features were the same, but there was nothing familiar about his expression. Jared smiled, and Bree saw a hint of sadness. Her heart shriveled a little more. A lone tear, of fear or pain, she didn't know which, escaped, trickling down her cheek.

Tilting his head, he studied it and then touched it with his finger, bringing it to his lips.

"Why, Jared?"

"Glory, power, the planet."

"You used me to get to Faelan. Why do you want him?"

"Because he tried to destroy me. Spying on me, tormenting me, trying to ruin my plans." Druan laughed, the sound jarring, coming from Jared's beautiful mouth.

Bree remembered him comforting her after the ordeal with Russell, sharing a glass of iced tea as they talked about his dig. Laughing over a funny movie. Then she thought about Faelan in the dungeon, beaten and bruised, his shoulder dislocated, dangling by his wrists. This thing wasn't Jared. He was only a cover for this monster. Everything they'd shared, laughter and grief, mysteries of the world, all of it was pretense. Her Jared had never existed.

"You humans are so blind. You think these wars and diseases come out of nowhere. The plague, cancer, AIDS," he said, bitterly. "You can't see what's in front of your faces."

He was right. She'd missed all the signs. Hair and eye color similar to Russell's. The dig so near where the time vault was buried.

"It'll be over soon, but I have a few surprises for the warrior first. Then he'll witness the destruction of humanity. And Michael will see what happens when he sends a warrior after me," Jared said, rubbing the scar on his palm.

She had to keep Druan talking, give Faelan more time. If Druan believed she had hidden Faelan, then he must have escaped. "What happened to your hand?"

"A souvenir from the charm the warrior wears," he said. "He'll pay for it before he dies."

A charm? Then he didn't know the talisman's power. "You killed Russell."

"Russell proved craftier than I expected. Tried to play the hero. Fool."

Russell had been trying to warn her, not harm her. "Was he human?"

"Pathetically so. Russell needed lots of money to keep the bad guys away. Human bad guys, which I worked hard to arrange. These addictions take time to create, you see. I stepped in and offered to pay his debts if he helped me find the key. Threw in the promise of a little glory, a little extra money, and he was mine."

Russell had stolen the key. What about the book? If Druan had it, the entire clan would be wiped out, whether or not the virus worked. Even if he didn't have the book, he knew about it. She'd mentioned it in the car. She'd told Faelan's worst enemy a secret his clan had successfully protected for thousands of years. If only there was a way to kill Druan herself.

"You shouldn't have freed the warrior. You'll pay for that."

"It was my destiny to free him." As she spoke the words, she knew they were true. The dreams and longings, so real they tormented her. Faelan was her destiny. Not only to help him fight Druan, but she belonged with him. With everything in her, she believed she was the mate foretold in the marks on his chest. She didn't care about some stupid rule. If she could get out of here alive, she'd fight Sorcha *and* Anna, his entire clan if necessary. She would make Faelan see they belonged together.

"I'm rewriting your destiny. I've waited a long time for you, little one. I watched you sleep, watched you

ANITA CLENNEY

grow. I made sure no one would have you but me. The only reason you're not lying next to Russell is that you're *mine*. But first you need a lesson in loyalty."

This was why Faelan had pushed her away. He was trying to protect her by putting distance between them. "You pretended to be an archeologist so you could search for the key?" She should've connected it sooner. She should've connected lots of things, but she'd never questioned Jared's claim after she'd heard her grandmother and Jared discussing the project. When he came by the house a couple of days after the funeral to offer his condolences, saying Bree's grandmother had agreed to let him dig, Bree had been so consumed by grief she hadn't questioned it. He'd started digging before she even moved in.

"The vault, the key. Nothing was where it was supposed to be." His face rippled then settled back into place. "I underestimated the warrior's brothers. You humans blow each other up on a whim, but this family bond thing brings out your protective side."

"If demons weren't breeding hatred, we wouldn't be blowing each other up."

"True. Your species is easily manipulated. I'll miss that."

"What will happen to humans?"

"Them... good-bye." He snapped his fingers and moved closer, cupping her cheek in his familiar, calloused hand. "But I've chosen you to give me offspring," he said as if bestowing a great honor.

She backed away, shaking her head. "Over my dead body."

Druan appeared shocked for a moment. "That can be

arranged," he said with a snarl out of his perfect, handsome face. "You can meet the same fate your grandmother did."

"My grandmother?"

"I'm afraid I got angry the last time I tried to persuade her to let me dig, and she saw my other side. I couldn't let her ruin all my plans."

"No." Bree shook her head, refusing to believe it. "She died of cancer."

"True, she had cancer, but—"

"You killed Grandma?" Something hardened inside Bree, like steel replacing muscle and bone.

"And Frederick, poking around where he didn't belong."

"You bastard!"

Druan's face chilled. "If you're not careful, I'll send you to join them. You think I've waited centuries just to sit back while humans try to destroy me? Infiltrating my camp, pretending to be workmen and campers? No one interferes with my plans. Not humans, warriors, or demons. Not even you."

Angus must have been working undercover at Jared's dig. Bree pictured him, bloodied and torn, and Faelan, who could be dead, both fighting to save the lives of humans who didn't know they existed. And her grandmother who'd welcomed every stranger with open arms. Innocent lives lost to Druan's evil.

Bree flew at him, catching him off guard. She clawed his handsome features, and the face began to shift. The eyes changed first, becoming narrow and yellow, the pupils reptilian. Bones cracked and lengthened, and smooth skin that had held her close and soothed her fears turned leathery and gray. He smiled, and where there'd been an orthodontist's dream, there were only sharp teeth and an odor so foul she couldn't breathe. The monster of her nightmares, worse than the thing in the chapel.

"Do you want to take me on, my human?" he asked, his voice deep, rumbling from his chest. He rose to his full height, towering above her.

Bree took a step back, trembling inside, knowing she didn't stand a chance, but she refused to let him see her quake. "You're the one who's pathetic, a hideous beast hiding behind human skin."

"My looks don't please you? That could make things interesting. I'd hoped you would come willingly, but I can take now what I didn't take before." He ran a sharp nail slowly down her neck, his stench caressing her face. "What I'm sure you've given the warrior. And I won't be in the pretty archeologist's form."

"You can go back to hell." Bree threw the only weapon she had, her flashlight. Druan screeched in rage and flew at her.

Chapter 31

"WE DON'T KNOW IF DRUAN'S USING THE SAME VIRUS or a different one, but he has to be stopped," Faelan told the warriors gathered in the bed and breakfast where he and Bree had stayed. It hurt just thinking her name. The others still believed she was innocent, that Druan was up to his old tricks. Faelan knew what he'd seen, no matter how much he wished he hadn't. He'd already lost everything in the world he cherished. There was no reason to hope he'd be spared this.

"I think there are others helping him. I saw five men in my dream," Sorcha said. This time there was no coy look slanted at Duncan. She'd been oddly subdued since Angus's death. "The faces were blurred. Two could've been Faelan and Druan, but who were the other three?"

"Tristol, Malek, and Voltar?" Duncan suggested, his gaze on Sorcha.

Faelan wondered if anyone else noticed how the warrior's eyes softened when Sorcha wasn't provoking him.

"The demons of old? Blimey. Don't even think it," Brodie said, crossing himself.

"They've probably all been secreted away working on this virus," Ronan said.

Faelan nodded. "If they're alive, and I know Druan is, you can be sure they're not sitting around idle."

"You have the shackles ready?" Shane asked.

Faelan studied the short blade of his *sgian dubh*, dreading to answer. His father had the dagger made as a gift for when Faelan came home from America. It had been locked away all these decades. Sean had sent it with Duncan. The *sgian dubh* had never been used, yet it looked older than the dirk he had in the time vault, the one Kieran had given him his first year as a warrior. "I'm not using the shackles. Druan's desperate. He'll be nigh impossible to suspend." He didn't tell them he had no choice, since Bree, or someone, had stolen the key along with the *Book of Battles*. If he told them, they'd have to kill her. He would find out where she'd hidden the things before anyone knew they were missing, and then… he didn't know what he'd do.

A knock sounded at the door, Mrs. Edwards again, asking if they needed anything. The woman was nosier than Bree.

"I agree with Faelan," Duncan said, after Mrs. Edwards had left. "There's too much riding on this to take a chance."

"Aye. Better off to blast him the minute you see him," Brodie added, "and pray the other demons aren't there."

"Cody's already at the castle, scouting the grounds, keeping an eye on the place." Faelan hadn't wanted to let Cody go in alone, but they both knew one man could hide easier than two. Besides Faelan, Cody was the most experienced of the group. Faelan pulled aside the ruffled curtain at the window and peered at the orange-pink sliver riding the mountain. He let the drape fall into place and turned back to face the others. "It's time. Let's move."

One by one the warriors filed out of the Victorian

bedroom, their weapons hidden in what looked like suit-cases. Warriors in his time used the secret compartment of a trunk, like the one in Bree's attic or a specially made box. They hadn't had swords that could collapse to the size of a dagger or these fancy gadgets and weapons. They went out armed with a talisman, a sword, strong senses, a *sgian dubh*, and a dirk. Occasionally a pistol or bow. Faelan was glad they still preferred swords for fighting. At least that hadn't changed.

Ronan gave Faelan a slap on the shoulder that he knew was meant to be comforting. In spite of butting heads in Scotland, Ronan had proven to be a good friend, even lent Faelan his sword. "Keep an open mind, Faelan. I still say Druan's up to his tricks. How could she be a halfling and make another halfling disappear or look at an open talisman? It's impossible."

Or trickery. She could've have lied about seeing the light. A human couldn't do those things either. He'd known all along too many things didn't add up, but he overlooked them, because of loneliness and lust.

"Faelan, I need to talk to you." Sorcha waited by the door, hands twisting the hem of her shirt. He looked at the lovely woman he felt nothing for, save respect. "What is it?"

"It's about Bree."

He didn't want to talk about Bree. His mind was already consumed with her. He hadn't slept more than an hour, tormented by her voice, pleading with him to hurry. When he woke up, Ronan was watching him, and Faelan knew he must have cried out. That was the last time he'd slept.

"I don't think she's a halfling, Faelan."

It angered him that they continued feeding his hope. "Why do you say that?"

"You know I sensed danger surrounding her." She looked uncomfortable and moved around the room, stopping to pick up a silver bowl from a table. She examined it in silence until he wanted to rip the thing from her hands. She put the bowl down and turned to him. "I shouldn't have acted as I did."

"Like I was your next meal?" He was rude, but he wanted this conversation over. He wanted to put an end to this mess. He needed to destroy demons.

Sorcha blushed. "I was just, I don't know what I was doing."

"I think I have a fair idea," he said, glancing at Duncan's retreating back. "I saw her in Druan's bed. The danger you sensed was because she's been hanging around for a hundred and fifty years waiting to kill us. She's probably the traitor Angus was talking about."

"Why didn't she kill us? No one suspected her. She was right there in the midst of some of the strongest warriors alive. She could've had us wiped out. She could've crept from room to room, killing us one at a time," Sorcha challenged. "What you saw had to be a trick."

"How could it be a trick? I met her in a different century, looking exactly the same."

"You said she claimed the woman in the picture was her great-great-grandmother. You were close to Bree. How could she hide something like that?"

"I saw her with my own eyes, in bed with Druan." He hadn't told anyone about the intimate smile he'd seen, a smile a woman would only give a lover.

"Men are so bloody visual. Things aren't always

what they seem. You should know that better than most. You've spent years battling demons hiding in human skin. He probably drugged her. Think, Faelan. Who could have released your chains except Bree? If she's a halfling, it makes no sense that she would wake you from the vault, help you find your family, feed you… take you to her bed. She could've killed you while the last thing on your mind was the hunt." Sorcha raised one eyebrow, and Faelan's cheeks warmed at the memory of Bree on top of him, her hips locked to his. "She could've killed you a dozen times over, and you know it."

He didn't tell Sorcha that Bree had kept his dirk hidden from him part of the time. She could have plunged it into him while he lay unconscious in her bed the first night. "I don't know what to believe." A flicker of hope warmed him, though, softening the armor he'd welded around his heart.

Sorcha rubbed both temples. "There's something bigger here. He despises you, but Bree figures into his plan somehow, and he's playing on your feelings for her. If I hadn't acted like a moron, things might be different." She looked troubled, and Faelan suspected this was the real woman hiding behind the vixen.

"We've got a battle to fight. Let's focus on that. Then we'll find Bree and get the truth." He would find her one way or another. If he was wrong, he'd misjudged Bree. Unforgivably. If she was a halfling, she had to be suspended. No. He'd make sure she was destroyed, so she'd simply cease to exist. He couldn't bear the thought of her being locked away for a hundred and fifty years awaiting Judgment. Faelan led the way toward the door, stopping when he glimpsed his reflection in the mirror.

Black shirt, black pants—combat pants they called
them—cuts and bruises that would've already healed, if
he'd slept. He looked almost as miserable as he felt, but
the outside didn't show the blistering fires raging within,
searing his body, mind, and soul until he feared there
would be nothing left but a shell, like the demons wore.
And there, with his hair pulled back for battle, for the
world to see, was the mate mark on his neck. Sorcha's
shocked gaze met his in the mirror, and she paled.

Druan held Bree in his arms, looking at the face he'd
grown so fond of. In his eight hundred years, he'd corrupted humans, killed them, manipulated them, even
eaten a few, but he'd never cared for them. Frail creatures. But her. There was something different about her.
He could feel the power emanating from her, an aura.
She must be special. Why else would Michael block
him from her dreams as he had nearly two decades ago?
Druan remembered the glow in her bedroom as she
thrust the cross toward him, gripping it in her small hand
in an attempt to cast him out of her house. And standing
behind her had been Faelan's ghost.

"Is it ready?" Druan asked the gangly youth who
approached.

"Yes, Father."

"You know what to do." He handed Bree to the boy.
A feeling of regret crossed his mind as her warmth left
him and her head drooped against the youth's shoulder.
He hadn't killed her, just knocked her out. She was
lucky. She wouldn't see her fate.

He thought about the century and a half of planning

nearly ruined because of her, and the key hidden on her mantel all this time. Had Bree bothered to tell him, her best friend, that she'd made her amazing discoveries? The key, the journal, the *Book of Battles*, the warrior. No, she hid them all and crept about like a thief, probably giving her body to his enemy. That book would have brought him all the power and glory he wanted, even without the virus and the time vault. There would have been nothing the Dark One wouldn't have granted for a gift so grand. Druan would've held Tristol's place of honor.

Come to think of it, Bree deserved some torment. Druan smiled and brushed his hand across her forehead. Her eyes flew open, and he saw a flash of recognition, an instant of relief, before she remembered who he was. She screamed. Her shrieks continued, then sudden silence.

A minute later, Druan's son dropped the key into his scarred hand, a scar even his human form couldn't disguise. Druan's constant reminder of Faelan and his cursed charm.

Now the warrior would die, but first he had to suffer.

Druan's half-human son stood proudly awaiting his next order. Druan shifted into his demon form. "Come here." He held out his hand, waiting until the boy was close before he struck. It was regretful. The boy had served him well, but he couldn't leave anyone alive who knew where he'd hidden Bree, and he could make another son. He dragged his son's body into the woods and dumped it into one of the holes he'd dug in the earth. He wouldn't need them anymore.

The pieces were in place. Soon the earth would be

his, and Tristol would be nothing but a smudge on history. Druan shifted to human and walked away from his son's body without a second glance. This last trick was almost too good, but he would miss her. Talking with her about human things, putting his arms around her as humans did for comfort, his human lips to her warm cheek. Later he might free her, let her make atonement for her betrayal by replacing the son he'd had to kill. He might even take on his human form from time to time. He knew she'd been fond of it.

Chapter 32

FAELAN PARTED THE VEIL WITH THE SWORD RONAN had lent him and stepped inside. The castle rose against the night sky, evil emanating from its towers like a curse.

Shane stuck out a finger. "Just like Conall said, a curtain."

"Quiet," Faelan called softly. "You can be seen and heard from this side."

Duncan put out his hand and stepped inside.

Ronan slung his bow over his shoulder and stepped through, joining Faelan and Duncan, looking at the others still waiting on the other side. "It's like a two-way mirror," he said.

"It runs a few feet outside the fence," Faelan said. After all the warriors had passed through the veil, they checked their weapons one last time, climbed the imposing fence, and dropped onto the other side. There were a few lights on inside the castle, but it was quiet outside. What if Druan had hidden the virus somewhere else, Faelan thought. No. He would keep it close, and what better place than here? A wind arose, swirling in the trees behind them. The warriors tensed, swords ready, but the disturbance settled as quickly as it had begun.

"That was odd," Cody said, slipping soundlessly behind them, the only one of the group aiming a gun.

"Blimey. I didn't even hear you coming," Brodie said to him. "Don't suppose you found the virus already?"

"No, but there's a pile of bodies, humans, torn to shreds. Must be minions."

"If the virus is ready, he probably doesn't need them anymore," Duncan observed.

"Something strange is going on here. A helicopter landed earlier, then several cars left," Cody said. "I've checked the outbuildings. Nothing there, but he could have it hidden underground."

"It's here somewhere," Faelan said, feeling the prickle of unseen eyes. "Let's get inside." They moved toward the small door on the side of the castle. "Locked."

"I can break it down," Niall said, testing the door.

"And announce that we're here?" Ronan pushed him aside. "Move over, muscle boy. Let me show you how it's done." He took a piece of thin metal out of his pocket and fiddled with the lock. "There."

They split up, Anna and Cody vanishing into the trees, as the others disappeared inside. Niall and Shane were checking the first floor, Duncan and Sorcha the second, Tomas and Brodie the third, and Ronan and Declan the towers. Faelan and Conall would check the dungeon and secret passages. They headed around back to the entrance Conall had used. The young warrior had gained a new respect. If not for his help, Faelan would already be dead, and the world would be doomed.

Conall lifted a wall of ivy aside with his sword, uncovering a small door. Holding their weapons before them, they entered a low, dark tunnel. Muffled noises filtered through the night, paws scurrying against stone, and another sound, still, but larger, the shifting of air. Faelan touched Conall's arm, signaling him to halt. There was nothing, not even breathing. But something was here. Faelan could feel it. Best get into the light. A few paces more and they reached a door that opened at the top of stairs leading to the dungeon.

"It's dark down there, nothing but a couple of old torches hanging on the wall."

"We'll have to rely on our eyes. We don't want them to know we're here."

Conall pointed to the opposite wall. "Over there's where I heard someone behind the wall, before I found you. I couldn't figure out how to get inside. The catch isn't like ours. I'm guessing it was Bree."

The pain of her betrayal hit Faelan again, but if he thought too much on what Sorcha said, that Druan was playing games, the distraction would be worse.

Tuning their eyes to the dark, they descended into the dungeon. Once they were in place, the warriors whispered their locations through their microphones.

"I don't understand what these demons want anyway," Conall said.

"They're pawns. Their master wants the human race extinguished. He's furious at God for casting him out and creating us."

With his back flat against stone, Conall slid around the corner. "No one here."

"Check every room. Who knows where it could be hidden. I suspect Ronan and Declan will find something in one of the towers. That room Bree was locked in was used for something. I should've checked it, but I had to get her out of there fast."

"Is there something between you two?" Conall asked.

"Ronan said you and Bree were… I guess I figured you and Sorcha would be mated. Have you felt the bond for one of them?"

Had Conall seen the mark on Faelan's neck? He'd untied his hair to hide it. He didn't want anyone asking questions he couldn't answer.

"Sorcha's nothing to me but a cousin."

"And Bree?"

Bree. He couldn't explain things he still didn't understand. The passion, the sense of belonging he felt with her, even when she was driving him barmy. Like he'd found a missing part of himself.

Duncan's voice came across the earpiece, sparing Faelan the effort of trying to explain. "Demons here. Six of them. Sorcha, look out!"

Before he could think, Faelan started toward the stairs. He stopped when Conall caught his arm. "Female warriors," Faelan muttered. He spoke into the microphone. "Can you take them?"

"Sorcha's already killed two," Duncan said over the screams. "Leave one of them alive… bloody hell, woman. I was going to question him."

"You should've said so," Sorcha grumbled. "I see a demon, I kill him. You need to take a chill pill, cousin."

"Stop calling me cousin."

Conall grinned. "I wouldn't want to cross her. Guess it was different in your time."

Faelan nodded. He'd never thought women inferior, as some men did. He always held them in high regard, but they were precious, to be handled gently. He couldn't imagine going into battle with one, but the other male warriors seemed to regard them as equals on the battlefield. He'd seen Sorcha and Anna at practice and knew they could hold their own.

Bree was just as strong. She'd opened his vault, fed him—no easy task in itself—and helped him find his family. She even saved his life with his own dirk. He wanted to believe he could've escaped if she hadn't destroyed the halfling holding him, but he wasn't sure. She tried to rescue him from the castle when he didn't need it and may have loosed his chains when he did. She'd excused inexcusable behavior and let him make love to her more than once.

"You okay? You don't look so good," Conall said, glancing up from the map in front of him.

He nodded. Had he made a mistake? He couldn't think about it now. It wouldn't do anyone any good.

"There's a metal door here."

"I'll go in first." Faelan entered the small empty room. There was another door at the back. Excitement started to build until he saw it was unlocked. Druan wouldn't leave his virus unsecured. Faelan stuck his head in. Stockpiles of swords and guns lined the walls, more than Druan could possibly use.

Conall moved in behind him. "Blimey. He's got enough weapons here to wipe out an army. Bet he's selling them to finance all this."

"Could be for his halflings." They couldn't summon weapons at will. Only full demons had that ability. "Or he's arming his supporters. You and I know human wars don't start with humans."

"If we set a small explosive here," Conall said, pointing to the door, "we can destroy the entrance without bringing the roof down on our heads. They won't be able to get to the stuff. We can come back later and destroy it or take it."

"It'll announce our presence, but if we can keep these weapons out of their hands, it'll be worth it."

"I'll put a delay on it so we have time to take cover." Conall planted the device, and they left, shutting the door behind them.

"We found a stash of weapons," Faelan told the others. "We're sealing off the door. In about two minutes the floor's going to shake. Let's stand back and see what bugs come running."

"This is where I found you," Conall said, pointing to a small room behind them.

Faelan moved inside. The scent of death hung in the air. He glanced at the heavy chains hanging from the wall and the pile of clothes in the corner. Kneeling, he turned the body over, wrinkling his nose against the smell. It was the man he'd found beaten in Bree's backyard. Russell. His injuries were worse. Druan must've worked him over again. Whatever part Russell played had sealed his fate.

"The dead guy had some kind of book under his sweater. Leather-bound, like a journal, but I didn't have time to take a closer look."

Faelan pulled up Russell's dirty sweater, not worrying about the stench. "There's nothing here."

Conall knelt and looked for himself. "It's gone."

"Damnation."

"What is it?"

"It was the *Book of Battles*," Faelan said.

"I thought you hid it."

"It was gone when I got back from Scotland. Russell

must have stolen it." Not Bree. What else had he accused her of that she hadn't done?

"I should've taken it," Conall said, "but someone was coming, and my hands were full."

With me, Faelan thought. "Don't blame yourself. I saw it on him too and didn't know what it was. He kept mumbling about protecting something. Must've been the book. I think he realized too late what he was up against."

Conall checked his watch and warned the others. "Thirty seconds till it blows."

"What's this?" Faelan asked, pulling an envelope out of Russell's shirt. It was addressed to Bree. Faelan stuffed it in his pocket and noticed the wound on Russell's neck. He scrubbed at it with the edge of Russell's sweater, uncovering two puncture marks. He drew back in shock.

"That looks like—" Conall's words were interrupted by the explosion.

Faelan leapt to his feet as footsteps sounded on the stairs "You ready?"

Conall nodded, glancing back at Russell's body. He drew his sword as the footfalls grew louder. Both men sprang out at the two newcomers, still in human form. They weren't even armed.

"Minions. This'll be messy." But it had to be done. Once they turned evil, it was too risky to trust them. Faelan plunged his sword into the minion's heart a second before Conall took the other one's head.

Both warriors stood mute, staring at the piles of dust on the floor.

Chapter 33

CONALL'S FACE WAS ASHEN. "BLIMEY!"

Faelan's head pounded. "We've got a problem," he said into his microphone. "We just killed two…" he looked at the dust again, "two vampires."

There was total silence. "Vampires?" Duncan said. "Must be one of Druan's tricks, like the invisible castle. Vampires don't exist."

"This is no trick. I'm looking at two piles of dust and a dead man with holes in his neck." Maybe the question wasn't whether Bree was human or halfling. Talismans wouldn't kill a vampire. But why would a vampire have been in Druan's bed? Vampires and demons were enemies. Then what were they doing in a demon's castle?

"Are you sure?" Ronan asked, his voice strained.

"Dead sure."

"I thought vampires were destroyed centuries ago," Niall said. "Shane! Behind you." There was a shriek. "What the… Shane's down!"

Faelan and Conall raced up the dungeon stairs two at a time, their footsteps pounding down the corridor as they followed the yells. Faelan rounded the corner and saw Shane slumped in an arched doorway. A high-pitched wail sounded from inside the massive room, a library, as Niall extracted his sword from a halfling a second before it disappeared.

"Bastard threw the knife from across the room," Niall said. "You're right. There was a bloody vampire right in the middle of a punch of demons. Shane stabbed him through the chest, and he sprouted fangs and tried to run. Three of them got away."

"We've got them cornered," Duncan said. Screams echoed from down the corridor. Sorcha and Duncan arrived minutes later, faces grim.

Faelan leaned over and checked Shane's pulse. "He's alive. Tomas, we need you here." He had the most knowledge of injuries. All warriors knew the basics of caring for wounds and illnesses. It was one of the things they learned in order to become a warrior, but some had special medical training. That had stayed the same. The clan still avoided outside doctors if possible.

"'Course I'm alive." Shane opened his eyes and reached down, yanking the knife out of his chest. "He wasn't that good." He gave a pained smile, but his face was sallow.

Faelan pulled off his shirt and pressed it to the wound. He remembered Bree doing the same for him after the chapel battle. "You need a doctor."

Tomas arrived and confirmed Faelan's opinion. "It's fairly deep. I can stitch it, but I think he'll be better off if we get him to a hospital. Tell them he fell on a piece of metal."

Shane protested, but Faelan wasn't taking any chances. "Another demon could finish you off before you recover. We need to get you away from here."

Sorcha sheathed her sword and knelt by Shane. "Cody said Druan has a chopper. I'll fly Shane out. If we can find the key."

Faelan's head tipped back. "You can fly one of those things?" Was there no end to what these modern women would try?

"You'd be surprised what I can do," she said with a suggestive wink.

Duncan scowled at her as Ronan and Declan arrived, Ronan with an arrow nocked in his bow, Declan wielding his sword.

"Tomas, go with Shane and Sorcha," Faelan said. "Niall, you're the strongest, get him to the helicopter. Ronan, cover them from the balcony with your bow. Cody and Anna, keep watch from out there. Cody has a gun. Use your talismans if you have to."

"Consider it done," Cody said.

Someone found a clean cloth and gave Faelan his bloody T-shirt back.

"Keep this tight against your wound," Tomas said, pressing the cloth into Shane's hand. Niall scooped him up as if he weighed nothing.

"Hey, I can walk."

"It's faster this way," Niall said, without looking down or breaking stride.

Faelan left his ruined shirt on the floor, and they all took their positions, watching as the warriors crossed the castle grounds. Niall put Shane inside the helicopter and closed the door. The key must have been there, because the blades began to whirl. Three demons ran out, but Cody destroyed the first one with a bullet to the head. The body disappeared as Ronan caught the second demon with an arrow in the heart. Anna killed the last one with a well-placed knife. Niall was back before the helicopter was out of sight.

"I expected a harder fight," Duncan said. "Either these bastards are afraid of us, or they're somewhere else."

"We found pieces of a body nailed to the wall in the tower where Faelan rescued Bree," Declan said. "If that's what he does to his own, I'm surprised he had anyone left."

"Get back to your positions and work toward the south tower. It's the only place we haven't checked. Niall and Conall, take the passageways. Cody, I need you inside. Meet us at the south tower. Anna can handle things out there." If Faelan needed help with Druan, Cody was probably the only one who stood a chance. "I'll take Ronan and Declan and head over to the tower." Faelan looked at Ronan, who seemed pre-occupied. "Everyone keep an eye out for the virus..." He pressed his lips together, only slightly swollen now. "And for Bree. I think you're right and Druan's playing a twisted game."

There were nods and relieved smiles.

Ronan hung his bow over his shoulder. "About time you got your head out of your ass. Let's find your woman," he said, sounding a tad more like himself.

He was the only one Faelan had told about the mate mark on his neck, although Faelan was sure Sorcha had seen it earlier. Odd that she hadn't mentioned it.

"Hold up, Faelan. There's something you'll want to see." Niall led Faelan to a glass case inside the massive library. A broadsword lay inside. His sword.

Faelan handed Ronan the blade he'd borrowed and shattered the glass with his boot. He lifted out the sword, closing his fingers around the hilt, relishing the familiar weight. He held it out and gave it a swing. It felt good.

Looked good, too. Faelan's heart felt lighter. A sword was like a woman. There was only one for him, and he would find her if he had to tear this castle down stone by stone.

Niall joined Conall by the fireplace. They opened the secret passageway and disappeared inside. Faelan followed Ronan and Declan down the empty corridor, testing his sword. Near the stairs to the second floor, they surprised two men. "It's him," one of them said, staring at Faelan, and they turned to run.

"After them," Faelan yelled. "Take their heads!" Too late, Ronan's arrow zinged past Faelan, lodging in the chest of the tallest one, pinning him to the wall. The man opened his mouth and hissed, exposing inch-long sharp fangs as he tried to pull free. Declan roared past the vampire, cutting his head clean from his body without pausing as he chased the second man to the top of the stairs. Another vampire. Ronan stared at his arrow lying in the pile of dust. He muttered a name Faelan didn't catch, but he knew the look on Ronan's face. Guilt.

"Where did these things come from?" Declan asked. "And what are they doing in a demon's castle? Demons and vampires are like oil and water."

Faelan rubbed at the headache building behind his temples. Was Druan forming some kind of alliance? If demons and vampires were unleashed on the world at the same time, humans wouldn't stand a chance. Vampires were nasty creatures, as bad as demons. They lived for their thirst. The legend was that they'd appeared a few thousand years earlier. From the stories he'd heard, humans had been as oblivious to vampires' existence as they were to the demons. It'd taken a special force of

Michael's army to wipe them out. Faelan wished they had one of the warriors now.

A hiss sounded from the top of the stairs. A short, squat demon started toward them, followed by several more. The lead demon stopped when he saw the pile of dust. His face convulsed, his body vibrating.

The warriors leapt up the stairs and struck hard. Faelan drove his sword into the squat demon, piercing another standing behind him. The first one disappeared into nothing before Faelan could even withdraw his sword. The second was wounded, but not dead. Faelan swung his sword without remorse. The head vanished before it hit the floor. He went for the next one, but a dirk lodged in the demon's chest before Faelan could swing. Cody ran past him and grabbed his weapon off the floor.

"There's something over here worth protecting," Faelan said into his microphone when the demons were dead, and for a moment he forgot about the virus, hoping it was Bree. When his sense of duty returned, he reminded himself that Bree's life depended on his stopping the virus, too.

When the group reached the final set of steps leading to the tower, more guards appeared. Some looked human, but most of them were huge, their faces and bodies hideous. These would be Druan's best. The virus must be up there. The demons positioned themselves along the stairs, dwarfing the space, swords drawn, ready to die for their master.

Ronan drew his bow and Declan readied his sword. "There are too many," Faelan said, pulling out his talisman. "Stand back and close your eyes."

Ronan grabbed Faelan's arm. "No. Save your strength for Druan."

Ronan was right. If Faelan wasn't strong enough, the talisman wouldn't work, and they'd all die, and if his suspicion was correct, his talisman was already weakened. With Cody's strength and experience added to Faelan's, it might be enough, but Faelan wasn't sure he wanted Cody to take that risk. They turned away as Ronan began to chant. The air grew thick; the vibration resonated through Faelan's legs. He saw the faint flash, even though he protected his eyes. When the screams were silenced, the stairs were empty except for two men looking for escape.

Declan leapt the steps three at a time, catching the closest one off guard, taking the vampire's head. The second one, a pale blond with icy-blue eyes, whirled and ran. Ronan nocked an arrow and let it fly. It hit the vampire's shoulder, and he vanished into the wall, arrow and all. Ronan bounded up the steps with Cody and Faelan on his heels and stared at the spot where the vampire had disappeared. "God forgive me," he whispered.

Faelan didn't have time to ponder why Ronan needed forgiveness. "We think the virus is in the south tower," Faelan said into his microphone. "It's heavily guarded. We've destroyed two dozen. Clear your areas and move over here."

Declan inspected the wall where the vampire had vanished, while Cody and Faelan tried to open the iron door. It was locked. Faelan could hear sounds within. "Let's kick it in," Faelan said. He and Cody got into position, and Ronan stood behind them with his bow raised, guarding their backs. With a quick nod, Faelan and Cody kicked the door.

"Damnation."

"What's that thing made of?" Cody rubbed his thigh.

"Niall, we need more muscle in the south tower," Declan said behind them.

"Almost there," came Niall's reply. "Bloody passages. Made for bairns."

They tried again, with Declan's help, but the door wouldn't budge. Faelan listened again to the scrambling sounds inside the locked room. "Bree," he called, trying to keep the desperation out of his voice. There was no answer. "We can't wait. Ronan, can you open it?"

"I'll try, but this one looks tricky. I think we're gonna need Niall." Ronan slung his bow behind his back, pulled the metal piece from his pocket, and knelt in front of the door. Faelan felt his sweat beading as he ticked off the seconds, imagining the horrors that could be taking place inside the room.

Niall burst out of a hidden door at the foot of the stairs, brushing cobwebs from his face. "Have you found it?"

"We think so," Cody said. "Door's locked."

"It's locked from the inside," Ronan said, rising. He stood guard while the others kicked the door on the count of three. It flew open, revealing a stark white room with tubes and machines and metal surfaces.

"Looks like a laboratory," Niall said.

"Same as the room in the other tower, except for the window," Ronan said.

They heard a gasp, and the white-haired man Faelan had seen when he came for Bree began frantically lowering something out the window, the thing so heavy it was about to take the old man with it.

"Stop," Faelan yelled. He ran toward the man, shoved him out of the way, and caught the rope. A large metal box dangled two feet from the bottom of the window ledge.

"He'll kill me," the old man said, struggling with Faelan, eyes wild. Declan grabbed the man around the chest, holding him back, as Faelan gripped the rope. Cody and Niall helped him pull the box up to the ledge and move it inside.

"I've found minions and a bunch of halflings hiding on the third floor, north side," Brodie called over the microphone. "I need help." In the background they heard screams.

"Go," Faelan told the others. "I have to do this myself."

"I'm on the way," Niall told Brodie. He and Declan took off at a run.

"I'll stay," Cody said. He had a look that said he didn't fear death, might even welcome it, but Faelan decided he couldn't have that on his conscience. He'd failed too many already. If he had to die to get this done, he wouldn't take anyone else with him.

"No, Brodie needs help. There could be others hiding. I'll destroy the virus—it's probably in that box—and meet you on the third floor. We can't let anyone escape."

"Are you sure?" Cody asked. "I'm willing to… stay."

And to die. "I'm sure."

Cody clasped Faelan's arm, his gaze somber, and then nodded.

Ronan held back. "Be careful, Faelan. It's not over."

But it was close. Ronan and Cody left. Faelan turned to the white-haired man. "What's in here?" he demanded, pointing at the box. It was heavy, solid. "Speak, old man."

"He'll kill me if I talk." He glanced from the box to the door with terror-filled eyes.

"He'll kill you anyway. That's what he does."

"He promised to take care of me after it's released. He's created a special place for those he wants to keep, like me." He raised a hand, rubbing at a nervous tic in his left eye.

"You're his sorcerer?"

"I didn't want to do it but I had no choice."

"There's always a choice. Are you human?"

"Half. I was born in 1720. I was an alchemist and a sorcerer when Druan came to me after his first sorcerer was killed."

"Why does he want me?"

"For revenge, and he needed to test the time vault, to see if it worked. He planned to wake you in time to witness his victory. He didn't realize it would take so long to create this new virus. He doesn't understand these things," he whispered, as if Druan could hear him. "Just like the mirror. I told him no one uses that spell anymore." He glanced at the door again.

"Did Druan tell anyone about the time vault?" If he had, their trouble wouldn't end with Druan's destruction.

"No. He protected his secrets. He was always afraid one of the others would find out."

"Others?"

"Them. The old ones. That's why he used this castle, so no one could see what he was up to, including his master."

"Are the other demons of old helping him?"

"No. They don't help each other. The league is a

farce. Druan wants rid of them as much as he wants rid of you."

League. The word Tomas had seen in Angus's notebook. "Did you cloak this castle?"

"No. I don't know who did it."

"Is this the virus?" Faelan pointed at the box.

"If I tell you and you destroy him, will you save me?"

He wasn't making any promises to a sorcerer who'd spent more than a century figuring out how to destroy humans and could pass the information on to someone else. "Is this it?" Faelan put his dirk to the man's throat.

"It's in there."

"How does it work?"

"It's a combination of virus and sorcery. It destroys oxygen on contact, feeds on it like fire, but faster. Everything human will die. One vial will wipe out this entire country. He brought demons here from all over the world to solicit their help in releasing it."

"They're here in the castle?"

"No, Albany."

The conference. "Is he working with vampires?"

"Vampires?" The old man looked startled. "Aren't they extinct?"

Everyone seemed to think so, except the vampires. If Druan had formed an alliance with the undead, he would have to keep it quiet. The Dark One wouldn't tolerate it. But it made no sense for the vampires to help Druan eliminate their food source.

"Druan wouldn't work with vampires if they did exist. He can barely tolerate his own kind."

Then what were they doing here? "Where is Druan?"

"I think he's with the woman. He had something urgent to do."

"The woman? Bree?"

"He didn't say for sure—"

Faelan lifted the man by his shirt, dangling his feet off the floor. "What has he done with her? Tell me now, or I'll kill you myself."

The old man trembled. "I don't know. I swear on my mother's grave. He just said he had something important to do. He doesn't trust me. He doesn't trust anyone."

Faelan dropped the man, swallowing back the pain. "Can you think of any place he'd take her? Somewhere hidden."

"The secret passages."

"We've checked there."

"I'd tell you if I knew. I tried to warn her when she called, but he almost caught me."

Faelan would have to get rid of the virus first, then find Druan, shackle him and force him to tell where Bree was. "Is this all of the virus?"

"It is. I packed it myself. Be careful. Once these vials are opened, nothing can stop it."

"The virus won't be released."

"How can you stop it? It'd take a miracle—"

"I know someone in the miracle business. Close your eyes." Faelan pulled his talisman from his shirt. "Better yet. Don't blink." He couldn't let this monster live to create another virus.

The sorcerer didn't hear him. He was staring past Faelan, his features twisted with terror. Druan stood in the open doorway, wearing his human shell, his gaze darting from Faelan to the box. The sorcerer ran toward the open window. Faelan grabbed for him, but it was too late. The old man plunged over the side with a scream, leaving Faelan with a torn piece of shirt in his hand.

"Good riddance. Saves me the mess." Druan closed the door. After glancing at the ruined lock, he lowered an iron bar that must have been there since the castle was built.

It took all of Faelan's willpower not to destroy Druan on the spot, but he had to find Bree first. "Where is she?"

"My human?" Druan laughed, but the sound was cold, hard.

"She's not yours," Faelan growled.

"Ah, but she is, warrior. I've watched over her for a long time. While you slept, I watched her grow. And after I rid this planet of its blight, I'll need a few mixed breeds for slaves. Bree will make an excellent mother, don't you think?"

Faelan wanted to shred Druan into pieces with his bare hands, feel his bones crunch and tissue tear. "Tell me where she is."

"Where only I can find her. You believed she was a demon, didn't you? When all she'd done was try to save you, which I'm punishing her for, even as we speak. Then I'll practice this forgiveness your God is so fond of and make her mine."

Every part of him seethed with panic and rage. Before he could judge the wisdom of it, Faelan sent his dirk sailing through the air. It struck Druan mid-chest, and the demon screeched. He ripped it out and flung it to the floor, hate oozing from eyes already starting to shift. His bones lengthened and skin bulged grotesquely, as he transformed into his natural form, towering over Faelan.

Faelan was no stranger to demons, but the sight and

smell was still repulsive. "Tell me where she is, or I'll destroy you now and find her myself," Faelan snarled, his hand twitching over his talisman, the other tight on his sword.

"You'll never find her in your lifetime. Not even two. I've saved the best trick for last."

"Did you hurt her?"

Druan threw back his gray head and laughed again, a slimy hissing sound. "Did I mate with her? Not yet. But I will. In and out of my human shell."

"You won't get the chance," Faelan said.

Footsteps pounded on the stairs. Druan smiled and moved toward the door. Faelan's anger numbed. He should have let Cody stay. It would be impossible to destroy Druan, the virus, and his horde of demons, too. But he could finish what he'd started before Druan came in. If the virus was gone, Druan might be easier to manage. Before he could raise his talisman, the air shifted. He heard screams and voices calling his name. He recognized Ronan and Duncan. The reinforcements were his. They'd destroyed Druan's demons.

Druan shrieked with rage. He whirled and came at Faelan, slashing with his claws. Faelan spun like a matador and sliced open Druan's arm with his sword. "That was for my father and Ian," Faelan said, trying to block the sulfurous smell.

Druan turned again, moving slower this time, calculating. "What about your sister, little Alana? I let her live... after I finished with her. But her firstborn son, how could I let him live, bearing your name?"

Druan had killed Alana's infant son? Faelan's anger merged into a fiery ball. The loss of his family, the death and destruction caused by a war that was no more than a distraction for Druan, the pain and heartache the demon had caused Bree. Faelan roared and lunged at Druan, striking again with his sword. A gash appeared in Druan's chest, close to where the dirk had struck, but it would take far more to kill him by hand. Faelan struck again, this time slicing deep into the demon's neck. Druan let out a terrible howl and swiped at Faelan. His claw caught on Faelan's talisman. Druan jerked his hand back when the metal scorched his skin. The cord broke, and the talisman tumbled through the air, landing in a corner with a thud.

"Another scar. I'll destroy that charm along with you this time." The smell of burning flesh mingled with sulfur, and the pounding in Faelan's head grew louder before he realized it was the door. It sounded like a hundred feet were kicking. Faelan moved toward the talisman in a haze. He had to get it back, or everyone he loved would die.

A whisper brushed his ear, soothing, balm to his pain. He didn't know if it was Bree, Michael, or even God himself who tried to quiet his rage, but he held on to it, pulled it inside. Used it to focus on what he had to do.

Druan moved closer to the corner. "What's so important about the charm, warrior? It gives a nasty burn, for a pretty decoration." Druan swirled and picked up the talisman by the cord, winding it around one claw, careful not to touch it. His ugly head turned as he scrutinized it. "I see writing," he said, inching toward the box. "Another trophy to replace the sword. I'll keep it with the *Book of Battles* to mark the day of your defeat."

Faelan's skin felt clammy. *Book of Battles*? Druan

had the book? His chest pounded like a cattle stampede. The demon was five feet from the box, bleeding from his wounds. Faelan had to destroy him. Now. Beheading a powerful demon was almost impossible, but it was that or wrestle the talisman from him. He'd already made the first cut. Faelan adjusted his grip on his sword and lunged for the demon.

Druan threw the talisman over Faelan's head and snatched the box. He reached for one of the vials as Faelan spun and dove for the talisman. He slid across the floor, snatching the talisman as it rolled. He opened it as he leaped to his feet, praying it had enough strength, and began to chant. Druan opened the vial and flung it across the room. The air sizzled, too thick to breathe; the floor shook. Faelan watched it happen as if in slow motion. The iron bar broke free from the wall and the door burst open. Niall rushed into the room, followed by the others, as green vapors clawed through the air like fingers. Faelan heard a warning cry and saw the warriors spin around, throwing their arms over their eyes. A boom sounded like thunder as brilliant white light met the green vapors in midair. Colors swirled, tumultuous and violent, and the white wound around the green, swallowing it like a snake. Druan screamed, his face distorted, as he reached for the virus. The light retracted, leaving nothing but the metal box and empty vials clattering in its wake.

The virus was gone.

Druan was gone.

Where was Bree?

Chapter 34

THE ROOM FILLED WITH WARRIORS, SWORDS DRAWN, chests heaving, some dripping blood.

"Are you okay?" Duncan asked, but all Faelan could manage was a nod.

"What in blazes was that?" Brodie asked.

"You almost kissed your ass good-bye," Niall said. "We all did."

Sorcha ran in, hair flying, then lowered her sword. "I'm too late."

The warriors circled Faelan, voices low with shock. Ronan put a hand on Faelan's shoulder. "You did it, brother. He's gone. The virus is destroyed."

"You need rest," Cody said. "We'll get Bree. Where is she?"

Faelan's legs buckled, too weak to support him, and he sank to his knees. "I don't know."

~~~

Four days later…

Faelan ran his fingers over the stone, leaving a smear of blood. He'd rubbed his skin raw. He kept his eyes off the bed as he moved to another stone, looking for a crack or hidden catch.

"Faelan?" Ronan stood in the doorway of Druan's bedroom. "Go home. Get some sleep before you fall over."

"I can't leave." Faelan pounded his fist against the next stone, but it didn't move. "I can hear her calling me."

"I know, but you killed an ancient demon. You're still weak. You need rest and food. We'll keep looking. You know that. He's hidden her somewhere. He was too obsessed with her to hurt her."

But where? Druan said he'd hidden her where only he could find her. The minions they'd captured had been no help. It was as if Bree had disappeared.

"Sean called a few minutes ago," Ronan said. "The McKenzie clan is searching Druan's last castle in Europe."

"What about the demons at the conference? Did they get them all?" The list Coira found on Angus matched the one they'd discovered in Druan's bedroom three days before.

"Most of them. They were still waiting for their vials. Warriors swarmed the place; only a few demons escaped, but they're being hunted down. Cody has a friend in the FBI who's covering our tracks. The public thinks it was a drug bust. More than a hundred demons have been destroyed in the last four days, thanks to you and Angus. This is the biggest joint operation in clan history. But you need to rest now, or you'll be dead before we find Bree. Ever hear of *Romeo and Juliet*?"

"He's right, Faelan," Duncan said, joining Ronan at the door. "Let us finish up here. Ten more warriors just arrived from Australia. They brought Skylar and Caleb, two of their best Seekers. And Ryan and Brenna are on their way from Rome. Their sense of smell is unequaled. We won't stop till we find her."

Faelan nodded and rose to his feet. They'd all worked tirelessly, especially Conall. The young warrior had sworn he would not stop looking until she was found. He still felt responsible for losing her.

"Here," Duncan said. "We found this hidden in the library." He handed Faelan a leather book. "It's her Grandma Emily's journal. I don't know why Druan had it."

Holding the book under his arm, Faelan trudged through the castle, ignoring the long looks and hushed whispers as he passed his clansmen surveying and cataloging Druan's possessions, some repairing the damage from the blast while others searched for Bree.

Since Angus had been followed, the Watchers decided it best to move some of the warriors from Scotland to make another home base. No one knew why Druan's castle looked so much like their own, or how it had been cloaked, but once they installed a security system, the place would be hard to penetrate, and by then every demon who'd helped Druan and knew the castle's location would be dead. Druan guarded his secrets well, as his sorcerer had said, even from the Dark One.

Faelan drove Bree's car to the house and sat in the driveway, dreading to go inside. Some of the other warriors had searched the place to make sure she wasn't there. Faelan hadn't had the courage to come back and face his guilt and pain. He sat there until it was too dark to see, trying not to suffocate at the thought that he might have to wake every morning without her, trudging through minutes and hours until the oblivion of sleep brought relief.

Why God had chosen to dangle her in front of his nose, the only woman he'd ever loved, and then yank her away, he couldn't fathom. There must be a reason. Michael might know. But as powerful as Michael was, he was still a servant, and some things God kept to himself.

Opening the door, he dragged himself from the car and forced one foot in front of the other until he stood in her bedroom. He wanted to collapse, but he was covered with sweat and dust. Her things were still scattered everywhere. He picked up clothes and draped them over a chair, closed drawers, and righted the photographs that had hidden his father's pocket watch. The last frame, one he hadn't noticed before, showed a gray-haired woman—he recognized Bree's grandmother from other photographs in the house—smiling at a dark-haired lassie who looked like a fairy from one of his mother's stories, with her green eyes and mischievous grin. The same lassie Faelan had seen huddled under the covers in his dream, the one Michael had sent him to protect. Everyone else had believed in her, but he, the one person who should've known better, who should've trusted her, had betrayed her. He trailed his fingers over her face. *Where are you?*

He stood under her shower, letting the water beat down on his head and run over his back, washing away the grime, leaving only guilt. He remembered her battling Grog with a broom, trying to get her hands on the swords, baking him a pie. Touching him in the tub. How shocked he'd been, how he'd thought he would die from wanting her.

Now he just wanted to see her, feel her breathe. He'd known her less than a fortnight, but she was bound to his soul. He turned off the water and stepped out. Wrapped in a towel, he walked back to her bedroom. A book lay on the floor by her bed. It was leather-bound, like the journal Duncan had found, but thicker. Isabel's journal? He picked it up and ran his hands over the rose engraved on the cover. He'd seen this book before, more than a hundred and fifty years ago. He remembered it falling at his feet outside the tavern. On the inside a name was written, Isabel Belville. Proof it *was* Isabel he'd met, not Bree.

Near the front of the journal was a genealogy chart. Above Samuel Wood, Isabel's father, was another name. Nigel Ellwood. Faelan leaned closer and rubbed his eyes in disbelief. Nigel Ellwood. It couldn't be. He was the missing Watcher who'd vanished before Faelan was born. The clan believed the Watcher had died. He'd obviously lived long enough to have a son, Samuel. Bree's great-great-great-grandfather.

Bree *was* part of his clan.

That's why Faelan bore the mate mark, why he had memories of Bree before he'd met her, even before she was born. It wasn't the time vault messing with his mind. God hadn't dangled her in front of him and taken her away. The whole thing had been planned. She was his mate. And he'd thrown her back in God's face.

Faelan grabbed the phone and dialed. "Sean, it's Faelan—"

"Faelan, my boy. I've been worried. I was ready to come over there myself. Have you found her?"

"No. We're still searching." For Bree, the *Book of Battles*, the time vault key. Vampires.

He'd told the clan about the key and the missing book, but they'd had no luck finding them so far. The

Council was meeting even now. He was grateful they were still trying to find Bree, with so many troubles weighing on the clan.

"They'll find her. They won't stop till they do. The whole clan owes her a debt for freeing you."

"Aye," he said, feeling the weight of guilt again. She risked her life for him, and he'd forsaken her, sent her from Scotland thinking he didn't care for her. Straight into Druan's trap.

"I hope you can forgive an old man for keeping secrets, but your mission was too important to get sidetracked by vengeance. Your father wouldn't have wanted that."

"I understand," Faelan said, not sure if he spoke the truth. "That's not why I called. Remember Nigel Ellwood?"

"The Watcher who vanished?"

"He had a son. Samuel."

"How do you know—"

"Bree is Nigel's descendent."

"Our Bree?"

"I found a genealogy chart with Nigel's name. Samuel changed his surname to Wood."

"Och, this puts things in a different light, it does. I've seen how you look at her. I'd wondered…"

"She's my mate. I knew as soon as I saw her, but I thought it was the time vault messing with my head. How could it be? We're from different centuries."

"God made time. I reckon he can manipulate it if He wants."

"But I failed my assignment. If I'd let those warriors stay with me, if we'd succeeded with Druan the first time, I wouldn't be here. I never would have met Bree. So how could—"

"Maybe this worked out the way it should. Could be it was meant for you to stop Druan in this time and not before. And could be there's something more for you to do. You said Michael warned you about the book. Why warn you and no one else?"

"He said something about a necessary sacrifice." His family? His father and brothers who'd died helping him, his mother, Alana? Or was Bree the sacrificial lamb?

"I don't know why Michael doesn't tell us everything. I suppose it's part of the journey. I think we'll know the answers when we're meant to know them. Stop beating yourself up over that war. It wasn't your fault. You were probably never meant to stop it, no matter how many warriors you had with you. Same goes for Druan. I know you blame yourself for not suspecting he was the archeologist, but anyone would have thought Russell was the demon after how he treated her. It was just bad luck that he resembled Druan's human shell."

Faelan rubbed at the knot of tension in his neck. Still, he should have insisted on meeting Jared. The demon had stood on Bree's front porch while Faelan hid in the family room, not fifty feet away.

"Don't give up, lad. We'll find her yet."

But they'd searched for four days. Did she have food and water? Was she injured? After he hung up, Faelan walked back to the bed. He picked up the earring in the marble cup, the mate to the one she'd lost in the crypt. She'd been so busy helping him that she hadn't taken the time to search for it. In the morning he would find it, as he'd told her he would. It might be the last thing he would ever do for her.

Faelan touched the earring to his lips and dropped onto the bed. He lay back, resting his head on Bree's pillow, and hugged her coat to his chest, wondering if she was cold now that the nights had turned cooler. Her scent surrounded him as her voice brushed his ear, pleading for him to hurry.

"I don't know how to find you," he whispered, staring at the ceiling until exhaustion overtook him.

~~~

Michael the Archangel stood before Faelan. Not the plump, androgynous thing with wings that graced masterpieces of art. This was the warrior angel. More than seven feet tall, glowing, clad in white and gold. Fierce, but beautiful, his presence so blinding he could come only in visions and dreams.

Each time Michael came with an order, Faelan was more humbled, more aware of how much help he and his clan needed to win these battles. It couldn't be done with swords and talismans alone, the same way human responsibilities weren't meant to be carried alone.

This time the archangel didn't bring orders but stood watching Faelan as he slept. Was he asleep or awake? Faelan didn't know. There was concern and kindness in Michael's face and an urging for him to do something, but Faelan was tired; he wanted to sleep, to forget.

"Faelan, wake. What you seek is near."

The pull of evil was strong, urging him to shut out the vision.

"Faelan, now." Michael clapped his hands once, and a noise like thunder pierced the dream.

Faelan sat up, surrounded by the strange glow. The archangel *had* been here. *What you seek is near*. What did it mean? Faelan had been sent to destroy the virus and eliminate Druan. Both were finished. Did Michael mean the book or the key?

Rubbing his hands over his face, he stood. The light of dawn was easing through the blinds. The earring lay on the table beside the bed. Bree thought she'd lost its mate in the crypt. He needed to go there anyway to send the time vault back. Even without the key, it was too dangerous to leave it here. He pulled on a T-shirt and his kilt and made his way to the kitchen, first cleaning up the mess on the floor, then swiping his finger through the jar of peanut butter. He didn't remember if he'd eaten yesterday or the day before, and he didn't care, but his body needed food so he could keep searching. After brushing his teeth, he left the house, his thoughts too dark to be warmed by the sun. He unlocked the crypt, wondering how he'd find something as tiny as an earring, and the words came again. *What you seek is near*.

Why would the archangel, charged with commanding the armies of Heaven, care about an earring? He must mean the book or the key. Faelan started to search, beginning with the floor. There could be a loose stone, like the floorboard in his bedroom. A sparkle caught the reflection from the sun coming through the door. The earring lay face down in a crack. Faelan picked it up and put it in his sporran, praying he'd see Bree wear it again. He continued searching for the book and key, but there was nothing here but the time vault.

Might as well send it back now. He couldn't take a chance on someone finding the key and figuring out what the vault was used for. Druan was no longer a threat, but the vampires had Faelan troubled. He'd blocked the steps to the chapel cellar until he could send that time vault back. The key still hadn't been found. It wasn't in Angus's things. Two missing time vault keys. Not something the clan should have to worry about with vampires on the loose, but Faelan didn't want to pull any of the Seekers away from looking for Bree.

The stone slab covering the vault slid easily. He pulled the talisman from under his shirt and lined up the symbols to return the vault.

No! The thundering command was clear. *What you seek is near*.

He'd searched for the book and the key. They weren't here. Faelan stared at the time vault, a terrifying thought piercing his mind. What did he seek above all else? Not a key or a book. Bree, his mate. Could Druan have done something so vile? He'd said Faelan would never find her, not even in two lifetimes. The key was missing. The perfect revenge. Faelan's body felt numb. He slid his hands across the prison, trying to feel if she was inside.

Hurry. Her voice brushed his mind, and his talisman grew warm against his chest.

She was in there. Druan had locked her in the time vault and it wouldn't open for a hundred and fifty years, assuming he found the key. Even if he did, he'd be dead by the time she could be released. She would wake as he had, with everything she knew gone, her family and friends dead.

"No!" His roar of anger echoed off the stone. He punched the wall with his fist. Druan had stolen everything else. He would not steal her. Faelan touched the engraved symbols, trying to reach her. He'd take another time vault and get one of the warriors to lock him inside, leaving a note so he and Bree could be awakened at the same time. He didn't care that it was breaking the rules. He'd face Michael when the time came. Who would do it? Ronan? Faelan's talisman grew uncomfortably hot.

He remembered the vision of the archangel, the kindness in his eyes, the voice leading him here. Why would Michael bring him to Bree if she couldn't be rescued? She wasn't ordinary. She'd saved the world. She'd survived looking at an engaged talisman and destroyed a halfling. The talisman was painful now. He had an idea, but if it didn't work, he risked killing himself and her, too.

Uttering one last desperate prayer, he readjusted the symbols, setting the talisman to destroy, and aimed it at the lock. The air grew heavy as the words flowed from his tongue. A rumble rolled up through the floor. A flash of white light shot out from his talisman, followed by a loud pop. Colors flashed, blue, orange, and green as Faelan was flung against the wall.

Chapter 35

FAELAN PULLED HIMSELF UP AND STARED AT THE TIME vault. He grabbed the lid and threw it open. Bree lay inside, her eyes closed, face bruised. A trail of blood ran from her neck, staining her collar. Faelan barely had time to recollect the puncture marks on Russell and the vampires hidden among the demons, when Bree's eyes flew open, and she screamed. Clawing her way out of the time vault, she shoved past him and ran for the door. Shock dulled his senses. She was halfway through the graveyard when he caught her.

"Bree, stop." He leapt and grabbed her, pinning her arms when she tried to struggle. They fell over a headstone and crashed to the ground. He rolled on top of her. "It's me, Faelan."

She stilled. He eased his hold and leaned back, giving her room to breathe. She lifted her face, but it wasn't red eyes and fangs he saw. It was terrified green eyes, human eyes that widened with recognition. And he could see the blood was from a gash on her neck.

A tiny sob escaped her lips as she touched his face in disbelief. "You're not dead. Oh, God, you're not dead."

Faelan sat up and pulled her against his hammering chest. She was alive. In his arms, safe. They sat there, clasped together, unable to find words.

"I can't breathe," she finally gasped, trying to pull away.

Had the time vault damaged her? Or his talisman? "Are ye hurt?"

"No. You're crushing me."

Faelan eased his hold. "I thought I'd lost you." He patted her face, her hair. "I'm sorry I let you go. I didn't want Druan to find you. To know how much you mean to me." His voice was raw, his face damp as he pressed it to hers. Her tears or his, he didn't know.

"I know." She wrapped her arms around him, squeezing tight, then leaned back and gripped his shoulders, panic in her eyes. "Jared is the demon, not Russell."

"You're safe now. He's gone."

"You destroyed him?"

"I had to. He released the virus."

Her eyes widened. "He released it?"

"My talisman was already open, or it would have been too late." She would've been the only human to escape annihilation.

"You did it. You saved the world. Wait… what year is it?"

"It's been only four days." Four agonizing days.

"What about one hundred and fifty years? And the disk? I heard the guards say Jared hid it in one of the towers."

"I used the talisman."

"You aimed it at the vault… while I was in there?"

"It was either that or get Ronan to put me in one, so I could wake with you a hundred and fifty years from now."

"You can do that?"

"I don't know. I was going to try. I couldn't let you go. Did he do this?" Faelan asked, looking at the cut on her neck.

She nodded. "I told him I wasn't interested in helping him repopulate the world with halflings."

Faelan remembered Grog and the other body hanging in the castle. Druan's obsession with Bree had probably saved her life. "Did he... hurt you?"

"I don't think so. When I woke, someone was carrying me to the time vault. I saw the lid closing and knew I'd never see you, even if you'd escaped." She looked back at the crypt and shuddered.

Druan had put her inside the time vault awake! Faelan stood and pulled her to her feet. "Let's get you inside and cleaned up. You'll need rest, and there are things I have to explain." He swung her up into his arms and carried her across the torn backyard, through the kitchen, and into her bedroom. He put her on the bed and pressed his lips against her forehead. "I'll be back. I'm going to get a washcloth. I want to clean your wound."

"I need a shower to wash off this blood."

"How about a bath after I clean you up a bit?"

She nodded.

"I'll turn the Jacuzzi on." He picked up the phone by the bed and took it with him, punching in the numbers as he walked. "I've found her," he said, when Ronan answered. "She's alive."

The whoop of joy on the other end made Faelan's ear ring. It was a welcome change from Ronan's silence. The entire clan was somber, but Ronan's reaction was puzzling, as if it were his fault. Faelan had been too busy searching for Bree to find out what disturbed his friend. Faelan found washcloths and first aid supplies while he listened to Ronan yell out the news.

"Where was she?" Ronan asked.

"The time vault."

"Inside? How the... *What* is she?"

Faelan wasn't sure himself. "Call off the search. Let Sean know, so he can get word to the other clans. Everyone should get some rest. I'll catch up later." Faelan knew Ronan wanted to ask questions, but they would have to wait. Faelan hung up and turned on the Jacuzzi, adjusting the water. He hurried back to her. "I called to let everyone know you're safe," he said, brushing her hair from her face. "They're all here, Ronan, Declan, Duncan, Niall, all of them. Even Cody refused to leave."

"My mother?"

"She doesn't know. We wanted to wait..." He'd planned to wait until he knew for certain.

"Did we lose anyone in the battle?"

"Only Angus." A fact that was remarkable in itself. Faelan cleaned the edges of the gash, cursing Druan when Bree bit back a cry. He wished he could bring the demon back for five minutes. "I'm sorry it was Jared. I know you cared for him. I should have insisted on meeting him."

"We were so sure it was Russell. How did you get out of the dungeon? I went back, but you were gone."

Faelan washed off the worst of the blood. "Conall followed you there. He found me."

"It must have been him trying to get in the secret passage. Is he upset with me?"

"He's too busy playing the hero." Faelan grinned, the first in many days, then grew serious again. "I'd be dead if not for both of you. Druan had been waiting all this time for me."

"He told me he'd been watching the place, and my family, for generations. He killed my grandmother because she wouldn't let him dig. And Frederick."

"He killed my father and Ian as well. And Alana's first son."

"Oh, Faelan."

"They didn't want to tell me until after Druan was gone, but I found my father's pocket watch in your bedroom." Faelan checked to see if the cut needed stitching. Probably not, but it might leave a scar.

"The only pocket watch I have belonged to... McGowan. He was—"

"My father." Faelan swallowed. "He used the name so he wouldn't be recognized."

"That's why he spent so much time in the graveyard, to be near you. Then it was your brother who found him. Remember, Isabel said he was so sad, and she thought she'd seen him somewhere."

"It must have been Tavis. He looks like me. And Isabel did see me, a few days before I was suspended. When I met Grog at the tavern, Isabel, Frederick, and another man, probably Samuel, were getting out of their carriage. Isabel dropped her handbag. Which, by the way, was nearly as big as that thing you tote around. I helped her gather her things. She had the journal with her."

"You met Isabel? Why didn't you tell me? What was she like? What did she say?"

She would drive him mad with her curiosity, but God, he loved her. "I wasn't paying much attention. I was too worried about Grog. Your bath is ready." He carried her to the bathroom and helped her undress, feeling guilty for how her naked form affected him when he should be satisfied she was alive. He eased her into the bubbling water, soaking himself in the process. He took off his wet shirt and sat on the side of the tub, tempted to climb in with her. She didn't need that now. She needed to heal. He discreetly adjusted his sporran and reached for her hand.

"There are things I need to say." How did he explain what he felt for her? It was too big for words. More than just wanting to make a home with her, see dark-haired babies at her breast, and grow old with her. His very soul was connected to hers. But what if she didn't want him? This was a different time. Women wanted more than a father for their children and a home. How would he survive if she turned him down? He took a breath for courage and spoke. "I can't go back to my own time. I wouldn't, even if I could. I belong here. With you. I know you're… independent, and I'll have to change the way I think about some things, but you're mine. I mean, I'm yours. We belong together."

"But what about mates?"

"You are my mate. I knew it the minute I saw you, but I didn't trust my feelings, since you weren't from my clan. Or my time."

"You saw it in my eyes, like Ronan said?"

Faelan frowned. "Why were you talking to Ronan about mates?"

"He and Coira were explaining how it works."

"I did see it in your eyes, but I thought it was the time vault messing with my senses. Then I got the mark on my neck. A mate mark. It didn't seem possible."

"What about the whole related-to-the-clan thing?"

"That's where it gets interesting. I found Isabel's journal. I'm sure you've read the genealogy chart in the front. Samuel Wood, his name was really Samuel Ellwood."

"Yes. Samuel's father, Nigel, was murdered, and his mother shortened the name to Wood. We assumed it had something to do with her husband's death. I'd hoped Isabel would mention something more about it in her journal."

"Nigel Ellwood was a Watcher from my clan. He disappeared before I was born."

Bree gasped. "Isabel's grandfather was related to you? That means I'm related to you."

"Distantly," Faelan said, feeling like his smile would touch his ears.

"This is incredible."

"Aye. It explains a lot of inexplicable things. You remember asking what I was thinking of in Alana's portrait? I don't know how, but I was thinking about you, even before you were born. I suspect I had been, all the time I waited for you to free me."

"Oh my. But what about Sorcha? I thought there was something—"

"Sorcha's a cousin. That's all."

"I saw you go into her room."

"She'd dreamed about you. She was afraid you were in danger. That's why I sent you away. I thought you'd be safer far from me. Then, when I saw you in bed with Druan in the castle, God forgive me, I thought you were working with him. Sorcha's the one who made me realize Druan was playing a game."

"I… I was in Druan's bed?"

"He did it to torment me." At least he hoped that

was why. "I know how foolish it sounds, now, but all the coincidences... I'm sorry. I betrayed your trust. I doubted you. If you can't forgive me, I understand, but know that I love you with all my heart, with all my soul, and I always will. If you'll have me, I'll get a job. I can raise horses, and I'll finish the house for you. Or we can move somewhere else." Sean had offered him the castle in Scotland, and told Faelan there was much to talk about. But Bree would most likely want to stay here. Where Bree went, so would he.

Her eyes glistened, but a smile teased her lips. "Well, I hear you're rich." She rubbed a finger over his arm, leaving a wet trail.

"I am?" he asked, confused.

"Ronan said your money's been invested all this time, and Nandor was a busy stallion."

"You've been talking to Ronan a lot. Why didn't he tell me?" Ronan had pointed out, in painful detail, every mistake Faelan had made with Bree.

"You'll have to ask him, but I suspect they didn't want you distracted."

Money had been the least of anyone's worries over the last four days. He didn't care about being rich, but it would be a relief to take care of Bree for a change, fix her house, repay her for the clothes and food, buy her gifts—starting with a wedding ring, he hoped—provide for however many babies she would give him. Assuming he could father children after more than a century in the time vault, and that Bree would have him. She still hadn't said.

"I'm kidding. I don't care if you don't have a penny to your name. I love you. I think I've loved you all my life." She raised a wet hand, placing it over his heart. He felt that odd tingle he sometimes got when she touched him. "'*God grant this warrior's aim be as true as his heart. Bend time and bring forward, his mate beside him, not apart,*'" she said, moving her hands across his battle marks as if reading Braille. "That's me. Not even time could separate us."

"Don't tell me you read my battle marks. No one can read battle marks."

"Maybe something happened to yours in the time vault, like with your talisman."

"There's nothing wrong with my talisman. Destroying Druan proved that. It must have been Michael."

"The warrior?" She frowned.

"The archangel."

"As in the Archangel Michael?" Bree blinked. "That's the Michael you were talking about?"

"He commands the warriors, gives us our orders."

"You're kidding! Michael's my favorite angel."

Most women had favorite books or dresses. She had favorite graves and angels. "He's the reason I found you," Faelan said. "I went to look for your earring, which I have here." He patted his sporran. "Michael showed me that you were in the time vault."

"Michael told you I was there?" She pulled in a quick breath. "He knows me... wait, does he kind of... glow?"

"Aye. He's very bright."

"He must be my shiny man, from my dreams. He was there when I was locked in the crypt."

Faelan stared at her. "You saw Michael?"

"When I was a kid, in my dreams, or whatever they were, he told me I was destined to find something great.

In the crypt, he told me my father had died, but he'd sent me another protector. He showed me your eyes. Then, you were there in one of my dreams with him. Druan was there too."

"Damnation. You wrote a letter and hid it underneath the floorboard where I found the necklace."

"Yes. But I didn't remember any of this until Scotland. I guess I blocked it out after the crypt. Michael must be the one who told me what your symbols mean. I know what the symbols on the time vault say, too, or some of them. *What lies within cannot be, until time has passed with the key*."

"How the…?" He didn't often shiver, but he did now. She'd done things no one in the history of the clan had ever done. "I don't know what to say."

"Then use those lips for something else and kiss me."

She loved him. He'd figure the rest out later. He dropped to his knees beside the tub, as she'd done days ago. "Yesterday was my *twenty-eighth* birthday."

"You're not a warrior anymore?"

"We're always warriors, but my duty is finished. I'm free to take my mate." He leaned closer. "I think you owe me something," he said, pressing his lips to hers.

"Birthday cake?" she asked, breathless.

"A wedding." And if he needed any help reining in her reckless streak, he had a family of warriors to back him up.

"Is that a proposal?"

"Aye, it is. *Tha gaol agam ort*," he whispered against her lips.

"Are you insulting me again?"

"No, lass, I'm saying I love you."

She leaned back a bit. "Enough to let me take one teensy picture of the inside of the time vault—"

"Damnation," he uttered, stopping her words with his mouth. It would take the whole clan to keep her out of harm's way. "You need something to take your mind off time vaults." He pulled off his socks and boots and stepped into the tub, kilt and all. He stood over her, water lapping at his knees.

"You're going to get wet." She lifted the edge of his kilt, holding it above the water, and peeked underneath. "Oh, my."

"Take my hand."

Bree dropped his kilt and took his outstretched hand.

He looked into deep green eyes that he needed more than he needed air to breathe. "I, Faelan Connor, born of the Connor Clan, offer you, Bree Kirkland, my hand in marriage, my heart in love, my sword in protection, and my soul forever. Will you have me as your mate?"

She blinked, eyes sparkling like emeralds, then she smiled, and he knew he'd found his way home. "Yes. I'll have you."

"This is the vow a warrior makes when he takes his mate. It's a separate ceremony, kind of like a handfasting. So consider yourself married... wife, with God as our witness until we can get to a church. Then I'll say the vow before a priest and the whole bloody world."

He grinned, stripped off his sporran and kilt, and sat facing her in the huge tub. Some things about this century were damned fine. She squeaked as he gently shifted her, pulling her onto his lap. "This is what I wanted to do the first time," he said, lowering his head. "Forget cake. I'll have you."

"You're sure about this, lass?" Sean's eyes crinkled as the bagpipes played in the background. "We're a strange lot."

"I've been accused of being strange a time or two, myself, but I can't think of anyplace I'd rather be," Bree said, gazing at the lovely old chapel on the grounds of Connor Castle in Scotland. The place was filled with warriors, many who'd helped battle Jared—Druan—and many who just wanted a glimpse of the Mighty Faelan in the flesh. How the clan had put a wedding together so quickly was a miracle. They could become wedding planners if they got tired of being warriors.

"Hold still," Anna said, tucking another strand of Bree's hair inside the wispy veil. "Isn't she the most beautiful bride, Sorcha?"

Sorcha tilted her fiery head and studied Bree's flowing, white gown with the small square of Connor clan tartan pinned at her shoulder and her dark hair knotted high. An impish grin lit Sorcha's face. "Ronan says she is."

"Ronan's going to get himself killed," Anna said, rolling her eyes.

Bree was enjoying her friendship with the female warriors, even Sorcha, who'd turned out to be not so bad. With so much of her time spent chasing dreams, Bree hadn't had many girlfriends.

"Wait. Your father's necklace." Orla fastened the repaired necklace around Bree's neck as Ronan walked through the door.

"If you don't get this show on the road, that soon-to-be husband of yours is likely to come back here and carry you to the altar. He's making the guests nervous with his pacing."

"He's waited more than a hundred and fifty years," Sean muttered under his breath, adjusting his kilt. "He can wait a minute more."

Ronan eyed Bree head to toe and lifted a dark, sexy eyebrow. "You could elope with me. I'm a lot younger— ouch," he said, as Anna swatted him with her bouquet. He stole a kiss from Bree and grinned. "Come on, Orla, I'll escort you to your seat."

"Wait. You need something from your mother, too," Orla said, her voice choked. She slid a tiny pearl bracelet onto Bree's wrist, clasping her hand for several seconds.

"It's beautiful, Mom. I don't remember seeing it before."

Orla looked away. "Hurry now, it's time," she said, taking Ronan's arm.

The bagpiper started a different tune, and Sorcha took a deep breath. "Ready, everyone? Here we go," she said, stepping inside. Anna followed, and when "Highland Wedding" began to play, Sean and Bree stepped up to the door. Sean had offered to give her away, since Peter was tied up with a rash of strange murders.

Bree stepped inside, blind to the smiling faces turned toward her, as she searched for *him*. Her breath caught. His hair was pulled back, highlighting his stunning face. He wore a white shirt, a kilt, waistcoat, and jacket, as did his groomsmen, Ronan, who stood next to him grinning like a wolf, and Duncan, his gaze only for Bree's red-haired bridesmaid. Bree moved down the aisle and took Faelan's outstretched hand, feeling his fingers clasp hers. "I love you," he whispered, dark eyes brimming with passion, as the minister began to speak.

After the vows had been spoken and Faelan had slipped a ring on Bree's finger, the ring his father had given his mother more than a century and a half before, the minister turned to Faelan. "And now, young man, you may kiss your bride."

Young, Bree thought. If only he knew. Faelan smiled, and her knees went weak. His head lowered, and her stomach rolled. An odd time for morning sickness to start. Faelan didn't even know. The feeling came again, stronger this time, and her vision began to blur. Faelan's grip tightened on her arm and his smile faltered. Behind him, Ronan and Duncan frowned. The floor wavered, and the faces disappeared.

A man appeared before her, his auburn hair streaked with silver. He ran one long claw over the yellowed pages of an open book. She could feel his longing for it, his lust. Bree shook her head, and the vision receded. She saw Faelan looking down at her, worry marring his handsome face.

"Are you all right?" he whispered.

Bree pushed the vision aside, refusing to let anything ruin this day. She touched her stomach and gave him a secret smile. Slipping the hand holding her bouquet around his neck, she pulled his lips to hers. "As long as I'm with you."

Her warrior. Her Romeo. Her mate.

Acknowledgments

There are several people I want to thank for helping me as I wrote this book. Austin, my real hero, who supported and encouraged me, running along beside me as I chased my dream. My wonderful children, who understood that Mommy had to spend a lot of time in front of the computer and sometimes forgot that real people need to eat. My parents, brother, sister-in-heart, and nephew, as well as my husband's family, who are a constant source of strength in my life. My incomparable agent, Christine Witthohn of Book Cents Literary Agency, who not only believed I had talent, but also helped me shape it. All the Book Cents babes and dudes, for their humor and support. My first instructor, Leigh Michaels, who opened the doorway to a dream. Margie Lawson, who helped me hone my writing skills. All the hard-working staff at Sourcebooks, and last but not least, my fabulous editor, Deb Werksman, for taking a chance on me.

About the Author

Anita Clenney writes paranormal romance and romantic suspense. Before giving herself over to the writing bug, she worked in a pickle factory and a preschool, booked shows for Aztec Fire Dancers, and was a secretary, an executive assistant, and a Realtor. She lives with her husband and two children in suburban Virginia not far from Washington, DC.

For more from Anita Clenney,
read on for an excerpt from

EMBRACE THE
HIGHLAND
WARRIOR

Available Fall 2011
from Sourcebooks Casablanca

Scotland, Present Day

SHAY PICKED HER WAY THROUGH THE HEADSTONES, grateful for the full moon, since she'd forgotten her flashlight in the car. Veering from the pebbled path, she pushed through overgrown tree limbs and the weeds brushing her ankles. A noise caught her ear. She tilted her head, listening. A whisper? Skin prickling, she turned. A statue stood in the corner. An angel watching over the dead? She didn't remember seeing it the last time, but that had been eight years earlier, and her head had been blurred with pain. A soft breeze ruffled her hair, stirring the dying October leaves rustling, not voices. Just leaves rustling, not voices. After the past few weeks, she jumped at every sound.

A few steps more, and she could see the tiny headstone nestled between two larger ones. Her throat tightened as she approached the grave. What did she hope to find? Reconciliation? Closure? To make sense of the lies? She traced the worn name under the angel's outstretched wing. *Dana Michelle Rodgers*. There should have been some sense of recognition.

After all, it was her grave.

Something flashed through her head, a memory, a dream... fire and pain. Shay shook her head and frowned. Some guardian angel. The clouds shifted, and a shadow crossed the angel's face, as if he didn't appreciate her disrespect.

Stones skittered, shattering the silence. She dropped to the ground, fingers digging into the chilled grass. What if it was *him*? She'd felt someone following her the past several days. The glow from the old-fashioned lamppost at the gate threw eerie shadows as she searched out the sound. It came from near the statue. Was someone hiding there? She squinted, watching in horror as the statue turned and looked at her. Shay swallowed a scream, rose from her grave, and ran like hell.

The bed shifted and Cody opened one bleary eye, looking at the woman beside him. Blond hair, slender back sloping into the curve of hips and legs that could outrun most men. He rolled over, snuggled up behind, and nuzzled her shoulder. "Shay," he whispered.

Her body tensed. She turned to face him, pulling the sheet to her chest. "Who's Shay?"

Cody stared into blue, accusing eyes. He flopped onto his back, head throbbing, disgusted with himself. Before he could apologize for his slip or pretend he'd misunderstood her name, his cell phone rang, the obnoxious ringtone blasting through the room as unwelcome as a fart. Damn Lachlan. The glaring woman stood, scooped up her clothes, and stormed into the bathroom, slamming the door. At least they'd only slept. He'd been too drunk for anything else.

"Yeah," Cody said sharply into the phone.

"Cody, it's Bree." Her voice was shaky, breathless.

Cody rubbed his eyes and glanced at the clock. "Aren't

you in Scotland getting married right about now?" He'd
been invited, but he'd had too many things to sort out,
and watching two people joining hands in wedded bliss
would've ranked right up there with castration.

Bree's response was drowned out by the bathroom
door slamming. The woman walked out, flung her blond
hair over her shoulder, gave him another withering glare,
and left the room, slamming that door as well.

Apparently he hadn't sorted anything out.

"I'm honored that you stopped the wedding to call
me—"

"There's a woman," Bree said. "I saw her beside you
in a vision the first time I met you. I don't know how
she's connected to you, but I've just seen her again. She
has blond hair and green eyes. She's in danger. Cody…
I think she's going to die."

call of the
highland
moon

BY KENDRA LEIGH CASTLE

A Highlands werewolf fleeing his destiny, and the
warm-hearted woman who takes him in…

Not ready for the responsibilities of an alpha wolf, Gideon
MacInnes leaves Scotland and seeks the quiet hills of
upstate New York. When he is attacked by rogue wolves
and collapses on Carly Silver's doorstep, she thinks she's
rescuing a wounded animal. But she awakens to find
that the beast has turned into a devastatingly handsome,
naked man.

With a supernatural enemy stalking them, their only hope
is to get back to Scotland, where Carly has to risk becoming a werewolf herself, or give up the one man she's ever
truly loved.

"*Call of the Highland Moon* thrills with seductive
romance and breathtaking suspense." —Alyssa Day,
USA Today bestselling author of *Atlantis Awakening*

978-1-4022-1158-4 • $6.99 U.S. / $8.99 CAN

WILD HIGHLAND MAGIC

BY KENDRA LEIGH CASTLE

She's a Scottish Highlands werewolf

Growing up in America, Catrionna MacInnes always tried desperately to control her powers and pretend to be normal…

He's a wizard prince with a devastating secret

The minute Cat lays eyes on Bastian, she knows she's met her destiny. In their first encounter, she unwittingly binds him to her for life, and now they're both targets for the evil enemies out to destroy their very souls.

Praise for Kendra Leigh Castle:

"Fans of straight up romance looking for a little extra something will be bitten." —*Publishers Weekly*

978-1-4022-1856-9 · $6.99 U.S. / $8.99 CAN

Highland Rebel

BY JUDITH JAMES

"An unforgettable tale." —*The Romance Studio*

RAISED TO RULE HER CLAN, SHE'LL STOP AT NOTHING TO PROTECT HER OWN

Daughter of a Highland laird, Catherine Drummond rebels against ladylike expectations and rides fearlessly into battle against the English forces sent to quell the Scots' rebellion. When Catherine falls into the hands of vicious mercenaries, she is saved from a grim fate by an unlikely hero. Jamie Sinclair only wants to finish one last mission for his king and collect his reward. But in a world where princes cannot be trusted and faith fuels intolerance, hatred, and war, no good deed goes unpunished...

"Complex, compelling characters and a good, galloping plot... Upscale historical romance at its best!"
—*Historical Novel Review*

"The romance is tender, yet molten hot."
—*Wendy's Minding Spot*

"Wonderfully written. It's captivating and heart wrenching." —*Anna's Book Blog*

978-1-4022-2433-1 • $6.99 U.S./$8.99 CAN

HIGHLAND HELLCAT

BY MARY WINE

✦

"**DEEPLY ROMANTIC, SCINTILLATING, AND ABSOLUTELY DELICIOUS.**" —Sylvia Day, national bestselling author of *The Stranger I Married*

HE WANTS A WIFE HE CAN CONTROL...

Connor Lindsey is a Highland laird, but his clan's loyalty is hard won and he takes nothing for granted. He'll do whatever it takes to find a virtuous wife, even if he has to kidnap her...

SHE HAS A SPIRIT THAT CAN'T BE TAMED...

Brina Chattan has always defied convention. She sees no reason to be docile now that she's been captured by a powerful laird and taken to his storm-tossed castle in the Highlands, far from her home.

When a rival laird's interference nearly tears them apart, Connor discovers that a woman with a wild streak suits him much better than he'd ever imagined...

Praise for *To Conquer a Highlander*:

"Hot enough to warm even the coldest Scottish Nights..."
—*Publishers Weekly* starred review

"I have read numerous Scottish-themed romances, but none compare to this amazing book." —*The Royal Reviews*

978-1-4022-3738-6 • $6.99 U.S. / $8.99 CAN

HUNDREDS OF YEARS TO REFORM A RAKE

BY LAURIE BROWN

HIS TOUCH PULLED HER IRRESISTIBLY ACROSS THE MISTS OF TIME

Deverell Thornton, the ninth Earl of Waite, needs Josie Drummond to come back to his time and foil the plot that would destroy him. Josie is a modern career woman, thrust back in time to the sparkling Regency period, where she must contend with the complex manners and mores of the day, unmask a dangerous charlatan, and in the end, choose between the ghost who captivated her or the man himself. But can she give her heart to a notorious rake?

"A smart, amusing, and fun time travel/Regency tale." — *All About Romance*

"Extremely well written…A great read from start to finish." —*Revisiting the Moon's Library*

"Blends Regency, contemporary and paranormal romance to a charming and very entertaining effect." —*Book Loons*

978-1-4022-1013-6 • $6.99 U.S./$8.99 CAN

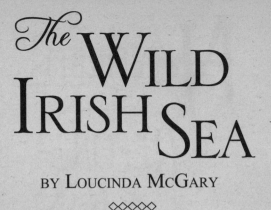

The WILD IRISH SEA

BY LOUCINDA McGARY

◇◇◇◇◇

DRAWN TO A FORCE HE CAN'T RESIST...

Former police officer Kevin Hennessey is running from his past—choosing to battle smugglers instead of dealing with his personal demons. When a desperate, rain-drenched American woman appears on his doorstep with wild tales of danger, Kevin is drawn to help her, despite his reservations...

SHE NEVER SAW HIM COMING...

Amber O'Neill knew without a doubt that her brother was in mortal danger. Rushing heedlessly to the rocky shores of Ireland, Amber was stunned to find her rescue mission derailed by a gorgeous, but deeply flawed Irishman...

The tumultuous sea, the intertwined fates of the coastal villagers, and unearthly tales of a hidden selkie prince bring Kevin and Amber together in a connection of mind, body, and soul that neither can deny...

◇◇◇◇◇

Praise for *The Wild Sight*:

"McGary never shortchanges the sizzling romance...
building to a dramatic, memorable conclusion."
—*Publishers Weekly*

"A masterful blend of mystery, magic, and romance."
—*Long and Short of It Reviews*

978-1-4022-2671-7 • $6.99 U.S. / $8.99 CAN

The WILD SIGHT

BY LOUCINDA McGARY

"A magical tale of romance and intrigue. I couldn't put it down!" —Pamela Palmer, author of *Dark Deceiver* and *The Dark Gate*

◇◇◇◇◇

HE WAS CURSED WITH A "GIFT"

Born with the clairvoyance known to the Irish as "The Sight," Donovan O'Shea fled to America to escape his visions. Upon his return, staggering family secrets threaten to turn his world upside down…

SHE'S LOOKING FOR THE FAMILY SHE NEVER KNEW…

After her mother's death, Rylie journeys to Ireland to find her mysterious father. She needs the truth—but how can Donovan be her half-brother when the chemistry between them is nearly irresistible?

UNCOVERING THE PAST LEADS THEM DANGEROUSLY CLOSE TO MADNESS…

"McGary never shortchanges the sizzling romance… building to a dramatic, memorable conclusion."
—*Publishers Weekly*

"A masterful blend of mystery, magic, and romance."
—*Long and Short of It Reviews*

978-1-4022-1394-6 • $6.99 U.S. / $7.99 CAN

The TREASURES of Venice

BY LOUCINDA McGARY

"Bursting with passion."
—Darque Reviews

An Irish rogue who never met a lock he couldn't pick...

With danger at every corner and time running out, Keirnan Fitzgerald must use whatever means possible to uncover the missing Jewels of the Madonna. Samantha Lewis is shocked when Keirnan approaches her, but she throws caution to the wind and accompanies the Irish charmer into his dangerous world of intrigue, theft, and betrayal. As the centuries-old story behind the Jewels' disappearance is revealed, Samantha must decide whether Keirnan is her soul mate from a previous life, or if they are merely pawns in a relentless quest for a priceless treasure...

"Lost jewels, a sexy Irish hero, and an exotic locale make for a wonderful escape. Don't miss this charming story."
—Brenda Novak, *New York Times* bestselling author of *Watch Me*

"A brilliant novel that looks to the past, entwines it in the present, and makes you wonder at every twist and turn if the hero and heroine will get out alive. Snap this one up, it's a keeper!" —Jeanne Adams, author of *Dark and Deadly*

978-1-4022-2670-0 •$6.99 U.S. / $8.99 CAN